Chasing Grace

A Novel of
Odd Redemption

Carol Costello

New Horizons
Library
San Francisco

New Horizons Library
825 LaPlaya Suite 426
San Francisco, CA 94121

www.newhorizonslibrary.com

Library of Congress Control Number: 2011934373

ISBN 978-0-9836837-1-1

Book Design by Kathryn Marcellino
Printed in the United States of America

Acknowledgements

Thank you to all who have supported me personally and editorially, especially Dianne Drosnes, Nancy Elkington, Emily Garvik, Jim Gilman, Carolyn Ingram, Jeff Leith, Tom LeNoble, Marsh Rose, Christine Schmoeckel, and Susan Snow.

Chasing Grace

A Novel of
Odd Redemption

Chapter 1

I first met God in 1956, when I was six, in Chicago's Indian Boundary Park.

Dad stood in a field of freshly mowed grass, smiling and waving, his red hair blowing in the wind. He held high above his head the most beautiful kite I had ever seen. One half was dark, fiery orange; the other half was a purple so deep and intense that I could feel it around the edges of my tongue. A lightning bolt of glittering gold slashed right down the middle.

The morning sun and crisp breeze made my eyes sting, but I smiled back at him and waved.

"Hold on!" he yelled over his shoulder, starting to run, and released our kite into the wind. It jerked away, whisking up and up, dragging on my stick, darting one way, then the other. The ball of string unwound so fast it pulled my breath up with it. Soon the kite was just a tiny, twisting dot against the sky—a sky that was shifting quickly from bright blue to the pearly green-yellow-gray that comes right before a storm.

I imagined the kite's purple, orange and gold up there, alive and fluttering noisily in the gusting wind far above us. I floated up to it, melting into the sunlight and the smell of cut grass and coming rain. Up there, far above the world, the sky seemed like a solid crust. Behind it, a brilliant, living light pulsed like bright clear blood, pressing to get through.

When I reached out to touch it, the brightness broke through the sky and flooded over me. I had never felt so happy or safe, so loved. That feeling of being home, exactly where I was supposed to be, sank deep down into my heart and spread all the way out to my fingertips. I called it *the bright*, because that's what it was. It made me part of everything. I belonged to something big and wonderful, something mysterious and good that I had wanted all along, without even knowing it. I knew *the bright* was not just behind the sky, but also behind Dad's smile, the trees, the wind, my playground gang—everything!

I breathed it in as far as I could and tried to make it keep racing around inside me—but when I breathed out, it escaped and was gone. The hole where *the bright* had been ached, like when she came into my closet and did the bad thing, then pretended not to see me the whole rest of the day. Without *the bright*, I was just Dead Girl, the small body on the mattress in the closet with nothing but darkness inside her. Or Ghost Girl, who got up and went outside to play with her friends, but was really just Dead Girl, walking around.

I tried for days to get *the bright* back—holding my breath, begging Dad to take me kite-flying again, running so fast I could hardly breathe—but it wouldn't come.

I had to have it! I would not be the Dead Girl, or Ghost Girl. I could not imagine how, but someday I would find *the bright*, wrestle it to the ground, capture it, and make it fix me.

∞

Our apartment was just a few blocks from Indian Boundary, in Rogers Park on the North Side. The building was old and crumbling, but friendly. The front was sooty red brick, but our "backside" was where people lived. All day long, the mothers moved up and down that crisscross of sagging wood stairways and landings, once painted dark putty gray—sauntering in and out of their tiny apartments, drinking black coffee or beer, smoking Camels, playing canasta, laughing loudly and calling to one another across the landings.

We kids played on a piece of cracked concrete below, a widening in the service driveway just big enough for the garbage truck to park. We ran around in circles, screaming wildly and throwing rocks at the "bad guys" that were really just rusty steel rods sticking out from the brick walls.

I was always the first kid down there. A few weeks after the kite-flying at Indian Boundary, I ran down after lunch and went right to my secret hiding place—a tiny space between two loose bricks where I kept my Popsicle stick. I had found it in a gutter a few weeks earlier and sharpened it on the driveway. I sat down and plunged the pointed end into a crack in the concrete, as deep as I could—then raked it toward me with all my might, keeping the downward pressure. Sandy, gooey dirt oozed up in a fantail from the crack, falling back on itself as I dragged on the stick. I stabbed again, and pulled. It made me feel calmer.

Peter Carmody's mother leaned over her railing high above and waved, pulling a Camel away from her mouth and leaving a bright red lipstick mark. She pushed her long, curly red-brown hair back away from her face. Her dark green skirt swirled as she shifted her weight from one black high heel to the other. I wanted a soft, pretty, smiling mother like her. Sometimes I dreamed that Mrs. Carmody married Dad, and he came home from the Loop every night and ate dinner with us.

"All alone down there, are ya, Cathy?" she called. I nodded, staring at the concrete. "No nap for you again today?" I shook my head and dug my stick deeper into the crack. When I looked up, she was gone.

Kevin Dolan was the first kid out after naptime, then Sheila Reagan, Peter Carmody, Jack O'Halleran, and Eileen O'Dowd. The big kids had gone off to Indian Boundary Park, so we had the driveway all to ourselves and started a game of stickball. Kevin and I snickered when Peter stepped up to the paper plate that we used for home base. Peter never hit the ball right. I sling-shotted a small stone at Kevin with my Popsicle stick and a dirty rubber band.

We all heard it at the same time and turned toward the footsteps pounding into our driveway. Pat Reilly, a big kid from our building, raced in from the street yelling, "Run, you guys! Joyce is coming with her gang. They've got knives and razor blades, and they're gonna cut you!" Joyce Ahearn was a "slow" thirteen-year-old girl from two blocks south who rode a two-wheeler with training wheels and had a gang of kids a few years older than we were. Once, she and her gang had stolen Timmy O'Malley's bike and beaten him up so badly that he'd had a broken arm and a concussion, and spent two days in the hospital.

"Aw, she is not," Peter Carmody said. "You're just tryin' to scare us."

"She's comin'!" Pat pushed him in the chest, almost knocking him down. "Get outta here!"

We heard wild shouting in the street, then the clattering of training wheels. Joyce Ahearn rounded the corner into our driveway, pumping her bike hard, bearing down on us with her long blonde hair streaking out behind her, all curly and dirty, and her pale blue eyes fixed on us. Three large boys ran alongside her. A knife flashed in one's fist. They raced toward us, making shrieking noises without words, blocking our escape to the street.

Kids ran in all directions, screaming. There was no way out. My eyes landed on the rotting wood door to the basement laundry room. It was black inside and off-limits because it was dark, slippery, and the mothers said rats nested down there, but it was the only escape. I heard my shoes on the concrete, felt the sweat on my hands turn cold as I moved through the air. My vision narrowed to that door—to the flaking gray paint, the weathered wood where the paint was missing, the tiny cracked window.

"Get 'em! Get 'em!" Joyce yelled. One of her boys was closing in on me.

I grabbed the rusty doorknob and pulled hard. Ducked in and threw the deadbolt. The dank air smelled like pee and mildewed clothes. Pools of liquid gleamed dully on the dark floor; something scampered under the feet of a washing machine. I stood up on tiptoe and peered out the grimy window into the driveway.

One of Joyce's boys held Peter Carmody's arms behind his back. She moved toward him with a knife, slowly waving the blade in front of his face. Then quickly, she flicked it down and sliced a three-inch gash on his calf. Blood poured over his white skin. He yelled and twisted in the boy's arms.

Teddy Cohallan, one of our big kids, sprang up behind Joyce's kid and pulled him off Peter. More of our big kids ran in from the street. Mikey Sullivan and Terry Shea tackled Joyce and sat on her, hitting her in the face and smashing her head into the concrete. Blood streamed from her nose.

My eyes moved away from the window to the doorjamb under my shaking fingers. I ran my hand slowly back and forth over the damp gray paint. I was trapped with rats in a dark place—but nothing, and no one, could touch me. I was safe, and would not be cut. I had saved myself. Something inside me had grown huge and *lifted* me. It had heard me when I said, "I need to be behind that door!" and helped me. I had moved like a grown-up, been smart like a grown-up, gotten what I wanted. My mind sped and raw energy surged through my body.

Then it happened again, just like it had at Indian Boundary Park. Something bright and warm, magical and *right* broke through from behind the flaking doorjamb. It poured into me and filled me up, made me feel happy, whole, and *big*. I was peaceful, and at the same time excited. I never wanted it to stop. For just that one second, everything was absolutely perfect. Even the blood on Peter's leg was beautiful. I breathed in *the bright*, watched Joyce and the boys scuffle as if they were playing, saw Mrs. Carmody starting down the stairs in slow motion—and then had to breathe out...

Screams shattered the air and kids ran in all directions. Mothers ran down the wooden steps and pulled kids apart. Joyce and her gang fled out the driveway, with Mrs. O'Dowd and Mrs. Carmody screaming after them. Our gang slowly appeared from behind piles of garbage and inside doorways, and followed Mrs. Carmody as she carried Peter up the stairs.

I stepped out into the driveway. A few big kids were still hanging around, but they ignored me. I looked for my Popsicle stick, but it was gone. I didn't care. I was different now. I had felt *the bright* twice. It liked me. Even if I couldn't make it come whenever I wanted, it could help me outrun bad things.

I couldn't think of anything else to do, so I slowly climbed the stairs to our apartment. She was waiting at the door.

ଓଃ

"I heard what happened," she said. "Are you all right?" She was acting like her nice self, the one who sat with the other mothers and ate cake at birthday parties.

"Yes," I said, stepping around her into the apartment. We had one room where they slept on a hide-a-bed, the kitchen, a bathroom, and my closet. She kept the windows and curtains closed all day, so it was always dark and quiet. It smelled funny, too. Salty and old, like things might be dying under the couch.

Dad didn't come there much. He was a lawyer and mostly stayed downtown at his office in the Loop. When I was little, I used to beg him to stay home. That made him nervous and cross, like when I asked him to make a rule that Mother couldn't come into my closet. After that, I only asked him "yes" questions, which made both of us happier.

She leaned back against the door with her arms crossed and frowned. I didn't like her looking at me, but I stared back. Her hair was kind of sideways on her head, like she'd been sleeping. It made the dark roots show beneath the yellow parts, and her skin looked even whiter than usual.

"Go to your room," she said. It wasn't loud, but it was scary. She stood waiting for me to move. I just kept staring at her, wondering if things would be different now that I'd met *the bright* not once, but twice! "Your father isn't coming home for dinner. We'll eat in an hour." I didn't want to go to my closet. I walked slowly across the room to the dark brown wing chair in the corner, climbed up into it, and examined my nails the way she always did. If I pretended not to hear, maybe she would just go into the kitchen.

"I *said*, go to your *room!*" In the end, I always had to obey. If I didn't, she would tell Dad and then I'd have nobody. I closed the closet door softly behind me, lay down on the mattress, switched on my little lamp, and pretended to read *Baby Ducks*. I knew what was coming.

The door opened in a few minutes, and her shadow came in before she did. I never said anything. I knew the rules by now, so I was quiet when she lay down half on top of me and started running her hand over my back and fanny, touching me all over.

"Turn over," she said in the rough, low voice that wasn't like the other kids' mothers. She moved her hand over my stomach and looked out the window above us, a small square cut in the wall. She always stared up there, like she was in a trance, even though all you could see were the red bricks of the next building a foot away.

It always happened the same way. Her hand would move down. She would touch me and rub me down there. If I tried to sit up, her other hand would clamp down on my shoulder, right between the bones, where it hurt. She would keep pressing down, even if I didn't move a muscle. I would make pictures out of the cracks in the ceiling—a dog, a knife, a building—and then fade up there myself. I would look out the window at the neighbors' bricks, then down at Dead Girl on the mattress. Finally, she would pull herself up and back out of the closet, pointing her finger at me, warning me.

We could never tell anybody what happened. Sometimes I wondered if *she* even remembered it. Each time she lay down on the mattress with me, I thought she might start to like me—but she seemed to like me even less. After she went away, I would lie there wondering how to fix myself. I would grip the cool white sheet until it was warm and damp in my fist, then reach for another handful of cool white, and another.

That day was different, though. I had outrun Joyce's gang! I had felt *the bright* twice. I was not Dead Girl. I couldn't look at Mother or tell her to stop when she said, "Turn over," but I could pretend she wasn't there. Just pretend I had to get up and go to the bathroom or something. Just keep getting up, even when she tried to pull me back down. Just keep getting up and slipping out of her grasp and moving away until before I knew it, I was out the door and into the hallway.

I didn't know where to go from there. It was almost dark, so I couldn't go outside—but I couldn't go back to the apartment. I walked all the way to the end of the hall and sat down on the thin, gritty brown carpet next to the stairs. That way, I was as far away from her as I could get, but could still see the apartment door in case she turned into her nice self again and wanted me to come back. I touched the carpet with my finger. It was sticky, and smelled like old feet and dogs.

I knew she wouldn't come crashing out of the apartment and yell at me. She was too smart for that. People would see her. She always waited until we were alone, and then glared at me with the jagged hazel lines snapping out of her eyes. I felt dark and horrible inside when she did that. I had no idea what she would do now. I had never slipped away from her like that. It broke off a corner of how we were together. She always said that if I misbehaved, I couldn't live with them anymore—so I might have to spend the night in Indian Boundary Park. Maybe start living there. I wished I'd grabbed my jacket on the way out of the apartment. I had been really nice to the people who owned the corner grocery store, so I could probably get food from them. Did anybody else live in Indian Boundary? People? Animals? I sat perfectly still on the scratchy brown carpet feeling scared, confused, horrified, and also a little excited. If I had to make it on my own in Indian Boundary, I was pretty sure I could do it.

I don't know how long I was out there, but at some point I got so nervous about Dad finding me in the hallway when he came home, and so hungry, that I stood up and started edging back toward the apartment. At least, I had to find out if I could still live there. I pressed the buzzer. The door opened, but she was already walking back to the kitchen by the time I got in. She didn't look at me and just stood facing the kitchen counter, squeezing raw meat loaf through her fists.

"You're too big for me to read you to sleep anymore," she spat over her shoulder.

I didn't think she would come into my closet again.

ᦉ

Late that summer, we moved to Elmhurst, a suburb where people from our building moved when they had "made it." Elmhurst was much too clean. The sidewalks and streets, even the trees and dirt, looked like they had been put out just for show, like they didn't really belong there. I missed the stickball gang and knowing where all the loose bricks and good hiding places were.

We had a house all to ourselves, a little square of red bricks with white shutters that didn't close. The tiny front yard was covered with bright green grass, and one young elm tree stuck up out of it, looking lonely and lost. Inside, "French Blue" carpet covered everything except the kitchen and bathroom. Walking on all that blue made me dizzy. It was hard to tell how far apart things were, and I couldn't get my bearings.

I had my own bedroom on the second floor, down the hall from theirs, with a real bed wrapped tightly in a yellow-and-white striped spread. Blue and yellow flowers climbed all over the wallpaper in baffling lines and patterns. The window looked out on an elm tree and the sky, instead of the neighbors' brick wall.

Everything in Elmhurst felt strange, fake, and confusing. Dad came home even less, since he had a longer train ride from the Loop.

She had not come in to "read me to sleep" since the day Joyce's gang chased us, but she was making up for it by being even meaner. On the way home from grocery shopping a week after we moved to Elmhurst, she pulled over to the curb in front of a vacant lot. She peered into the lot as if she were looking for something and stretched her index finger out toward it. The hand was inches from my face. Blue veins stuck up from the back of it, like on an old lady's hand. I wondered how long it would take for her to get really old.

"That's where your father and I will leave you if you don't behave yourself," she said, as if she were explaining something as simple as how to tell time. I stared into the field. Overgrown grasses the color of straw, patches of dry gray dirt, a few cinder blocks strewn around. I imagined building a shelter out of the grasses and cinder blocks, but resolved instead to be three steps ahead of her and never do anything wrong.

She snorted as we pulled away from the curb and turned toward home. The backseat was crammed with brown paper bags full of Wonder Bread, jars of peanut butter, chicken and roast beef wrapped in plastic, a large bag of Idaho potatoes, leggy celery, and Hostess Cream-Filled Cupcakes. She loved those, and she ate a lot of them. They put her in a kind of trance, a lighter version of the trance she used to get in my closet.

I just bided my time. Pretty soon, I would start school. That would change everything. The two things I knew for sure about school were that I would be away from her all day, and that I would learn to read more than just simple kids' books. That meant getting my hands on all kinds of information, including how to capture *the bright* and make it do what I wanted, and how to deal with parents.

The night before my first day at Immaculate Conception Grammar School, I lay on the yellow-and-white-striped bed, looking through *Beginning Reader*. It was about a really dumb family who lived in a town just like Elmhurst. I kept glancing over at my new uniform hanging on the closet door—a very serious-looking navy jumper and a crisp white short-sleeve blouse. I couldn't resist and hopped out of bed to try it on again.

I stood in front of the mirror, looking at this new, official person. Skinny white legs above white socks and saddle shoes. Long white arms. Long brown braids. Pale face and freckles. I stepped closer to the mirror and looked into my own eyes. Green, but kind of muddy. It was like looking at a picture in a book. Who was that person? *What* was it?

I stepped back and looked myself up and down. I didn't think anybody else would see the terrible blackness that Mother saw. I looked all white, brown, and navy blue. Dull, but everybody else would be wearing the exact same thing. I would fit right in. Maybe. Slowly, I took off the uniform, hung it up, and pulled on my white T-shirt and pink-and-blue plaid shorts. Dad had brought them from the Loop for my birthday. Mother hated them. I found them exciting, beautiful, and dangerous. I smiled at myself in the mirror before slipping back onto the bed with *Beginning Reader*.

I didn't even hear her in the hall. The door just swung open, and she was in. Before I could move, she was standing over me. I jumped up, holding *Beginning Reader* to my chest and facing her across the bed.

"What's the matter with you?" she asked.

"Nothing."

She sat on the bed. I backed away a few feet. She had on black slacks, a tan blouse, and brown oxfords—what she called her "suburban clothes," although I hadn't seen anybody else in Elmhurst dressed like that. Her yellow hair was pulled back into a tight bun that she called a "chignon" and she had on bright red lipstick. She sighed, shook her head, and picked at the bedspread as if there were tiny specks of dirt on it. Her mouth shook a little, like she was cold.

"Tomorrow you start at that God-awful school."

I nodded. We had driven by Immaculate Conception the day before and seen big, scary women wrapped in billowing black cloth from head to toe striding around the parking lot with scrunchy faces and enormous chains of black beads strapped to their belts. Whips? Mother had frowned at them through the windshield. She was a Protestant. Officially a Catholic because she had to convert to marry Dad, but she hated "mackerel snappers," as she called them when he wasn't around.

"I'm warning you, don't believe a word those old witches tell you," she said, glancing up at me but continuing to pick at the bedspread. "They're the spawn of Satan, and you'll go straight to hell if you believe anything they say."

The nuns had looked frightening, but if she thought they were God-awful and the spawn of Satan—whatever that was—they seemed a little more interesting. Mysterious, and even kind of thrilling. I just nodded and tried to make my face a total blank. That was always best until you knew how she wanted you to feel. Then, suddenly and for no reason that I could see, she put on the nice face and even a small smile.

"I'm just trying to help you, Cathy," she said softly. Then she stood up and came toward me. I made myself stand still. She reached down and, very gently, patted my shoulder. I looked up. She had the squiggly smile, which meant she was trying to be nice but having trouble. I smiled back, but not too much. Did this mean she liked me now? No. She went back and forth, seeming to like me and then not. This was just a "forth."

"Now go to bed," she said. I stood still and waited for her to move. She looked very sad, and walked out with her eyes glued to the blue carpet. I listened to her clump down the hall, close her door, and start crying. Really loud. Like she didn't care if I heard her. Or maybe like she *wanted* me to hear her. I couldn't tell which. Before I changed into my nightgown, I pulled over the chair from my little desk and propped it up against the door. It wouldn't keep her out if she wanted to come in again, but it would make a noise and warn me.

I pulled the white sheets up to my chin and stared out the window at the stars. How far away were they? How far back did the black stuff behind them go? Where did *the bright* hide at night, and those times when I couldn't get *at* it? Why didn't it come whenever I wanted it? Who or what was out there, holding everything up? How come, all of a sudden, I had my own room with a bed and a window that looked out on a tree and the sky, instead of a mattress on a closet floor with a window full of bricks? Everything was stumbling forward faster than I could figure it out.

Tomorrow sizzled around me. The nuns, with all their strange power. Being away from Mother almost all day. My uniform. Learning things. Maybe how to make her like me, or else how to make her fall down and never get up. Maybe how to catch *the bright.* Or how to be the me that I was with Dad. I wanted to catch that me, hold on to it, and stuff it down inside of me forever.

The stars got fuzzy...then the deep, black water swept over me and I sank into it.

Chapter 2

She drove me to school in our tan Buick coupe. I sat in the passenger seat, gripping the armrest with a sweaty hand. She scowled. Neither of us said anything.

Immaculate Conception Grammar School was a large, solid brown brick building connected to a huge brick church. Cement angels hovered above the big arched doors. The school, the church, and the parking lot covered a whole block.

Kids swarmed over every inch of the blacktop, a sea of girls in navy jumpers with white blouses and boys in navy slacks with starched white shirts. They all ran around in circles, screaming and acting "like banshees," as Mrs. Carmody used to say. In a strange way, they were more frightening than Joyce and her gang. I had no idea where to stand or what to do.

"Where should I go?" I asked Mother.

"How should I know? Go ask her." She pointed to a young-looking nun standing perfectly still in the midst of it all. I climbed slowly out of the car. The door shut and the Buick rolled away. Only then did I realize I had no idea how to get home. I tried to remember the turns we had made, but couldn't with all the screaming and just froze in my tracks.

The tide of kids swept me up, pushing me left or right as they moved. I looked again for the young nun, but couldn't find her. Then suddenly, I felt *her* looking at *me*. The sun was in my eyes as I walked toward her. She was a black silhouette against its brilliance, even when I came to within a couple feet of her.

"I'm Sister Mary Celeste," she said, spreading her arms out to her sides. I half expected her to take a bow, like the cast of *My Fair Lady* had done when we saw them in the Loop. "Which of God's children are you?" she asked, tilting her head to one side. I had never seen anything like her. Enormous, frightening, yet strangely friendly. I couldn't imagine what she was talking about, but figured I couldn't go too far wrong with basic information.

"Cathy Callahan. I'm in first grade."

"Ah! Then God has sent you to *me*! I'm the first-grade teacher!" she cried, bending down to get a better look. Now I could see her face. She was beautiful, with creamy skin like the angels in Marshall Field's

Christmas windows, brown eyes, and pink cheeks. She grinned at me, then stood up and called to a girl with curly black hair and dark skin.

"Lisa Delgado! Lisa Delgado, come here please."

The girl hurried over. It was odd to stand next to someone who was wearing exactly the same clothes I was. "I've taught five of Lisa's older brothers and sisters. Haven't I, Lisa?"

"Yes, S't'r," the girl said. She smiled at me with big white teeth.

"Lisa will show you where to go, Cathy. Go on now, girls." She waved us away and moved toward two older boys who were fighting. When they saw her, they froze in place and stood with their heads hanging.

"Kevin O'Connell and Timothy Fagan, come here this minute!" she commanded. They skulked toward her. Lisa Delgado seized my hand and pulled me along with her into the building.

ଔ

The centerpiece of our classroom was Sister's massive wood desk, which stood on a riser about a foot high. It looked like an altar. Behind it, stretching across the entire front of the room, was a blackboard so old that chalk dust seemed to puff out of it even when it wasn't being used. The walls were a peeling yellow-gray. Statues of Jesus, Mary, and various saints in all sizes and poses covered every surface.

I sent a silent thank you to my Aunt Maureen, Dad's sister, who had grabbed me one day when we were visiting them in Peoria, shoved me into her car, and driven me over to their local church. "Your parents may be heathens, but you can't grow up ignorant of your heritage!" she had said darkly as she led me around to every statue and point of interest in St. Simon's—altars, votive candles, Communion rails, tabernacle, you name it. Without that half-hour crash course in Catholicism, I would have been completely at a loss in Room 3 of Immaculate Conception Grammar School.

Ninety miniature wood desks were bolted to the brown linoleum floor, in nine rows with ten seats each. After some shoving and scrambling, I grabbed a seat smack in the middle—fifth seat, fourth row—so I didn't stick out. When all the seats were taken, six kids were left standing. They darted from one occupied seat to another and finally huddled together forlornly in the back of the room.

Sister breezed in, waving a thin white finger in the air. "Sit! Sit, please, little children," she sang. Then she spied the six kids in the back of the room. I looked over my shoulder at them. One boy's stained and wrinkled shirt had popped out of his slacks. A girl was trying to wipe her face with her pudgy hand, but only spreading the sweat and dirt all over her blouse. Another hugged her lunch box desperately to her chest. They were what Mother would call "a mess."

"You six children, come here, please," Sister said, waving them forward. She grouped the disheveled kids about her and somehow managed to get her arms around all six of them. "These children are like the little children to whom Our Lady of Fatima appeared. They are loved by Our Blessed Mother. You other children are like the evil villagers who did not believe that the Fatima Children had actually seen Mary. Cruel and unkind!"

I glanced around. Eyes were wide; jaws were slack. Across the aisle from me, Lisa Delgado's chin quivered.

"Yessssss," Sister hissed. "Very selfish, you are, to let these poor little children stand in the back while you lounge around in your comfortable seats." The whole room shifted in their hard straight-backed wooden chairs. "You and your lazy ways!" she murmured softly, so we had to strain to hear her. The words were harsh, but her tone was almost seductive and her presence was hypnotic. Just beneath the surface, she seemed very pleased with the effect she was having on us.

"Now, who will give up their seat to one of these little Fatima Children?" She scanned the room. It felt like she was reading every thought that passed through my mind. The tension was unbearable. Kids squirmed and looked around, confused and starting to panic. I was mesmerized. What power she had!

"Who will give up their seat and become a Fatima Child?" she asked again, holding her arms up to heaven. I had no idea what she meant, but at that point any action seemed better than none. I watched in horror as my hand rose into the air.

"Cathy Callahan! Cathy Callahan will be a Fatima Child! Come up here, Cathy!"

As I twisted out of my seat, twenty more hands shot up, all waving frantically for attention. A few kids punctuated their hand-waving with urgent cries of "S't'r! S't'r!" These kids were quick studies. Now everybody wanted to be a Fatima Child.

Just then, the classroom door flew open and in marched a huge nun, half again as tall and wide as Sister Mary Celeste. Folds of fat fell around her face. Her eyebrows were completely gray and met in the middle. In one deft motion, Sister Mary Celeste slipped her hands inside the folds of her habit, took a step backward, lowered her eyes, and bowed.

"Is everything all right, Sister?" the new nun bellowed, pivoting her massive frame from Sister, to us, and back to Sister.

"Oh yes, Sister. Class, this is our principal, Sister Thomas Aquinas."

Sister Thomas Aquinas eyed us suspiciously. Sister Mary Celeste whipped us up into her net of high emotional energy and said pointedly, "What do you say, class? You say, 'Good morning, Sister Thomas

Aquinas.' Let's try it all together now. 'Good morning, Sister Thomas Aquinas.'"

There was some confused mumbling along with Sister as Lisa, and apparently a few other kids who had older siblings and so were vaguely familiar with Immaculate Conception rituals, tried to step up to the plate. Sister Thomas Aquinas did not seem impressed. She grimaced and shook her thick fingers at the sides of her head, where her ears would have been. Then she cast us a disparaging look and said, "Class, put your heads down on your desks while I talk to Sister."

Again, the kids with older siblings took the lead. Lisa Delgado folded her arms on the desk and rested her cheek on them. We Fatima Children pressed together in the front corner by the chalky blackboard as the two nuns conferred. A moment later, Sister Thomas Aquinas stomped out with the other six, and Sister Mary Celeste shooed me back to my original seat.

"Well!" she said, dusting imaginary chalk off her hands. "That's that! Sister has found desks for the Fatima Children in the other first-grade class." The *other* first-grade class? There were two rooms full of first graders?

"First things first, class," Sister sang, extracting from the depths of her habit a large clicker. It was bright kelly green, with a leggy red and black cricket painted on it. She held it above her head, and sharp cracking noises bounced around the room. A few kids in the front rows jumped and put their hands over their ears.

"When you hear this"—she clicked again—"it is your signal to be completely silent. Is there anyone here who does not understand 'completely silent?'" she asked, sweeping the room with her gaze. I was awed, terrified, in love.

"Good!" she proclaimed. "Then we'll have no trouble at all! You children will learn your lessons and not wind up working in coal mines or smelting factories." This seemed to baffle even the kids with older brothers and sisters. In suburban Chicago, you didn't hear a lot about coal mines or smelting.

I couldn't wait to learn. I looked around the classroom at the shelves stuffed with faded, tattered books, at the statues of people so holy that they had been made saints, at the other eighty-nine children who I suspected had a lot to teach me, and at the magnetic presence of Sister Mary Celeste, who was now printing her name on the blackboard, carefully holding the folds of her enormous black sleeve away from the chalk.

This would suit me just fine.

Sister ran down our "Daily Schedule," a series of classes in Religion, Spelling, Reading, and Arithmetic punctuated by recesses and lunch. However, we would soon discover that anything, even an Arithmetic problem, could turn into Religion class in a flash of Sister's eye:

"Little children, if you ate a bite of hamburger on Friday and were damned to Purgatory for ten years, but then you went to Mass every day for a month and got two years off your time in Purgatory, how many years would you spend burning in agony without being consumed, but with the certain knowledge that you would one day be happy with God in heaven, eating ice cream?"

We quickly learned to think along these lines. It was all about one thing: learning how little children could best "know, love, and serve God," the mission set out for us in the Baltimore Catechism.

By three that afternoon, I was on board. This whole place was devoted to God—who, it turned out, was the one who held the stars up! Also who created the darkness behind them, the earth, all of us, and everything that existed—even *the bright—out of nothing*. Who knew? The best part was, God could do or fix anything! Boy, did I have plans for Him. Anything you wanted, Holy Mother the Church had a saint or a prayer or a penance that would do the trick. I could not believe my good fortune.

The main thing you were supposed to want was to get out of Purgatory, and on your way to heaven, as quickly as possible. You did this by stacking up "indulgences" with little prayers or holy actions. Then, after you died and landed in Purgatory, and just as you were about to be flung into the fiery chasm, you simply presented these little indulgence credits for two months off, a year off, or whatever, and got released into heaven sooner!

Sister always talked about heaven in terms of ice cream, but I decided that it was like being surrounded by *the bright* all the time, forever, completely happy, with everybody liking you and God smiling down on you.

☙

By Wednesday, Sister had pretty much abandoned Arithmetic, Spelling, and Reading in favor of Religion class. She had ninety squirmy, overheated kids on her hands, and the only air-conditioning came from six large windows without screens. She needed a few more arrows in her quiver.

"And now, little children," she said late one afternoon, rolling her eyes, "Sister Thomas Aquinas has asked me about your reading skills, so we will have Reading class." She stepped to the blackboard and wrote in letters about a foot tall, "OFFER IT UP!" This, it turned out, was the answer to any discomfort, frustration, pain, or outright evil you might ever encounter in life. I was riveted. Here, at last, was how God and *the bright* wanted me to deal with Mother.

"Offering it up" was simple. When bad things happened, like poor Sheila Connerty being allergic to chalk dust and sitting in the front seat of Row 5 where she was enveloped in a cloud of it all day, you just called God's attention to the fact that you were suffering in silence—and He had to give you time off Purgatory!

"We could change your seat, Sheila," Sister said solicitously, shaking her head slowly from side to side, "but you would be giving up a magnificent gift—the chance to show God how much you love Him and get out of Purgatory sooner. You might spend hundreds of years burning in Purgatory while your classmates were happy with God in heaven, eating ice cream. Shall we change your seat, Sheila?"

"No, S't'r!" Sheila choked out between sneezes, tears streaming down her face. "Thank you, S't'r."

When hordes of flies and mosquitoes swarmed into Room 3 each afternoon for their daily buffet of sweaty first graders, and we "offered it up" instead of swatting at them "like windmills," as Sister said, we again got time off in Purgatory. She reminded us constantly to keep an eye on our heavenly balance sheets, and never miss a chance to earn credits.

"Seize the moment, little children," Sister admonished, shaking her index finger high in the air. "You never know when you'll be run over by a freight train on your way to school, killed instantly while in a state of mortal sin, and spend the rest of eternity burning in the fires of hell!"

The system kept us on our toes and worked greatly to Sister's advantage. In fact, it was almost as if Holy Mother the Church's complex ledger of gains and losses, indulgences and sins, heaven- and hell-oriented activities had been designed with our first-grade class in mind.

As a practical tool for dealing with my mother, I didn't know how well "offering it up" would work. Sure, I would get a lot of time off Purgatory if I just looked at the floor like a saint when she told me I looked "gaudy" in my pink-and-blue plaid shorts, or that I was so skinny nobody would ever want to marry me, or that nobody really liked me—even Aunt Maureen—and people just talked to me because they felt sorry for me. Yes, I wanted to be happy with God in heaven, eating ice cream—but if I just sat there, silent and smug, when she said mean things, it would only make her madder and cause more trouble.

I wanted my new access to God's magical powers to make things *better* at home, not worse. I understood "offering it up" and planned to take full advantage of it at school, but decided that at home, a blank face was still the best bet.

Holy Mother the Church had a million tricks. It was just a matter of time before Sister revealed one that would work with Mother.

"So you see, little children," Sister went on, "offering it up is an investment in your immortal souls."

She began pacing slowly down one aisle, up the next as she urged us to be on the lookout for opportunities to offer things up. Her closeness, her presence in our midst, was unnerving. She smelled like soap—and something else, something holy. Her beads swayed as she took each step and rustled in the folds of her black serge habit. A tiny piece of the black cloth brushed against my desk as she moved by. I breathed in her smell as she passed and held my breath, as I had with *the bright*. It was almost as good, and lingered in the air long after she was gone. I had trouble looking at her, but could not look away. Her tone got familial, even conspiratorial, when she came among us like that.

"Those of you who offer up your burdens may even become saints one day," she said softly, looking right at me and then casting her eyes to the linoleum floor. I couldn't tell whether she was talking about herself, or about *me*! In my mind, an unknown Sister-of-the-future spoke, "Class, open your *Lives of the Saints* and turn to the page on Cathy Callahan."

Sister resumed her place at the front of the room and pointed with her long white index finger, like a ringmaster presenting the next act, toward a foot-high plaster tableau that sat on the corner of her desk, facing us. In the scene, a young woman had fallen half out of her bed. Blood gushed from crimson stab wounds all over her long white dress and pooled on the gray stone floor. She had apparently bled out. Angels hovered to either side of her, looking distressed and holding their hands in the air, but not helping.

"This is St. Maria Goretti, little children. A virgin and martyr who was stabbed twenty-seven times while defending her purity." Sister glanced up at us with a look that told us just how important this girl was, even though we might not know what "virgin," "martyr," or "purity" meant. She let the look and the shiny crimson paint do their work, then walked slowly to the blackboard and laid her white finger on one word, then the next, and the next. "OFFER...IT...UP." The silence was deafening.

To wind up "Reading class," Sister toured us around about twenty other saint statues that stood poised on every surface of our classroom. She glided serenely from one figure to the next, giving brief life histories, pointing out which of their virtues we might want to emulate, and occasionally sharing her personal appreciations for special favors they had granted her.

"This, class, is our wonderful St. Jude!" she said, sweeping her hand in the direction of a slitty-eyed, thin-haired, glum-looking version of

Jesus. "St. Jude was beaten to death with a club and then beheaded. He died a glorious martyr's death!" We quickly learned that where martyrdom was concerned, the bloodier the better.

"St. Jude is the Patron Saint of Lost Causes, class." Here she let her voice fall and said almost inaudibly, looking at the floor, "Also, a special friend of Sister's."

We all leaned toward her as she stood by the window, laying one pale, translucent hand on St. Jude's shoulder and with the other, twirling the pull-cord of a massive tan window shade. She stared up at the ceiling, apparently giving herself over to some secret reverie about St. Jude. Lisa Delgado's brown eyes were huge and fixed on Sister. Even Terry O'Hara, a freckled kid whom I'd already identified as the class bad boy, sat completely still and stared at her.

"Yes," Sister went on, "when I was about your age, my mother gave me money for the butcher. I walked three miles through a blizzard to shop, but when I reached into my pocket for the money, it was gone! Sister walked right out into the street and fell to her knees in the snow..." I pictured a seven-year-old girl in a nun's habit groveling in the dirty, sludgy snow of a Chicago sidewalk. "I lifted my arms to heaven and prayed, 'St. Jude, help me!'"

Sister raised her arms to heaven, reliving the moment, and Lisa looked around at me. I thought she might jump across the aisle and huddle with me in my seat.

"At that very instant, little children, I saw the five-dollar bill on the sidewalk ."

A group gasp, punctuated by a few "Oh's!" from the girls and "Uh's!" from the boys.

"That, class, is how Sister found her vocation." I imagined her walking directly from the butcher shop to the convent, which was probably right down the street.

Then, before we could recover ourselves, she was on to St. Joseph, St. Teresa, and all the way around the room. My head was spinning by the time she got back to her desk and St. Maria Goretti. The saints were worth studying. They had, after all, made it with God. There was no telling what He might be persuaded to do if you were a saint, or even if you had access to some of their powers.

ଔ

On Friday we had our first Visit to the Blessed Sacrament—a treasure trove of indulgences! Sister told us we had to look like "decent little children" when we entered the Presence of God, so we practiced marching in the parking lot. Within ten minutes, she had all ninety of us walking lockstep in pairs, starting on one click of the green cricket clicker, stopping on two clicks. This was a useful skill, since we had to move to and from the parking lot twice a day for recess, to and from the cafeteria for lunch, and to and from the sites of any field trips Sister devised, like the Visit.

On our second tour around the parking lot, Terry O'Hara started dragging his shoes on the blacktop and making scuffing noises. Sister had his ear between her left thumb and forefinger before the third scuff, clicking twice to stop us and dragging him out of line, so that we could all see him.

"Class, Terence O'Hara was scuffing his shoes, showing disrespect!" She tweaked his ear and Terry winced. "What happens to disrespectful children, Terence?" Terry looked at the blacktop. "Cat got your tongue? Answer when Sister asks you a question!"

"I don't know, S't'r," he mumbled.

Her white hand flashed in the air and slapped across the back of his head so quickly I wasn't even sure she had hit him, except for a dull CRACK and his neck snapping.

"Now go find your place in line, *if you can*, Terence."

Then, as if nothing had happened, she clicked the cricket once and sang, "Follow me, little children, into the House of God!"

If anyone had not understood "complete silence" before, they understood it now. The only sounds as we moved across the parking lot to the church were the shuffling of our saddle shoes on the blacktop and the brisk fall wind in the elm trees.

As we crossed the church threshold, we entered a world that was hushed and shadowed, thick with incense and sacredness. The altar was a massive white marble slab draped in dark green silk and lit from above. Soft light drifted in through stained glass windows in deep, rich colors—purple, gold, dark greens and reds. Banks of wine-red votive candles flickered under an enormous statue of Mary on a side altar. The presence of something sacred and mysterious tingled in my fingertips. *The bright.* Or God. It didn't matter.

"Stand to the side, children," Sister said as we entered, gently waving her hand from side to side. "Girls to the left, boys to the right...Girls to the left, boys to the right..."

Very quickly, we were all standing crunched together at the back of the church, our eyes wide and fixed on Sister. She stood beside the holy water font, seeming about a foot taller than she had outside the church. Her silky white hand descended like a ballerina's toward the font. Only the very tip of her middle finger grazed the holy water. Then, dramatically, she raised that hand and made the sign of the cross on her forehead, heart, and shoulders. Finally, her hands came to rest together in "prayer position" and she bowed her head. Several girls gasped, and a few boys grunted quietly.

"Now, children, each of you will bless yourselves and move to the front of the church. Quickly. Quietly." With that, she headed off toward the altar.

After a moment of panic, we muddled through blessing ourselves and scuttled forward. Sister's gaze from the front of the church was like a tractor beam. Within minutes, we were neatly arranged in the first ten pews. Sister stepped silently to the front of us, her hands folded inside the cape of her habit. She scanned us silently for a moment, gathered us up into her invisible web, and began to speak in a way that was strangely soft and intimate.

"You are in God's house now, little children. You are God's own children, and this is His house..." We were putty in her hands as she went on about God's majesty, His power, and His love. Everything about Him was infinite. Anything other than God was pretty much a waste of time, except as it brought you closer to Him. "Small potatoes," was how she put it.

"God loves you more than you can imagine, little children." I felt that sharp pain when tears get into your eyes before you know they're coming. Sister reached out to somewhere and brought God right down into our midst. I felt tingling all over my body. As I stared into the hundreds of pulsing red votive lights, shimmering flecks of light began floating in the air. The greens and golds of the altar linens turned into brilliant lights and shadows instead of colors. My heart felt warm and relaxed, just like it had when I first felt *the bright.* Only now, I knew it was God—and that Sister said He loved me.

From that moment, I had no more doubts about God being the most important thing in life, or about Sister and the Church being the path to God and *the bright.*

Now I just had to figure out how to drag the whole package back to 221 Fairgrove. As we marched back to Room 3 after our Visit, I pondered how this might happen.

It sounded hard, but God could work miracles and I was determined to be first in line for them. Now that I knew He really was *the bright,* or at least in charge of it, I wanted Him to lift me out of my terrible nervousness, make me okay, change me into someone who was good inside, and real. Take away the darkness that Mother saw—and sometimes that I felt, too. Like when I lay in bed and wondered what it would be like to steal a policeman's gun while he was writing up a parking ticket, and take it home and point it in Mother's face and pull the trigger. Watch her fall down, and keep shooting at her face until she had no head. At that point, I always jumped out of bed and got a drink of water so I wouldn't be that girl.

Or maybe God could change Mother. I tried to imagine her smiling when I wore my pink-and-blue plaid shorts, just because they made me happy. Sister smiled all the time. Starting with my triumph as a Fatima Child, I seemed to do everything right at school, just as I seemed to do everything wrong at home. Sometimes the same thing was right at school, but wrong at home. Like winning a spelling or math contest. That was good at school, but if I came home excited about it, Mother spat, "You think you're so high and mighty. You and the mackerel snappers. They'll figure you out pretty soon. They'll see you're a rotten apple."

Maybe they would! Maybe God already *had*! Or else—and this would explain a lot!—maybe God saw me through Sister's eyes when I was at school, but *through Mother's eyes* when I was at *home*! I could not have that! If God thought I was bad when I was home, then I couldn't *be* home.

It seemed an impossible dilemma, but just as we were about to enter Room 3, the most simple, obvious, elegant solution struck me. Ghost Girl could take over at home! The real me would be the one who went to school, did everything right, racked up indulgences, made people smile, pleased God, and had everything going for her—grades, friends, the saints, Sister, Visits, everything! I would be that girl! Then, the minute I walked in the door at 221 Fairgrove after school, I would just dissolve like a Fizzies tablet in water and Ghost Girl would take over. Ghost Girl would deal with Mother. She could handle it. She didn't feel, didn't think. She would be fine.

It was a brilliant plan. I made a mental note to put my pink-and-blue plaid shorts in the bottom drawer of my dresser when I got home, way in the back. Ghost Girl knew better than to wear them.

Chapter 3

Over the next few months, Ghost Girl did a great job. Nothing Mother said got to her. She was quiet, well behaved, empty, and put her feet in all the right places—just like the footprints in the newspaper ads for the Arthur Murray Dance Studio. She lugged the "A" volume of the *Encyclopedia Britannica* up to her room, and began slowly working her way through it. She still couldn't read very well, but she could look at the pictures and start figuring things out. She got lost in it for hours on end, and that became her refuge.

Luckily, everything she learned transferred to me, so I was getting to know a lot about words that began with "A." I became a superstar at reading, the saints' stories, arithmetic, and especially Religion. Sister knew I always had the right answers, and often smiled at me before calling on someone else "to give everyone a chance."

Our classroom routines became familiar and comforting, even when they weren't exactly pleasant. Every day after lunch, for instance, we extracted from our Spelling books long laminated strips of gray-green cardboard, one inch wide, with the letters of the alphabet printed one below the next. Like little novice nuns and monks, we chanted rhythmically in a high, keening tone to which Sister cued us: "A goes a, a, a. B goes buh, buh, buh. C goes cuh, cuh, cuh..."

It was excruciating. Hard for us, because it was repetitive, boring, and we had just wolfed down as much as we could of whatever was left after a thousand other little children had rampaged through the cafeteria. Hard on Sister because there was little opportunity for turning the horrible phonics mantra into a Religion class. Sometimes she tried, calling out at A, "St. Anthony!" At B, "St. Bonaventure!" This confused the dumber kids, though, and our cadence fell apart. Once lost, it was difficult to recover. We were all relieved when it was over and we could move on to afternoon Religion class.

"Tomorrow, class, you will have your first chance to become soldiers of Christ!" Sister began enthusiastically. "You will start to fight Communism and lead Holy Mother the Church's crusade for Jesus in Poor Countries! You will become *missionaries*!"

That sounded exciting, but the word "missionaries" was a caution. In the Saints-O-Rama Tour around Room 3, Sister had described in detail how St. Isaac Jogues, a French Jesuit *missionary*, had had his fingernails pulled out by Iroquois Indians—"one by one, little children, until his fingers were bloody stumps"—before being scalped and tomahawked to death.

"Not far from Chicago," she had added, as if his suffering (and presumably, his time off Purgatory) might somehow accrue to us. At the mention of our becoming missionaries, several kids cast furtive glances at St. Isaac Jogues, who stood on the windowsill next to the pencil sharpener. He had a pointy gray beard and always looked at the floor, as if he might know something about being a missionary that we didn't.

"Tomorrow," Sister continued, "you will have a chance to buy your first Pagan Baby! Tonight, little children, ask your mothers for one small five-dollar bill, so that your very own Pagan Baby will receive rice and milk from our mission in Honduras, and clothes to cover its nakedness." Terry O'Hara and his cohort, Denny Quinn, eyed one another at the word "nakedness." I could see Sister considering whether to deal with them, or to press forward with her pitch. The missions won. "In due time, with the help of our holy missionary fathers and sisters, they will become good little Catholic children—and you will come closer to God."

Bottom line, I needed five dollars by tomorrow. For kids like Lisa, whose families knelt down in the living room each night to pray the Family Rosary together, and whose parents competed to give time, money, and old clothing to Holy Mother the Church, this would be no problem. However, I could not imagine an argument that would convince Mother it was a good idea to give me five dollars to buy a Pagan Baby in Honduras so the Church could cover its nakedness, give it rice, and spread Catholicism across the globe.

When Dad went to Mass on Sunday—on those rare weekends when he came home—she spent the whole time he was gone blasting Protestant hymns at full volume on the radio, marching around the kitchen singing the alto part to every song and smacking appliances with a wooden spoon while she made blueberry muffins. I hid in the dining room, watching in horror.

"A migh-ty fo-or-tress i-is our God!" WHAP on the avocado refrigerator. "A trus-ty shi-ield and we-e-ea-pon." WHAP on the innocent white toaster.

I looked over at St. Jude, the Patron Saint of Lost Causes, who had been so helpful to Sister with the butcher money—but he had shed some of his glamour since that first heady afternoon and now appeared to be sleeping while standing up, his knees locked like a horse. He did not look back at me.

છ

That night Mother fixed leg of lamb with mustard glaze, my favorite. She had been pretty quiet lately. Sometimes even nice, like tonight. I was tempted to send Ghost Girl packing, and take advantage of Mother being in such a good mood. Maybe something had changed, and she liked me a little now. How could she not, if she made leg of lamb with mustard glaze? I told Ghost Girl to get lost.

"I love lamb," I ventured, trying to smile a little but not too much. She stared at me, then twisted her mouth into the squiggly smile. Trying to be nice, but having trouble.

"What did you learn at school today?" It was the first time she had ever asked anything about school. Maybe I could ease into the subject of Pagan Babies after all, but I didn't want to start out with anything too Catholic. That was hard because practically everything at school was very Catholic. I grabbed the first thing that came to mind.

"A goes a, a, a. B goes buh, buh, buh. C goes..."

"Really! Is that all they teach you? You sound like a goat!" She spat the words out like her old self, her bad self. How could she switch so quickly? I offered it up and kept staring at her as if it didn't even hurt. She took a long swig of water. Her fingertips left little sweat marks on the glass when she put it back on the table. "You make me sick. I can't even eat! I'm going to talk to your father. We're getting you out of that place and putting you in a decent school!"

She stood up and stomped out. I listened to her steps on the staircase, stunned. How could she be so nice, and turn mean so fast? It seemed a little crazy. "Crazy" was a word my classmates used a lot. It meant wild, scary, unpredictable, witch-like. She was all those things. If she went to an insane asylum, what would happen to me? Could I sleep on the floor of Dad's office, and take the train to IC every day?

Ghost Girl had watched the whole terrible scene from the corner, her arms folded, her foot tapping, looking like, "I told you so." I shooed her away. Ghost Girl's job was not to feel and not to think. She was good at that, but it meant she wasn't much of a problem-solver. She was certainly not up to figuring out how to get five dollars for a Pagan Baby, let alone finding a way to stay at IC.

I cleared the table, put everything away in the refrigerator except the leg of lamb, which was too heavy for me to carry, and washed the dishes. Then I put a piece of aluminum foil over the lamb and checked out the cookie jar. Chocolate chips. I didn't even ask if I could have one, just stuck my hand in and took it. I got a paper napkin so I wouldn't leave any crumbs, and leaned against the kitchen counter.

I could not, would not, leave IC. If necessary, I would run away. I couldn't go to Dad's office. He would just make me go home. He never went up against Mother. No, I would sleep in church under a pew and sneak up to the girls' washroom to wash my face in the mornings. I would tell Sister I needed a toothbrush for a poor child I'd met sitting in a gutter on the way home from school. I would find objects like bottle caps and rubber bands on the sidewalk, and sell them for lunch money. I would figure it out.

The more immediate problem was the Pagan Baby money. There was money in the house. In her purse. Taking it would be a sin, of course, and there would no doubt be some Purgatory time involved—but it might be worth it. Maybe it wasn't a sin if the money went for Pagan Babies. Or if the person you stole from was crazy, or hated the Church. Sin or not, I had to have it. I had to have Sister, God and the Church on my side. A little Purgatory time was a small price to pay. Besides, nobody in Room 3 would even know about the extra Purgatory time. All they'd see was that I was a good little child, willing and able to buy Pagan Babies.

I wondered what Sister would do in my place—or St. Maria Goretti. Well, Maria Goretti hadn't had to worry about Pagan Babies. She had lived in a farmhouse in Italy, where they probably didn't even *have* Pagan Babies. For all I knew, she might have *been* a Pagan Baby! In any case, Maria Goretti was too busy with her purity to think about the missions.

Besides, she probably hadn't had a mother with a brown purse, sitting right on the kitchen counter. Or a black fake leather wallet inside with one-, five-, and ten-dollar bills all lined up and turned the same way. It was like watching someone else's hand slip in and extract the clean, crisp five-dollar bill. Like watching someone else fold it over and over, making it as small as she could, flattened it against her palm with her thumb so that the hand would look normal if anybody saw her.

By the time I got to my room and closed the door, the five-dollar bill was wet and sticky. My heart pounded and my cheeks felt hot. I pulled the bill flat and hid it inside my Speller, in the pouch with the cardboard phonics stick.

I huddled under the sheets that night, looking out the window at stars pulsing far away against the enormous darkness. My world had changed a lot in the months since I had first seen them.

How did God keep track of everything—holding up the stars, Sister and all the things she knew, playing host to people making Visits to the Blessed Sacrament, all the while keeping track of everybody's Purgatory time as it jumped up and down with all the praying and sinning? It was all I could do to wrap my mind around my first months at IC—learning a system that could mathematically guarantee you a place in heaven and access to God, St. Isaac Jogues and his bloody stumps, St. Jude and the five-dollar bill, the dramatic head-whapping that kept everybody alert and watchful, phonics chanting, eighty-nine new acquaintances, my brief stint as a Fatima Child, Pagan Babies, the clicker, and of course Sister herself.

Surely God wouldn't pay much attention to one seven-year-old girl taking Pagan Baby money from a mother who hated the Church.

ଔ

As all ninety of us pushed and shoved into Room 3 the next morning, Sister stood serenely behind her desk, waving us in with one hand and clicking her green clicker with the other. Ignoring the chaos, she spoke serenely above the roar. "Come in, little children, and find your seats. Quickly, quietly. No talking, please. Terence O'Hara, tuck in your shirt! Quickly, quietly! The Blessed Mother is watching you!"

This was the morning she had promised to tell us all about the Blessed Mother and the enormous power she had to intercede on our behalf with her son, Jesus, for reduced Purgatory time and a host of other favors. I checked the five-dollar bill tucked securely in my Speller pocket and put a well-behaved, expectant look on my face.

Sister clicked three times for "complete silence" and got it immediately. She raised her eyebrows and, without a word, pointed in the direction of a life-size statue of the Virgin Mary looking down at us from a pedestal in the front corner of the room. The Blessed Mother wore a white wimple just like Sister's and a sky-blue mantle that draped to her feet over a white dress cinched at the waist with a gold rope. She stood on a little globe, and her bare foot crushed the head of a snake. That looked kind of dangerous, but Mary didn't seem worried. She held her hands out to us, palms up. There was a little chip in one corner of her mouth, which made it hard to tell whether she was smiling, frowning, amused, or annoyed. She had a dusting of chalk on the shoulder nearest the blackboard.

Sister approached the statue and did a scaled-down version of the little bow she'd given Sister Thomas Aquinas. Then she turned to us and held up her hand toward the plaster statue. I half expected Mary to break into a tap dance.

"The Blessed Mother watches all little children, all the time," Sister began. "Our Lady wants you all to get an A in Behavior." She did a quick rundown of the Blessed Mother's life, qualities, and special skills, just as she had in the Saints-O-Rama. "She knows everything, little children, so don't try to fool the Blessed Mother!" Our Lady seemed to be staring right at me as Sister said this. Her smile had turned a little funny. My hand moved involuntarily toward the Speller on the corner of my desk.

I hadn't anticipated this, and decided that the best strategy was to throw myself on Mary's mercy. I prayed silently, "Blessed Mother, please don't let anybody find out about the money." There was something wrong with that prayer. I couldn't tell exactly what it was, but I took another stab. "Blessed Mother, forgive me for taking the money. Help the little Pagan Babies and make everything okay." That felt more on target for catching the Blessed Mother's attention, even if it wasn't quite as clear or as truthful.

In a nod to academics, Sister had us take out our *Dick and Jane* readers. I loved reading—it gave you access to the school library, the *Encyclopedia Britannica*, and everything you might ever want to know about anything—but I hated Dick and Jane. The dog, Spot, was okay, but the parents were awful and fake. Father came home every night, all the way from wherever he worked, and sat at the dinner table with Dick, Jane, and Mother. Mother smiled all the time and was always hugging Dick, Jane, and even Spot. It was disgusting.

Sister called on Lisa to read—she already knew who the "go to" kids were—and I followed along with my pencil. Lisa was a great reader, but after a few sentences I watched my pencil come to rest on the picture of Dick and Jane's mother. On her forehead. Then my pencil pushed down all the way through the paper and into the next page. I felt my cheeks turn hot and red. When I looked up, Sister was staring right at me, watching. How much had she seen?

I looked over at the Blessed Mother for help, but she had her eye on Terry O'Hara. I turned around just in time to see Terry lean across the aisle and punch little Squeaky O'Connor in the arm. Squeaky yelped and adjusted his black horn-rimmed glasses.

Sister was on top of them in an instant, holding Terry's right arm in her left hand and smacking it over and over with the red plastic ruler that she always kept handy on the corner of her desk. I counted nine times. Terry screamed in pain. Squeaky stood up in the aisle, his hands over his mouth, yelling incoherently.

Finally, Sister stopped and looked around the room. "Eyes front, little children," she said quietly. Talk about complete silence!

"John O'Connor, go to the boys' washroom and wash your face." Squeaky slunk out of the room, and Sister returned to her desk. She picked up her book and said, as if nothing had happened, "Lisa Delgado, continue please."

Lisa stared at Sister a minute, glanced at Terry, then started reading. "See Jane run..."

Yikes! I slipped my thumb over the hole in my page and peeked over my shoulder at Terry. His eyes were as red as the bumps on his arm, and he was sweating. Lisa read on. After a few more pages, it really did seem like nothing had happened. I hoped Sister had forgotten about seeing my pencil slip, too.

"That will do, Lisa! Little children, one day you will all read as well as Lisa Delgado," Sister smiled, raising the red plastic ruler above her head and waving it in joyful little circles. A few kids in the front rows flinched.

ভ

"Now, little children," Sister announced when Squeaky had returned from the boys' washroom, "the most wonderful part of our day!"

She ducked out of sight behind her desk, rummaged around in its bottom drawer, and reappeared struggling under the weight of a large gray metal box, which she let drop on the desk with a loud THUD. She smoothed her hand over the lid, then rapped it twice with her knuckles.

"This, little children, is our Mission Box. It is here that we keep your Pagan Baby money, and the record of how much you have helped Jesus and Mary save the souls of heathens around the world!"

She sauntered over to the enormous faded globe in the corner opposite Mary and gave it a good spin, letting her fingertips trail over various heathen countries as she glanced at Mary, then eyed us sharply. "The Blessed Mother is very pleased with little children who help save souls."

Lisa began fingering her change purse as Sister mounted the riser and sat grandly at her desk.

"You will come forward now, little children, one by one. You will give Sister your Pagan Baby money. We will begin with Row 1. The rest of you, take out your phonics strips. Sheila Connerty, stop your crybaby sniffling. Stand and lead the class!"

Sheila rasped, as if in the grip of a death cold, "A goes a, a, a. B goes buh, buh, buh…"

Phonics acted like a drug on us. The rhythmic chanting seemed to put us in a light trance. "C goes cuh, cuh, cuh and sometimes sssssssssss. D goes duh, duh, duh…"

I watched as kids climbed up on the riser and approached Sister with their crumpled five-dollar bills. Sister whisked the money away, arranged the bills in her box, and made little notes on a huge sheet of paper.

Row 4 started, and I saw my hands begin to shake. I took the five-dollar bill from the Speller and laid it on my desk, so it wouldn't get wet from my hands. The more I tried to stop feeling flushed and shaky, the worse it got. Alice Casey, the redheaded girl who sat behind me, poked me in the shoulder. I took my place in the line edging toward Sister's desk.

She started watching me when I was still three kids away, taking little glances in between scooping up money and making notes on her big white paper. I held the five-dollar bill by the corner to keep it dry. Maria Delfino. Jackie Haggarty. Me!

I couldn't look at her, so I just slid the bill onto the edge of the desk. She didn't take it right away, so I looked up. She was staring at me. Her eyes squinted a little, like she was trying to figure something out. I thought how nice it would be just to blurt everything out, to have her tell me what to do so I wouldn't burn in hell, and to know that everything would be all right.

"Please thank your mother for Our Lady, Cathy," she said in a way that was kind of friendly, but also kind of like she didn't really mean it. She picked up the bill, turned it the same way as all the others, and was about to place it in the little nest of bills in her box—but instead, she turned and looked me right in the eye.

I felt like I was being electrocuted, and imagined every hair on my body standing on end. Could she tell I was a thief? A disobedient little child who flew in the face of Our Blessed Mother and Sister? A liar whose sins were compounding by the second? I began to see sparkly lights in front of my eyes. Not *the bright*, but like when you're really hungry and stand up quickly and everything goes swirly...

"Cathy?" I heard, from way far away.

Then an explosion of terrible stinging up high in my nose and a pain in my arm as I came awake on the linoleum floor at the foot of the riser. I looked up into the faces of Sister and about ten kids.

"Step back, little children," Sister said firmly. "Cathy Callahan has fainted, and Sister has brought her back to life with smelling salts." She made a broad sweep toward them with the smelling salts. They jumped back in all directions, putting their hands over their noses. "Take your seats immediately!" They scrambled to their seats. "Sheila Connerty, continue the phonics, please!"

The chant began. "M goes muh, muh, muh..." Sister looked at me suspiciously.

"You are fine now, Cathy," she said, not asked, and pulled me to my feet. "Good as new."

"Yes, S't'r." I felt dizzy, but okay.

"Take your seat now. I will speak to you after school today. Don't leave with the others." I stumbled back to my seat, feeling humiliated until Lisa smiled at me. I smiled back, but shakily because now Sister must know I was a thief.

The phonics trance settled over us and the Pagan Baby line started moving again. What would she say to me after school?! Like the Blessed Mother, she probably knew a lot more than I thought she did. How much more, though, and how much should I reveal? Should I tell her my mother hated Catholics and marched around the kitchen singing "A Mighty Fortress Is Our God" and other, more brimstone-y Protestant hymns? Confess what had happened in my closet when we lived in the apartment? Or would that make me seem bad, too? I felt guilty whenever I thought about the closet, but that whole time was starting to seem like a dream. Sometimes, I wasn't even sure it had happened.

Could Sister really tell me what to do so I wouldn't burn in the fires of hell, as she often assured us she could? I needed a plan that would keep me connected to IC, Sister, and God, and at the same time make Mother like me, win her over to Catholicism, allow Ghost Girl to retire, and get everybody on the same page—hopefully, without my actually having to tell Sister too much, without Mother discovering that I was using the Church's magical powers on her, and without anybody finding out that I was stealing money for Pagan Babies.

Walking that tightrope was tricky and involved semi-lies to everyone, but anything else seemed like certain disaster.

That afternoon, we had a thunderstorm. At about the time we were reciting, "W goes wuh, wuh, wuh..." the sky turned dark gray, with tinges of green and yellow. Lightning flashed in several places at once and thunder rattled the huge windows. Kickball was canceled. Squeaky O'Connor redeemed himself by winning the spelling bee. Dick and Jane went with Father and Spot to the park. I pictured them all huddled together in a gutter with no food, since Father apparently didn't work. I wondered how much hugging Mother would do then.

By 2:45, fifteen minutes before dismissal, I thought I might throw up. At three o'clock, Sister rousted everybody with the clicker and said, "Everyone rise except Cathy Callahan, and line up!"

All eyes shifted warily to me. I busied myself putting away my books. The last kids marched out, with Sister riding herd on them like a lone cowboy on a cattle drive. I sat alone in the room. Rain slashed against the windows. Streaks of lightning cut across the gray sky, followed by rolling thunder. All the saints seemed to be eyeing me. I half expected them to relax their poses, dust themselves off, and start milling around, chatting with one another like the adults did at my parents' cocktail parties. St. Jude, the Patron Saint of Lost Causes, looked at me sorrowfully. I peered up at the Blessed Mother, but couldn't tell whether she was grinning or wincing.

My gaze drifted, as if often did, to the Family Rosary that sat on the windowsill next to a stack of chalky erasers. It looked like any other statue—a tableau of Our Lady of Fatima with the three children in the grotto where she had appeared to them—except that it was made of a waxy, yellowish-white substance that Sister had assured us glowed in the dark. It was about a foot tall and two feet wide and always looked moist, as if it were about to melt.

The week before, Sister had showed us its many miraculous features. She had held it aloft and slowly, slowly pried open the bottom. Out slid an enormous rosary, bigger than the black one she wore on her belt! It was about three feet in diameter, and made of the same yellowish waxy stuff as the statue itself. She held it high above her head for our amazement and delight. It was like a huge, soft albino snake. I had an urge to put it in my mouth. She told us about the many blessings and indulgences that you and your family could get if you knelt down after dinner and said the Family Rosary together—maybe even a miracle, *like the conversion of a family member.*

Sister's footsteps echoed in the empty hallway. She swooped in and headed straight for her desk, gesturing for to me to join her. I ascended her riser and stared down at St. Maria Goretti with her twenty-seven stab wounds. I would have traded places gladly. Sister sat with her elbows leaning on the desk and looked at me, her head angled to one side.

"Do you want to help Mother Mary and Jesus save souls, Cathy?" she asked.

"Uh, yes, S't'r." So far, so good. She pursed her lips and tilted her head to the other side.

"Does your mother want to help the Church convert heathens as well?" I could hardly say "No," but anything else would be a lie that Sister would detect immediately.

"My mother is a convert, S't'r." Her eyebrows flew up and her mouth formed an "Ah!" I had learned from Lisa that converts were either rabid Catholics, doing too much of everything, or they didn't really want to be Catholics at all. Usually, like my mother, they had been forced to convert in order to marry the other parent.

Sister nodded slowly and tapped her fingers lightly on the desk, searching my face. I thought I might faint again.

"Is that sometimes difficult for you, Cathy? Your mother being a convert?" She seemed eager, as if *of course* it was difficult, but she could help.

"Yes, S't'r." I felt like one of the witnesses on my dad's favorite TV show, *Perry Mason*, trapped in a line of questioning that was leading somewhere far beyond their control.

"In what way, Cathy?" Sister pressed, leaning toward me. I wasn't exactly sure where we were going, but when she reached over and took my hand in hers, the whole story came falling out. I told her all about "A Mighty Fortress Is Our God," the threat of being taken out of IC, and Dad never coming home. I made myself stop there. I could not tell about what had happened in the closet, especially with St. Maria Goretti bleeding out only inches from where I was standing.

"There, there," Sister said and put her arms around me for a minute. It felt like God's arms. Then she held me by the shoulders and stared into my eyes. "Would you like Sister's help in staying at our school and bringing your mother to the One True God?"

"Yes, S't'r!"

"Good! Then bring me the Family Rosary!" It felt like we were moving to dangerous ground, but I did as she commanded. I reached up to the windowsill and gingerly grasped the Blessed Mother's shoulder, pulling her and the children down into my arms. Sister smiled at me as I lugged the huge contraption back up the aisle, climbed the riser, and placed it on her desk. She tapped the inscription etched across the ground where the children knelt: *The family that prays together, stays together.*

"Can you read that, Cathy?"

"Yes, S't'r."

"Do you believe it?"

Ever since I had learned to pray at IC, I had knelt by my bed each night and prayed for my parents to get divorced. Ideally, Mother would just go away somewhere. Failing that, maybe I could go live with Aunt Maureen in Peoria. Sister was no fool. She took one look at my face and switched tactics.

"Would you like your family to be happy in God's grace, and win indulgences for yourself and for them?"

"*Yes*, S't'r!"

"Then you must take home the Family Rosary, and pray it with your family every night for a week," Sister cried triumphantly. She assured me that the Family Rosary could not fail. Mother would receive a "full conversion," start being nice to me, and we would all live happily ever after not only here, but also in heaven. She smiled and nodded encouragingly, gently edging the Family Rosary toward me across the desk.

"Take it! Take it! Go ahead!" She pushed it until it toppled off the desk into my arms. "The Blessed Mother will help you, Cathy!" she smiled, as if success were certain. "Tomorrow you can tell Sister all about praying the Rosary with your family!"

She waved as I moved toward the door, staggering under the weight and awkward configuration of the Family Rosary. I waved back with as much of one hand as I could safely remove from the statue, wondering how I would ever make it home and what I would do when I got there.

◌

All the way to 221 Fairgrove, I thought how stupid I had been to go along with Sister's plan. What was I thinking, to bring home the Family Rosary, with Sister believing that Mother and I would actually kneel down together on the French Blue carpet and say Catholic prayers?

I wondered what the Blessed Mother would think if she actually showed up in Elmhurst one afternoon, like she had in Fatima and Lourdes. I imagined her and Mother sitting on the cotton chintz sofa— Mother in a tan housedress, the Blessed Mother in her white dress with the golden belt and long blue mantle. Mother would hate Mary's bare feet, but would be polite and offer her coffee and a cigarette from the little box on our new "oak veneer" cocktail table. The Blessed Mother would give her that confusing look—part sympathetic smile, part smirk, part disapproval—and that would make Mother *furious*. She would lash out at Mary with the crackling eyes, but Mary would just pull *the bright* around her. No problem for her. Mary might even suggest that instead of having coffee and cigarettes, they kneel down and say the Family Rosary...

Ghost Girl could never handle this.

The shades were drawn when I got home. I heard her in the kitchen and felt a tight ball gather in my stomach as I crept through the dining room. She was swishing a mop back and forth over the linoleum floor, but spun around when I appeared in the doorway, holding the Family Rosary.

"What's that monstrosity?" she asked. My instinct was to run, but that was a course of action that absolutely nobody in *Lives of the Saints* would have pursued. I stood my ground, determined to "defend the faith." Mother came to within inches of me. I stared at her, and she stared at the Family Rosary. Suddenly, she grabbed Mary's head and yanked hard. As she pulled up, and I tried to hold on, the bottom fell off and the Rosary clattered down to the damp linoleum, making little squeaking sounds as it skidded across the floor.

"It's the Family Rosary!" I yelled, louder than I'd ever spoken to her, and lunged to rescue it. She kicked it across the floor toward the avocado refrigerator. "Let me have it!"

I hurled myself over the wet, sticky floor after the waxy beads— horrified by her sacrilege and by what might happen to both of us if anybody in heaven were watching. My hand flew out and grabbed the Rosary, now covered with a faint green Spic 'n Span sheen, just as she kicked at it again. Sharp pain shot from my wrist up my arm. She stood staring down at me with her feet planted wide apart, hands on her hips, the Family Rosary casing still dangling from one fist.

"Sister says that if we pray the Family Rosary together, we'll be happy!" I pleaded, near tears.

She walked slowly over to the new stainless steel flip-top trash can, slammed her foot down on the pedal, and tossed the Family Rosary casing in among the celery tops and coffee grounds.

"That's what I think of Sister," she spat. "We're already happy! We're the happiest family I know! I'm going to tell your father we have to get you out of that school this week!"

That absolutely could not happen.

"You can't do that!" I heard my voice scream, as if it were someone else's. I think it startled her as much as it did me. She turned and marched out. I heard her running up the stairs, and started trying to fix things fast.

I reached into the trash, gripped the Blessed Mother's shoulder with my thumb and forefinger, and extracted her and the children. A butter wrapper clung to the side of the grotto and obscured some of the kids. Catsup smeared all down the front of Mary's dress. Coffee grounds spattered over all of it, and clung to the catsup and the butter wrapper.

I got the little stepladder from the pantry and ran the Rosary and its casing under warm water in the sink, hoping everybody in heaven understood that I was just trying to clean them, not drown them. My hands were shaking. I had to get this done quickly. I dried everything with paper towels and reassembled the Family Rosary.

Now what? How to save the Family Rosary from further desecration, without taking it back to school and admitting to Sister that I'd failed? In a flash, I knew just what to do. Criminal behavior was coming more and more easily. I stuffed the Family Rosary under one arm like a football and ran upstairs to my room, shut the door quietly behind me, and pushed the chair up against it.

In the very back of my closet was a small wooden door that led to an unfinished crawl space. I pressed it open and, as gently and reverently as I could, placed the Family Rosary on the rough wood floor. It really did glow in the dark! It was horrifying to watch myself toss the Blessed Mother into the slammer like that, knowing that I was going to keep her on ice for a week. She and the children would just have to offer it up. As I replaced the door, I tried to justify it by focusing on the unspeakable alternatives.

I absolutely could not let my mother get her hands on Mary again— and clearly, we were not going to be kneeling down on the French Blue carpet and saying the Family Rosary. It would be much, much better just to tell Sister about all the miracles the Family Rosary was working. How my mother now loved receiving Holy Communion, how I thought our kitchen faucet might actually be giving out holy water, and how the only reason she didn't see Mother at Mass was that Mother had developed a special devotion to St. Elizabeth of Hungary, so she went to St. Elizabeth's over in Glen Ellen.

Mother would be easier to handle. She already had what she wanted. The Family Rosary was gone, and I would be making myself scarce for a while. Even Ghost Girl would have to lie low. I could go to the library in Wilder Park after school, or play kickball with the regulars— anything to stay out of sight.

In a week, the Blessed Mother and children would be back on the windowsill in Room 3—or in some other little child's home, actually being used to pray each night. I would look like a champ, and nobody would be the wiser. I promised myself never again to take over for Ghost Girl at home, and told her she would have to get a whole lot ghostlier, just like I would have to get a whole lot smarter—because now I was stealing at home and lying at school.

Sister seemed to buy the whole story about the Family Rosary, after a brief moment of eye-narrowing and a weird smile just like the Blessed Mother's, and never again had me stay after school.

I breezed through the rest of first grade, a star at saints' names and stories, math problems, "sounding out" words, and whatever else went on at school—even kickball and the budding clique system. I knew what life was about now: being the best at everything at IC, and using my connection with Sister and the Church to get a better grip on God. God wanted me to know arithmetic? Done! A home run in kickball? Done! Offer it up? Done!

At 221 Fairgrove, Ghost Girl's eyes looked at Mother, but didn't really register her presence. Her ears heard Mother's words, but she was getting better and better at crushing any sad, mad, or bad feelings. She disappeared into her room, made brief appearances at dinner, said little, and disappeared again. She read the *Encyclopedia Britannica,* lugging volume after volume up to her room. At school, all her wisdom was mine.

"You have a very large vocabulary, Cathy Callahan," Sister mused when I mounted the riser to receive my end-of-the-year report card, a sea of As. I smiled thinly and pushed down the urge to tell her all about the *E.B.* The less said about life at home, the better. Sometimes she stared at me as if she knew everything, but I doubt that she wanted to discuss it any more than I did.

In second grade, I got off her radar completely.

Chapter 4

Sister Cyprian was our second-grade teacher. She was ancient and fat, with folds of dark flesh pillowing out from her white wimple. Her eyes were dark brown and set deep in her frowning face. Kids whispered that she was crazy.

It was her job to shepherd us through our First Holy Communion. She had to transform ninety squirming kids in dirty, disheveled uniforms into little angels in white dresses and veils, pressed navy slacks, white shirts and navy clip-on bow ties who marched "quickly, quietly" to the altar rail to receive Communion for the first time—hopefully without fainting, hitting one another, speaking, throwing up, gawking, or committing one of the many mortal sins to which receiving Holy Communion exposed us.

The reason Holy Communion was both so exalted and so dangerous was that once the priest had "consecrated" the thin little wafers of bread by saying, "This is my body. This is my blood," they were *the actual body and blood of Christ*! That meant nobody could touch them except the priest. We had to kneel at the Communion rail, bend our heads back, and stick out our tongues at an angle exactly parallel to the floor so that he could pop the little hosts into our mouths without dropping them.

I had only to glance around our second-grade classroom at characters like Terry O'Hara and Sheila Connerty to see how terribly wrong that process could go.

The preparation was an ordeal for all of us, especially Sister Cyprian. In the weeks before the big day, she prowled up and down the aisles as we did arithmetic problems, chanting, "The body and blood of *Christ*...the body and blood of *Christ*..." She had a slight lisp and trouble with her "r's," which was doubly unfortunate, given her name. Gina Galletti cornered me one day at recess and asked, her brown eyes wide and fearful, "Who is *Kwithe*?"

Sister brought in some unconsecrated hosts and showed them around. That afternoon, they were just shiny little white wafers about the size of quarters. They looked more like ultra-thin plastic tiddlywinks than unleavened bread, whatever that was. I could not get my mind around them becoming the body and blood of Christ. Which part? The finger? Which Christ? The Baby Jesus? The mostly naked man hanging in agony on the Cross atop the blackboard in the front of the room?

This particular magic trick was a hard sell, even to those of us who were eager for more God, more lore, more power. We looked at Sister with slitty eyes, unable to mask our skepticism. Terry O'Hara asked, "S't'r, if you cut open a consecrated host, would blood come out?" My question, exactly! I could easily imagine Terry stealing a consecrated host, running it out to the parking lot, laying it down on the blacktop, and slicing it open with the switchblade knife he had shown us at recess.

Now it was Sister's turn to squint. She was nowhere near as canny as Sister Mary Celeste had been.

"No one knows, Terence," she said enigmatically, letting a silence fall as we each pondered our own version of the priest tripping and accidentally dropping the gold-lined cup, or ciborium, in which the consecrated hosts were kept, and hundreds of tiny white wafers falling all over the marble sanctuary floor and bursting into bloody little bombs, and the blood flowing down into the pews and flooding the church, and everybody squishing home in blood-soaked Mary Janes and saddle shoes.

"It is a fate too horrible to contemplate," Sister said quietly. She relied on this phrase a lot. Without Sister Mary Celeste's ability to read minds, she had no way of knowing if people were asking real questions or just being "smart-alecky," so she fell back on something that evoked a general sense of uncertainty and dread.

Every year, the solemn First Communion ceremony was marred by mortifying, and often messy, incidents. Kids burst into tears, overcome by the thought of God seeping around amid the rubber bands and metal of their braces. Others fainted from hypoglycemia, since you couldn't eat or drink anything except water before Communion. Still others suffered nervous gag reflexes and vomited. Medical emergencies were common among First Communicants, and Sister did her best to ward off the worst of them by suggesting that if you suffered one, it was because the Devil had entered your body and your mind. Another tough sell, since suffering was usually encouraged.

"Let Sister know if the Devil has entered your stomach and you feel unwell," she said, holding aloft a small plastic bucket that she had decorated for the occasion with white crepe paper, a large white satin bow, and a small crucifix.

When the big day actually arrived, I was torn between the thrill of having God actually inside my body (Would I see *the bright* all the time? Would I stop lying to everybody and being two people?), concern about what would actually happen to the host once I swallowed it (I had reached "Digestion" in the *Encyclopedia Britannica*), and most importantly, how to keep looking holy and perfect even if the host got stuck to the roof of my mouth. (We had done some practice rounds with unconsecrated hosts and experienced first-hand how easily this could happen with the glutinous little wafer.)

At the moment when the host was actually placed on my tongue, God was the farthest thing from my mind. I just kept moving the wafer around in my mouth so it wouldn't stick anywhere before it melted. I didn't feel much of anything, let alone experience *the bright*. Mostly, I just focused on Sister's final, dramatic admonition before she released us into church for the big show. As we stood waiting in the back vestibule, she pulled herself up very straight, drew in her breath, raised her arm with one finger pointing to heaven, and said so loudly that many of the people sitting in the back pews heard it and turned to stare at us, *"And don't chew the Baby Jesus!!"*

It was a good thing our First Communion was in the spring, because the stress was too much for Sister Cyprian. The next week, she dislocated Denny Quinn's shoulder after she caught him stealing Pagan Baby money. We never saw her again. Rumors flew that she had been sent to a home for insane nuns.

For the last two weeks of school, we had Sister Mary Celeste. She questioned us over and over about the lead-up to our First Holy Communion and the incident with Denny, implying that Sister Cyprian's breakdown had somehow been our fault. Her first-grade class was given to a novice sister who left the convent that summer and moved to California. Sister Mary Celeste stopped calling us "little children" and started calling us "people."

"People, you are in for a rude awakening in third grade! You will learn the multiplication tables and long division, and Sister Patricia Marie will not coddle you!"

Denny slumped in his seat, cradling his arm in its sling, and shot Terry O'Hara a dour glance. I caught Lisa's eye and smiled. After all our academic and spiritual triumphs, and with the certain knowledge that no two people understood or played the system as well as we did, it would take a lot more than multiplication, long division, or Sister Patricia Marie to scare us.

ॐ

Sister Patricia Marie was a little rabbit of a nun. She was barely five feet tall and had a white face, watery blue eyes, a pink nose, and a pinched mouth. If I stood on tiptoe, I was taller than she was.

She did not coddle us. She taught us the multiplication tables and long division, but there was something about her not towering above us that made her seem less magnificent and powerful than Sister Mary Celeste, and less scary than Sister Cyprian.

It made for a rather dull, workaday year. We learned more about Holy Mother the Church, got better at kickball, solidified our friendships and cliques, got more smart-alecky and also better at disguising it, put on inches and pounds, became more adept at managing both our schoolwork and—with the help of more sophisticated math—our sanctity status with the Church.

I developed the habit of doing long division problems with numbers that ran all the way across the page to pass the time while Sister explained things for the fourth time to the dumb kids. It made me feel a little like Ghost Girl, but that was okay. I didn't mind Ghost Girl coming to school sometimes. She knew how to blend in and stay out of trouble—and was really good at putting her feet on the Arthur Murray footprints, even at school.

I had a lot more information about God now, more do's and don'ts and magic tricks, but I hadn't actually felt *the bright* much since first grade. In fact, I hadn't felt it at all. More and more, it seemed like God was something way far away and definitely outside me, not something that swirled around inside me like *the bright* had. Knowing that God was the most important thing, and having less and less access to Him, made me even more nervous than I usually was. I wondered if maybe God didn't let me feel *the bright* anymore because He didn't traffic with girls who stole and lied, and then sent poor Ghost Girl home to deal with Mother.

Sister Patricia Marie's most memorable words were spoken on the sweltering last day of third grade: "Next year, people, you will have Sister Agatha. Sister Agatha has lived in New York!" She paused and scanned the room from atop her desk riser. Whatever she was trying to tell us, we weren't getting it. She followed up pointedly with, "People from New York are different from those of us with *Midwestern roots.*" Again, a swing and a miss. "*Your horizons will be broadened!*" I wasn't sure what that meant, but it sounded good.

o&#x8;

I had that summer pretty well covered. The librarian at the Wilder Park Library had helped me sign up for "summer camp" programs on "Arts and Crafts" and "Nature Lore." Between that and swimming classes at the Elmhurst public pool, I would be away from home most of the day.

Home didn't change much. Ghost Girl had become very skilled by her third year in the driver's seat there. She didn't feel at all, rarely thought except about things in the *Encyclopedia Britannica*, and managed everything pretty well. She was solid even when Lisa's mother came to pick me up for a "boy-girl party" at Terry O'Hara's house. Mother stood at the door with her arms folded as I went out in my party dress, which I had borrowed from Lisa's older sister and which I thought made me look very pretty for the first time in my life. As I passed in front of Mother, she hissed, "You look like a basketball player!" Ghost Girl just stared at her and walked out the door.

The problem was that in the summers, it got confusing who was Ghost Girl and who was me. Before, the difference had been that I felt *the bright* and God, and she did not. Now that *the bright* wasn't around, I started to worry that somehow over the summer I might sink into Ghost Girl, and she might sink into Dead Girl, before I realized what was happening. A little string of fear started growing inside me like the line of mold in our garage. More and more, I blamed God's absence from my life on the darkness that Mother saw in me. If she were right about that, she might be right about everything. If that were the case, there was no hope for me.

In July, Sheila Connerty died in a car crash. She and her mother were on their way down to Bloomington to visit her grandparents, and they had a head-on collision with a drunk driver. Lisa said, "She's happy with God in heaven." I flashed on all the time off Purgatory that Sheila had piled up by sitting in the cloud of chalk dust in Sister Mary Celeste's class. That night, as I lay in bed watching the stars out my window, I wondered where Sheila really was. Her body was already starting to rot and turn to dust, but where was *Sheila*? I tried to imagine her in heaven with God, smiling and eating ice cream, but the picture wouldn't come.

Most of our class attended Sheila's solemn high funeral Mass. I knelt at the consecration of the hosts, determined to get back to where I had been with God. I wanted desperately to feel *the bright* again, but Ghost Girl didn't like being pushed aside and kept trying to make me go numb. During Communion, she made me start thinking about getting together with the gang in the parking lot after Mass, and about how she might like to start coming to school with me more. Before I knew it, Mass was over and I had lost my chance to connect with God again.

That same summer, I started having dreams that woke me up at night. Mother was coming into my closet again—only I was paralyzed. I couldn't move even one little finger, or get up into the cracks in the ceiling. Other times, I was standing inside an enormous Mason jar with holes in the lid, like the ones people used to catch lightning bugs on hot summer nights. Mother was pouring water into the jar. The water got higher and higher. I swam and swam. Finally, my head pressed hard against the top of the jar, but the holes were too small to climb out and the water came up over my nose so I couldn't breathe. I jerked awake all sweaty.

In other dreams, I raked her over and over just like Dad did with leaves in the fall, only the rake was really sharp. Her skin came apart and flew into the air. Then her blood spurted all over me until, again, I couldn't breathe and woke up gasping for breath.

I couldn't deny my darkness when I startled awake like that. I hated it, hated that I didn't know how much of me was the darkness and how much was something else, maybe something good. Hated that I didn't know how to fix it, kill it, lose it, or somehow become better than it. Hated that I didn't really even know what it was. On the other hand, I was pretty sure Mother and I were the only two who saw it. The two of us and, of course, God.

When school started, the dreams came less often. I was determined not to let Ghost Girl push me around anymore, and to spend the year getting back my closeness with God. He would either have to take away the darkness, or get used to it. I thought about finding a way to fool Him, too, but realized that was impossible. Besides, I was exhausted. I didn't think I had it in me to keep one more plate spinning.

∛

Sister Agatha and I turned out to be kindred spirits, even though she was from New York and did not have Midwestern roots. She was just a little older than Sister Mary Celeste—and very athletic, smart, and matter-of-fact. She often leaned back in her chair reading a novel by Charles Dickens or Henry James while we copied our multiplication tables over and over in our notebooks or "worked ahead" in our new fourth-grade history books. Sometimes she took the eraser end of a pencil and idly scratched up under her wimple as she read, pulling forth bright red hair when she withdrew the pencil. She had pale, pale Irish skin like mine. I thought she looked like I probably would look at her age. She often gave us extended recesses and, when there were no other nuns around, took a turn at kickball herself.

Now that we were in fourth grade and expected to know certain things, like that the Earth was round and 7 times 9 was 63, we actually did study subjects other than Religion. Still, Sister Agatha was always ready to toss out the Revolutionary War in favor of our increasingly complex, and increasingly sexual, questions about Religion. Sister Agatha loved rules—the more byzantine, the better—so Holy Mother the Church was just the place for her. The more sexual our questions became, the more deliciously arcane the Church's answers got.

Helen Pulaski, a lanky, morose girl who looked like she'd been born in one of our school uniforms, asked unexpectedly one afternoon during

History class, apparently apropos of Washington crossing the Delaware, "S't'r, if you were riding in the car with your mother and thinking maybe you might kiss a boy if you had the chance, but you were pretty sure you wouldn't have the chance, and then as you were crossing the railroad tracks a train hit you and you died instantly, would you still go to hell, even though you were on your way to Mass and planning to buy your mother a rosary at the church store?"

"Of course," Sister replied, barely looking up and flicking a speck of dust off The Infant of Prague, a chubby little Baby Jesus with a miniature crown and red cloak. Helen might as well have asked if 6 times 8 equaled 48.

Sister Agatha believed that both good and bad behavior deserved instant, dramatic response. I guess she figured that if she could balance our "records" a little here on earth, God wouldn't have so much to do when we died. If we behaved well or gave some promise of one day mastering the 12-tables in multiplication, she could be jolly. Sometimes she even read to us from one of her novels.

If we misbehaved, the results could be sudden and electrifying. One day that spring she caught Mary Frances Kennedy reading a Wonder Woman comic book when we were supposed to be writing the names of states on a blank map of the United States. There was a brief tug of war, which Sister won, then a moment when Sister realized she was holding the scantily clad Wonder Woman in her very hand, and then a terrible smashing of the comic book into the waste basket.

"You and your impure magazines!" she sputtered. "Sins of impurity...sins of disobedience!" She made MaryFran hold out her hands, palms up, and whacked them three times with the ruler. Hard. Then, after a slight hesitation, two more times. She pushed MaryFran back into her seat, turned, and strode to the front of the room. MaryFran whimpered softly. I had an urge to pat her trembling shoulder, but thought better of it.

☙

The next day, Sister gave a pop quiz in Catholic Geography, which was supposedly far more accurate than regular Geography. I was delighted. It would showcase a brilliant system I had designed that year for passing notes in class. Mostly, the note-passing system was just a way to show everybody that I wasn't a goody-goody, even though I was smart. Plus, I was kind of bored and tired of being perfect—or pretending to be perfect. Long division wasn't as fulfilling as it once had been.

The note-passing system was based on a procedure that was already in place. Whenever assignments or tests were passed out, the first person in each row took a sheaf of papers from Sister and walked down the row, placing one on each person's desk. What my note-passing system added was that the "passer" surreptitiously collected from people in his or her row little scraps of paper with vital messages scrawled on them: which boys "liked" which girls that week, speculations on what the nuns did and wore when they went back to the convent after school, and invitations to "come over" after class.

The "passer" deposited all these notes in a miniature mailbox made of three-hole lined notepaper, slung under the desktop of the last person in the row. (The little mailboxes weren't necessary, but they highlighted the cleverness and bravado of my scheme.) When the last person in the row collected the tests or assignments, moving from back to front, he or she distributed the notes. The only flaw was that you could only pass notes to people in your own row, but I was working on that.

That afternoon, the first person in each row took a handful of pop Catholic Geography quizzes and walked slowly down his or her aisle, handing one quiz to each kid. Three people in my row slipped tiny scraps of paper to the "passer," who left them in the little mailbox under the last person's desk.

The quiz asked us to match two columns: Places and Saints. A tiny bend of the Mississippi River was where St. Isaac Jogues had gotten his fingernails yanked out. Maryland was where Fr. John Carroll had founded the first Catholic Colony. The quiz was a snap, even with many of the saints under consideration peering over our shoulders. I finished early, and started a long division problem that stretched the width of my notebook paper.

"STOP!" Sister cried, as if we were contestants on *The $64,000 Question* and our futures rode on these quiz scores. "Collect the papers!"

The last kid in each row stood and moved forward, picking up quizzes and delivering the illegal notes. I had advised them to sort the notes according to where people sat, so that they would always be delivering the top note, and to hold the deliveries in their left hand while they collected papers with their right. Some kids didn't seem to get this, even when I demonstrated it at recess, but there was only so much you could do with the kids Sister called "dumb-bunnies."

Suddenly, a scuffle broke out over in Row 7. Squeaky O'Connor stood over Helen Pulaski's desk, pulling on her test paper as she tugged at his note-carrying hand. In the confusion, five tiny wads of paper scuttled to the linoleum. Leave it to those two!

Sister was on the scene so quickly I hardly saw her move.

"John O'Connor, stand back! Helen Pulaski, stand up!" Squeaky edged back, staring in horror at the scattering of crumpled notes on the floor. Helen pulled herself up and glared down at him. Sister's eyes moved slowly from the floor to the other kids delivering notes—who now stood frozen in the aisles, trying to hide their fistfuls of wadded scraps in their pockets, under their belts, or down their shirts. Terry O'Hara raised his hand to his mouth and started eating his.

Sister often reminded us that she was "not born yesterday." She grasped the situation immediately. A plot of gigantic proportions had been hatched against her authority, against the link she provided to us with Holy Mother the Church, against God Himself. Squeaky and Helen were now only small dots on an infinite field of black. Her gaze shifted from Terry, to Denny, to the other usual suspects. Somehow, she seemed to sense that they were not to blame.

She moved from one standing kid to the next, holding out her hand for evidence. Each kid deposited on her palm a nest of sweaty little scraps of paper. She glided to her desk and placed the notes in her top drawer. She wanted us to know that they would be read later, and perhaps trigger a second wave of her anger.

"Who is behind this?" she asked darkly. Nobody moved a muscle. She waited. Silence pulsed through the room, palpable and terrifying. Adrenaline shot in electric lines from my stomach all the way out into my toes and fingertips.

This could not be happening. I had only intended to have some fun and keep people from thinking I was a goody-goody. It had seemed so innocent. I had never thought about how it would look through Sister's eyes, and I didn't see why I should take the blame for something I hadn't really intended. Maybe I wouldn't have to. I could wait this out, as long as nobody ratted on me.

"Everyone take your seats," Sister said in a low voice. The shamed note-deliverers skulked back to the last seat in each row. "Whoever is behind this has committed a mortal sin—*worse* than a mortal sin because it was calculated to make fun of God. And Sister! Calculated by some evil and devious mind...a mind taken over by the Devil! Whoever has done this, stand and confess your sin!"

I would not, could not, have my connection with Sister severed. I might not be feeling God's presence much lately, but my whole life rested on IC and its trappings. Without that, I was nothing. Worse than nothing. I was Mother's. It felt like my soul was shriveling into a dark wrinkled thing the size of a pea. I stopped breathing. Part of me wafted out the window and sat on a branch of the tree just outside, looking in on the horror.

"Who was it, Lisa Delgado?" Lisa stood and stared at the floor. I knew I should confess and save her, but I couldn't. "Then you are as guilty as that person! Who is it, Helen Pulaski?" Helen stood and stared at the Blessed Mother, obviously seeking intercession. It was clear that Sister would go all around the room, calling each kid to his or her feet and asking the question. With each kid who committed a "sin of omission" on my behalf, my Purgatory got worse. It might already be hell. How could I have done this? What had I been thinking?

At some point, she was going to call on me. Neither I nor Ghost Girl was capable of standing up, looking Sister in the eye, and telling a huge, mortal-sin-level lie. Maybe I could redeem myself by confessing. She would have to admire my courage, at least. Finally, I couldn't stand it anymore. I raised my hand. Sister's eyes bored into me, and she nodded without speaking. I stood and said, "It was me, Sister."

She stared for a long minute, then picked up the red plastic ruler and began walking slowly toward me.

"Class, Cathy Callahan has been fooling us. She has tried to make us believe that she was a good student, a good child of God—but we see in her the Works of the Devil. Works of the Devil!" She smacked the ruler against the side of my head, so hard I almost fell over. "Hold out your hands."

I held them straight out, palms up. The red plastic ruler rose in the air and sliced down onto my hands. Up, and cut down with a soft whistle. Pain seared up my arm. Up again, and down on my forearm. She hit my hands and the insides of my forearms eighteen times, as hard as she could. The counting kept me from passing out. Red bumps started rising on my arms, and smears of blood oozed around them. I was far outside myself, but tears still rose in my eyes.

Finally she stopped and stood staring at me, breathing hard, her face contorted and deep red. I looked at the Blessed Mother, not for intercession but so I wouldn't have to look at Sister.

"Your sin is so large that God may not forgive it," she said, not screaming anymore, but loud enough for everyone to hear. "It is even worse because you did not confess immediately, but let your classmates suffer." She shoved my shoulder. "Do you understand?" she yelled.

"Yes, S't'r," I whispered.

"*What?!*"

"Yes, S't'r," I said more loudly.

"Go home now. Sister Thomas Aquinas will call your mother. She will want to see you and your parents tomorrow, I am sure. Leave us!" she said with dark finality.

I looked around the room. Nobody looked up at me, not even Lisa. I walked out to the parking lot in a daze. My arms stung and throbbed. I considered making a Visit to the Blessed Sacrament to ask what to do, but I would not be welcome there. I slunk past the huge wooden doors of the church, under the eyes of the cement angels, away from IC.

C*

My mind was all static and white noise, flying out in every direction. The welts and cuts needed mercurochrome, or at least washing, but I couldn't go back to the girls' washroom. I was damned in the eyes of Sister, the Church, and IC. Maybe even God. *Probably* God. I couldn't show up at home until after school was out, or Mother would get suspicious. Maybe I couldn't show up there at all, if Sister Thomas Aquinas had put in her call.

So I walked. Through Wilder Park, past the greenhouse and playground and library, heading in the general direction of 221 Fairgrove, my arms held out a couple inches from my body, my mind screaming things I couldn't quite hear. It made me dizzy to look at the slow swelling, the beginnings of purple splotches under the crisscross of dark red stripes.

On Grove Avenue, a sprinkler swung a huge fan of water lazily back and forth over someone's front lawn. I stood at the end of the sweep and held out my arms. The blood thinned and dripped into the blades of grass. When I looked up, a curtain fell back across the window where a lady had been watching me. The door flew open and she came toward me across the lawn, frowning. Maybe to help, but I couldn't take the chance. I ran. For five blocks, until I had to stop and catch my breath. I hid in some shrubs until I saw kids walking down Elm Park Avenue. School was out.

I took the back way to 221 Fairgrove, edged along behind the garage, and washed my arms again with our garden hose. It hurt, but it was a good thing to do. I grabbed my bike and headed away from the house, pedaling fast and trying to think. My arms were deeper red and purple now, with pinpricks of blood and yellow liquid still pushing out of the welts. They burned and ached at the same time.

As I pumped farther and farther away from the house, my situation slowly began to sink in. Everything at IC was over. Holy Mother the Church, Sister, God, indulgences, heaven, *the bright*, everything. Even if the school took me back, I would be an outcast. Sister would treat me the same way she treated Terry O'Hara, like a rat who had somehow gotten enrolled in school with the good little children, but who didn't belong there. I couldn't go back, even if they let me.

All I had left now were Mother and Ghost Girl. That was worse than nothing. Without the connection to IC and God, however tenuous it had become, I would sink quickly into Ghost Girl, then into Dead Girl, then into whatever terrible state was beyond that.

From my left, down Prospect, a dog barked frantically. Then, a sickening moan. I stopped. Sweat gathered on my face and legs as I leaned forward on my handlebars. Halfway down the block, I spotted Brendan Higgins, a skinny redheaded kid from our class who caught baby squirrels and pulled off their legs. He was running across their front yard with a big stick, chasing something. I rode slowly down the other side of Prospect and stopped two houses away. He had Maxine, their collie puppy whose tail fur he had brought to school, trapped under a manicured hedge against the white picket fence between their yard and the neighbors'. He was stabbing viciously at her with the stick, and there was blood on her shoulder.

Maxine could have run sideways along the fence, under the hedge, until she cleared the yard and was free in the street—but she didn't. Her high-pitched yelps made me shiver. Tingles crawled all over my body and I felt dizzy again.

Then, in one breath, I knew exactly what to do. I rode back to our street, hid my bike in the bushes four doors away, and walked as normally as I could up the concrete steps to our front door. The house was dark and cool inside, and smelled like furniture polish. I ran upstairs and changed into navy shorts and a white T-shirt. I grabbed my red jacket from the front hall closet and crept through the living room. I could see her out the window, in the back yard, digging in the garden. Frowning, pushing dirt on top of purple petunias, slapping it down with a trowel.

Her purse was on the hall table. My hand was moist and shaky as I reached inside for the sharp-edged black wallet. A flush came over me as I pulled it out and opened it. I took every cent, $36.87. It was like someone else was doing it, somebody older, smarter, better prepared, and more practiced.

That person moved back into the living room and took the photo album down from the bookcase, carefully extracted a picture of my dad and me, looking at one another and smiling, and stuffed it into my pocket next to the money. I moved silently out into the sunlight.

My knees felt liquid as I pulled my bike from the bushes, ripped the clothespin and playing card from the wheel, pressed them into the dirt beneath the bushes, and rode away.

At the stone quarry, I covered my bike with gravel and made myself walk, not run, out to Route 83. Outlaw skills seemed to come easily to that older, smarter person inside me. I hid in a field of tall dry prairie grass and watched the cars fly by, thinking that some of them must be on their way to Colorado or Montana, or at least Wisconsin. I didn't want to spend a lot of time by the side of the road with my thumb out. A ten-year-old hitchhiker in a red jacket attracted attention, even if I was tall for my age and looked much older. I had to avoid regular people in family cars. They would turn me in, and I'd be dragged off to jail—or worse, home.

I climbed up to the road and crunched slowly along the gravel shoulder as if I were just taking a walk, but meanwhile sizing up each oncoming car out of the corner of my eye. A beat-up old red pickup truck looked okay, so I stuck out my thumb—but too late, and not like I meant business. The truck whizzed by, and the driver craned around to look at me.

I had to get off the road, fast. A white truck with PIE painted on it came barreling toward me. A whole truck filled with pies! I took it as an omen, stepped out into the road, and waved both arms above my head so he either had to stop or run over me. The truck screeched off to the shoulder, leaving black skid marks on the hot pavement and sending up the sharp smell of burning rubber.

I ran to the cab. The driver frowned down at me. His face was lined and deeply tanned, his hair dirty, gray, and longer than I'd ever seen on a man.

"Whatsa matter with you, kid?" he bellowed.

"Please, please, I need a ride right away!" I tore off my jacket and held up my arms. "Somebody beat me up and I have to get home!" He narrowed his eyes.

"What am I supposed to do about it?" He scanned the field, I guess looking for an adult who was attached to me.

"Take me HOME!" I screamed and started to cry. "PLEASE! PLEASE!"

"Pipe down!" he yelled. Then, after looking around again, "Come around the other side." He opened the cab door a crack. I was up the steps and beside him in a flash, crying more now and holding out my arms. He looked at them, lit a cigarette, and stared out the window while he took a couple puffs. Then he looked back at me.

"Where do you live?"

"Where are you going?" I glubbed through the tears.

"North Side." He was going into Chicago! The wrong direction! Still, I was off the road. He could at least take me out of Elmhurst, and I kind of knew my way around Chicago. Or I could figure it out from the little maps at the El stations.

"Me, too." I sobbed.

"What're ya doin' way out here?"

I started crying more loudly and wrapped myself around the red and blue anchor tattoo on his right forearm.

"PLEASE! PLEASE! Take me home!" I screamed incoherently, at the top of my lungs. That seemed to get to him.

"Pipe *down*! Okay, okay. I'll take ya home. Stop crying!" He put the truck in gear and we roared back onto the road. I huddled against the passenger door, sobbing quietly and sneaking peeks at Elmhurst trailing away behind us out the window. I felt empty, relieved, excited, and terrified all at the same time.

I quieted down to reward him and buried my face in my hands, hoping he'd just leave me alone and drive. It worked for about three minutes. Then he started in again. Parents. "The Smiths." School. "Public." The more questions he asked, the worse my answers got and the more he smoked. Each time he flicked a Winston out of the red pack, I thought he was going to kick me out of the truck.

"Whereabouts on the North Side?"

"You can drop me anywhere."

"Yeah, but *where*?"

"State and Madison." Even I knew that wasn't on the North Side, but it was the only street corner I could remember. He looked at me sideways and lit another cigarette.

"Kid, I don't know what you're up to. I do know you're lyin'. I'm takin' you to the cops."

"No! If you do, I'll tell them you kidnapped me!"

He thought a minute, then said, "You're comin' with me."

I didn't like the sound of that. Sister had warned us that most strangers, especially Protestants, were intent on selling us into white slavery. It wasn't clear what white slaves did, but it was very bad and smacked of impurity. Maybe I should jump out of the truck, run back to Sister, and demand to be taken in as a nun in training so I would be held safely in God's arms forever—but I'd made them hate me. They had seen the dark thing inside me. Instead of being Sister's pet and God's favorite, I was the prisoner of a grisly stranger, bouncing around the cab of a truck rumbling toward the North Side of Chicago.

He revved the engine and we started going faster. I couldn't do anything until we stopped, but then I'd make a run for it. I could outrun any kid at school, and I bet I could outrun him. As we entered the city, rickety old buildings started to fly by—dark brown brick and cement, dingy gray wood. We wound through neighborhoods with signs in Italian and German, old men sitting on stoops in their undershirts with beers dangling from their fingertips.

He looked over at me and glared.

"You got me in some trouble, and now I gotta fix it. Shit!" He slammed the steering wheel with his palm. I stared straight ahead and pretended not to hear. Just like Ghost Girl would, except I felt alive. Scared, but alive. He turned on the radio real loud, then snapped it off, lit another cigarette, and slammed the steering wheel again.

I had no idea where we were, but the signs over stores got grimier and the streets got more potholes. He pulled into a big lot surrounded by a chain-link fence, and parked so fast that before I realized what was happening, my door was slammed right up against the metal fence. I couldn't open it! The only way out was through him, on the driver's side. I lunged like a football player, but he caught me by the shoulder of my jacket like he'd expected me to make just that move.

I pulled and squirmed, pushed and kicked, but he grabbed me by the shoulders and put his face two inches from mine. I winced from the cigarette smell. He said, very low, "Listen to me. Shut up and calm down. You just pretend like we're friends while we walk over there." He gestured up the street. "One peep out of you, I'll call the cops and they'll throw your ass in jail so fast...You hear me?"

I nodded.

"Anybody asks, you're my niece. Right? Okay?"

I nodded again. He grabbed my wrist, almost like we were holding hands but so I couldn't slide away. We walked up the cracked, dirty sidewalk past a bar with a neon "Pabst Blue Ribbon" sign sizzling in the window and people laughing and yelling inside, past a launderette, and past "Mollie's Bakery" into a narrow alley. I would have run at that point, but his hand was too tight around my wrist. He started dragging me up a grimy putty-colored staircase that climbed up the back of a dark brick building.

I did not want to be inside with him, and flashed on the wolves who gnawed off their legs to get out of traps.

"Let me go!" I screamed, and pulled hard at my hand.

"You want the cops?"

Maybe I should let him call the cops—but they would take me home for sure, and I might as well be dead if that happened. I shook my head. On the second landing, he knocked on the door. I was shaking and grabbed the wood railing. I could throw myself over it and carry him with me to the alley, but it was too far down. I would never survive. He knocked again, harder this time.

The door swung open. A large woman in a floor-length jade green silk robe stood with one hand on her hip, the other holding a cigarette and an amber-colored drink with a maraschino cherry bobbing on top. The robe was covered with tiny red and black dragons and open at the top so her powdery white breasts spilled out. She looked about as old as my mother, but with blue-black hair piled on top of her head, red rouge and lipstick, and spider-web mascara. My mother would have called her "brassy." She looked from him, to me, and back to him.

"Good Lord, Stan, what have you done now?"

Chapter 5

"I found her by the road, Moll." He raked his hand back through his hair, taking little steps like he didn't know where to put his feet. "She made me take her."

"Yeah?" She threw her head back like a tough movie star, a glamour girl who was kind of old and very tall. "Well, you both better come in where I can protect you from her."

She pulled me gently inside and replaced the chain lock. Her hands were soft. The smell of Jergens hand lotion, perfume, cigarettes, and alcohol made my nose twitch. When she saw the welts and bruises on my arms, she looked at Stan like he was the one who was in trouble—not me.

"You wait here while I talk to Stan." She led me over to a rough wood table twice the size of our dining room table in Elmhurst. Above it hung big copper bowls and spoons, spatulas and whisks and other stuff I didn't even recognize.

"See that window in the door?" Moll pointed across the kitchen to a swinging door with a glass rectangle across the top. Her fingernails were the same dark red as her lipstick. Vermilion. I nodded. "I'll be right on the other side, keeping my eye on you. Hear?"

I nodded. She squeezed my shoulder and pulled out one of the eight chairs around the table. I sat. She might be a white slaver, but something drew me to her. She was strangely comforting, and definitely in charge. I liked how she bossed Stan around. I had no doubt whatsoever that she would be "keeping her eye on me." As she herded Stan into the hall, she looked back over her shoulder. I watched my hand go up in a small wave. She raised an index finger back at me.

The kitchen was huge. Pale yellow with gleaming white trim, not grimy like the rest of the neighborhood. There were three big ovens and two double sinks. I smelled cookies, and spotted a rack of ginger snaps cooling on the counter next to a pan of brownies. An angel food cake, half covered with dark chocolate icing, stood on a little pedestal by the sink.

Only a few feet away from me, right in the center of the table, glistening under the big ceiling lamp, were eight apple fritters on a big white platter. My mouth watered for them. They looked like they were fried just right, with lots of nooks and crannies and a thin layer of sugary frosting. My stomach growled.

I had planned to be far away by now, in a fast car with anonymous and disinterested people, flying West into the sunset—not locked in a dirty building in a bad neighborhood with people who were unlike anybody I'd ever met. If I didn't watch myself, I'd wind up slung across a deathbed, bleeding out like St. Maria Goretti.

I glanced at the chain lock on the door. I wasn't sure I had enough courage or strength left to run again, and wasn't even sure that running was a good idea. All I really wanted was something to eat and a place to lie down. I tightened the sleeves of my jacket around my waist and looked up at the glass rectangle. Moll's face appeared. I clasped my hands in front of me on the table like the Protestants did when they prayed, in a two-handed fist. It was a good bet these people weren't Catholics. No crucifixes or saints' pictures. Way too much makeup, and too much skin showing to be connected to Holy Mother the Church.

In a minute, Moll came and sat next to me, rearranging our chairs so we faced each other. Stan had apparently been sent out another door.

"Let's see those arms." As I shifted to show her, two quarters and a dime clattered out of my jacket to the hardwood floor. I scrambled for them.

"I can pay my way out of white slavery! See?!" I showed her all my money. "How much does it cost to get free?" She looked almost like she was going to laugh, but instead passed her hand over her mouth and got kind of fake serious.

"Your money's no good here," she said, waving it away. I stuffed it back into my pocket. "Let's see." She turned my arms over and frowned. The welts were huge and purple now. Blood and clear liquid still oozed from the corners of the red marks. Looking at them made them hurt more. "Who did this?" she asked casually, like it happened every day and she was just wondering who won the Cubs game.

"My parents! That's why I'm here!" Before the words were even out, I knew that she knew I was lying. My cheeks felt hot. Lying usually made me feel smart, not ashamed. It wasn't even a smart lie—just the opposite of what I'd told Stan—and I hated her knowing that I'd tried to fool her. She leaned back in her chair and resumed her tough girl look.

"What's your name?"

I didn't want to lie again. It made me feel too awful. Anyway, every third kid in Chicago was named Cathy.

"Cathy."

"Cathy what?"

I turned the welts down and stared at the tops of my arms.

"Well, Cathy, you and I have a problem." She lit a cigarette and exhaled smoke through her nose. I watched, transfixed. She was so large, so odd. So sinful, yet somehow good. She treated me like I was an adult, maybe even one of her friends. "Don't we." It was a statement, not a question.

I worked up the courage to look her in the eye. Hers were brown, and very steady. I nodded slightly.

"I don't know if I can help you, or even if I want to. Here's the deal. You lie to me one more time, I call the cops and you go home. They'll find it, wherever it is." She rolled the ash off her cigarette inside a red plastic ashtray. "I want the whole story," she said. "No more bullshit." I'd never heard that word spoken aloud before. "Why don't you have a fritter while you think about it?"

She pushed the plate toward me. I chose the one with the most peaks and valleys. It was darker than the others, which meant it was more deep fat fried. "That's a good one," she observed, picking out one for herself. She got us both big white cloth napkins, and ate her fritter slowly while I ate mine. Her lipstick rubbed off, so each bite she took had a little red smear on it.

I had never eaten anything that tasted as good as that fritter. I could do a whole lot worse than this. Already had, just this afternoon, being dragged around a slum by a dirty old truck driver who now seemed pretty dumb! I either had to run now, make a break for it out that back door, or play it her way. My usual tactics, lying, clearly wouldn't work here. Not only would Moll know if I tried to "bullshit" her, but I sensed that she meant business about calling the cops.

I saved the most fried and sugary clump for last, and let the crunch and sweetness explode together over my tongue. When I finished, I wiped the sugar off my mouth and laid the napkin on the table.

"Well?" Her eyes were like my mother's chinchilla coat.

I told her everything, at least everything that had happened since we moved to Elmhurst—even about being afraid I'd wind up like Maria Goretti if I stayed there. When I said that, she sucked on her Pall Mall and blew a smoke ring up into the kitchen utensils. It was like Confession was supposed to be. I felt washed clean, and exhausted.

She asked some questions, like was my mother a drunk and did she hit me, how come my Dad was never home, and where exactly did we live. I told the truth, even about our address on Fairgrove Avenue. Then she circled back and asked the same questions another way, I guess trying to stump me. Finally, she seemed satisfied.

"Well, one thing, Cathy. We can be pretty sure you won't wind up like St. Maria Goretti." I didn't know whether or not to believe her. Maybe she was just trying to soften me up, so I'd let my guard down.

"That's good," I said, playing along.

"Yes, it is." She pulled another Pall Mall from the crinkly red package and snapped her Zippo lighter shut as she exhaled. "So you're looking for...what?"

"A place to stay until I can get to Montana or Colorado."

"Ah! Just passing through..."

I nodded tentatively. She played with the Zippo, turning it over and over. I waited.

"Tell you what," she said. "You stay here a few days, let me check things out." I must have looked panicky. "Don't worry. For now, we'll keep this between you and me—but you have to stay out of sight while I figure this out. I'll give you a room, but you have to stay in there. Can you do that?"

It might be a trick, the first step on the road to white slavery. I could be deep in the hull of a ship headed for Shanghai by morning, but I was pretty sure about one thing: This lady would not send me back to Elmhurst. I saw the look in her eyes when I talked about my mother and Sister. She might sell me to a Chinese warlord or mob boss, torture me, give me to the cops, or send me to an orphanage—but unless I really blew it, she would keep me away from 221 Fairgrove Avenue and Immaculate Conception Grammar School. That was a step ahead of where I'd been this morning.

"Okay," I said. She stamped out her cigarette in the ashtray and stuck out her hand.

"Okay. My name's Mollie." I shook the hand. It was enormous, soft, and very warm. "We have a deal?"

"Yes."

She led me down to the end of a dark hallway that creaked when we walked on it, and opened a door. I stopped in the entrance. The room had bars on the windows. She flicked on a light and pulled me in. Except for the window bars, the room was cozy. The walls were the same light yellow as the kitchen, with a dark green bedspread, a big adult desk with a file cabinet, two packed bookcases, a dresser with a mirror, and a large easy chair with a reading lamp. Mollie left and locked the door behind her.

She was back in an hour with pot roast, mashed potatoes, gravy, and green beans with butter and little almond slivers. Real beans, not canned. It was the best meal I'd ever eaten. She gave me a toothbrush and put ointment on my arms. Then she brought me a slinky peach-colored nightgown that didn't even cover me up on top, so she tied knots in the spaghetti straps to make it come up over my chest.

"Remember," she said before she left. "You stay in here and be quiet. I'll bring you three squares tomorrow." With that, she leaned down so her face was only about a foot from mine, and put her hand on the top of my head. Even her smell was warm. "Big day, huh kid?"

I nodded and watched her leave. Again, she locked the door.

I crawled under the sheets. They smelled like Mollie. Beyond the bars, the window looked across the alley to another brown brick building. It reminded me of the view out my closet window in the apartment building, before we moved to Elmhurst.

I was different now, a girl who could run away. A girl who could make friends with powerful people. A girl who, in a matter of hours, had killed a bad life dead and found a place to stay where at least they served apple fritters. Maybe I would become a junior Mollie, wandering around the back alleys of Chicago in slinky clothes and robes from an opium den, drinking Old-Fashioneds—which is what she called her drink—puffing on Pall Malls, bossing around men like Stan, talking out of the side of my mouth, baking pot roast dinners, God knew what else...

God. Where was he now? I would never find him in a place like this. Did He even want me to find Him? I wanted to pray—that I was doing the right thing by running away, that I would be okay, that some good thing would find me—but could only imagine God sitting with his long white beard on the golden throne, surrounded by hordes of saints, the Blessed Mother and Baby Jesus, and all of them shaking their heads sadly at what I had done. Disobedience. Disrespect. Lying. I could see St. Isaac Jogues' fingertips starting to bleed again, St. Teresa's stigmata acting up, her "wounds of Christ" beginning to ooze rose-smelling blood...

I would have to get to Confession somehow, so that I wouldn't go straight to hell if a truck happened to run over me, as it easily could in this neighborhood.

I stared out the window. Light rose up from the street. In the bar, they were singing "Happy Days Are Here Again." I wasn't so sure about that. People shouted down in the alley, scuffling and swearing like they were fighting. I tried to listen, in case they climbed up the fire escape and attacked me, but the dark river came to take me and I fell into it.

೧೫

In the morning, Mollie appeared carrying a huge tray of bear claws, a melt-in-your-mouth puffy pastry that she called "popovers," creamy butter, coffee for her, milk for me, and two copies of the *Sun-Times*. This became our morning ritual for the next several days. We would eat silently and read the paper while Mollie drank cup after cup of black coffee and "woke up."

Then we would discuss the news of the day and "get to know each other." Mostly, this consisted of Mollie grilling me about world events and her favorite subject, Chicago politics. She remembered the names of all fifty aldermen, showed me a map of how all the wards were laid out, and seemed actually to have attended most of the meetings in "smoke-filled back rooms" where the real business of Chicago was conducted. She loved political gossip and, I could tell, hoped that some of her savvy would rub off on me so she would have someone with whom to rehash the details of City Council floor flights. Mayor Daley was her hero for his raw power and mastery of the political machine, even though she sometimes called him "that thug."

"What do you think Hizzoner would say to *that* resolution, Cathy?" she would ask to test my budding political acumen.

It felt like I'd slipped into some *Alice in Wonderland* hole. What was I, a ten-year-old runaway, doing lounging around each morning in a North Side walk-up, eating pastries in bed and talking politics with a woman like Mollie? I could only guess that she really did want to get to know me, that she didn't have much experience with children, and that this was all she knew to do.

She acted like there was nothing unusual about our arrangement. I just went along. I didn't want to spend the rest of my life locked in a room—but for now, at least I had a roof over my head and "three squares," as she said. I kept telling myself just to let the dust settle, not to do anything until I got the lay of the land. The less I did, the less chance there was of upsetting her, or of doing something that showed her the darkness inside me. I didn't know exactly what I wanted from her, but I needed to keep my options open.

She wanted to know more about my life in Elmhurst, and even asked about the time before we moved to Elmhurst, when we lived in the apartment. I looked out the window, trying to figure out what to say. That got her radar going, of course, and in five minutes I'd told her all about the closet, too. I felt ashamed that I had been part of such a bad thing. I had never told anybody about it and even wondered if, after all these years, I might be making it up. Mollie just nodded and ate another bear claw.

She picked out books for me to read during my long days in the room, so that we could talk about them: *Black Beauty*, *Little Women*, and *A Midsummer Night's Dream* from the humongous *Works of Shakespeare* book. I had to stop reading *Black Beauty* when people mistreated the horse until it fell on its knees and got "ruined." I wondered what made a person get "ruined," and if it had happened to me. *Little Women* was just as bad, with all those sisters cuddling up together with Marmee and nobody hating anybody. It made me horribly sad, so I moved on to *A Midsummer Night's Dream*. That was just baffling. Even when I read it aloud to myself, I had no idea what they were talking about. Mollie picked out other books, ones with lower emotional content: *Road Atlas of the United States,* which seemed like a very helpful gesture, and *A Child's Guide to Birds of America,* which was boring and seemed fake because all I ever saw were pigeons.

I loved to read, but not all day, every day, so she brought me a 200-piece jigsaw puzzle of the Rocky Mountains and set up a card table where I could work on it. It seemed like she was trying hard to find things a ten-year-old girl might enjoy while locked in a room all day, so I took pity on her and pretended to like the jigsaw puzzle. The next day, she brought another one of the Garden of the Gods in Colorado.

I spent a lot of time just lying on the bed, staring at the white ceiling, my arms folded across my chest and tears sometimes leaking down into my ears, the warm soft smells of bread and cakes and chocolate chip cookies wafting down the hall and under my door.

What had I done, running away? Maybe I should have made Dad...do what? He always changed the subject when I brought up anything about Mother, and seemed to have lost interest in us completely since we moved to Elmhurst. He hardly ever came home, and seemed distant when he did show up. When it came to solving my problems, he was as useless as Ghost Girl. Maybe I should have called the cops, but Mother would have acted nice when they came around, and they would have left me there. Talked to some other Sister? The nuns stood together, and Mother's prediction had come true. They had seen my darkness, and knew that I was a rotten apple.

Could I go back? I fantasized about showing up at our house, walking into the dark dining room and seeing Mother setting the table. She looked up at me like I was a large, ugly snail—then swept up from beneath the table a big sack of salt and hurled it at me. Every inch of my skin scalded and shrank, and I melted into a terrible, mangled version of myself. It would be worse than it had been before.

Somehow, I had to find another nest or "purchase," as they said in *A Child's Guide to Birds of America*. A place to be. Then figure out what to do about God.

છ

When Mollie wasn't telling me the inside story behind every newspaper article or quizzing me about my life, she talked about baking and Ping-Pong. It turned out she had been the Ladies National

Champion. She showed me a newspaper clipping of her wearing a navy blouse and shorts, a Ping-Pong paddle raised high above her head at the end of a follow-through, looking so excited and triumphant I thought she might burst. Another picture showed her opponent, a short Chinese woman with a bowl haircut, catapulting through the air in a vain attempt to reach Mollie's sharply angled slam. Mollie tried to hide her smile when she showed me the pictures and to pretend it was no big deal, but she didn't fool me.

I wondered why someone like her would risk keeping me around, even for a while, but kept quiet and waited.

I found out some other things about her, too. She was the Mollie of "Mollie's Bakery." A couple girls rented rooms from her at the other end of the hall, which explained the voices I sometimes heard at night—men and women laughing and, I figured, drinking because it got pretty loud. She had lived in the neighborhood ever since she'd moved to Chicago after her divorce.

"How long will I have to stay in this room?" I asked as politely as I could after four days. She nodded and lit a Pall Mall, tossing the crumpled pack across the room into the waste basket.

"We may get some answers today. Then we'll talk."

I was no longer afraid of her, except for the power she held to keep me or kick me out. I wanted to stay with her, but not be locked up. She was smart, and might help me get some money before I moved on. Or maybe I would stay with her longer. As she stood up to leave, I asked if she would pick me up a *Daily News*, one of the afternoon papers. This pleased her immensely, as I knew it would.

That afternoon, I watched from my window as a cop car pulled into our alley. Mollie hurried down the back stairs in a powder blue cotton shirtwaist dress and blue flats, almost no makeup, and her hair smoothed down into a simple pageboy. She carried a white vinyl purse and didn't look anything like herself. She slipped into the front seat of the cop car and they sped away.

As soon as she was out of sight, someone knocked on my door. I knew Mollie wanted me to keep hidden, but she hadn't told me what to do if somebody knocked.

"Yoo hoo, little girl?" a woman's voice sang. She sounded friendly enough. I crept over to the door and looked under it. Lime green high heels. "Yoo hoo! Are you in there?" How dangerous could she be, in those shoes? Plus, Mollie must have told her I was in here—so I wouldn't be giving away any secrets.

"Yes?" I answered softly.

"Oh good! I'm gonna unlock your door and come in for just a sec. Okay?" The lock turned, and the door opened on a young blonde woman with pale white skin, bright red lipstick, and green eye shadow. She wore lime green Capri pants that matched the shoes, a clingy white blouse, and a hot pink bow in her hair. She carried a bulging Kresge's bag.

"Hi, hon! I'm Julie. I brought you some clothes," she said with a big smile, holding up the bag as if my main concern while locked up had been my wardrobe and I could finally rest easy. She clattered into the room, threw her arms around me, and actually pinched my cheek, which I hadn't known people did in real life. Then she turned the Kresge's bag upside down over the bed. Out tumbled a riot of brightly colored clothes—shorts, dresses, tops, and hair bows. They all leaned toward a look that was a smaller, dark-haired, pre-makeup, pre-puberty version of herself.

"This is so cute!" she squealed, grabbing up a turquoise sundress. She held a lime green hair bow against it, raised her eyebrows, and grinned at me for confirmation that it was the cutest thing I'd ever seen. I smiled weakly, worried that Mollie wouldn't want me talking to anyone. "Now don't you worry, hon, I'll tell Mollie it was all my fault. I just couldn't stand to think of you cooped up in here, wearing the same old thing every day." She put her finger to her lips, as if it were our secret, and backed out the door. I put all the clothes back in the Kresge's bag and slipped it under the bed, so Mollie wouldn't see it when she came back from her mysterious mission.

That night, it was Julie who showed up with a hamburger, broccoli with a big pat of butter, and scalloped potatoes runny with cheddar cheese.

"Mollie called, hon, and I told her what I did." She mugged, putting her hands over her eyes, and continued, "She was kinda pissed, but then I guess she figured it was okay, since I already broke the ice and she was tied up wherever she is, I might as well make myself useful and bring you dinner so here I am."

She threw her arms wide, and somehow knew to look under the bed for the Kresge's bag. She laid all the clothes out on the bed again. While I ate, she created outfits. She went through each item, and told me what blouse went with what shorts and hair bow, and even wrote down a list of combinations I could put together. Then she made me put on the turquoise sundress and lime green hair bow.

"Oooo. You're so *cute*! I have a dolly to dress up! I hope Mollie lets you stay!"

So Mollie had talked to Julie about not letting me stay! Where would I go if I couldn't stay with her? What would make her decide one way or the other—and what was she up to in that blue get-up with the cop? Julie didn't seem like someone you would turn to for these kinds of answers, so I just said, "Me, too."

She talked on and on about clothes and makeup and sales at stores in the Loop and how she hoped Mollie wouldn't make her work in the bakery on Saturday because she had a new boyfriend and they wanted to drive out to Morton Arboretum for a picnic. My parents had taken me to Morton Arboretum last fall, and we'd watched all the beautiful crimson and gold and orange and brown leaves swirl around in the wind. The kind of leaves we had drawn in second grade.

Inside, I felt like a game of 52 Pickup, where you just threw the cards into the air and they scattered every which way. When you asked someone if they wanted to play 52 Pickup, you were usually playing a trick on them.

೫

When Mollie resurfaced the next morning, she looked like herself again. She swept through the door with our breakfast tray wearing her dark red silk robe with the black trim and big pockets for her cigarettes. I grabbed a bear claw and reached for the *Sun-Times*, but she waved my hand away and shook her head.

"Let's talk," she said, as if she didn't really want to talk. A bad sign. I replaced the bear claw. "No, eat!" she barked. I didn't feel like eating. She leaned back, crossed her legs, lit a cigarette, and fixed me with a steady look that made me squirm.

"Well, you and I have some decisions to make, kiddo," she began. I nodded, trying to look attentive and hopeful. "I've done some checking and asking around. I don't think you need to go back to Elmhurst, if you don't want to."

Relief flooded through me, but also a wave of panic. I didn't want to go back—or worse, have her *send* me back—but it meant shutting a door that I'd left cracked open.

"Did you go there in that cop car?" It seemed a brazen question, but I had to know. She frowned, pursed her lips, and shifted her weight around the chair. Then I guess she decided to follow her own advice and be honest.

"My friend Bill drove me out to Elmhurst. We talked to some people we know, took a look around. You know…" I imagined Mollie prowling around Elmhurst—up and down Fairgrove Avenue, following Mother into the Piggly Wiggly, watching her select pork loin, ears of corn, paper towels. Then heading over to IC and posing as somebody's mother, scrunching into a desk at the back of Sister Agatha's classroom, witnessing something like the Wonder Woman incident with MaryFran.

(Mollie actually looked something like Wonder Woman!) The thought of her touching my life in those strangely intimate ways was horrifying, but fascinating.

"Don't worry. Nobody saw me. I wore a disguise."

Oh, brother. Even in the blue shirtwaist and white vinyl purse, Mollie looked nothing like an Elmhurst housewife.

"Did you see my mother?"

"Oh yeah, I got a good look at her." I waited, but she didn't volunteer any more. If anybody could figure why Mother hated me, or why she acted so strange, it was Mollie. This seemed like my last chance to find out.

"What did you think?"

"Does she get drunk a lot?"

"I don't think so." Unless she did it after I went to bed, but I never saw any bottles or anything.

"Take a lot of medicine?"

"I don't know."

Mollie kind of snorted.

"Well, she's a very unhappy woman."

That much, I already knew.

"Where did you see her? Did you hide in the bushes in our back yard? Did you..."

"Hey! Enough. I saw her, all right? I got the picture."

Mollie either didn't understand it herself, or didn't want to tell me about it. *I got the picture.* It wasn't very satisfying, but it was all I was going to get.

"Are the cops after me?"

"Yes and no," she said carefully. I felt like I was going to faint, and held on to the edge of the bed. Yes and no? Hadn't my parents called the cops? I nodded, but the bed, the room, all of Chicago felt like it was falling out from under me.

"I don't understand about the cops," I said, on the verge of tears but trying to make my voice sound calm and polite, adult and easy to get along with, so maybe she would keep me. Mollie acted like she didn't want to say any more, so I shut up and just *watched her wheels turn*, as Dad always said he was doing with me. Finally she shook her head, shifted in the chair, and lit a cigarette.

"Bill has a buddy on the Glen Ellen force. Next to Elmhurst?" I nodded. Did she think I was an idiot, or was she stalling for time? "He asked this guy to feel out the Elmhurst cops, make up some story to find out if they knew about you. Turns out your dad called, but he sounded kind of crazy. When they asked him why he let days go by, he said he didn't know you were gone. Is your dad kind of crazy?"

"No, but he might not have known I was gone. Like I said, sometimes he doesn't come home from work." Mollie nodded and glanced at the ceiling.

"How often does he not come home?"

"Lots. Maybe four or five nights a week."

"Okay." She looked like she knew something I didn't, but wasn't about to tell me.

"Do the cops have a dragnet out for me?" She kind of looked down and put her hand over her mouth.

"Well, not exactly a dragnet. They looked, didn't find you, and nobody answered their alerts. Oh! That nun? Sister Annabelle?"

"Sister Agatha."

"The cops went out to your school, and she's gone."

"Where?!"

"The missions, they said. Where's that?"

"Honduras," I said, as if I actually knew. Mollie nodded. "What about my dad? Isn't he doing something? Calling the cops back? Hiring private eyes?"

She took a long drag on her cigarette.

"The whole thing is quieting down now."

"What else is he doing?"

"He may be doing a lot, but he's not talking to the Elmhurst cops about it. So unless you make a big mistake, like running away from here, you're on the other side of trouble—if you wanna be."

It was hard to believe. Things were a lot easier when you had powerful connections, like Mollie did. Like I did, now.

"What about Bill?"

"Bill knowing is like me knowing. Don't worry about him. Or any of our cops."

Our cops? She said it like she meant the whole Chicago police force, and maybe that was true. I picked up the *Sun-Times* and held it up in front of my face, pretending to read page one. There was a picture of Mayor Daley pounding on the podium at City Hall, but I didn't read the story.

A huge river had opened up between me and Elmhurst. I felt almost safe on this side of the river. Dad was on the other side, but maybe he didn't care about me anymore, backing off like that. I lowered the *Sun-Times*. Mollie looked at me as if she'd been watching me right through the paper.

"*So.* Like I said, we have some decisions to make." I nodded. "We can do this a couple ways." She lit another cigarette, even though the old one was still smoldering in the ashtray. "First, you can go home if you want to."

She looked out the window. I followed her gaze to the brown bricks of the building across the alley. Morning sounds drifted up from the alley and the street below—people walking briskly along the sidewalk to the El station, muffled conversations, the roar of an El train clattering along its creaky tracks a block away, rushing people downtown. If I said no, I could never get back to the other side of the river. But they didn't want me back.

"No," I heard myself say. It was like somebody else was talking. Mollie's shoulders shifted, like she'd been holding her breath and now she could relax. She tried not to smile, but she seemed a little happy and that made me feel good.

"Okay. Here's another possibility. There's this really nice place, Holy Angels Orphanage. You could get a great education. The only problem is, it's a Catholic school, so there's a chance you'd get caught there. Bottom line, I think the nuns are more likely to get you than the cops."

Mollie would send me away? To nuns? She must have seen my panic, and held up her hand like a traffic cop.

"The other choice is, you can stay here with me and go to regular school. Either way..."

"I'll stay here!"

"Not so fast. Don't you want to go look at Holy Angels? I can take you this afternoon..."

"*No!*" She seemed surprised, but pleased, and took a minute buttering her popover. She had that same trying-not-to-smile that she had gotten looking at the clippings of her Ping-Pong triumphs.

"Well, then you have to do something. You might not like it, but it'll keep both of us out of trouble." I teetered on the edge of the bed, eager to show I would do whatever was necessary. She bit into the popover and took her time chewing. Then finally, like she thought it would make me jump out the window or something, she said to the popover, "You have to, uh, be someone else."

She took a big swig of coffee, watching me over her mug, and started talking real fast. "Like a disguise. It'll be fun! That way, there's no Cathy Callahan for them to find, whatever your dad may or may not be doing!" She sucked on her Pall Mall, like the idea of me becoming someone else would be terrible for me.

I'd been doing that all my life. The only difference was that now I had a co-conspirator, and a smart one at that! The one problem was that disguises seemed to be about the only thing Mollie wasn't very good at. I imagined her designing something out of the clothes Julie had bought.

"Uh, who would I be?"

"Well, that's the beauty of it," she said, like she was almost out of breath. "My niece Mara was just your age, and she died last year in a tractor accident. My sister has all her things, like her birth certificate. You could use it. You could become Mara, my niece who came here to live with me from Montana. See how that throws 'em off?" She grabbed a bear claw and began slathering it with butter.

"You have a niece?" She had never mentioned a niece, or even any siblings.

"My sister and I aren't exactly on speaking terms, but you know me. I'll find a way." She frowned at the bear claw. I decided to let it alone.

"She lived in Montana?" I asked slowly, trying to take in the idea of becoming a girl who died in a tractor accident. Had she been cut up into a million pieces? How strange that she had lived in Montana, where I wanted to go. Mollie nodded.

"We'd just, you know, pretend you were her. I'd tell you stuff you needed to know, and you'd…uh… look different."

"Different how?"

"Hair, clothes, Julie…" She waved her hand in the air as if this was the least of our worries, and I supposed it was. I could be a whole new person. One from Montana. Maybe even one with no darkness inside her. Mollie's world would be my world. Dirty streets. The bakery. The bar next door with the sizzling Pabst Blue Ribbon sign. My mother would definitely not approve. It was a grown-up world. Mollie would be kind of like my mother. Or something. I felt the Ping-Pong smile playing around my own lips.

"Why are you helping me?"

She reverted to her tough glamour-girl self and barked, "Ha! You think you're the only one who ever ran away from something?" Then she picked up the paper and pretended to be engrossed. I looked around the room, which would probably become mine. Filled with books. My eyes fell on the *Road Atlas*. Mollie had known I wanted that before I did. She had thought about what I might want, and brought it to me.

"Want to see a picture of her?" she asked finally. I nodded. She pulled an old photo out of her big pocket, like she'd had it all planned.

I cradled it in my hands. The girl had short hair, blowing every which way in the wild Montana wind. A ragged white T-shirt and smiling cheeks. She looked like she lived outdoors. I would look like that if I'd been born in Montana. In a funny way, it felt like we were the same person, living the same life from two different angles. I put my finger on her happy cheek. *The bright* hovered around me, just on the fringes. I wanted to be this girl. Had a right to be her. Actually *was* her, in a way. I looked up at Mollie. She had little tears in her eyes, and was sneakily wiping them away. I didn't say anything, and looked back at the photo. This girl wanted me to be her. I smiled at Mollie, and she smiled back at me.

Five days later, a small brown package arrived in the mail. Mollie riffled through it, noting each paper until she came to an official-looking one with a gold seal and a curly border. She snapped it out of the pack and held it up between her index and middle finger.

"We're in business, Mara!"

Chapter 6

When I became Mara, Mollie and I had to push out the sides of the bubble where we floated together to include her two boarders, Julie and Loreen.

Loreen had olive skin and flat black hair that she dyed every other Thursday night. She wore only black—black nightgowns ("negligees," she called them), black dresses, black jeans, black blouses, even black underwear. Julie told her, "Hon, you look like the Addams Family's gone-wrong cousin!" Loreen was sultry and rarely spoke. I sometimes heard her crying in her room.

Mollie made them swear to uphold the story of my being her niece Mara, but they just shrugged. Cathy, Mara, it was all the same to them. All they knew was that Mollie had put a strange little girl in their midst, and it was everybody's job to take care of her.

Julie and Loreen had many boyfriends. Sometimes they would have two or three dates in one night, little "parties" in their rooms with lots of drinking and squealing. Mollie had boyfriends, too, but not so many and older. Her men friends also included "pals and pols." The pals were guys like Stan and Bill the cop, who came by during the day to drink coffee and smoke cigarettes at the kitchen table. The "pols" were fatter, balder guys from city politics who talked all the time and had booming laughs. They seemed to worship her, and she held court in our parlor most nights, passing around drinks and telling stories. I would inch silently down the hall and peek around the corner to watch them, amazed at how jolly and loud everybody was compared to the people at my parents' parties.

It was Loreen's idea to dye my hair. The four of us stared into Mollie's bathroom mirror. Julie held the black and white picture of the Montana girl up against it, so we could compare her to me.

"Honey champagne," Julie said.

"Raven," Loreen said.

"Perm," Mollie said.

I leaned in and peered at the photo.

"Red," I said. That was the spirit of the hair. That smiley, breezy Montana girl with the wind in her hair knew who she was and what she was about. She had two feet planted firmly on her very own place on earth. Red hair suited her. Besides, it seemed more Irish and I was desperate to get a foothold somewhere. I felt like a snake being pulled out of its skin. The old skin had to go. I wanted it gone—but if it had to go so fast, I needed something to hang on to.

None of the other three faces in the mirror seemed to understand any of this. Loreen looked perplexed. Mollie, curious. Julie actually looked upset.

"*You're* blonde, and you'll always be prettier," I said to her. She smiled. There was something like an indulgence system for getting out of Purgatory here, too.

"Red it is," Mollie said, smiling slightly.

"And short!" I said.

"No!" they all screamed.

I wanted to be the tousled tomboy in the picture. No more Cathy Callahan with her tight braids and nervousness.

"I hate my braids! My dad's private investigators will be looking for braids!"

They all kind of eyed one another and looked sideways at me. A few hours later, I had a thick mop of short red hair. I looked in the mirror and tossed it to the left, then to the right. It felt carefree, almost reckless, to flop it from one side to the other and let it fall any which way. I was unleashed, loose, and could do whatever I wanted.

Mollie wrapped my braids in tissue paper and put them in a box on the top shelf of her closet. I watched, wondering why she did that, but didn't say anything.

She told me to put on my bright pink sundress and white sandals, because we were going to Mr. Kelly's to celebrate and listen to jazz. She gave the guy at the door a twenty-dollar bill, and he didn't seem to notice that I was smaller than they were. A waiter in a white coat and black bow tie brought them all drinks with gardenias in them, and set in front of me a fizzy pink soda with a green umbrella. I felt like someone in a movie. Not myself, but glamorous and better, one of the gang.

As the lights came down and the jazz trio began playing a slow, winding version of "Chicago," I looked around the table. Julie's bright, wide smile focused on the musicians, and she tapped her hand against her drink. Loreen stared at the table and looked like she was thinking about something very unhappy and far, far away. Mollie leaned back, one arm hooked around the back of her chair, and took a long sip on her drink. She stared into space in the general direction of the trio, looking happy and sad at the same time, like she was thinking about something far away, too, and let her head drift lazily back and forth in time to the music. It was the first time I'd seen her when she didn't know I was watching. It didn't last long. She turned around to me, gave me a big smile like we were on the same team, and lifted her glass. I saluted her back with my pink soda.

The set of our movie felt a little creaky and unsteady, but I hoped nobody would turn up the lights just yet.

ભ

Over the summer, Mollie and Julie started teaching me to bake. I wanted to make chocolate éclairs because they seemed so mysterious.

"How do you get the custard *in* there?" I demanded.

"Magical powers," Mollie said, not taking her eyes from the saucepan where she was slowly stirring the dark chocolate icing. Had she been raised as a Catholic, too? I decided not to pursue it.

"Yeah, but *how*?"

"Master the cookies, then I'll tell you."

By the end of the summer, I was making all of our cookies for the bakery. For dessert one hot August night, I made a special plate of oatmeal raisin fresh from the oven and chocolate double chip that I'd cooled in the refrigerator. It was a huge hit.

"Oh my God, she's gonna take over this place!" Mollie said. Julie made a face like she was in ecstasy and shook her long, bony fingers around her mouth like she couldn't even speak, they were so good. Loreen smiled wanly.

Everything about the bakery suited me, not just the baking but taking care of customers. For starters, I got to work the cash register! I loved the KA-CHING noises it made and tallying up the receipts at the end of the day. It amazed me that we made pies and cakes and cookies, and people gave us money for it. There was something enormously satisfying about that, and about having all the numbers match up at the end of the day. Doing those endless long division problems to entertain myself at IC paled before working with numbers that represented actual *things* like dollar bills and cookies. Now I knew what math was *for*.

Mollie made sure I was a neighborhood fixture in short order. "Mrs. Gambini, this is my niece Mara, come to live with me," she said. The woman's dark, deeply lined face broke into a gap-toothed smile, and she made vague welcoming gestures with her gnarled hand. Soon I knew everybody in our German-Irish-Italian mongrel immigrant neighborhood—the old German housewives in their sweat-stained housedresses, the aging Irish spinsters in their shawls even on the hottest summer days, the cops who came in every morning for free Danish, the skinny, red-faced guy who owned the tavern next door and bought a loaf of raisin bread every morning.

"Where does he put it?" Mollie sighed. She struggled with her weight and was always on some weird diet that involved grapefruit or drugs. Everybody admired my red hair, and nobody blinked when Mollie introduced me as her niece.

I learned to ride the El and did errands for Mollie—the butcher, the dry cleaner's, grocery shopping—until I was an expert on North Side geography. I pored over maps of the city and the El system at night while the parties raged in the parlor.

One day on my way home from picking up Mollie's re-heeled shoes, I got off at Holy Angels Orphanage. It was a U-shaped brown brick building that covered three sides of a block, with a playground on the fourth side inside a locked chain-link fence. I hooked my fingers through the fence and stared in. A few pale, listless kids were tossing around a softball and shooting baskets without much enthusiasm. They wore dark green serge skirts and slacks with starched white cotton tops and seemed very tired.

Suddenly, a nun broke out of their midst and started bearing down on me. I ran, darting behind buildings, weaving a roundabout path back to the El platform. I jumped on the next train and rumbled home feeling both relieved and distressed. I was glad not to be living behind that chain-link fence, but vaguely nervous to be locked out of something as solid, predictable, and permanent as Holy Angels seemed to be. I still hadn't done anything about God.

That night I lay on my bed, staring at the high white ceiling and listening to the laughing and talking in the parlor. Somebody was playing "When Irish Eyes Are Smiling" on the piano. That nun had worn a different habit from our nuns', with a smaller white wimple that seemed to crush her face. I'd run from instinct, but when I thought about it, she hadn't actually looked mad. Maybe she was just coming to see if I was an orphan, trying to get in. Maybe she was really nice to those kids. Took care of them when they got sick, comforted them when they cried for their dead parents. Taught them all about God and how to go to heaven.

How would I learn all that now? It was the most important thing, and I was cut off from it. Would *stay* cut off from it, since I would be going to public school with the doomed "little Protestant children." Mollie never said anything about God, except when she swore. That couldn't be good. Maybe God didn't even *want* me to know about Him anymore. I might not deserve Him now—but maybe one day He would want me back, and I should be ready if that day ever came.

I closed my eyes and pretended to be sitting at Mass at IC, letting the incense waft through my soul and swoop me up into God's arms. Imagined the priest lifting the host high above his head at the

Consecration, the altar boy ringing the bells to let everyone know this was the most sacred time. Felt the soft, familiar shifting and shuffling of my classmates around me, all dressed exactly alike and saying the "Our Father" together.

My eyes stung and tears began seeping out. I closed my eyes, crossed my arms, and cried until even my mouth felt swollen. I asked God what to do, but heard nothing back. Just more laughing and shouting from the parlor, and "Daisy, Daisy, Give Me Your Answer True." I was on my own.

I got up, went down the hall to the bathroom and splashed water on my face, then came back to my room and found the old red jacket I'd worn the day I ran away. I folded it into a square and put it on top of the bookshelf, then laid the *Road Atlas* on top of it. Then I found the picture of the sea anemone in *Our Oceans* and propped it open on top of the *Road Atlas* like the huge missal on the priest's altar.

I felt a kinship with tide pool creatures—swept every few hours into a dangerous new world, crashing against the rocks and clinging desperately to whatever was within reach, grabbing for food and trying to get steady, then sucked out again into the wide and surging sea.

Leaning up against *Our Oceans*, I carefully placed the picture of the real Mara and the genuine leather change purse, made by Indians in Wisconsin, that Mollie had given me to hold the $36.87 I'd taken from Mother. She said never to spend it, just hold on to it. Then I rummaged around the "everything" drawer in the kitchen for two candles, and put one on either side of the altar. Next to it on the bookshelf, I put the diary Mollie had given me (also genuine leather, made by Wisconsin Indians) in case God decided to tell me anything.

I didn't know quite what to do with the altar, but it was comforting to see it every morning when I woke up. Sometimes I pretended to say Mass, walking reverently around the room and genuflecting like an altar boy, taking down *Our Oceans* and reading aloud about tide pools like the priest read about Jesus in the big missal. Other times, I knelt and prayed that something wonderful would happen to prove that running away had been the right thing to do. Still other times, I just sat in the chair and stared at the altar. Occasionally, all the colors would fade away and I would see only sparkly light and dark shapes. *The bright* would play around the edges of me, but not go inside and take me over like it used to do.

In that silence, I often heard Julie, Loreen, or Mollie talking in other rooms.

"I'm sorry, Mollie. I needed the money," Loreen whimpered after a particularly noisy night, and Mollie grumbled about getting "a real job."

I'd never heard of people paying to come to parties. Puzzling half-pieces of information like that floated all around me. I just stashed them away. Eventually, the other half might float in and everything would make sense. If you asked questions, people got careful and you didn't learn anything.

One morning, I came back to my room after brushing my teeth and found Mollie staring at my altar. She hardly ever came into my room, now that I was out and about in the world. I froze and frowned at her. Looking at the altar through her eyes, it seemed childish and humiliating. I thought about what had happened with the Family Rosary, and steeled myself. I didn't say anything, just stood there in my slinky peach nightgown, glaring at her. She stared back at me a minute, then looked kind of embarrassed.

"Okay, I shouldn't be looking at your things. But hey! There you go!" Then she stalked out. I was astounded. It was like *she'd* done something wrong.

That Sunday morning, she knocked on my door at five thirty. I startled up, thinking maybe the cops had come for me after all. She glided into my room, holding a finger to her lips for me to be quiet.

"Get up, we're going to six o'clock Mass," she hissed. I stared at her. "C'mon. We have to be back by 7:15. Julie's opening up, but she has to leave by seven thirty to go on some damned picnic."

St. Anne's was an old neighborhood church built long ago with pennies scraped together by immigrants whose only hope rested with the Church and their children's education, which were one and the same. It was a dark, cavernous, and moldy place. The slightest noise—a cough, weight shifting from one knee to the other on the ancient wooden kneelers—reverberated over and over through the vaulted ceiling so that everybody knew everybody else's slightest move.

Mollie brought along a babushka for me to wear, and I felt like one of Mrs. Gambini's thirteen great-grandchildren. She covered her own head with a black lace mantilla, which I thought was much more stylish and beautiful than the boxy little pastel hats the neighborhood women wore—and certainly in a different league from the Kleenexes bobby-pinned to the heads of women so harried and forgetful that they came to church without a hat.

The Mass was exactly like the one at Immaculate Conception, and utterly different. At St. Anne's, I was a stranger. I didn't go to the school, didn't know everybody in church, wasn't privy to talk about indulgences and which saint's feast day it was. I was on the outside, in disguise, a far cry from being one of the Church's "little children"—but just in case I had made a terrible, terrible mistake and a truck hit me before I'd figured it out and fixed it, I went to Confession after Mass. Technically, my sins were forgiven—but walking home, I felt empty and sad.

"Didn't you like it?" Mollie asked. She seemed disappointed. "I thought you might miss going to church…"

"It's not the same," I shrugged, and turned my face away. I felt bad that she felt bad. "You and Julie don't go to church, and you're happy."

"Julie's twenty-three years old, for God's sake. A child."

"Well, I'm only ten!" Then it hit me. I wasn't ten anymore! I'd forgotten my birthday. I was eleven years old! "Hey wait! I'm eleven!" She looked at me sideways.

"Oh yeah? When's your birthday, Mara?" I fixed my eyes on the sidewalk. The snake skin tore. "September 17," she said softly and took my hand as we pressed through the bakery doors. Julie was doing a land office business.

C3

By September 17, I had twelve days at the public school under my belt. Jefferson Grammar School was a big, square brown brick building with an American flag out front—a pale and lifeless place compared to all the drama at Immaculate Conception, where the smallest thought or action might plunge your immortal soul into the searing fires of hell for all eternity, or where a secret word or gesture from Sister might foreshadow the exaltation of sainthood.

Worse, there were no uniforms. I hated having to pick out different clothes to wear every day. Julie got me more outfits for fall, but Mollie made her take most of them back.

"She looks like a goddamn stick of cotton candy! Loreen, you take her!"

The upshot was that I wore a lot more black than most fifth graders, with splashes of hot pastels. I flatly refused the hair bows. I had enough on my hands, with the dumb "publics" who couldn't even diagram a sentence and were completely lost with basic grammar and math, but who giggled and squealed over fifth-grade boys—most of whom were far more interested in catching and tearing apart bugs, learning new swear words, and beating each other bloody than they were in the shrieking fifth-grade girls. I had gotten even taller and more gangly over the summer, and felt like a black-and-neon grasshopper among the pretty little ladybugs.

Plus, they were mean. They called Mollie a "crazy witch" and Julie and Loreen "bad women." They didn't ask me over to their houses or to the movies. That was fine with me, because I worked in the bakery after school and on weekends and made fistfuls of money. I was smarter than they were and, besides, had beautiful nails because Loreen taught me how to push back the cuticle and use an emery board.

I got so good at the cash register that Mollie had me check over the books every month. I always found mistakes, so she started paying me extra to keep them myself. I socked away all the money. Mollie took me to the bank and I opened a savings account. They gave me a small red passbook with my name, Mara Sheehan, written right on it. (The real Mara's last name had been Spencer, but we changed it to Mollie's last name at City Hall. That put another step between me and anybody who might be after me, and Mollie said it was the natural thing to do when a niece came to live with her aunt.)

I rearranged my altar a lot, replacing the Indian change purse with a weathered piece of green bottle glass I'd found on the beach, the red jacket with some dry Queen Anne's lace I picked up on our picnic at Morton Arboretum. The last week in November, I found myself staring blankly at the orange, pink and gold sea anemone clinging to his dark green rock, his tentacles extended imploringly, looking scared and quivery even though he had no face, about to be swept back into the depths. I slowly closed *Our Oceans* and returned it to the shelf. In its place, I propped up my savings account passbook. I had moved out of the tide pool into some temporary inland sea, and in an odd way had actually morphed into Mara Sheehan.

Our Oceans said the first rule of evolution was "change or die." I knew that! The next two years, as I floated on the inland sea—working and saving money, reading anything I could get my hands on, getting smarter in the way Mollie was smart ("street smart," she said)—I never forgot that rule. Despite my new "family" and the relative comfort of our raft, I kept one eye on the horizon.

ↂ

On my thirteenth birthday, Mollie fixed leg of lamb with mustard glaze, green beans with slivered almonds, and scalloped potatoes. All my favorite foods. We had a hot, muggy Indian summer that year and September 17 was "a scorcher," as Julie said, so we ate dessert out on the landing. Sweaty double chocolate cupcakes with buttercream frosting, rhubarb pie a la mode, and angel food cake with lemon cream icing, strawberries on top, and thirteen lime green candles. I figured Julie had a hand in that.

Stan, Bill, and a couple other cops stood down in the alley and sang "Happy Birthday" to me in harmony, like a barbershop quartet, then climbed up the rickety wooden staircase and helped us eat the desserts.

"She's a teenager!" Mollie beamed, pouring more champagne for the adults. She was more excited about it than I was, but as I looked around at all of them—smiling and leaning against one another, kidding and joking, enjoying the hot evening just because they were together—I felt happy and lucky to be on their raft.

Later that night, I got my period for the second time.

"Hey, are we in luck or *what?*" Julie cried. She had given me a box of Tampax for my birthday and stood outside the bathroom with Loreen and Mollie, all of them yelling instructions and encouragement, pouring glass after glass of champagne as I grappled with a fistful of cardboard, cotton and string. Finally, I got it in! I could tell the whole sex thing was going to be very troublesome—but figured I'd come this far, I'd find a way to muddle through.

After they all went to bed, I sat up with my altar—by now, stripped down to the red passbook, two white candles, and *The Works of Shakespeare,* which to me meant great wisdom, sophistication, and something just beyond my reach. I couldn't make the shimmering silver light come that night. I had been edgy for weeks, maybe months, as if some part of me knew we were coming to the other shore of the inland sea and I had no idea what lurked on that beach.

I loved Mollie, Julie, and Loreen. Slowly, like suturing together the edges of a wound, I had knit myself into this little family—or been knit. Mollie didn't seem to see the darkness inside me. I hadn't thought about Ghost Girl in years. No need for her now. I could think or feel just about anything I wanted. Like when Mollie caught me using a red pencil as lipstick and screamed at me. I froze. Literally, could not move. Could not think or feel. She looked surprised, then shocked, then came toward me and wrapped her arms around me, stroking my short red hair and rocking me back and forth as we stood there. Finally, I could move. She took my face between her hands and said, "No lipstick until high school, okay?" I stared at her. "*Okay?*"

"Can I still live here?" I asked. She grabbed me again and hugged me tight, then put her hands on my shoulders.

"People scream, babe. Don't take it so personally." With that, she sauntered down the hall to the kitchen. She didn't hate me, even though she had screamed at me. It took me weeks to figure that out.

I had done a good thing by running away. So why did I feel so restless and dissatisfied? Mollie and the girls had noticed it, too.

"Cranky," Mollie had said.

"Hormones," Julie nodded.

"Teenage angst," Loreen added knowingly.

Something was missing, or looming, I didn't know which—but I had a feeling it had to do with God. Nobody talked about God at home or at school, and as busy as I was, I didn't think much about *the bright* or anything divine. In quiet times, though, when I stood still for a minute and looked, I could see that there was a hole in me. Right where the most important thing had been.

I didn't have any new information about God, and the old IC system seemed very far off the mark now. The careening elevators full of indulgences and sins, all those saints with their wild antics, the crazy nuns with their red plastic rulers and head-whapping—none of it seemed very reliable, real, or practical.

I grabbed my journal and stared at its creamy paper. In large letters, I filled a whole page with the bottom-line dilemma:

> *"God—*
>
> *Who is he?*
>
> *What does he want?*
>
> *How can I get at him, and his stuff?"*

How had I gotten so sidetracked? Why had I put the most important thing on hold?

I resolved to get down to business with God, but then I started at Penn High School. I worked longer hours at the bakery and made even more money, began going out on dates with guys, and kind of went to sleep again as far as God was concerned. From time to time, I woke up panicked that I hadn't done anything—but then a term paper would be due, or some guy would ask me out, or Mollie would get sick and I'd have to work more hours. I always vowed to get back to God just as soon as the crisis was over, but I never really did.

Without meaning to do so, I floated on the inland sea for four more years, until I was almost through high school.

Chapter 7

Julie was painting her toenails "Shivers Pink" and I was frosting a Quintuple Chocolate Cake for my classmate Dorothy Dillinger's seventeenth birthday—devil's food with chocolate chips, rich raspberry reduction between the layers, and white, milk, and dark chocolate icing.

"Looks gorgeous, hon!" she said, jabbing the nail brush at it.

"Twenty-five bucks. Go, Wildcats!" Dorothy was a cheerleader at Penn High. I would not be invited to her party. Dorothy was one of the cool kids; I was more of a skulker with a turned-up collar and a DA haircut. I smoked, necked behind the gym during pep rallies, and went to great lengths to hide my reading habit from the leather jacket crowd. I probably had the reputation for being much more of a "bad girl" than I actually was.

Joe Rafferty was the closest thing I had to a boyfriend. I had first spotted him slouching against the gym wall with his hoodlum friends at one of the Friday night dances—a lineup of sulky James Dean types in dirty white T-shirts, jeans, and black boots. Elvis began "Love Me Tender" and it was a ladies' choice. I stood in front of him, looking as tough as I could, and extended my hand. He took it, and within twenty minutes we were behind the gym.

I was sick of listening to the other girls squeal about sex and its antecedents and determined to find out what the big deal was. Joe seemed like an excellent starting point. He was bad, outlawish, dark! Often seen luring girls back to the make-out area behind the gym, so presumably experienced. The groping felt good and was kind of exciting, but so far I was not very encouraged about sex as an ultimate source of happiness—at least the kind of rapturous, everlasting happiness that I was after. But then, I hadn't gone all the way yet and was withholding judgment until I had.

Joe and I rarely spoke outside of our frantic make-out sessions. The most profound thing he'd ever said to me was, "Yo! Mar! Got a C in History! Whaddayathink, babe?"

It was his crowning academic achievement and our most intimate moment—and came only after a half bottle of Southern Comfort. Still, he was taller than I was, and his thigh muscles bulged through the oil-covered jeans he wore both to school and to work at the garage. He had long black eyelashes and a way of rolling his cigarettes up into the sleeve of his thin white T-shirts that conveyed a confidence and certainty about life to which both of us aspired.

Mollie eyed my hoodlum friends skeptically, but didn't say much because anybody could tell just by looking at her that she'd probably worn a leather jacket in high school herself. Besides, she probably knew my heart wasn't in all the toughness. It was just another place to hang out while I waited—for what, I wasn't quite sure—and also a way to show everybody I was grown up and a force to be reckoned with.

"You don't fool me," Mollie had said a week earlier when I appeared in the kitchen before going out in a tight black skirt, a black sweater that looked like it had been spray-painted on, more makeup than Julie, and a brassy blonde streak in my now-black hair. She put down her *Daily News*, removed her reading glasses, held out her arms, and smiled. "C'mere and give me a hug before you go!" I had rolled my eyes at the time, but I smiled as I remembered it.

"Anyway, all frosted and done," I said to Julie, pushing Dorothy's birthday cake aside and flopping down at the table to check our ad for the new Summer Picnic Cookie Box in the *Ravenswood Review*. It had been my idea—assorted cookies in a red box that people could take on picnics. The ad looked good, and my eyes drifted down to the one just below ours. It began with a big "3" with little squiggles coming out of it.

Special Invitation
Highest Spiritual Teachings of the Ancients
Suk Baba is an enlightened teacher who achieved nirvikalpa samadhi after eight years of study with his guru, Swami Chidakashananda, in Bombay, India. He has committed his life to teaching the Vedanta to Westerners.
Suk Bhavan, 4652 N. Racine
Beginning meditation class, Wednesday nights 7-9 PM
All are welcome   Love offering

"What's a love offering?" I asked Julie. She looked embarrassed and grabbed the paper.

"Lemme see that!" She frowned as she read. "What's a nir...kal...ma...di?" She quickly turned the conversation where she always turned it—to the sorry state of my social life. "Hey, you oughtta go to this!"

"Nah."

"You never go anywhere, except with those hoodlum kids. You should have a nice boyfriend. When I was your age..."

"This doesn't sound like a sock hop."

"Wear something nice. Not the jeans!"

୧

Suk Bhavan was only a few El stops away. I had half expected an Indian-style building, kind of a miniature Taj Mahal tucked in between the brownstone walk-ups—something with wild colors, filigreed minarets, and maybe even a small reflecting pool. Instead, 4652 N. Racine was a regular Chicago brownstone. I skimmed down the names on the intercom. All normal people, except for one that read "Hari Om!" That sounded kind of Suk-y. I pressed it. Somebody buzzed me in without even asking who it was! Boy, they meant it when they said, "All are welcome!" I would have to clue Suk Baba in on the realities of life in Chicago.

I pushed open the door and stepped into a dim hallway with a musty, threadbare burgundy carpet and a dark wood banister winding up to the second and third floors. As I rounded a curve, I caught a flash of white fabric on the third floor landing. The incense was so thick I could actually see it curling past me down the stairs. The door to the third-floor flat had a brass copy of that strange "3" symbol from the *Ravenswood Review* ad bolted to the door. Suk Baba was in for a rude awakening when his landlord visited.

Before I could knock, the door opened. A man with curly auburn hair stood naked except for an immaculate white floor-length sarong, very tight and slung low on his hips! He was about thirty and tall—taller than I was—with a chiseled jaw and brilliant blue eyes that were both gentle and compelling. I could not stop looking at his chest, his shoulders, his arms. I knew it was rude, the very definition of what Sister Agatha used to call "impure glances"—but he had wonderful, perfect muscles everywhere, with absolutely no fat around them. I had never seen a man that young and good-looking, that well built, without a shirt on, up that close. I couldn't speak.

"*Om shanti*," he said softly, looking deeply into my eyes, sliding his hand under my elbow, and drawing me into the vestibule with him. "Would you like to remove your shoes?" he asked with a graceful gesture toward the floor that made his chest and shoulder muscles ripple. He talked like an American. In fact, like a Chicagoan, maybe from the South Side.

Five pairs of shoes lined up on the polished oak floor. I took off my sneakers and placed them next to a pair of cheap K-Mart running shoes, which were next to the kind of black low-heel oxfords worn by nuns and our German housewife customers. Then came a pair of fake jeweled metallic sandals like something Julie would wear, brown loafers, and a pair of shiny black wingtips. This was not a group of shoes you would find anywhere else I had ever been.

"What is your name?" Now he had the tiniest trace of an Indian accent.

"Mara."

"How beautiful! Mara, the goddess of death!"

What?! I was named after the goddess of death? How could Mollie have done that without checking it out? I must have looked crestfallen.

"Death is good! The death of the ego, the death of all that is false," he said encouragingly. "Come." He smiled and held back the curtain of sandalwood beads between the vestibule and living room. I walked beneath it into a vast expanse of off-white carpet with about ten large, brightly colored Indian pillows strewn around the room. Dark reds and oranges, brilliant turquoise and jade green, sequined gold. At the far end of the room was a little pile of pillows, like a throne. Candles flickered in large amber glass jars to either side of it. Another squiggly brass "3" symbol hung above it on the wall, no doubt secured with molly bolts. More landlord problems.

Three other people hunkered awkwardly on pillows, presumably the owners of the shoes. The naked man introduced me around, leading me from one person to the next. He introduced each one as a "Brother" or "Sister," which they seemed to find as embarrassing as I did, gave us a few details about one another, and made brief small talk.

Brother Simon was a pretty, wraithlike young man who wore a black yarmulke and worked in his parents' dry cleaning business. The oxfords, I guessed, belonged to Sister Janet, an overweight retired truck dispatcher in navy polyester slacks and a white peasant blouse with red cross-stitching around the neck. She looked as if she hadn't sat on a cushion in fifty years, if ever, and was already regretting her foray into the exotic world of ancient wisdom. She smiled wanly and shook my hand.

Brother William was about forty and a lawyer, just like my dad! He'd taken off his suit jacket and laid it on the floor in the back of the room since there was no furniture other than the pillows, let alone a coatrack. Otherwise he was dressed for the Loop in a white shirt and red and black striped tie. His hair was a little gray at the temples, and he looked tired. He smiled sheepishly as he took off his black socks and walked them back to his suit jacket. It was very hot, and the overhead fan didn't help much.

"Tell us about yourself, Mara," our host said, folding his arms so that his biceps and pecs jumped.

"I'm a student." That was general enough that even if William had lunch with my father every day, he'd never know. It occurred to me that I didn't really have to hide anymore, that my wariness was just a knee-jerk reaction, but I couldn't think about that. There was only room for one thing in my mind: the man in the sarong.

"Wonderful!" He herded us into a little semicircle closer to the pillow throne, then glided over to it and sat down. This guy was apparently Suk Baba! Or his opening act.

"I am Suk Baba," he said pleasantly, and casually folded his legs beneath him at angles I didn't know that human joints would go.

My first thought—after dragging my eyes away from his chest and regaining some sort of cognitive function—was, "Oh yeah? You look more like someone named Timmy O'Rourke from the South Side." What was he doing, pretending to be an Indian swami or something with the weird name and that getup? My skepticism softened when he extended his arms to put his palms on his knees, and all the muscles rippled again. It looked like his ankles would crack off from sitting in that twisty way, but he seemed utterly serene.

He took a deep breath, exhaled hard three times through his teeth, and stared intently at the back wall as if in a trance. Sister Janet snuck a peek over her shoulder to see what he was looking at, so I did, too. Another brass "3" on the wall, and a picture of an old Indian guy with huge gold-and-black glasses, a salt-and-pepper beard that straggled down to his waist, and a wide, exultant smile that showed a gold tooth. He seemed to be gazing into a bright light, and on the verge of screaming with delight. Janet squirmed back around and narrowed her eyes at Suk Baba.

"OOOMMMMM!" His chant thundered through the flat for at least a minute. Then, almost in a whisper, *"Om nama Shivaya. Om nama Shivaya."*

William echoed quietly, *"Om nama Shivaya."* He must have been here before and come back! Then, as if nothing had happened, Suk Baba lapsed back into the happy guy with the curly auburn hair who had greeted me at the door.

"Welcome to our new brother and sisters!" He took a long look at each of us. Simon squinted up his eyes and met Suk Baba's gaze. Janet looked down and picked her toenail. I blushed.

A tall woman in a white sari swept in from what must have been the kitchen, carrying a glass of water and a cup of tea on a silver tray. She arranged it all reverently on the little table next to Suk Baba, stooping like a supplicant and never turning her back to him.

He smiled broadly at her and said to us, "This is Saraswati." She turned and gave us a quick, mildly contemptuous glance.

Saraswati, my ass! That was Wendy Schotz, who had just graduated from Northwestern and whose mother was a regular customer at the bakery! In a sari, with a dark red caste mark on her forehead, her long dark brown hair done up in a bun at the nape of her neck, and dangly Indian earrings with a hundred tiny pieces of hinged metal! Running around the neighborhood in metallic fake-jeweled sandals! I looked right at her, but her eyes were now riveted to the white carpet.

"My assistant," Suk Baba beamed, stroking her hand.

Suddenly, I wanted a sari and an Indian name.

ك

Suk Baba began the evening with a short course in Advaita Vedanta, the spiritual system he taught. I began the evening mulling over the presence of Wendy Schotz in a place called Suk Bhavan—in disguise, gotten up as an Indian girl named Saraswati who was in a caste! Did Suk know who she really was? Did her mother know she was here, and in costume?

If those were her fake jeweled sandals in the vestibule, then maybe she didn't actually live here. Suk's shoes were there as well, though—presumably the loafers, not the K-Mart runners—so I couldn't tell. She could be living in sin with him. Right under this roof, probably in a bedroom down the hall, the one to the left...

"Mysticism, in all religions, is the direct experience of God," Suk was saying, as if he were delivering a weather report—sunny, with a light breeze off the lake. "In this experience, we not only *know* that there is only one of us here, we *feel* it. We *are* it. Oneness. Everything that exists is just one energy, one force, and we are all that infinite I AM that people call God. The universe is nothing more, or less, than that force shaping itself into different forms, vibrating at different speeds. We are all just the waves, small and temporary fluctuations in the ocean of the One."

He looked around the room with hooded eyes, apparently giving himself over to the bliss of Oneness. "The walls, the light," he said, gesturing gently at the ceiling fixture, a standard frosted globe with three dead moths lying in the bottom, then let his gaze drift out the window. "The buildings. The sky. Even you and me. We are all one substance, appearing to be different and separate from one another."

He turned his eyes right into mine when he said that. I tried to look deep, as if I had actually understood what he was saying—perhaps had known about it all along—and of course, completely agreed. After lingering awhile with me, he moved his gaze to William.

Suk had a deep, soft voice. He laid out everything he said on a thick marble slab of slow certainty that made you inclined to believe it, or at least to give it the benefit of the doubt. Maybe that's why William was still around. He didn't seem like the mystical type, but he was listening intently. If a downtown lawyer bought this, who was I to dismiss it?

Suk shifted on his pillows and leaned forward, his elbows resting on his knees above the twisted legs and feet. It felt like he was having an intimate conversation with each one of us.

"Mystics of all faiths—Christian, Hindu, Buddhist, Muslim, others— learn to quiet their minds. They go deep within themselves to that place beyond the everyday chatter, the place where there is no separation between themselves and other people, or anything else. They know that *there is only one of us here*, and everything that exists is *that one*."

Huh? What about garbage? What about my mother?

"The whole universe. All One. The I AM, shaping and reshaping itself into different physical forms. The New Physics is beginning to prove this."

I made a mental note to sign up for Physics next year and tried to get my mind around everything being only one thing, vibrating differently. My mother, Suk, Sister, Stan, Julie's boyfriends, Mollie, serial killers, éclairs, Mayor Daley, the El tracks, the saints, Lake Michigan, and Wendy Shotz in a sari were all one thing? It seemed vaguely true, but was that just because of Suk's muscles? I yearned after something about the I AM Oneness idea, and could almost get my mind around it—but then it slid out of my grasp.

"This is the essence of Advaita Vedanta, and that's what we'll be studying here. Investigating. Practicing." He rested his hand lightly on the little stack of books on his table. I could read three of the titles: *The Bhagavad Gita*, *Vivekachoodamani*, *The Upanishads*.

Oh brother! Was any of this stuff in English? So in case I couldn't put up with Wendy's posturing, or in case Suk himself turned out to be stupid enough to be dating her—let alone living with her—I could get it on my own?

"Any questions?" he beamed, holding his palms open to us as if he were about to catch a basketball. Janet raised her hand tentatively. "Yes! Sister Janet!"

"What about family? Life isn't about all that woo-woo stuff!" she spat. "What about loving my kids?" She nodded conspiratorially at me and William, as if she knew we were thinking the same thing. I looked away pointedly, then smiled smugly at Suk, as if I felt his pain in having to deal with the unwashed.

"It's *all* love, Janet, but not personal love. That only ends in sorrow. This is *agape*"—he pronounced it *ah-**gah**-pay*—"the universal love that embraces all beings equally. You love the checker at the supermarket just as much as you love your family or spouse, your boyfriend or girlfriend or children."

Deep lines appeared between Janet's brows. She hardened into someone who, if I owned a trucking company, I would definitely want telling my drivers what to do.

"I'm a good mom," she said defiantly. "If I don't love my kids and grandchildren more than the checkout girl, what is my life about?"

Suk tilted his head back just slightly and smiled as if he had her right where he wanted her. I wondered where compassion fit in with Oneness, if at all. "Is your life over because you aren't a truck dispatcher anymore?"

"No," Janet had said suspiciously.

"Well, your true identity has no more to do with being a mother than it does with being a dispatcher. You *are* the infinite I AM!" Janet returned to picking her toes and wouldn't look up. Suk gave her a quick, dismissive glance and moved on.

Seconds later, as he was launching into a riff about Krishna being "the light of a thousand suns," Janet muttered pointedly, under her breath, still engrossed in her toes, "Am *not*!"

William and Simon cast horrified little glances in her direction. If Suk heard her, he ignored it.

"I want to show you something," he said, scanning our ragtag group. I smiled encouragingly. "Saraswati," or "Saraswendy" as I'd started to think of her, had been off to the side giving him moony looks and sitting in the same twisty-footed way that he was. I would have to learn to do that. Now she came forward holding a big cone of butcher paper, rolled up like a megaphone, and a flashlight. She half bowed as she handed them to him, then wafted over to the light switch by the door.

He shined the flashlight into the narrow end of the cone and nodded to her. The room went dark except for the light shining up through the cone. The white paper had tiny holes punched in it. He placed a book over the wide end, so that you could just see the light inside the cone and pinpricks of light coming out through the little holes.

"Each of these holes is one of us. You see the little specks of light?" We all nodded in the dark. "Each hole is different, individual. It looks like it's a separate little ray, but the light coming through each hole is the same. It's the flashlight. Just the way the I AM Oneness shines its light through each of us. Our true nature is the light, not the little holes."

He paused a few minutes to let this sink in. Janet stared at the ceiling. Simon cocked his head to one side and frowned. William looked mesmerized. It made absolute sense to me, but it seemed too simple. My mind raced back and forth between two opposite reactions: Wow! So? Wow! So?

"Knowing that our true nature is Oneness is the only thing that can make us completely, permanently happy. It's the only thing that is infinite. Everything else either disappears or disappoints eventually—money, relationships, art, even our own bodies."

He flashed Saraswendy a stunning smile, and she turned on the lights.

"Let's try a little meditation," Suk said smoothly. "Just let your eyes close if you feel comfortable doing that..." He seemed to move into a different place within himself, just as Sister had during our first Visit to the Blessed Sacrament. His eyes fell shut, and I could almost see his energy stretching out and enveloping us, making everything vibrate a little faster and, at the same time, slowing everything down. When he spoke again, his voice was deep and soft.

"What if you could move beyond your smaller mind, your personality? What if you could actually feel that infinite I AM inside you? Swim in it. No pain or lack. Only love. Joy. Peace."

He said it slowly, like a chant. The room seemed to tilt slightly and fill up with soft, caressing shimmers of energy. I had been looking at his left biceps, and it literally jumped in my vision to about a foot from where it had been. The walls dissolved into glowing columns of light. I felt a little dizzy, but amazingly relaxed. A filmy curtain lifted inside my mind, and suddenly it really did seem like I was part of everything and everyone, and that they were part of me. It lasted only an instant, but in that tiny slice of time, I actually *was* Suk. I was even Saraswendy, Simon, William, and Janet—and the floor and walls and ceiling. It was as if I had pulled up out of myself and, literally, *was everything.*

It was tremendously unsettling, but also the most thrilling thing I had ever experienced. Even after it ended, I felt suspended in a soft, golden, pulsing light. My right hand felt the softness of the carpet as I reached down to steady myself.

I looked up to see Suk watching me, an ecstatic look on his face.

"That is *samadhi*, the direct experience of I AM!" He paused and gazed into my eyes. The room began to shimmer again. "That is why we practice meditation, to get to that place where we experience ourselves as the One."

The way Suk kept looking at me, it seemed like he'd had something to do with my being in that state—or thought he had. Now that it had passed, I felt a little woozy.

It reminded me of the night I ate a whole bowl of chocolate chip cookie dough. I had wanted to do that forever, but when Mollie finally let me, the experience was overwhelming—not just to my stomach, but to some internal emotional barometer. Mollie sat watching me until I finally licked the last buttery, chocolate-chippy, sugary smear off the spatula. As I sat there, green around the gills, she ruffled my hair and smiled, "Well, kiddo, howdaya feel? I guess you can do any damned thing you want, right? Now what? What are ya gonna do now?"

In retrospect, that sounded kind of Suk-y. He would have said, "You've exhausted the capacity of that finite cookie dough to make you happy. Obviously, that is not the source of happiness. What is?"

Suk held my eyes a moment, then said to the group, "When you feel comfortable, you can open your eyes."

I stared at him, astounded that I had experienced *the bright* again— actually, something far beyond *the bright*—in this strange setting, and in the presence of someone claiming to be named Suk Baba, who could apparently make it appear at will.

Suk seemed to know instinctively just how much mysticism our little group could take at one sitting. After forty-five minutes of saying these same things over and over in different ways, he grinned and leapt to his feet.

"Let's have some refreshments!"

It took both William and Simon, working together, to crane Janet to her feet. Her chubby legs unfolded with difficulty, and she limped badly as she made her way through the swinging door to the kitchen.

There, laid out on a table covered with a the same white butcher paper as the Mystical Cone, was a spread of raw carrots, cucumber, and celery sticks, accompanied by oddly colored condiments strongly flavored with curry and cumin. Next to that, a large bowl of soupy lentils, some yogurt with flecks of cucumber, crispy crackers flaked with black seeds, and fried vegetable dumplings so spicy they singed my tongue when I bit into one. It seemed like overkill for just the four of us, and neither Simon nor Janet looked eager to dive into the bizarre Vedantic mini-buffet.

Saraswendy presided over it all, looking grim and a bit pained to be among the un-saried. She gestured for people to take a paper plate and plastic spoon, then march on down the food line until they arrived at a stack of red plastic cups.

She moved silently among us, topping off everybody's red plastic water cup. I figured she was keeping quiet so we would assume she was recently arrived from some Himalayan cave, didn't speak English, and/or had taken a holy vow of silence—or else was so enlightened that even speaking to us would somehow mess with her vibration. Certainly, she didn't want us to think that she was just another girl from the North Side. The sari flowed around her body as she moved. I made small talk with Simon about the dry cleaning business and kept waiting for one of her swishing tails to land in the dark yellow curry condiment—but it didn't.

She avoided me, so I walked up to her and stuck out my plastic cup. She focused intently on pouring.

"Hi, Wendy," I said pointedly. She stared right through me. "Mara Sheehan. I work at Mollie's Bakery?"

"Oh yes," she said with a wisp of Indian accent, and turned away from me to Simon. I followed.

"You're back from Northwestern?"

"Yes, I've started my new life with Baba," she said. Now that she was an Ascended Master carrying around Oneness Cones, she didn't seem to want anything to remind her of the old life when she was just a regular person and bakery customer.

"You live here?"

"Of course." Now she seemed a little smug, which catapulted her quickly from the Oneness of the Flashlight to way out to the periphery, where she was just a small, pathetic little hole in the butcher paper that thought it was the source of its own light. Just another gal marking turf. "I've devoted my life to Baba's service."

I bet she had.

"So this is your job?" I gestured toward the dumplings and carrot sticks. She narrowed her eyes and started rearranging celery on the platter.

"Well, I have a job in The World to support our work." She hadn't wanted to go there, but neither did she want me thinking she couldn't do anything beyond crudités.

"Oh? Where do you work?"

She hesitated, then spat it out.

"J. Walter Thompson." Saraswendy worked at an *ad agency*.

"How great! What do you do?"

"Receptionist." Her Oneness was wearing thin. She turned again, this time to offer William more cucumber yogurt. Having just bitten into a fiery dumpling and unable to speak, he gratefully scooped about two cups of the cooling yogurt onto his plate. I joined them, patting William on the back.

"Do you wear your sari there?" I asked Saraswendy in the most innocent, casual tone I could muster. She turned on her heel and huffed off toward Janet, who was slumped in a chair in the corner, coughing over her dumpling.

Suk turned toward me, celery stick in hand. He seemed to glow, and I had a funny feeling he'd been eavesdropping on my conversation with Saraswendy.

"Mara." He took my free hand. I wished I hadn't taken any food. "Don't mind Saraswati. Her *kundalini* is..." I nodded knowingly. I was going to have to get a Sanskrit-English dictionary, fast. "Did you find tonight interesting?" He *knew* I had, knew what had happened for me. Acting like it had just been a regular information-packed evening somehow made our connection deeper. Sexier.

"Very," I said, trying to be cool and sophisticated, but at the same time suffused with Oneness. Looking into his blue eyes seemed to make the walls jump around.

"I hope you'll come back next week."

"Oh, I will," I smiled.

"I'm so glad!" Then, with what might have been a caress of my palm or maybe just an accident, he glided over to Janet, who by now was having trouble breathing through the searing spices. Suk laid a hand softly on her shoulder. Immediately, she stopped coughing. He seized the moment.

"Janet, do you see the healing power of knowing that there's only One of us here, and understanding that everything is just the love of that One?"

"I love my children!" she screamed and scrambled for the door, knocking over the runny cucumber yogurt that Saraswendy had called *raita*. It flew in every direction, splattering over the table, the cabinets, and counter before hitting the linoleum floor. Saraswendy stared in horror at the mess in her godly kitchen.

William followed Janet out with an apologetic glance over his shoulder and a signal that he would make sure she was all right. Simon grabbed his chance to leave as well—which left me, Suk, and Saraswendy staring at one another over a sea of raw vegetables, the spilled *raita*, and stacks of torrid dumplings. It seemed like a good time to end the evening.

"Thank you so much," I said with a huge smile, embracing all of creation in the bounty of my Oneness. "I'll see you next week." Then I turned with what I hoped was a graceful swirl and headed for the vestibule, leaving Saraswendy in the servant's role of cleaning up the *raita* and veggies.

As I was putting on my shoes, I noticed a little box on another small table that hadn't been there before. (Where did all those little tables come from? Maybe the bedroom was stacked high with them. That certainly wouldn't be very romantic!) The box was dark wood, carved with all kinds of Indian signs and letters, with a small slot cut into the top. Scotch-taped next to the slot was a three-by-five recipe card with LOVE OFFERINGS written in black magic marker. Aha! The Love Offering was the price of admission. I peered through the slot, but it was too small to see what others had left. Clearly, neither Janet nor William had paused to feed the kitty.

How much was a love offering? How deep were my *agape* pockets? I figured three dollars and slipped the bills into the slot. If they needed more, Saraswendy could put in some overtime at JWT.

Riding home on the El, I tried to tamp down my excitement. How could so many good things have happened in one night? I had felt something way beyond even *the bright!* It might have been connected to the surge of adrenaline I felt when Suk looked into my eyes. Still, if what he said was true—and it was hard to argue with the *samadhi* experience I'd had after only forty-five minutes of exposure—then he would be holding in his beautifully manicured hands the answers to a lot of my God questions. Maybe he and I would live in India. Or found a spiritual community in Colorado or Montana.

First, though, I had to deal with Saraswendy. Before I went to bed that night, I looked up "kundalini" in Mollie's *World Book Encyclopedia*.

"In some Tantric (esoteric) forms of Yoga, the cosmic energy that is ... pictured as a coiled serpent lying at the base of the spine. In the practice of Laya Yoga ("Union of Mergence"), the adept is instructed to awaken the kundalini...through a series of techniques that combine prescribed postures, gestures, and..."

I couldn't read any more. Tantric meant sex, I knew that much. Saraswendy had a coiled serpent rising from the base of her spine and was practicing the Union of Mergence. That could only mean one thing! All those prescribed postures, gestures and techniques could not be good. Saraswendy was an adept at sex, and I knew nothing about it! I was doomed.

ଔ

"So hon, how was the Suk party?" Julie asked at dinner the next night. "Tell us everything!"

Mollie eyed me as she scooped huge portions of chicken parmesan onto our plates. Loreen didn't eat with us much anymore. She mostly stayed in her room and looked ashen when she did emerge.

"Very interesting," I said, spearing a floret of broccoli. I had made some inquiries at school so I'd know more about what was going on at Suk Bhavan myself and be better prepared for exactly this conversation. Mr. Davidson, the Social Studies teacher whom kids called Mr. Gray because his face, his hair, his beard, and most of his clothes were gray, had seemed startled and vaguely fearful when I cornered him after class. I demanded to know all about the Vedanta and what he thought of someone like Suk Baba, who claimed to have learned it in India from a guru. He said a lot of "Westerners" were going to India, learning meditation and ancient wisdom, and yes, the Vedanta was legit. He said he expected all these *sanyasis*, or students, to come flooding back soon and "capitalize" on what they knew, and that Suk was probably just the vanguard of what would become a huge wave of Americans running around in sarongs, which he called *dotis*. He wanted to know more about where and when the whole Suk Bhavan experience was, but I told him I'd forgotten and fled. I didn't need any teachers from Penn High looking over my shoulder.

"Whaddya mean, 'interesting?'" Mollie asked. Julie flashed me a conspiratorial grin. I felt the need to shock them. I was sick of being the amusing kid.

"I may have met the man I'm going to marry."

Mollie gaped, the serving spoon suspended motionless above Julie's plate. Julie practically jumped out of her chair. She put on a big smile, but her eyes were wide and wild.

"Hon! Who is he?"

"He's enlightened. A guru," I said, hoping to appear blasé. "All kinds of people come to Suk Bhavan to hear him." I said "Suk Bhavan" as if it were commonplace for me to speak Sanskrit, or Hindi, or whatever it was. "I think he's famous." I grabbed the salt shaker and pelted my chicken parm. Without looking up, I added, "He's also very good looking, and doesn't wear a shirt."

"Oh Lord," Mollie said.

"The only problem is,"—I was talking fast now—"Wendy Schotz lives with him! She's pretending to be an Indian girl from a Himalayan cave and wears a sari! I think he's training her to be an adept of some kind."

"Oh Lord," Julie said.

"Anyway, I'm going again next week."

Mollie's eyebrows flew up and she started to speak, but Julie shot her a look and she closed her mouth.

"That's great, hon! Good for you! How old is he?"

I hesitated. It wasn't a good question.

"I don't know. In his twenties maybe."

Mollie frowned. "What did he talk about?" she asked.

"Oh, enlightenment stuff," I said airily, implying that it was probably way beyond them. "There's only one of us here, and we're all made of the same light. We just seem to be separate from one another, and from tables, because our energy is vibrating differently." When Suk said it, it made perfect sense—even seemed like the answer to everything—but it didn't sound the same, coming from me.

"Wow!" Julie said. "What color are his eyes?" Now Mollie shot *her* a look.

"Blue. Bright blue."

"What's his job?" Mollie asked. Another bad question.

"Wendy pays the rent! She works at J. Walter Thompson." At least we would all agree that Wendy paying the rent was a terrible thing, even though their reasons might be different from mine. "I'll find out more next week."

"You have to do the books next Wednesday night," Mollie said.

"I do not! I can do them anytime. I'll do them Tuesday, or Thursday morning before school!"

Mollie glared at me across the table. We ate in silence. For the first time, she seemed old. The lines in her face seemed deeper, and there were little crow's feet just above the cleavage that pressed out of her dark red robe. For that matter, even Julie was starting to look kind of saggy. Her lime green robe showed a couple bulges when she stood and poured more wine for herself and Mollie. Maybe they were just jealous! I might not be prettier than they were, or know as much as they did, but I was a whole lot younger and most guys on the street would probably pick me over them. There were even tiny wrinkles on Mollie's forearm as she reached for a cigarette.

"The books on Wednesday," she said in a low voice as we finished eating.

"No," I said to the last few bites of my chicken parm, trying to sound soft but certain, like Suk. Then I said in my own voice, "No! This is my life. This is what I want, and I'm doing it!" I had never spoken to Mollie like that. We were both surprised, and glared at one another again.

Julie looked from me, to Mollie, to me.

"Well, we have plenty of time to think about next Wednesday," she said in a smooth, creamy voice. "Hon, I'm glad you had a good time."

Then she gave Mollie another look that said Shut Up! "Baby, you do the dishes tonight. I want Mollie to help me hem my blue skirt." With that, she practically picked Mollie up and carried her out of the kitchen on her shoulders.

I did the dishes slowly. It ached to be on the outs with Mollie, and to know that I'd hurt her. The worst part was, she was usually right about things—and she didn't like Suk, Suk Bhavan, or any of it. Not at all.

I had jostled us out of our usual places with one another, like when I tapped the mobile of plastic pastel bunnies that hung in Julie's window and all the pieces went out of balance. What if I had to run away again?

After I put away the last plate, I did something I'd never done before. I walked over to the cabinet where Mollie kept her booze, pulled down the Cutty Sark, and poured myself a juice glass full of neat Scotch. I lit one candle on the kitchen table, turned off the lights, sat back, and took a sip. After the second or third swallow, that wonderful feeling of being relaxed, a real and normal person, began coursing through my veins. It had happened the first time I drank vodka with Joe behind the gym, and every time since then. I felt confident, like I could walk right into Suk Bhavan and order Saraswendy back to her mother's house.

I tapped one of Mollie's Pall Malls out of its pack and lit up. I had never smoked or had a drink at home, in my own domain. My first real, personal cigarette, and my first personal drink of hard liquor, right under our roof. I took a bigger sip. Maybe this was what Loreen was doing in her room all the time.

Julie sauntered back into the kitchen a half hour later. She glanced at my drink and got down two Old-Fashioned glasses.

"Do it right if you're gonna do it, hon." She sat next to me and put her arm across the back of my chair.

"Where's Mollie?"

"She went to bed early. She just loves you, hon, that's all. She doesn't want you to get hurt."

"I *won't*." She gave me a quick hug and looked like she was going to say something, but I beat her to it. "Jules, you gotta help me. Wendy knows everything about sex and she went to college and I don't know anything. You've gotta help me so I won't be an idiot." She took my hand. "You *gotta*!"

"Hon, you'll be fine..."

"No, I won't!"

She frowned. "Wait a minute. Those boys at school...You didn't...?"

"No! I don't have any idea what I'm doing, and Wendy does."

"Oh." She sipped her Cutty Sark and swirled it around in the Old-Fashioned glass. After a few minutes, she said, "You know what? You should hit the sack, too." She picked up my Scotch and dumped it into hers, then hauled me to my feet and pushed me out of the kitchen. "'Night, hon. Don't let the bedbugs bite."

I walked down the hall to my room and flopped onto my bed. Screw them! I hadn't come this far not to fight for the most important thing in life! This is why I ran away. I *had* to have it and would fight through Mollie to get it, if I had to. I would do anything! Screw them!

Chapter 8

I went back to Suk Bhavan the next Wednesday, and the next and the next. Mollie was grim and thin-lipped about it, but mostly she just seemed sad. I was determined to *show her* by becoming enlightened in record time and spreading godlike vibrations all over our apartment and the bakery—which would probably also improve our bottom line and make her less tired and worn out than she had seemed lately.

It felt great to be completely, 100 percent committed to Suk—and through him, to *the bright*, God, *samadhi* and whatever else was out there running the show, able to make me happy, ensure that I was on the right track, fix whatever was wrong with me, and smooth out anything that wasn't right between me and the divine after the IC debacle. Even at IC, I'd had only had nine toes in the water, what with all the lying and stealing and faking. Now I had both feet in and was going the right direction.

I became a regular at Suk's and quickly mastered all things Suk-y—the shoe lineup, the snaky-legged way of sitting (which turned out to be the lotus posture), the fiery dumplings (*samosas*), esoteric dipping sauces, and even *samadhi* itself. I sat on a pillow front and center, just feet away from him. William and Simon came occasionally, but I was the star student.

Everything outside Suk Bhavan faded to gray. Being there with him was like running my hands through piles of blood-red jewels, lolling around on gold satin sheets, sipping heavy apricot elixir. I loved the things he said and the way the air got all rich and electric when he said them. Loved how my mind thinned out, fell silent, and relaxed into a bottomless peace as I stared into the cream-colored candles undulating in their amber jars beside him. Loved *samadhi*, those fleeting seconds of being *not me*, but *everything*.

If Suk were all mine, then all that peace, all that truth, all that shimmering energy behind the candles would be mine as well. If I had to put up with Saraswendy and her spicy condiments for a few more weeks until I overtook her spiritually and he saw the light, I could manage that. Then I would be *his*, and locked into all the good stuff he had.

Besides, the Vedanta was a lot more sensible than that wacky Catholic stuff. More adult, and far more ancient. Even those books, the

Bhagavad Gita and *Vivekachoodamani,* made sense when Suk explained
them. When we meditated on Wednesday nights, I truly did feel "the
light of a thousand suns" inside me. It was all I'd ever wanted—and
unlike at IC, where everyone was presumed guilty until proven innocent,
Suk actually seemed to think I was something special.

One night after class, I even told him about my experiences with *the
bright* as a kid. (I did not extend my religious history to include Sister's
ruler, buying Pagan Babies, or the Purgatory yo-yo.) He took my hand,
leaned in with his shoulders and his eyes, and said, "That's wonderful,
Mara. I have a feeling you've come to exactly the right place." I was
thrilled.

"Come with me," he said quietly, leading me down the hall while
Saraswendy cleaned up the kitchen. "I have something for you." His
smile made me feel softer, kinder than I actually was. It helped me slide
into Oneness and the love that came with it. The closer I got to him, the
more often I would be in that state.

He turned into a room lit only with one large candle in a dark red
glass jar. I hesitated in the doorway, but he reached back for my hand
and pulled me in as he turned the rheostat and made the room glow with
a soft amber light. In the corner was a king-size mattress covered with
shiny Indian fabric in deep jewel tones—forest green, teal, ruby, dark
bittersweet orange, and gold. Brightly colored pillows were scattered
over the white carpet.

On the opposite wall was a tapestry depicting the young Krishna
dancing with his *gopis*, the Indian milkmaids who were completely
smitten with him. It was supposed to represent the love between the
One True Self and all of us little junior selves, whose job it was to reunite
with the One—but it looked a lot more sexual than that to me, a lot more
like the kinds of things that happened behind the gym after bonfire pep
rallies. Both Krishna and the *gopis* had wild, ravenous looks in their eyes
that didn't exactly go with the Peace that Passeth Understanding.

Directly in front of us, next to the red candle, was a small altar
silhouetted against a pale ivory satin sheet tacked to the wall. Suk glided
toward it and reached into a little wooden box like the one used for Love
Offerings, only without the slot for money. He extracted seven sticks of
incense. The air thickened with the scent of sandalwood and what I
imagined was myrrh because it seemed so exotic. He slowly, gently,
pressed the grainy sticks into my palm, folded my hand between his
hands, and gazed into my eyes.

"Take these home with you, so you will always be close. When you
burn them, they'll remind you of being here."

"I love being here." I put my other hand over his, in a way that could have been just warm and friendly but wasn't. He pulled me into an embrace, and electricity flew between our bodies. I felt my breasts on his chiseled pecs, his hands on my back, my hands running over his shoulders.

Then suddenly, he was standing apart from me, smiling gently. His arm went around my shoulder and we were out in the hall. Then his arm dropped and we were walking separately back to the kitchen. What had happened? Had I done something wrong?

"Saraswati." He caressed her with his voice as warmly as he had me with his hands just a few seconds earlier. "Can we help you?"

She turned toward us from the sink, a foaming Brillo pad grasped in a huge yellow rubber glove. Her hair streamed out of its bun and tamarind sauce dotted the front folds of her white polyester sari. She seemed on the verge of tears—far, far from Oneness. He took the Brillo pad from her and stepped up to the sink. She stood behind him and put her arms around him, nuzzling the back of his neck, and shot me a self-satisfied look as I stood alone in the hallway, watching.

It was *wrong*. They did not belong together, especially not in that dark, sensuous room. Things had to change. They *would* change—but in that instant, all I wanted was to be away from there. The El tracks thundered beneath me all the way home, drowning out everything else as I plotted how to drive them apart.

℃

I arrived early the next Wednesday, quickly found a pillow, and stretched myself into the deepest *samadhi* I could muster. The overall impression I hoped to create was one of mystery, high-powered sanctity, and indispensability. Suk would have to see that I, and not Saraswendy, had the better spiritual goods. I'd seen her scurrying around the kitchen, oogling Suk, and handing him tea and Mystical Cones—but I'd never actually see her in *samadhi*. I would make it impossible for him *not* to see that I could reach higher states than she could, and then he would *have* to choose me.

William came in and sat down quietly, followed by a new young couple in jeans and matching purple T-shirts with gold sunbursts on the backs. Both had bright red hair. They could have been brother and sister, except that they held hands and gazed longingly into each other's eyes, even after they sat down on their respective Indian pillows. Wildly inappropriate! It made me look even better.

Suk glided to his cushion throne in the front. He wound himself into the lotus posture, did his breathing and huffing thing, then sat for a few minutes transfixed on the OM symbol in the back of the room. Finally, he let loose with a big, bellowing, "OOOMMMMM!" The redheaded couple jumped. It sounded kind of like a bagpipe.

Then, without missing a beat, Suk relaxed into his real self and flashed us a heart-melting smile.

"Welcome!" he said, looking right at the sunburst twins, then glancing to include William and me. Our eyes held for a moment while he looked to the depths of my soul. I tried to make it seem pure and holy.

He gave his little intro to the Vedanta, touching on its incredible depth, simplicity, and power, and noting with some disappointment, "I wish the whole world could be here tonight to share this with us. It's just us five, though"—a faint, brave little sigh—"six with Saraswati, who will join us later." Then in an apparent nod to karma and Accepting What Was, he almost whispered, "Just as it is meant to be..."

My God! Suk wanted more people, more students. He wanted to fill this room! *I could do that*, probably better than Saraswendy. She only knew her mother's matronly pals from the neighborhood, maybe some graduates of Northwestern, and other staffers at JWT. Not a promising crew. I had all of Penn High School at my fingertips, or at least enough of them to look impressive in this room. We were probably just talking about warm bodies, not junior gurus who actually took this stuff seriously. I ticked off the possible markets in my head: Joe and his hoodlum friends; the nerdy boys in my Accounting class; the whole Coke-bottle glasses crowd of girls who were very smart but definitely not pompom squad material...

I became lost in marketing thoughts, rather than *samadhi*, as Suk began his transition to the meditation part of the evening and finally invited us into the kitchen for post-*samadhi* veggies. I had decided to snag him at refreshments and ask casually if it would be all right to bring some new people next Wednesday—but when he came up to me in the kitchen and put his palm softly against my cheek, I didn't have any words. I just looked into his eyes.

"Your heart is unwinding. It's very sweet," he whispered, taking my hand.

Saraswendy's hand curled around from behind him and clenched his upper arm. "Baba!" she said pointedly, "I need you to bless the food before we eat." He looked at her as if she had offered him a rat.

"You can do that, Saraswati." She glared at me and flounced off to bless the *samosas* and carrots.

I pulled my wits about me and asked, "Would it be okay if I brought some friends from school next week?" He put his other hand over mine and looked into my eyes more deeply than anybody ever had. Now I understood Oneness.

"Of course." It was so soft that I didn't actually hear the words. Just saw his lips form them.

❧

The next Wednesday, I showed up with eleven people in tow. Or rather, I claimed them as they straggled in, standing next to Suk at the door so I could introduce them and make sure he knew they came from me.

"Yo! Mar!" Joe flung his arm awkwardly around my shoulder, grabbed me and released me so quickly that it was more like a jitterbug step than an embrace. Then he leaned his head back, slid grimy fingernails through his greasy black hair, thinned his eyes, and muttered skeptically to Suk, "Yo."

Joe's best friend, Charlie James, hovered just behind him, as always. Charlie slunk in with a brief nod to Suk and me and—this simply could *not* have happened, but it did—a deliberate clutching of his balls.

Suk didn't bat an eye. I supposed he'd seen worse in India.

"Welcome," he said with a soft smile. "*Om shanti.* Please come in." He held an open hand out toward the little bench where people removed their shoes, which made his pecs ripple. Charlie scurried over to Joe and whispered something as they removed their heavy black boots. They dissolved into giggles, shoving one another back and forth. No doubt Charlie had suggested that Suk was a "homo," what with the sarong and all. He and Joe didn't run into many bare-chested, *doti*-clad gurus. A dense odor rose from their socks.

Next came the three smart Coke-bottle girls from my Analytic Geometry class who kept up a continuous flow of conversation among themselves and seemed magnetized together by its electric buzz. Leticia Albacranz wore pastel polished cotton shirtwaists that emphasized the huge perspiration stains always seeping from under her arms. Alice Simpson slept with her hair wound around orange juice cans to create a Rosemary Clooney pageboy, but they must have gotten rearranged during the night because some of the pageboy curls always wound up vertical instead of horizontal, giving her the look of a milking machine. Clara Reinhartz smelled pungent, like rotting pears.

Their buzzing crescendoed when they saw Suk. They flew past him to the bench, hovered for a moment to remove their saddle shoes, then rose as one and headed for the living room. They stopped dead in their tracks when they saw Joe and Charlie, who visibly shrank from them and plastered themselves against the wall.

Jonathan Snickley and Richard Armat from my Accounting class showed up in their school clothes—starched white short-sleeved shirts with pants that were belted at the waist and barely reached their ankles.

One of Richard's ballpoint pens had bled deep-blue ink through its plastic pocket protector, and the dark stain crept slowly across his shirt. As they sat on the bench, Jonathan handed him a Kleenex, which he had thoughtfully moistened with spit.

I was starting to question my strategy in just going for warm bodies to fill up the room and vowed to find some better students for Suk next week.

The gang from Penn High was rounded out by Miss Rumford, our gym teacher, who brought with her a short woman named Patty who never stopped smiling. Miss Rumford was five-foot-two and built like a fire hydrant. She wore her gym shorts and a clean white T-shirt, but thankfully had left her lanyard and whistle back at the gym.

"Margaret Rumford," she smiled broadly, sticking out her thick paw to Suk. He took it and covered it with his other hand, smiling beatifically.

"Suk Baba, Margaret. Welcome." She looked up at him and actually batted her eyes. He grinned. It was surreal.

"Hi, Miss Rumford," I put in, just to make sure he knew she was there because of me. She nodded curtly and lumbered over to the bench.

"Hey Suk, can I keep my socks on?" she bellowed.

"Of course, Margaret," he cooed.

The final two were Paddy and Kitty Murphy, retirees whom I'd hauled out of Kilkenny's Tavern down the street from Suk Bhavan to push my total number of guests into double digits. Passing Kilkenny's on the way from the El station to Suk Bhavan, I'd had an instinct to run in and grab a few more souls to save—and thanks to Mollie sending me on errands to odd places all over Chicago, I felt comfortable just pushing into the tavern. I walked up to Paddy and Kitty like a long-lost daughter, leaned my elbow on the bar, and asked them if they'd like to have some fun tonight. I told them it was something that might change their lives, and even bring them closer to God. They burst out laughing, threw back their shots, and agreed to meet me at Suk Bhavan.

These were my people. Suk moved among them, rounding up their energy into one semi-cohesive ball and getting them situated. He was a genius. We were a great team.

ॐ

Suk knew better than to open this particular evening with his usual huffing and startling "OOOMMMMM." Instead, he was smiling and affable, making people feel so comfortable with small talk that, after a few minutes, Joe actually smiled over at Kitty Murphy as if she were his long-lost grandma.

Suk was everybody's doting brother or son—except that he'd spent eight years in an ashram with his swami and, of course, didn't wear a shirt. I wondered what he would do when winter came. Maybe Julie would teach me to knit, and I'd knit him a sweater. White, to match his *doti*. The image of him in a cuddly white sweater that I had made myself was so exciting that my palms began to sweat.

He launched into his Vedanta intro, reorienting it and watering it down on the spot for the desire-ridden and spiritually clueless crowd from Penn High and Kilkenny's tavern. Kitty beamed at him with pursed lips and twinkling eyes. Joe and Charlie were at least paying attention, which was more than they ever did in school. Suk seemed thrilled to have so many people.

I was happy with my results, but already thinking how to tweak them for a higher quality crowd next week. It was far too stressful to stand at the door with Suk, imagining how the Penn High kids might look through his eyes, or how they might react to the Ultimate Wisdom of the Ages. Tonight's apparent success had been dumb luck, and I didn't want to chance it again—or press Suk's social skills too far. Next week, I would tap some new markets. Maybe put up fliers in city colleges, coffeehouses, neighborhood businesses.

Suk paused suddenly and grinned, spreading his arms out to the sides as if to embrace us all. "Isn't this wonderful?" he asked the ceiling. His joy was infectious. Even Charlie flashed his lopsided grin. "All of us here tonight, talking about what is real. Important. Thank you for coming." He seemed almost on the verge of tears. The Coke-bottle girls leaned together and tittered. "Thanks to you, Mara, for bringing us all together." Low rumblings of assent all around. "Mara and I are partners in this evening, partners in bringing this ancient knowledge to the world."

I was stunned. First embarrassed, then so excited I thought I would float off my pillow. Partners! It was huge. Well, that's what we *were*! Still, I couldn't believe he had actually said it aloud, in public. I tried to keep my eyes humbly glued to the carpet, but when I peeked up he was smiling broadly and starting a round of applause. The others joined in, slowly and a bit awkwardly, but I could see that the Penn kids were impressed.

Then he invited us all to close our eyes and join him in meditation.

"There's no trick to it," he soothed. "Just let your eyes shut and think about something that makes you happy."

It started well. After a few darting glances at one another, most of them appeared to follow instructions—even Joe and Charlie. I closed my eyes, hoping to melt into a deep *samadhi*, to let myself sink into that place inside where there was no mental chatter, just vast, undulating Peace...

Then I smelled it. I knew that odor. Julie had once gotten lost in a phone conversation and forgotten about the doughnuts bubbling away in hot oil. If the *samosas* weren't already in flames, they would be soon. I opened my eyes and met Suk's. He glanced toward the kitchen, an intimate signal for me to check it out on his behalf.

I rose silently and moved as gracefully as possible toward the swinging door, feeling his eyes on me and glad I'd worn the tight jeans that nipped in my waist. As I pushed on the door, there was a dull thud on the other side and it stopped cold. I'd hit something! Hard! I pushed again, gently this time, and the door opened to reveal Saraswendy sprawled on the floor. She had been listening at the crack and gotten smacked when I'd come to investigate! She clutched her forehead, and her mouth gaped in a silent scream. Her hair had fallen out of its bun and stuck out in all directions. Her face was splotched and tear-stained, the white sari smeared with dark ocher curry. She glared up at me with clenched teeth. As she started pulling herself off the floor, the sari began to unwind. She snatched at its folds and stuffed them desperately back into place.

Horrible crackling noises rose from a smoking pot on the stove. It glubbed wildly, spitting hot oil onto the counter and floor, so overheated that it rocked back and forth on the burner. I quickly turned off the flame and grabbed a couple of towels for hot pads—but just as I touched the pot, I saw Saraswendy out of the corner of my eye. She shoved hard on my shoulder, sending me flying a couple feet. Hot oil splashed onto the stove. A couple drops hit my forearm. I endured it in silence for the sake of Suk's powerful *samadhi* on the other side of the swinging door. I pushed her back, hard enough to put her on the floor again, and took the pot off the burner. The blackened *samosas* shrank into themselves and slowly disappeared through the brown oil to the bottom of the pot.

Smoke filled the kitchen, so I opened all the windows and turned on the fan. Saraswendy was on her feet again and hurled herself at me. Mollie had taught me how to grab someone's wrist and turn their arm so it really hurt and you got control of them—or at least kept them from getting at you. I grabbed Saraswendy's wrist and twisted. Then twisted a little more than Mollie had taught me. Maybe it wasn't something a partner in salvation like myself would usually do, but I needed control of the kitchen. I was, after all, in service to the Great Knowledge of the evening and its purveyor, Suk—and Saraswendy was trying to screw things up. When she started making shrieky, squealing little noises, I had to release her.

"OOOMMMMMM," came the long chant from the living room, louder than usual. Suk was trying to distract them from the kitchen noise.

"Shut up!" I hissed at Saraswendy. She was snuffling and moaning, holding her shoulder. I soaked up the oil on the stove with a towel and grabbed some ice cubes from the freezer. Holding them to the burns with my left hand, I grabbed her wrist with my right hand and looked at her like if she didn't keep quiet, I'd twist again. She cowered and shut up.

"What's the matter with you?!" I whispered.

"How dare you come in here and ruin everything?" she whimpered.

"You're the one who practically set us all on fire!"

"Stop trying to fool poor Baba! Bringing all those hoodlums and misfits, and pretending you're helping!" she hissed. "Go home to your whore aunt and her friends and shoot up some heroin, why don't you!?"

What?! I filed that away for later and focused here, now, on what was in front of me in the kitchen. If she had been listening at the door, nothing I could do or say would hurt her as much as what she had heard Suk say. She wrenched her wrist out of my grasp and fled down the hall to the bedroom.

The smoke had pretty much cleared, so I turned off the fan. I took the whole pot and stuck it into the oven to hide it and minimize any further smoke, then laid out the crudités that Saraswendy had cut before her breakdown and glided back to my pillow just as they were doing their final "OOOMMMMM" after the meditation.

Suk gestured for me to come up to him. I waded through the pillow-sitters to his little throne, every inch the handmaiden that Saraswendy had been only a few short months earlier. He took my hand, right there in front of everyone, and pulled me down to whisper in my ear, almost touching it with his lips.

"Is everything all right?" I steadied my breathing. Nothing upset or moved the ineffable I AM. Nothing touched the self-effulgent One. Suk looked up at me expectantly. I turned to whisper in his ear.

"Saraswati burned the *samosas*." I guess that must have been obvious, because he still looked expectant. "I put the pot in the oven." He nodded slowly. "Saraswati's resting in the bedroom." He nodded again, then gazed up as if he understood everything.

"Uh...Is the food ready?" he asked.

"Yes." He covered my hand with his other one and squeezed.

"Thank you," he said with great relief.

I returned to my pillow and sat humbly, just one of the students, as if nothing had happened. As if I hadn't just saved the whole evening, possibly saved Suk Bhavan from burning to the ground, actually *created* the whole evening by bringing all these people. As if I hadn't been called Suk's partner, easily made a nice little buffet in the kitchen with one hand tied behind my back and—on top of everything else, and unlike Saraswendy—been willing to share Suk with the world!

Saraswendy stayed in the back during the little social after class, and I played hostess. I kept the crudités coming, schmoozed around with the water pitcher, and chatted people up. At one point, I found myself over in the corner, cutting up more carrot sticks, face to face with Vishnu, the Preserver part of the Hindu godly trinity. He stared at me from the brightly colored picture on the wall with heavy, slightly disapproving eyes as he reclined on the great serpent Ananda in the Ocean of Milk, the lotus of creative power springing from his navel.

"What's it to you?" I thought, glancing around at the various Hindu gods and goddesses who traipsed about or stood frozen in awkward poses in pictures or statues around the kitchen. Krishna playing his flute for the *gopis*, Arjuna standing in his chariot getting solid advice from Krishna, Shiva dancing the Nataraj, winding through the cosmic cycles of creation and destruction, flicking back the Veil of Illusion with his foot. I flashed on the Saints-O-Rama at Immaculate Conception. Maria Goretti's twenty-seven stab wounds. Isaac Jogues' missing fingernails. These folks had nothing on the Catholic saints. Been there, done that. I was in a whole new league now. Not a supplicant, but a mover and shaker.

It was an early evening. The Penn/Kilkenny's crowd wasn't big on raw vegetables, and most were reeling from their first encounter with esoteric wisdom. Plus, the smell of charred *samosas* still hung heavily in the air. They didn't stay long.

Finally, Suk and I were alone in the vestibule, staring at the door. For a moment, he had that beatific Suk-y look that gazed into the center of the universe and saw God. Then our eyes met and he was a real person who probably had a name other than Suk Baba. He threw his head back and laughed, "Oh my *God*!" His laughter got kind of hysterical and I giggled along. "What a night!" he shouted. He bent over with his hands on his knees, still laughing, shook his head, then stood up and threw both arms around me. Our bodies melted into one another and, slowly, he stopped laughing and just held me tight.

Saraswendy came flying out of the bedroom. Her hair was back in place and her sari rewrapped, but not cleaned. She had a large Indian cloth bag slung over her shoulder and froze when she saw us, then put her head down and swooshed quickly past us toward the door. Suk reached out to stop her, but she pulled away violently, gave him a withering look, and slammed the door on her way out. I thought of Janet that first night, spilling the *raita* and running out into the night. Where did they go when they fled Suk Bhavan? Kilkenny's? I pictured

Saraswendy hauling herself up onto a barstool next to Paddy and Kitty, ordering a neat Scotch, and telling them what an evil bitch I was.

"Let her go," Suk said softly, more to himself than to me.

He cradled my cheek in his palm and kissed me, not like Joe did, but softly, sensuously. Chills spread across my shoulders and down my spine. He kissed me again, more deeply, and I pressed into him. He pulled away, took my hand and started leading me back to the bedroom.

I didn't move and pulled back on his hand. I had no idea what to do once we got there, and I didn't want to look naive and stupid. I wanted him to keep touching and kissing me, but I didn't want to wreck the whole thing by making some huge, dumb mistake. I squeezed his hand, but wouldn't go down the hall with him.

"Not tonight," I said, like I knew what I was doing but just wanted to make it sexier by delaying it. Or like I was just afraid that spiritual midget, Saraswendy, would come sniveling back up the stairs and interrupt us—which, come to think of it, she might. Or like I was so exhausted from saving the world and cleaning up Saraswendy's mess that I needed to rest and couldn't bring to our lovemaking all the incredible energy and skill I had. Or something.

He put his arms around me and held me close, in a way that was safe rather than sexy.

"Have you ever done this before, Mara?" he whispered in my ear. I felt myself flush with embarrassment, and at the same time loved him more for seeing me, *knowing* me like that and still wanting to put his arms around me. I buried my face in his shoulder and held on tight. He swayed back and forth like he was rocking me.

"I love you," he whispered. I pulled him closer, then realized he might be talking about *agape*, the impersonal God love—not real love. I pulled away and looked him in the eye. "I want you," he said, kissing me softly, then harder. "Do you trust me?"

"Yes." He brushed back my hair.

"I love that it's new to you," he said softly.

We walked down the hall with our arms around each other's waists and then just sat on the bed making out, except that every kiss, every movement of his hand seemed to say that he loved me, that I was wonderful and special, cherished. I had never felt like that—cherished. I guessed Mollie and Julie and even my dad had loved me, but this was different. My whole mind and body pushed into it. A raw, fiery need surged up from some dark, unknown place and focused on him.

He loved how beautiful I was, he said. How much I loved God, how powerful and sweet and pure and innocent I was. My soul drank it in, overcome by the feeling of being treasured and precious by someone who knew God, was *like* God. Lying naked next to him in the dark with the deep red candle throwing our shadows against the wall, I felt like I was inside the exact moment for which I had been made. I reached out into the smells and tastes, pulled in the feel of his skin on mine, breathed with him, and gave over into being so wanted. When I came, my fingernails bit into his back and I screamed. We clutched at one another so hard, it felt like our two bodies had actually become one. It was terrifying and exhilarating. He wrapped himself around me and stroked my face.

"Sweet baby," he whispered. He turned onto his back with one arm around me and the other tucked behind his head, staring at the ceiling with a big smile on his face. When I looked at him, he turned back on his side and put his arms around me again. In the candlelight, his blue eyes seemed black.

"I love you," I whispered, embarrassed as soon as I heard the words. It was true, though. Partly to cover the embarrassment and partly because it felt so odd to have had sex for the first time with somebody named Suk, I asked, "Hey, is your name really Suk?" He laughed and touched his forehead to mine.

"No, it's Jeff." I shrieked. "Jeff Hackney!" He said it like it was a huge joke, and we both started laughing.

"Oh my God! Where are you from?" We were hysterical now, both of us blowing off steam.

"Madison!"

"No! No!" I banged the pillow with my fist. "How old are you?"

"Thirty-two!"

"Did you ever really go to India?"

"Yes." He seemed suddenly serious, even earnest. "Everything about studying the Vedanta is true. It's my life. It's all I want to do." It was all I wanted, too, and now I had a way to do it.

"I know," I said softly. "We'll make it happen. You'll see."

He nestled into my breast and, unbelievably, was sound asleep in about two minutes. I held his head against me, stroked his auburn hair, ran my hands lightly over his back. I couldn't have slept to save my life.

He was still asleep when I woke up at five thirty. I thought he might wake up, too, but he was all scrunched into himself, curled up like a baby, snoring. I tiptoed into the kitchen and found a purple flier for the Wednesday night class. I folded it in half with the print side in, drew the outline of a heart with a red magic marker, tiptoed back, and stood it up on my pillow. I kept thinking he might wake up as I dressed, but he didn't. I had never slept that soundly, or *seen* anyone sleep that soundly, in my life. I let myself out about six thirty.

A crisp October breeze blew in off the lake and swirled around in the sunlight, grabbing dead leaves and old newspaper from the gutters and tossing them in all directions. Everything seemed bright, new, and fresh—alive with energy and possibility.

The only other person in my El car, going north against the rush hour that early, was a heavyset old woman in a mauve housedress, thick gray sweater, nun shoes with gray wool anklets, and a babushka. She sat facing me with her huge brown plastic purse balanced on her lap, her legs splayed apart. She looked me up and down, then smiled at me as if she had witnessed at close range everything I'd done in the past twelve hours. I grinned back.

ॐ

Mollie was waiting when I walked in, slumped at the kitchen table over a cup of black coffee and a half-filled blue ceramic ashtray that I'd made in Crafts at Jefferson Grammar School. There were dark circles under her eyes, as if her mascara had melted down. Her skin was pale gray-green against the low-cut black robe. I was shocked at how old she looked. We just stared at one another for a moment.

"Are you okay?" I asked finally.

She looked me up and down like the El lady had, but didn't smile.

"Are *you*?"

"Yes."

She pursed her lips and pulled herself up, walked slowly over to the wall phone and dialed a number. "It's me. Everything's okay. Thanks, Jim."

"You had the cops out looking for me?"

"We didn't know where you were."

"You should have!"

She sat and motioned for me to sit. Her vermilion-tipped fingers shook slightly when she poured cream into her coffee.

"I don't want to fight with you," I said, scrambling for high ground.

"I bet you don't!" She lit a cigarette. I reached for the pack, but she snatched it away.

"I love him." She rolled her eyes and watched the smoke rise toward the ceiling.

"You don't know your ass from a hole in the ground," she said quietly, her eyes suddenly clear and level.

"I do, too. I've got God now. I've got a man. A *spiritual* man. You're just jealous."

"What you've got is a half-naked charlatan who's going to hurt you." I stood up and turned away to pour my coffee, but really to hide the tears stinging in my eyes. "Shit!" she said. I heard her chair push back, and her steps on the hardwood floor. She put her arms around me from behind, but I went stiff and turned to face her.

"You should be happy for me! This is the best thing that's ever happened to me!" All she had to do was look at me, but she said it anyway.

"I doubt that. Not the best thing." I felt ungrateful, but didn't want her to ruin everything by making me feel like a naughty kid.

"I'm sorry. I am, but I'm grown up now." She raised an eyebrow.

"It's not grown up to stay out all night and make us worry."

"Okay—but from now on, when I go over there, I may not be coming home."

She looked at the coffeepot and shifted her weight to the other foot. "I love you, kid, but you're dead wrong on this."

"I'm gonna do it. You can't stop me."

She shrugged. Then glared at me. Then shook her head. Then coughed. Then put her arms around me. I wrapped myself around her, suddenly aware that I was taller than she was and that it felt like I was holding her, instead of the other way around. Tears stung in my eyes again, and I held on tight.

Chapter 9

That winter was glorious. We had long weeks of crisp, cool sweater weather with stunning blue skies and bright, polarized colors everywhere you looked. The dark green trees in Lincoln Park against the teal lake, the deep orange and purple neon sign buzzing above the dry cleaner's. Even the traffic lights shimmered with an energy that was unearthly and exciting. Being in love changed everything.

I shuttled back and forth between home and Suk Bhavan, flushed with new feelings and sensations. Julie and I did most of the cooking, cleaning, and baking, since Mollie couldn't throw off the flu and often stayed in bed coughing. Our cop friends started picking up Loreen more and more often as she sank deeper into her heroin addiction. They sometimes left her in the holding cell overnight as an incentive to get clean, but it didn't work. Despite all that, I loved the safety and comfort of home almost as much as the thrill and newness of being with Jeff.

I stayed with him every Wednesday, Friday, and Saturday night. He and I were a couple. I was an adult. I had found God. Nothing could really ever go wrong again, because I had everything that mattered.

The first week of December, we got sparkling white snow and Jeff finally put on a shirt. Or rather, white *kurta* pajamas—loose white slacks and a long top that came to mid-thigh—but I could get my hands on those wonderful pecs whenever I wanted.

We never saw Saraswendy again. Even without a sari, I became his mainstay—not just the cook and assistant, but his soul mate, confidant, and caretaker. Nobody understood him, his concerns, his work, his glory as fully as I did. I reveled in being his partner, in being one as well as One with somebody, and in knowing that I'd been born to do *just this*, to support this wonderful person who gave the world its most important message.

I was very good at what Jeff called "godly public relations" and was starting to put Suk Bhavan on the map. I didn't exactly know what to do, but Mollie had made me fearless about moving around in the world and approaching strangers. If it seemed like more people would come to class if the newspapers did a story on Jeff, I just called up their main number and asked whoever answered how I could make that happen. After a while, I got the hang of it.

I'd invited a reporter from the *Sun-Times* to the Wednesday class and she had written a mostly good story about Suk Baba and his work. We now had about thirty regulars, with new people coming all the time—not just from the fliers I continued to post around the city, but from word of mouth. We were even thinking of renting a bigger place for Wednesday night class. I could afford it, with all the money I'd saved from working at the bakery. Besides, if we started having classes at one of the more liberal, ecumenical churches, we could draw even more people!

Best of all, *samadhi* was coming more often as I went about my normal life. It was like *the bright*, except wider, deeper, and it had a philosophical foundation in the Vedanta. I felt it, and then could explain it to my mind through the idea of Oneness. Then it reappeared again as an experience, even more thrilling.

As I waited on the El platform in driving sleet one day, my eyes fell on a young girl's dirty turquoise ski cap. I sank into those fibers, dissolving into the cap, into her, into the people around us and the freezing wet air, the soft rotting boards beneath our feet, the whole city, the world and beyond. There was nothing more to do—just revel in that vast silence. I touched and merged into the spark from which everything sprang into being.

The next week, I was cutting up vegetables in the Suk Bhavan kitchen and swept into that same place where my hand, the knife, the cutting board, the carrots, and the people who would eat them were absolutely One.

Jeff and I lay in one another's arms, talking about our future. We would build a huge base for "the work" in Chicago. Then travel the world, giving people the secret to happiness. For the first time in my life, everything made perfect sense. God, me, the world, and why I was here. Finally, I could relax. My heart unfolded into what Jeff said was a beautiful flower. I had become somebody.

ひ

We had our "grand opening" in the Pine Room of the Unitarian Church in April. It was a Saturday night kickoff for the ongoing Wednesday night classes, which we were also switching to the church.

A pancake house had opened in the neighborhood that winter to wild acclaim, and I modeled our debut on its success. I took out ads in the *Ravenswood Review* and other neighborhood papers, then got the *Daily News* and *Chicago* magazine to do stories on Jeff, "Chicago's homegrown guru." They were mostly flattering, with only a few swipes at the OOOMMMM-ing, the brightly colored sequined pillows, the patchouli incense, and the other Hindu trappings surrounding a guy who obviously didn't grow up in Delhi. I leafleted for the grand opening outside El stations, restaurants, movie theaters, and nearby churches, buttonholing passersby and talking about the glory and fun of exploring this new route to happiness.

The Unitarians let me create a backdrop of gold fabric—well, yellow sheets—and hang one of our big brass OM symbols against it. Stan made a platform that I also covered with sheets so Jeff could sit in the lotus posture on a stack of pillows and still be seen by everybody. Finally, I got the funeral parlor down the street from the bakery to loan me two potted palms and put them on either side of the platform.

We stood at the back of the room that afternoon, and he held me close as we looked at what I'd done.

"Sweetheart, you are so wonderful. Thank you."

"I love you."

"I love you, too. So much." He stared at the stage, his eyes shining.

I wore a long black skirt and black sweater to the Unitarian Church that night, which wasn't as weird as wearing a sari but did have a certain nun-like aura and contrasted nicely with what I'd bought for Jeff—a white Nehru jacket and white slacks. I'd considered white buck shoes, but realized that would get too complicated, what with the lotus posture and all. Better to leave him barefoot.

At 6:45, he hoisted himself up onto the platform and sat on a blood-red pillow, falling into a deep *samadhi* to "tune up" the room while I put on a tape of sitar music. I watched him for a moment, wallowing in my good fortune, and curled my energy into his before opening the doors to the crowd that had been standing outside for fifteen minutes.

By seven o'clock, I counted 168 people sitting in states ranging from skepticism to mild interest to outright reverence. I tried hard to maintain at least a light *samadhi* myself, but was so thrilled with the turnout that I kept pacing in the back of the room like a caged tiger. Finally, I forced myself to stop and channel energy to Jeff, seeing him and everyone in the room as One.

"OOOMMMMM."

It reverberated through the room, a strong but gentle sound tonight. He had taken to heart one reporter's comment about it scaring people and toned it down into something more Midwestern—a sound your parish priest might make, less aggressively foreign and more a commanding homage to the God we all shared. Also, mercifully brief.

"Welcome," he said softly into the microphone, his voice caressing each soul as if he or she were the only person in the universe. He was so good at this! I would have to get him a bigger venue. He gave the same basic talk he always did—overview of the Vedanta, a short meditation to get them high (*very* short, with this larger and less focused crowd), and an invitation to come back on Wednesday nights.

He closed the program with another resounding OOOMMMMM, and I stepped to the stage to invite everybody for refreshments in the smaller Sunset Room down the hall—carrots, celery, and tahini dip I'd brought over from Suk Bhavan that afternoon—socializing, and a chance to meet Suk Baba.

About half of them actually stayed. The Sunset was a dark, elegant, wood-paneled room with a thick carpet that muffled sound and made the gathering seem both intimate and holy. People milled around munching carrots and celery, asking what the dip was, then what tahini was, then smiling gamely when I said, "Ground sesame seeds." They didn't stay long, but most left with fliers for the Wednesday class.

As the crowd thinned out, I spotted Jeff over in the corner, talking to a short blonde girl. Woman, actually. Maybe twenty. She wore tight jeans, a bright red Chanel jacket, and expensive black patent leather stiletto heels. She grinned broadly, tilted her head to one side and flipped her hair back. He reached over and touched her arm as they laughed. A chill spread from my shoulders down my arms. I headed in their direction.

"Mara! This is Sally. Sally, this is my assistant, Mara."

"Hi!" Sally chirped. "I was just telling Suk Baba..." She giggled. "Is that what I should call you? Or Suk-y?"

"'Baba' is fine." He smiled softly. "For now."

"Anyway, I was just telling Baba, my Dad is an investment banker in the Loop, and he could get you funded so you could do this in bigger places. Maybe even McCormick Place." She giggled again. "You could do that! You're really good!"

"You two should talk!" Jeff said to me, arching his eyebrows. My veins filled with hot lead, but I smiled in a way I hoped was at once gracious, mysterious, holy, and frightening. I resisted the urge to link my arm through his. It would have appeared clingy, attached, un-One. Desperate.

"Wonderful," I cooed, reminding myself that this was my turf. It wasn't like she was going to slip into a deep *samadhi* any time soon or be able to distinguish Oneness from a hole in the ground. She turned and shot Jeff one last glittering smile before turning to leave.

"Well, bye-bye!" she chirped over her shoulder at us, "See you Wednesday!"

Jeff was quiet as our shoulders jostled together on the El going home.

"Are you okay?" I asked. He nodded.

"Just tired."

"You were the best you've ever been tonight!" He smiled and took my hand, stared out the window at the dark brick buildings streaking by, dimly lit by streetlights. I put my hand over his and stroked it. The El rumbled beneath us.

That night was the first time he didn't want to make love.

&

In the morning, I got up early and made tea for us. He stumbled into the kitchen wearing the fluffy white bathrobe I'd given him for his birthday. He kissed me on the cheek, sat down at the table, and buried himself in a yoga magazine.

"You were great last night, honey," I said after a while. I wound my arms around his shoulders from behind and kissed his neck.

"You were, too," he said sleepily, craning around to kiss my cheek again. "I'm gonna go sit, sweetheart." He stood up with his tea and the magazine, and headed down the hall to the small meditation room we'd set up across from the bedroom. "Have a good day at work." It was Sunday, and I was taking Julie's early shift behind the counter.

The door to the meditation room closed behind him. It felt like he had slapped me across the face, but I didn't want to make a fuss. Maybe he really was just depleted by the strain of holding more people's energy in the new, bigger place. By Wednesday, when I saw him next, he would be himself again. Besides, it was my job to make his life easier, not harder.

I made the bed, got dressed, and straightened up the bedroom. As I lifted his new Nehru jacket from the floor, a little card fell out of the pocket. It was pale blue, with dark blue lettering:

Sally Slater
Kappa Kappa Gamma
1871 Orrington
Evanston, Illinois 60201
(312) 448-8037

A sorority girl, and another one from Northwestern! I thought about burning it with a black candle, or shredding it in the garbage disposal, or ripping it to pieces and leaving a neat pile on the floor—but decided that voodoo, the violence of whirring disposal blades, and the passive-aggressive pile were probably all bad karma. Worse, through Jeff's eyes, they would all look childish, reactive, and far removed from Oneness. I decided to play to my strength and Sally's weakness—holiness.

I took the card between my thumb and index finger and placed it carefully on the little table beside our bed, lining it up perfectly with the corners. It screamed, "I found this in your clothes but was so unaffected, so generous, so open to anything that might support our work, that instead of being upset, I put it where you could find and use it easily."

I felt shaky all morning and waited on customers with one eye on the phone behind the counter, but it didn't ring.

I finally called him on Tuesday, but he was on his way out the door. In a big hurry. We agreed to meet at five o'clock on Wednesday afternoon at Suk Bhavan to cut up vegetables before class at the church, but I had another plan. I was going over a couple hours early, and taking some of my famous lemon tarts with the sumptuous crust and ultra-rich custard. They were his favorite. I always brought them over on weekends. We ate them in bed after we made love.

An afternoon together would make everything right and prove that there was nothing to worry about. After class, we would spend the night together to cement our relationship. People gave him their business cards all the time. My fears were unreasonable.

I felt a little queasy on the way over, but walking the familiar route from the El platform to Suk Bhavan calmed me down. The trees were starting to bud, and Micky Kilkenny waved to me from inside his tavern as I passed.

"What're ya doin' here so early, darlin'?" he yelled.

"A surprise!" I held up the pink cardboard box of lemon tarts, tied with a white string and a red plastic heart. He smiled and nodded from the darkness as he wiped down the bar, the bright orange Schlitz sign glowing above his head.

I let myself in quietly so I could surprise Jeff—but as I slipped off my loafers, my eyes fell on a pair of shoes I'd never seen before. They were small, about a size 5. Shiny brown alligator, four-inch heels. The blood rushed to my face. I considered sneaking out and coming back at five when I was due, but instead walked with my pink box to the kitchen.

I set it on the table and made a lot of noise getting out the big wooden cutting board and taking the celery and carrots out of the refrigerator. I found our sharpest paring knife and started cutting carrots as if my life depended on it, emptying my mind of everything else. I focused completely on their bright orange color, the paler veins that ran through them, and exactly the size I wanted each piece to be. They should be short, so people wouldn't double dip into the tahini, and also so I could make a better arrangement on the large platter. I liked alternate circles of carrots and celery, in a spiral shape that...

"Oh hi, Mara!" Sally stood in the doorway between the kitchen and front hall. She wore jeans and a kelly-green silk blouse, buttoned wrong. Her feet were bare. I turned with the knife in my hand, feeling like one of the Jets in *West Side Story*. She looked smirky, or maybe it was just that she never stopped smiling.

"Sally!" It was the voice Mollie used when she wanted to make sure I knew she was the boss.

"Hi! What can I do here?" It was as if she belonged there, as if she'd been invited, as if she might even be in charge.

"You can cut up the celery." I felt dizzy, almost on the verge of fainting. It helped to focus on the carrots and celery. Orange and green vegetables that needed to be cut up into little pieces.

"I came over to see if I could help," she said smoothly, without looking up. "Baba was picking out a book for me to study." At least she wasn't calling him Jeff yet. I nodded and forced a smile. Maybe she really *had* come over to cut up vegetables, and Jeff really *was* just giving her a book to deepen her understanding of Oneness. With my temples pounding so hard, I didn't trust myself to figure it out.

Jeff appeared in the doorway, shifting from one bare foot to the other in his Nehru outfit. What was he doing, ready to go to the church this early? He kissed my cheek and stood between us at the counter, peering left at the carrots, right at the celery.

"I'll make the dip!" he said with a big smile, bouncing over to the fridge and hauling out jars. Nobody spoke. Sally and I chopped. Jeff mixed and stirred.

"All done!" Sally sang. "Hey, I have an errand to run. How about if I meet you guys at the church?"

"Sure!" Jeff said eagerly. She moved toward the shoe rack in the vestibule, and he followed. "We'll see you there. Don't be late!" His voice sounded unusually loud.

"I won't." Hers, on the other hand, sounded muffled.

By the time he came back, I had all the vegetables and dip packed up and ready to go.

"Let's go to Luigi's for dinner!" he said brightly.

"I can cook here. I brought lemon tarts." He looked at them, then back at me. They were definitely an "after sex" food.

I wanted to run to him, burrow in his arms, smile up at him, and feel loved—but I wasn't sure what I'd be running into. Instead, I stood frozen a minute, then turned and started cleaning the cutting boards. I wanted him to come to me, to put his arms around me and tell me that Sally was a new student, and a little taken with him, and had just showed up without being invited. I turned around, half expecting to see all this in his eyes, but he was looking out the window.

"Let's let Luigi do the cooking tonight. I want some lasagna." Maybe I should have brought lasagna.

Over dinner, we talked about the big interview I'd set up with a reporter for the *Tribune*'s Sunday magazine. I was hoping for the cover. I stared into the red candle melting over a Chianti bottle, wanting to ask him about Sally, but not wanting him to see how attached and unsure I felt. He seemed oblivious, calmly chewing his lasagna, even smiling occasionally. Was I nuts? Maybe everything really was okay. Surely he would say something if he didn't want to be with me anymore.

Back at Suk Bhavan, we had the lemon tarts for dessert—but ate them at the kitchen table, not in bed. We had to be at the church by six and were running late.

༄

The Sunset Room barely held the sixty-eight people who showed up. Sally sat in the front row, gazing up at Jeff. Again, with the red Chanel jacket. A flashy color, inappropriate to the sacred space. I caught his eye and smiled. He smiled back. I relaxed for a second, then caught myself watching to see if he smiled at her as well and trying to make him look at me again. I imagined him introducing me to the class, saying how important I was to his work—anything to link us together and hold our connection in place.

After class, I passed among people pouring water, explaining about tahini, and watching Jeff and Sally. Where were they standing? Were they looking at one another? No, she was talking to a man and woman in business suits. He was talking to the *Tribune* reporter, a short woman in a gray pantsuit with a huge tapestry satchel.

I was replenishing the veggies when I saw them move together out the door, into the hall. They walked in step with one another. His hand rested softly between her shoulder blades—which might not have been sexual, but seemed intimate. A silent, burning scream rose up in my throat. I poured water for a woman in a purple peasant skirt and spilled some on the Unitarian carpet. I moved from one person to the next, chatting, pouring water, my energy stretched out the door after Jeff and Sally.

He appeared back in the room about ten minutes later, moving easily into the crowd, talking and mingling, smiling. As people started to leave, he came up beside me and smiled over what was left of the crowd.

"How do you think it went?"

I looked up at him. How could he pretend that everything was normal? I might be holding it together on the outside, but inside I was scratching and scrambling, snatching at shreds of attention and validation. I felt insane. I *must* be insane, because he seemed fine. I couldn't let him see how undone I was.

"It was wonderful!" I said, shuffling carrots and celery into their plastic containers. He beamed as if he hadn't really known it was good until I told him. He did need me!

That night, we made love. Rather, we had sex. It was the first time I realized the difference. Making love was the delicate chemistry and artistry of an angel food cake—adding the ingredients in just the right order, folding in the egg whites, letting it rise slowly over time. Sex was just throwing everything into a pan and tossing it into the oven.

Afterward, he seemed *gone*. I was definitely gone. I wanted to hit him, then to have a crying jag. I thought about Julie's current boyfriend, a cop named Ed, who had told us about his partner getting caught in crossfire between drug dealers and cops in a parking garage. Ed and the other cops had been pinned down behind some cars and had watched helplessly as a pool of blood spread out from this guy, inch by inch over the concrete, getting deeper, wider, and thicker as he lay motionless and bled out before their eyes.

For hours, we had been doing all the same things we'd been doing for eight months—at Luigi's, at the church, at Suk Bhavan—but in some gruesome way, I was bleeding out.

C8

At two o'clock each Saturday afternoon, old Skelly O'Connell appeared outside the Tribune Tower on Michigan Avenue. No one knew where Skelly lived, or what he did the rest of the week, but he was always there at two o'clock on Saturday afternoon to sell the early edition of the Sunday *Trib*. For years, my ritual had been to take the bus downtown and pick it up so that Mollie, Julie, and I could read it late Saturday afternoon. Now, of course, so Jeff and I could read it—especially this week, since the story on him was supposed to be in the magazine.

Skelly touched his grimy maroon ski cap with a bent finger when he saw me crossing the street.

"Hiya, Mara."

"Hiya, Skelly. How's it going?"

He nodded as the huge brass doors opened and three burly men tossed six bundles of the *Trib* roughly out onto the sidewalk. Skelly cut a white plastic tie and, in one smooth movement of his wrist, extracted a huge Sunday paper, rolled it up, and stuck it under my arm. He extended the other hand. I laid three quarters on his palm.

Normally I turned and headed back to the bus stop, but I couldn't wait. As Skelly watched, I flipped open the paper and rummaged for the magazine. There, on the cover, in full color, was a picture of Jeff sitting on the platform at the grand opening. It was taken from far enough away that you could see the whole platform, the gold fabric, his crimson pillow, and the OM symbol—but close enough that you could also see his irresistible smile. I imagined having to rent Soldier Field for the hordes who would now flock to see Suk Baba.

Skelly was staring at me. I held up the magazine and pointed at it.

"This is my boyfriend!"

He moved closer and squinted at the picture of Jeff, then looked suspiciously at me, then back at Jeff. He forced just enough smile to reveal three missing teeth.

"You be a good girl."

What the hell did that mean? Crazy old man. I packed up the paper and climbed back on the bus, hugging to me the proof that everything was okay, that Jeff and I were all right, and that we were meant to be together forever.

The bus chugged north along the Outer Drive. Sunlight glinted off little whitecaps whipping up on the lake. I took apart the paper and read the story. Again, it was mostly good stuff about Jeff's studying with his swami in Bombay, the "spiritual thirst" of the carrot-and-tahini crowd at the grand opening, Suk Baba's personal charisma and the way he could look anybody in the eye, "including this reporter," and make them think they were going to heaven—maybe even before they died. There was a brief mention of me, the "lanky, black-clad, redheaded 'assistant' who promotes our own Chicago guru."

The story was a terrific coup, and I had made it happen. I had planned to spend the rest of the afternoon doing errands—a better gold backdrop for his platform, more paper plates for the larger buffet to accommodate the growing crowds—and get back to Suk Bhavan around five, just in time to cook dinner. Instead, I decided I couldn't wait to show him the magazine.

Micky waved as I passed Kilkenny's, but I didn't stop to chat as I usually did. I felt oddly nervous, and noticed as I got out my keys that newsprint had bled all over my sweaty fingers. I slid the key in the door and turned it. Kelly-green pumps. A flush spread out over my whole body. My mind stopped working. I couldn't think, just moved numbly down the hall and slowly opened the bedroom door.

They were naked, writhing slowly, sensuously on the floor like snakes behind the thick glass at Lincoln Park Zoo. So absorbed that they didn't even see me at first. I stood in the doorway, holding the paper, watching, feeling my heart turn inside out, blood pounding in my neck and temples. My eyes were looking at something that absolutely could not be happening. At something that made me not *me*, and him not *him*.

He saw me first and snatched up the colorful Indian bedspread to cover both of them. He just stared at me. She squealed and clung to him.

"Mara!" He staggered to his feet, using the bedspread as an improvised *doti* and tearing a sheet off the bed for her. "Honey..." He came toward me. I held out the paper. "What's this?" he asked, taking it and staring for a moment at his picture. Then quickly, he tossed it on the bed and came toward me. Sally grabbed her clothes and scurried into the bathroom. As she brushed past me, I saw her secret smile.

I couldn't speak. Couldn't scream. Couldn't feel. Ghost Girl came careening back wildly over the years. The whole world filled with gray static. It was strangely comforting, even though its edges were sticky with humiliation.

"Honey, she was just here and things got away from us." He reached for my arm, but I pulled it back. "I love you," he said softly. "I need you. Please forgive me."

My eyes fell on the white carpet. I dove down into the soft fibers and let them hide me, soothe me, envelop me. Gray static inside the soft white carpet.

"I love you both."

"What?!" My voice sounded small.

"I love you both. You and I, we know the Truth. Sally does, too. We're all beyond jealousy. We know that we are One."

"What?!"

"I still love you. But I love her, too. Things have changed, that's all. *Agape*, real love, knows no limits. We're a family. A family in the One." Searing pain broke through the static.

"You want to sleep with her, and with me?" I sounded more like me, but an angry, bitchy me. An un-One and unenlightened, desperate me.

"There's only One of us here," he said softly, as if speaking to a child or a new student. "Being jealous means you think you're separate. You know better than that!" He took my hand between both of his and kissed it. "Don't you?"

Yeah, I did. Oneness was true. If I didn't stand by that, then everything had been a fake. Grasping, selfish, possessive feelings were the mark of someone who didn't live the Truth. Maybe this was a spiritual test for me. He somehow got closer and kissed my cheek. Then my lips. It didn't feel right to let him love both of us, but it *sounded* right. More right than being jealous and smothering.

Behind me, I heard Sally moving down the hall and out the door. Jeff put his arms around me and tried to pull me toward the bed, but the gray static came back and filled up my brain. I turned out of this grasp and would not look at him. I felt nauseous and could barely stand.

"Are you okay?" He looked concerned. It felt like, in the space of about ten seconds, I'd come down with the most terrible flu I'd ever had. My body and mind were on completely different pages. My mind was almost willing to try the new arrangement; my body could not do it.

"I don't think so. I need to go home."

"Let me take care of you." I could not stay there and was already heading toward the door. I would figure it all out and make it work, but later.

"I've gotta get out of here," I said. "I've gotta think."

He patted my arm, following me down the hall.

"Okay, sweetheart." He seemed almost relieved. As if he couldn't wait for me to go, so he could read the *Tribune* story. Or get Sally back there. He closed the door softly after me.

Outside, the wind cooled my face and hands. Had I done the right thing? Maybe I should have stayed, but I couldn't trust myself to act enlightened. I might have kicked and screamed about betrayal and demanded my "rights," which would have made him hate me, maybe want to leave me, and washed away everything that made me good.

I didn't want to see Mollie and Julie right away and couldn't just stand around on the street, so I ducked into Kilkenny's.

"Mara! Darlin'! You'll have your regular Coke, will ya?" Micky yelled, pulling down a glass, filling it with rum and splashing some Coke on top. I practically chugged it.

"It's a little sweet, Micky. Do you have the Coke without the bubbles?"

He knew what I meant, and pulled down the Cutty Sark. An hour later, Paddy and Kitty Murphy came in and dragged me away from the bar, over to their table. I told them groggily about the *Trib* article, about finding Sally there—leaving out any reference to sex, since most Irish Catholics in their generation had been virgins until they married at thirty, so it sounded like I'd walked in on a hot game of Parcheesi. I told them about the gray static and not knowing what to do. Kitty put her arms around me. Paddy clucked.

Finally, they rode home with me on the El and delivered me to Mollie, who put me to bed, covered me with a comforter, and quietly closed the door.

Chapter 10

The smell of thick, rich chicory coffee wafted into my dark world. I forced open crusted eyes to see Mollie walking through the door as if it were her room instead of mine, carrying a tray that she set down none too quietly on the table by my bed. She pulled up a chair, sat down, crossed her arms, and watched me. I preferred looking at the tray to meeting her eyes. A pot of coffee, a Bloody Mary, four apple Danish, and the Sunday paper. It was like the trays she had brought the first week I arrived, but customized for a grown-up with a crushing hangover. The room swirled when I pulled myself up from under the covers into a sitting position. My head felt three feet across. My tongue was thick and furry.

Mollie handed me the Bloody Mary, but I waved it away.

"That's how I got this way." My voice was gravelly.

"Drink it. The hair of the dog. You'll feel better, and you can tell me about this." She held up the magazine and pointed to Jeff's picture on the cover with a bright fake smile. I just narrowed my eyes at her and took a sip of the Bloody Mary. It was delicious—soft and soothing in my mouth. I sipped some more and watched as she made a big show of reading the article, occasionally saying a word or phrase aloud.

"Lanky assistant! Ha! Our own Chicago guru...spiritual thirst." She looked over the top of the magazine. "Wanna talk?"

I shook my head. "Can I have the Metro section?" She handed it over and we read in silence.

That afternoon I walked along Lake Michigan, hoping the strong breeze would clear my head and the dark blue water would unwind my mind. The waves rolled in, one after another, cresting and breaking, cresting and breaking. I loved the instant just at the height of the crest, when the top of the wave turned almost transparent, then pale bottle green, and then crashed into wild white foam.

I could do this. I could make this work. Just keep doing everything I'd been doing, and pretend it didn't hurt. Become a paragon of Oneness. Look good, and maybe even become so immersed in the One that it actually did stop hurting. If Jeff saw that I could do that and Sally couldn't, then he would have to choose me. I would be incredibly kind to her. Look beyond what a spiritual cretin she was—how sly, perky, and shallow she was—and see her as part of the One. Then even if I didn't get Jeff, I would get God.

For something that sounded so simple, Oneness was a lot of trouble.

℞

Over the next weeks, the three of us spent time together at Suk Bhavan—something that Jeff insisted we do because we were a "godly family," but that I don't think Sally liked much better than I did. Sometimes she stayed over, and sometimes I did. The three of us often had dinner together, and Sally and I competed to cook the most extravagant, the most vegetarian, the most holy meals.

I made a point of engaging Jeff in deep spiritual questions that were way out of her range. If he lost interest and his eyes started following her around the kitchen, I raised my voice and became more passionate about karma, or Oneness, or *samadhi*, or whatever. It felt desperate and clingy, but I didn't know what else to do. The more I pressed on him and tried to control the situation, the more I could sense him pulling away from me. Still, I couldn't stop.

Ever since I'd caught them together, the old darkness had been rising up inside me again, bigger and stronger than it had been when I was a kid and much more difficult to control or hide. I called it *the dark*. The name seemed childish, but that's how I felt when it was around. I felt hateful, so I acted in hateful ways, which made me feel even more hateful. I didn't know what *the dark* was—other than an amorphous mass of shame and rage—or how it got inside me. I only knew that it was a twisted, brutal sort of evil that was mine alone.

The dark made me insist on staying the night with Jeff, even when I knew he really wanted to be with Sally. It made me act sullen or snide whenever he paid attention to her. It made me pick up hot pans at the bakery without thinking and burn my hands, and then made me lash out at Mollie and Julie.

Ghost Girl, who had come running when I first found them on the floor together, was no match for *the dark* and quickly disappeared into the night. *The dark* flailed around inside me, furious and desperate, filled with vengeance, wanting only to strike out and *hurt*. The stronger it got, the more I tried to control it or at least hide it. The more I tried to control or hide it, the wilder it got and the more it took over.

Plus, I had the world's worst case of PMS. It hung on and on, impervious to teas, Midol, and aspirin. I felt nauseous and depleted all the time. Finally, I made myself turn back the months on my Montana wall calendar at home. June. May. April. Finally, a red circle around a date. My last period had started April 21. It was June 19. That could not be. Maybe I'd forgotten to circle the May date. Either that, or all the stress was making me late.

Julie leaned in my doorway, slinky in her long pink silk robe, her hair in curlers, halfheartedly filing her nails.

"Whatcha doin', hon?"

"Just looking up my period." Our eyes met. "How do you make your period come when it's really late?"

"How late?" She came in and stood next to me. I pointed to the red circle around April 21. She turned to me, eyes wide. "You're using those rubbers I gave you, right?" I did not want to have this conversation. "*Right?*"

"Well, we didn't want to take a stand against trusting the universe. We knew our intention was clear, and since all is One, and we're detached from any positive or negative outcomes, and we know it's all karma anyway and whatever happens is an opportunity to polish the spiritual diamond..."

"Oh my God!" Her eyes were huge, horrified.

"Jeff didn't like them! We used something. It was just, you know, more...etheric!" My hands were sweating. I couldn't take my eyes off the red circle.

"Oh my God," she breathed.

"Don't say that!"

"Oh my God." She patted my shoulder over and over. I wanted to hit her. "We're going to see Dr. Siegel on Monday."

୬

Julie held my hand as we rumbled home on the El from Dr. Siegel's office. The gray static had started again. I could not get my mind around the idea that there was a tadpole growing inside me, or that one day it might become a person. I tried to think of it as Jeff's baby, and imagined a minuscule version of him wearing a tiny white *doti*, flexing well-formed miniature pecs. I wanted to throw up. Again. Julie put her arm around me.

"When we get home, hon, you just go to bed. Let me talk to Mollie." I nodded, did as I was told, and lay in bed staring at the white ceiling.

Every move I had made since finding Sally and Jeff together on the floor, and especially after succumbing to the Oneness Family idea, had been focused on making him pick me over her. This was a whole new piece to the puzzle. It might make him want me *more*. Or *less*. I did not see how I could kill the tadpole—I didn't need Holy Mother the Church to tell me that was murder—so I had to make it work to my advantage.

That night, Mollie cooked meat loaf, double-baked potatoes, and asparagus spears with clarified butter. It all tasted like metal.

"What's one more mouth to feed?" she beamed, stuffing out her cigarette and helping herself to a large piece of meat loaf. "A little baby!" I was shocked that she was so happy.

"We might get married," I said, trying to sound like I had even the vaguest notion what I was doing. "When he finds out, he'll want me to move in."

"Oh, yeah?" She drizzled butter on her asparagus.

"I'm telling him tonight."

Mollie and Julie looked at one another. Julie cut through the cheese on top of her double baked potato and inserted a pat of butter. Mollie cut her meat loaf into uniform little pieces.

Jeff called during dinner and I took it in my room. He wanted to cancel. He said he was tired, but I could hear dishes being washed in the background.

"I have to see you!" I tried to be calm and loving—but instead sounded like a fishwife.

"Not tonight. I'm going to bed early."

"When, then?"

"Tomorrow. Before class."

"Okay, I'll come over about four."

"No, let's meet at the church."

"I want to see you at home."

"The church is easier. I'll see you there at five."

The line went dead. I walked slowly back to the kitchen and slid into my chair.

"What's up?" Mollie asked.

"We're going to talk tomorrow."

Again, they looked at one another. I wanted to slam their heads together.

"Who's up for Monopoly?" Julie asked.

Mollie lifted her wineglass to us. "Have another potato, Mara. You're eating for two," she beamed.

ଔ

The Sunset Room was dark when I arrived at 4:45, in case he showed up early. At 5:15, I went out into the lobby to wait for him. I picked up a Unitarian brochure and pretended to read, but then it occurred to me that he might have come in the back door and be waiting for me in the Sunset Room. I ran back, my footsteps echoing through the empty corridor, but the room was still dark and silent. The faint smell of incense hung in the air. We could be getting married right here, in this room, in a matter of days or weeks. I sat down and tried to meditate.

His footsteps were sharp in the hallway. He strode in, fell into the chair next to me, and started taking off his shoes.

"What's so important?" he said brusquely.

"It's 5:35. Where were you?"

"I was busy. What do you need?" He was all business. Yeah, well, me too.

"I'm pregnant." He froze with one hand on his right shoe. I wanted to rip his face off and at the same time appear steeped in *samadhi*, so he would see that my Oneness was perhaps even higher than his now and that *he* needed *me*.

"Are you sure? Have you seen a doctor?"

"Yes!" He put his head in his hands. Finally, he rubbed his palms up and down his cheeks and looked at me.

"So, this doctor. Can he help you take care of the baby?" What was he talking about? A doctor doing child care?

"Mollie and Julie can help me take care of the baby, but I was thinking you and I might..."

"They can give you an abortion? At home?" He seemed eager, as if this were wonderful news.

"No! They can help me raise the baby, but you and I could..."

His eyes were suddenly hard.

"You can't have this baby, Mara." He said it like he was telling me I couldn't rob banks. Just a fact. Something everybody knew. I couldn't breathe.

"Why not?"

"I can't have a baby around. Not now. You wouldn't want to raise it on your own, would you? Even with Julie and Mollie..." I stared at him. "Look, I won't be manipulated into anything. You and I are having problems. If you have that baby, we can't be together. I'm sorry. That's just how it is." He paused, glanced up at me, and quickly looked away. "Why don't you go home and rest? Take the night off. Sally can fill in for you."

I felt *the dark* rise inside me—thick, black, and huge. If I stayed in that room, it would come raging out of me and he would see it. I stood up without a word and looked down at him. I wanted him to stand up and hug me, at least, but he focused on his shoes, glancing occasionally at the door. Finally, he stood and walked to his platform as if I had become invisible.

The smell of incense suddenly made me nauseous. I moved slowly toward the door, down the hall and out into the spitting rain. Along the street, up onto the El platform, into the train. By the time I got back to the bakery, I was drenched.

ೞ

It rained for three days. I stayed indoors, shuffling up and down the stairs—baking, working behind the counter, and spending long hours in bed staring at the ceiling.

Abortion was murder. It would be nightmarish, but then it would be over. If I didn't kill this baby, I would lose Jeff forever—and we had to be together. *The dark* wanted to get on with it, get it done and out of the way, get back to making him choose me. I embraced the gray static when it came now, welcomed the numbness, hoped it would stop the surges of fear and revulsion. Scotch helped. I wanted to be Ghost Girl again, but she seemed far away.

Mollie coughed down the hall to the bathroom. She was sick again, this time with some terrible chest flu. It seemed like she caught every disease that came along. Last winter she'd had pneumonia. On her way back to bed, she wandered into my room wearing her jade green satin robe with the crimson dragons. It seemed at odds with her being so sick all the time. She picked up the tumbler from my table and sniffed it.

"You shouldn't be drinking."

I shrugged. I would be a terrible mother, anyway. I should put the thing out of its misery before I treated it like Mother treated me. They said that happened. Mollie sat down on my bed and took a sip of my Scotch.

"You look awful," I said. "You should go to the doctor."

She nodded and examined the sash of her robe.

"Yeah..."

Then out of the blue, she reached over, put her arms around me and held me close. I think she was crying—or trying not to. She pulled away and patted my shoulder gingerly.

"I love you. You know that?" I was dumbfounded and took her hand.

"I love you, too, Mollie." Then *I* started to get tears in my eyes, and she fled down the hall.

ೞ

Four days after the "procedure," as Dr. Siegel called it, I still felt too sick to get up, let alone leave the apartment—but I hadn't seen Jeff in a week. I decided to take some lemon tarts over before class. I wasn't surprised to find Sally there. In fact, I was relieved to find them sitting at the kitchen table instead of in the bedroom. Sally's hot pink silk blouse was buttoned all the way up, with all the right buttons in the right holes. She gave me a quick, stiff little smile before heading out, saying she had to pick up napkins and would meet us at the church.

I pulled a chair over to sit closer to Jeff than she had been sitting, but he turned his chair so we were facing one another.

"How are you feeling?" His eyes seemed gray, rather than blue, and kept shifting away from mine. He hooked his right elbow over the back of his chair and stretched his legs out in front of him. He wore the white slacks from his Nehru costume and a loud purple, green, and yellow Hawaiian shirt, which seemed strange. Frivolous. As if he were headed for a luau instead of a *satsang*. As if he and Sally might be catching her father's private jet to Maui right after class. I took the hand he'd left on the table.

"Pretty good. How are you?"

He rolled his eyes and forced a smile, as if life had dealt him a tough hand but he was dealing with it as well as could be expected.

"You know. Good. People keep coming. The work is going well. That's all that matters. It's why I'm here on earth." He seemed different—not just Hawaiian, but like he was sitting on the pillow platform while he was talking to me. As if I were just some pesky student, trying to siphon off his spiritual energy, his *shakti*.

"What's the matter?" I asked.

"Mara, things have changed."

I felt sick to my stomach.

"Like what? What's changed?"

"Sally and I have decided to formalize our Oneness. We're getting married." I couldn't breathe, couldn't speak. "I know this is hard, but I told her you'd understand. It's what's best for the work, Mara. I know you support that."

Wait. I had gotten rid of the baby. Now we were supposed to be together. I could not grasp where he was going with this.

"So...do we all live here together?" I asked hesitantly. He pulled his hand away, folded his arms over his chest.

"Sally's dad is getting us a place on Lake Shore Drive. It'll be better for the work."

"We move to Lake Shore Drive?" That was upper crust, expensive. It would give people the wrong idea about the work.

"Uh, just Sally and me." I stared at him. "That's what I mean by things being different. I think your path is taking you somewhere else now, Mara. You're much too tense and anxious for this work. Frankly, you're getting in the way of what we're doing."

"Wait a minute. I just killed this baby for you!" My voice sounded shaky, and very loud.

"You'll always be special to me, Mara, but I think it's better if you're on your own now."

"Are you telling me to get out?" I was on my feet. *The dark* rose up, powerful and hateful. At least it made me feel stronger. He backed his chair away from me.

"Calm down! I thought you were evolved enough to hear the truth." Now he was on his feet and shouting, too. "I can see that you aren't. You need help, Mara. I can't deal with this. I can't do the work if I have to deal with you, too."

"I put you where you are!"

"I can't have anything around me that doesn't support the work. You're just too much trouble." He stood up. "I'm going to ask you to leave now." His eyes were like steel. I grabbed his arm, but he pushed me away—hard. "Get some help!" he shouted.

With that, he turned and walked down the hall toward the bedroom. I stared after him, *the dark* coursing through me. I wanted to run after him and kill him—or else run after him and *make* him love me—but I didn't let myself move.

This could not be happening. I would go home, have a drink, go to sleep, wake up, and everything would be fine. I sat on the little bench and put on my shoes, then headed for the El platform as if in a trance. Micky waved from the tavern, but I just stared at him.

When I got to the bakery, an ambulance stood out in front with the lights still twirling.

೫

Mollie stayed in the hospital a week. It was frightening to see her leaning back against the big white hospital pillow, thin and ashen, helpless and still, tubes going in and out of her. The cancer was everywhere. The doctor said she had a week to a month.

After a few days, she rallied and asked about Jeff. She squeezed my hand weakly when I told her, but she seemed very far away. I sat in the room with its pale gray walls and eerie fluorescent lights, its ticking machines and Mollie's shallow breathing, and went numb.

Julie and I shuttled back and forth between the bakery and the hospital, taking turns baking, working the counter, and sitting with Mollie. Loreen had been spending less and less time at home and had disappeared completely about a week before Mollie's collapse.

"Good riddance!" Julie said, slapping the kitchen counter with the palm of her hand. "She'll die shooting up in some alley on the South Side." Two days before Mollie left the hospital, Julie's prophecy came true. The cops found Loreen, literally, in an alley on the South Side.

We scurried to get the funeral done and Loreen buried before Mollie came home. I hadn't been to St. Anne's since the Sunday Mollie took me to Mass there. It was darker than I remembered, smaller and more somber. I hardly recognized Loreen. She was skeletal, and looked like she might have lost her soul long before she left her body. Julie and I were the only two people there. What did it mean that Loreen had even lived? What would happen to Mollie when she died? She couldn't just melt away. What had happened to the little baby?

I called Jeff twice that week, thinking he might have changed his mind and just need me to reach out to him. He was calm and distant, clinical. Part of me was so hurt I couldn't even look at the wound; another part was relieved. Even the terrible void of not seeing him was better than the searing pain of having him talk to me like I was insane or evil. His final words, in our last phone conversation, were, "Leave me alone, goddamn it!"

"Do it!" Julie said. "Good riddance! Fuck him!"

Yeah, fuck him. I didn't really feel that way, though. I felt burning emptiness and *the dark* hiding somewhere inside the gray static. I took down the Shiva statue, incense burner, and candles from my altar and let it stand bare. I tried to meditate, to recapture *samadhi*, but could not get my mind to quiet down. All I could feel were anger and humiliation. It wasn't clear to me now that there even *was* a God—and that might be a good thing, given who and what I had become, and the things I had done. It occurred to me that the high of the *samadhi* might have been nothing more than the false high of loving Jeff. I wanted no more to do with any of it.

ॐ

When Mollie came home, she mostly stayed in bed. Her limp salt-and-pepper curls flowed out over her pillow. She hardly ate, no matter what we fixed. Each day, she seemed smaller and weaker than she had the day before.

"I'll have my eye on you," she said one night. I looked up from the book I was reading. I'd thought she was asleep. "I'll be watching out for you," she said weakly. I smiled a little. I couldn't stand to think about her being somewhere else. She drifted off for an instant, then started up as if she'd been in a deep sleep. "Hey! I'm leaving you some money." She gestured around the room. "This, too. The building. The bakery. You and Julie." I was aghast.

"What about your sister in Montana?" I hesitated. "Mara's mother." Mollie waved that away.

"No." She said firmly, shaking her head. She closed her eyes, then opened them and seemed more present than she had in days. "Promise me one thing."

"What?"

"Don't think about that baby. It'll kill you."

I took her hand and nodded, knowing it was a promise I would not keep. That, like everything else, was on hold. I had a lid on all of it now. Even so, I could feel *the dark* churning beneath the surface like a snaky underground creature. I kept my eyes averted, but sometimes I would reach down inside myself and could feel its back moving under my hand. It was awful but, in some strange and twisted way, reassuring.

Julie came in and took down the old brown leatherette photo album from Mollie's closet shelf. We climbed into bed on either side of her and turned the pages slowly. There were old black-and-white photos—now brown-and-white—with pinking-sheared edges of Mollie's high school graduation, of her as a trashy-looking teenager wearing bobby socks, a pleated skirt and a tight sweater, sitting on a bench near some lake with a guy in a sailor suit, their arms around each other. Then some of her and Julie and Loreen around the house and bakery, and down at the Grant Park band shell with some guys.

Then I appeared. There was one of me as the Elmhurst girl, before we cut and dyed my hair, washing the dishes in the kitchen, looking blank and startled. Then my twelfth birthday party, when we had all danced around the living room in diaphanous pastel dresses that Julie had made.

After Julie went to bed and Mollie drifted off, I took the album to my room and turned to the very beginning. The first picture was fuzzy around the edges, ancient and blurred sepia. Two little girls. The one with black curls smiled into the camera; the other looked over to the side, worried and stern. They stood in front of a sagging old barn. In the distance were vast, high mountains with snow on top and rolling white clouds above them. I took the picture out of its little glue-on corners and looked on the back. "Sarah and Mollie by the barn, ages 7 and 5."

I found the picture of Mara, Sarah's daughter, that Mollie had showed me when I first got there—the one in the T-shirt with the wild Montana wind in her hair. There was another of Mara with a stiff, sour looking woman, sitting on a piano bench in an old-fashioned living room. She wore a dress and looked unhappy. I turned it over. "Sarah and Mara, age 9." Just before she had died in the tractor accident.

I closed the book and put it on my altar. All night, I dreamed of wandering around the prairie by that old barn, looking for something but having trouble remembering what it was. I would catch glimpses of Mollie as a child, of Mara, of sour Sarah, and finally woke up exhausted at about six o'clock knowing that something was wrong.

I ran down the hall to Mollie's room. She was all sprawled out on the bed, her ruby nightgown and colorful shawls flowing around her. Her face was a pale gray-green. I knew she was dead. I tried to find a pulse like Julie had showed me, and put the small mirror under her nostrils. Nothing. I just sat down on the bed like we were going to have a talk, and stroked her arm. There was nothing inside her. My whole body was in shock. Finally, I went to get Julie.

☙

The wake was raucous. Aldermen, precinct captains, cops, and people from the neighborhood milled around our living room talking, drinking, telling jokes and stories, laughing, playing the piano, and singing. It started at three in the afternoon and went on until people left early the next morning.

For a few weeks, Julie and I baked and sold, baked and sold like zombies. It kept us occupied with things we knew how to do. Then one day Julie went on a shopping binge at Carson's—textured stockings and wool skirts for herself, cocktail dresses for me, bathing suits on sale, other wildly inappropriate things that we would never wear.

"Whaddaya think?" she asked, spreading them out on her bed. I stared.

"I think you're nuts!"

It seemed to break the spell. We laughed until we cried, then fixed Rock Cornish game hens for dinner and got drunk on red wine.

"Whatcha gonna do, hon?" she asked as we finished the apple-rhubarb pie.

"About what?"

"Your *life*. You wanna bake muffins for the next forty years? How're ya gonna meet anybody? You gotta get outta here."

I lit up one of her cigarettes. I wanted desperately to be away from everything in Chicago.

"I can't leave you. How would you do everything? Who would do the books?"

"Well, smarty pants, funny you should ask! You remember my girlfriend Gloria, who worked in Accounting at Field's? She came to Mollie's wake? She got laid off, and her lease is up. We were thinking she could move in here. I'd teach her to bake, and she could do what you do." Her eyes were large—as if she were afraid I wouldn't go for the plan. "Well, not as *good* as you, hon, but if it's okay with you...Whaddaya think?"

I grabbed her and hugged her tight. I couldn't imagine life without her gum-snapping banter, her wild colors and her kindness. I needed to go, and she had found a way for me to do it.

"I love you, Jules."

"I love you too, hon. Whaddya think?"

"I'm going to Montana!"

I hadn't known where to go until I heard myself say it. I had thought off and on about Mollie's sister, Sarah, and wondered if I could make a place for myself where Mollie—and the real Mara—had lived. Sarah ran the Big Sky Dude Ranch outside Whitefish, Montana, right next to Glacier National Park in the northwest corner of the state.

That's all I knew about her, but it gave me a place to go and a reason to get out of town. It was a whole lot better than making doughnuts and thinking about Jeff, Mollie, the baby, and what kind of a person I had turned out to be.

Before I left, I bought a red Ford Falcon and made two pilgrimages. I drove out to Elmhurst and parked a half block away from the red brick house on Fairgrove, but nobody went in or out during the twenty minutes I sat there. It felt dark and still, as if its energy had fallen in on itself.

Then I drove over to Immaculate Conception and watched hundreds of shrieking kids in dark blue uniforms run around the parking lot, with about ten nuns milling around among them. For a moment, I became the Elmhurst girl, alive with God and desperate for more. Finally, I drove out to the spot on Route 83 where I'd stuck out my thumb and stepped into the path of Stan's truck. I wanted to feel all those things again and rub them over me before I left.

The other place I went was my father's building in the Loop. I dressed like an office girl—nylons and a burgundy suit—and lurked in the hallway outside his office around the lunch hour.

When I saw him, it felt like my blood was sending out little emanations into his blood. The experience was so physical I thought for sure he would recognize me, but he looked right at me and didn't. His hair was thinner and he was fatter, but it was the same Dad. My fingertips tingled with the desire to touch him. I edged closer as he stood waiting for the elevator with a redheaded woman in a dark green suit, black nylons with seams up the back and black high heels. He smiled his "charmer" smile and put his hand on the small of her back as they stepped into the elevator.

Early the next morning, I loaded a suitcase and my pack into the red Falcon. Julie handed me a pink cardboard box full of éclairs and sobbed so hard she could barely speak.

"You write, hon." I hugged her close and said I would. Her pal Gloria stood on the steps that went up the back of the building and waved. I pulled out of the alley and headed out toward Route 83, éclairs on the passenger seat beside me.

Chapter 11

The sky was dark and low as I drove out of town. It looked like rain, but there were no drops yet. Just whippy winds scurrying around before they brought the storm. From the expressway, I looked out over miles of old red brick warehouses with faded ads painted on their sides for bubblegum, cigarettes, and candy...telephone wires snaking up the backs of dark gray and brown bungalows... railroad yards with intricate mazes of dull steel tracks...church spires jutting up every four or five blocks.

I loved this town, but everything here was too real. I couldn't see Chicago without seeing myself. I wanted to be on the road, in transit— going somewhere, but not there yet, floating far above the miasma of Jeff, killing the baby, Mollie dying, Mother, Sister Agatha, and all those gods that hovered around them. Maybe I could even leave *the dark* behind to slither among the buildings and alleys, looking for me where I wasn't.

The Mississippi River flowed below me like flat, slow, muddy molasses. I imagined St. Isaac Jogues getting his fingernails ripped out along its banks, maybe on the exact site of the Dairy Queen where I had just eaten a large chocolate-dipped cone.

The sun came out just as I crossed over to the other side of the country. In my mind, I saw pioneer families fording the river in covered wagons, juggling babies and rocking chairs, wearing sturdy boots and shaded bonnets, their eyes dancing and determined, headed for a new life where they could do whatever they wanted, live by their wits, be stronger and smarter and freer than they had ever imagined being, and make everything up as they went along. Reinvent themselves. Leave anything that was chasing them far behind. Chase something themselves for a change, even if they didn't know what it was.

In Rochester, Minnesota, I ate a double burger, fries, and a chocolate shake in the car. In a park across the street, young mothers lounged around picnic tables wearing pastel polyester slacks and windbreakers, their hair carefully parted and curled. They rummaged in brightly colored plastic satchels for bottles, clean diapers, pacifiers, and other baby items, talking and laughing with one another in a smug, self-satisfied way.

Suddenly, out of nowhere, I realized that Mollie was dead. It hadn't really hit me until that moment. A deep brown river of grief swept me up and carried me in its current. I leaned my forehead on the steering wheel and cried until my eyes were practically swollen shut. Then, as quickly as it had come, the river dried up and set me down. I didn't feel anything.

I gathered up the trash from my lunch and took it to a bin in the park. Down the street, I spotted a liquor store and sent Julie a thank you over the miles. Her going away gift to me had been an exact duplicate of my driver's license, except that the date of birth was changed to make me twenty-two years old.

"You don't wanna make it twenty-one," she explained. "See, that's like you're trying to pass, ya know? Just squint up your eyes and look sad. You can do it."

I walked into Roy's Liquors trying to look world-weary, found the Scotch, and selected a fifth of Cutty Sark. I took a deep breath as I moved toward the cash register, casually examining items as I passed them—as if I strolled through liquor stores every afternoon and was just looking for a little something to break the monotony.

Roy had wispy gray hair combed straight back over his papery freckled scalp, gray-white skin, and a thin gray mustache. A half-smoked cigar lay extinguished in an ancient brown ashtray by the cash register. I plunked down the Cutty and a twenty on the counter. He coughed and looked up at me from his stool.

"ID?"

I opened my wallet to the twenty-two-year-old me, tucked snugly and officially behind the little plastic frame.

"Take it out."

I did, and held it up for him to see, looking right at him. He looked up at me, and I didn't let my gaze wander. He kind of smiled out of one corner of his mouth, palmed the twenty, punched the register, and gave me change. Then he tilted his head to one side, no longer smiling. "You visiting us?"

"No, Sioux Falls by tonight." He nodded.

"Well, be sure you keep that in the trunk if you open it. Wouldn't want the cops to stop you."

"No."

He half smiled again and, in what seemed an odd gesture, stuck out his hand. I took it and we shook up and down twice.

"Good luck," he said.

I felt warmed as I walked to the car—but it occurred to me that there was someone out there now who knew my name and where I was going, and suspected that I had a fake ID. I would have to be more careful. I told myself I had every right to drive from Chicago to Sioux Falls, but suddenly I felt ten years old again. On my own, on the run, scared, and not knowing much except that I had to get *away*. That girl in the red jacket who planted herself in the path of Stan's truck had it all over me, though. She was clean, clear, one-pointed, and innocent. Too young to be a fool or to kill, and *the dark* was still just a tadpole inside her. She hardly even knew it was there.

ᘓ

Route 90 was a straight line across the bottom of Minnesota, all wooded lakes and farmland with huge expanses of prairie. I imagined vast herds of buffalo thundering through a rainstorm at night, lightning flashing above them. Warriors in feather headdresses riding paint ponies at a dead run, bows at full draw. Pioneer farmers sweating all day in the wheat fields and lumbering back to their sod houses to sleep while the sun was down. Wheat and corn husks stacked in the fields under a harvest moon. Indians dancing around enormous bonfires on cold October nights. Simple, pure, brave things.

I pulled into Sioux Falls just after dark and swung in under a sputtering red and blue sign: *Sioux Falls Motel, Cheapest Rates, TV, Vacancy.* The lobby was about ten-by-ten with two filthy green plastic chairs. The dark brown floor was littered with gum wrappers and cigarette butts. It made sticky, ripping sounds each time I took a step.

The manager appeared behind a window of thick glass that separated the lobby from his little office. He must have weighed 400 pounds and wore black horn-rimmed glasses, a dingy white T-shirt that stretched across his stomach, pajama bottoms, and flip-flops. He lifted a hot dog wrapped in aluminum foil to his pudgy mouth. Pickle relish and mustard oozed out onto his hand.

"Thirty-nine bucks a night," he spat at me over the intercom, still chewing. I put a fifty in the small metal drawer. He pulled it quickly over to his side of the glass, replaced it with change and key, slid it back, and said, "Number 3."

The room had brown and orange plaid curtains, made of some material that was partly plastic. It reeked of stale cigarette smoke and Cheetos. There was a small television, but it was all snow. I found a slightly opaque drinking glass in the grimy bathroom, perched precariously on the edge of a pale gray sink, and ran it under hot water. The Cutty Sark would kill anything really bad. I filled the glass with Scotch, listened to the traffic, and plotted tomorrow's route. I filled it again and thought how great it would be to have Julie there so we could play gin. I thought about digging around in my pack for some paper, so I could plan the rest of my life. I filled it again, and...

ᘓ

Sun knifed through the plastic drapes. I was still wearing my jeans and red shirt. Every muscle in my body ached. My head throbbed, and my tongue and teeth felt like they were coated with dried paste. I pulled myself out of bed, inched my way stiffly to the bathroom, and drank glass after glass of water without letting my eyes fall on the mirror.

I threw back three aspirin and gathered up my things, moving very slowly. The world seemed to tip on its axis each time I took a step. I staggered out to the parking lot, reached for the car door handle—and saw it. A jagged streak of gray metal cut through the red paint. It ran from the front of the door all the way to the taillight. Somebody had run a key, or something sharp, the length of my new car. My first car. My getaway car. No windows were broken. They hadn't even tried to break in. They had just done it to be mean. I was furious, and terrified. I wanted to hit somebody, to slash *them* from top to bottom.

I knew I should just get in the car and drive, but my body was already on its way to the office, powered by *the dark,* pushing aside my aching muscles and slamming head. I yanked open the door. The same fat guy stood behind the glass, shoving a chocolate-covered doughnut into his mouth.

"Hey! Somebody keyed my car!"

He glanced up, then picked another doughnut out of a large cardboard box—glazed, this time—and shoved it into his mouth. He glanced up at a TV mounted on the wall, some local morning news show. *His* TV worked!

"Hey! What are you gonna do about it?" I yelled through the glass.

He pointed to a filthy, ragged sign taped to the window—*Not responsible for lost or damaged items*—and turned away. He'd done it! Who else even knew me? I pounded on the glass. He turned slowly toward me. I couldn't see his eyes behind the fat folds and the glasses. He leaned his bulk toward the intercom.

"Get lost, lady, or I'll call the cops." A voice inside me said to leave, but the rage had taken over.

"*I'll* call the cops," I screamed. "That's a new car! I paid good money for that car. What are ya gonna *do* about it?" I banged the palm of my hand on the window again, pushing down the nausea and headache.

He faced me and opened a drawer under the counter. His hand came up wrapped around a gun, which he pointed at the center of my chest. I ducked and ran as fast as I could, out of the office and across the parking lot. Jumped in the car, leaned down low behind the wheel, and screeched into the street. I turned right, then left, then left again, then right, trying to lose someone I knew probably wasn't even following me. Five minutes later, I thought I was going to pass out and pulled over in front of a laundromat. What a dumb-ass! I needed to get a lot smarter—and a lot calmer. I needed a gun. It was a long road, and I was only a few miles out of Minnesota.

I spotted a phone booth, riffled through the yellow pages, and found an address on the same street as the motel. In fifteen minutes, I was standing in front of a display case. A young guy with dark skin and a long black ponytail ambled out from behind the brown curtain. He wore a clean denim shirt and tight jeans with a leather and silver belt. Our eyes met, and it was almost as if I recognized him from somewhere. He lived outside the white picket fence, too. I knew just what I needed to happen here, so I did exactly what I'd done that first night at Mollie's because I'd been too scared to do anything else. I told the truth.

"I need your help," I said. "I'm traveling alone and somebody just pulled a gun on me. I have money. What kind of gun should I buy?"

He didn't bat an eye. It was as if I'd said I wanted a green sweater, size medium.

"This is what you want," he said, pulling out a small, stylish, but deadly-looking gun. "S&W Model 60 LS, 'Chiefs Special Stainless Lady Smith.' This'll do ya. Come on out back. I'll show you how to use it."

ଔ

I drove all day along the southern border of South Dakota, past the Rosebud and Pine Ridge reservations, the gun secured in a pouch inside my pack. The road stretched out into mile after mile of undulating amber wheat, tan prairie, and dark green stands of trees under a clear blue cloudless sky.

I rolled down the window and let the hot wheat wind rush through my hair and burn my face, breathed in air rich with sunlight and the smell of grain, held my arm out the window like an airplane wing. My mind began to unwind and ease out into the distance. The prairie swelled up into small, then larger hills amid the clear lakes and tumbling streams. I spotted a road sign for the Badlands, and that sounded like just the place for runaways and outlaws. For girls who carried guns, who were trying to outrun *the dark* and just needed to be outside for a while, to lean back, rest, and breathe.

I drove through the Badlands at sunset. The pinnacles and spires, peaks and gullies, buttes and canyons were smeared with red and orange, tangerine, purple and mauve, with splashes of what seemed like gold. I could hardly look, it was so beautiful. My heart began to sting, like my eyes did just before I cried. I felt something moving out there, hovering up near the high crags, scuttling over the buttes, flowing down through the canyons, just out of reach. It was conscious and enormous, but not like the other gods. It didn't want anything from me, didn't even seem to care whether or not I wanted it. It just pulsed within itself, aware but disinterested, throbbing in its own glory, beautiful beyond belief.

og

Coming out of the Badlands into Rapid City was like shooting forward a hundred years, catapulting from a raw, stunning, dangerous world into rush-hour traffic.

I chose a mid-range motel that looked like the kind of place where you wouldn't need a gun and spent a whole week exploring the Badlands and Black Hills—hiking, driving, and just sitting, looking out at the mountains. I watched the sunset paint each crag, each horizontal ribbon of stone, a different color. Apricot, purple, gray, rust, and everything in between. I hadn't known there were so many colors and hated even to blink, for fear of missing one. In the moonlight, they became paler and finer, more purple and dark blue—but the color never completely died.

Again, I felt something alive out there on the high horizon, inside the sheer granite walls, bouncing along in the rushing creeks. I couldn't see it, but it began working its way into my cells—a softer, deeper cousin of *the bright*. It moved just beneath the surface of life, whispering in the pine needles, running through the cool dark valleys, pulsing softly deep down inside the earth, washing over me like a warm, comforting cascade of water.

I would not call it a god. I called it Spirit. That reminded me of the native people and spoke to something that shimmered inside everything. It seemed safe to let it calm me down and help me breathe. Spirit only touched me when I looked at it. When I was out on the trails, it hummed inside me, swept me into itself along with the mountains and streams and trees and the crisp, sparkling air—but it didn't seem to like being inside. It disappeared whenever I was in a motel room or a convenience store. I liked the fact that it stayed put, where and as I left it, and that nobody seemed to be in charge of it except maybe the National Park Service. Maybe this was what I'd been after all along, in all that chasing after *the bright*, the old graybeard IC God, and the patchouli-laced *samadhi*.

The Black Hills were more lush than the Badlands. Thick forests of Ponderosa pine, aspen, and spruce stretched out for miles. The Lakota Sioux called the Black Hills "Paha Sapa." The brochures said that meant "hills that are black"—they actually do look black from a distance—but that the deeper translation was "the heart of everything that is." Spirit.

I stopped to picnic one day on a large boulder that jutted out over a roaring creek, and sat looking up into miles of soft green pines, ribbons of fluttering yellow aspen, and white-barked birch. The wind in the trees and the rushing creek drowned out all other sounds. Sunlight bounced off the dancing water and made little rainbows in a damp spiderweb between two rocks. I pressed thick chunks of sharp yellow cheddar into fresh bread, added salami, and bit into the fat sandwich, staring upstream as I chewed.

I didn't see him until he lifted his head from drinking in the creek. An enormous rack of antlers moved slowly above him as he turned toward me. A stag! I stopped breathing. He looked right into my eyes, stared a second, then slowly turned back into the trees.

I hardly spoke to anyone that whole week. Spirit cleaned away everything but the bigness, the openness, and the beauty of the Badlands and Black Hills. At night, I drank Scotch and cried—for Mollie, for being lonely and probably bad, and also because Spirit had touched me.

The night before I left, I dreamed I rode bareback through the Badlands on a paint horse, looking for something. I searched through ravines and buttes until I forgot what it was. Then I would remember, panic, and head off again at a gallop. When I woke up, I had again forgotten what I was looking for—but was astonished and delighted that I'd been able to ride a horse.

That morning, I felt strangely calm and ready to move on, as if my mind had recalibrated and reset itself. I stopped for breakfast at a greasy spoon nestled between a tire shop and a hardware store. Three eggs scrambled hard, sausage, hash browns, and brush-buttered white toast for $3.98. I drank my coffee and stared out the window.

At the gas station across the street, a young couple leaned against their pickup. It had probably been white once, and both of them had probably been on their way to graduating from high school. That was the story in my mind as I watched them. He was hunky and good-looking in a klutzy, country boy way. He wore a T-shirt, even though the temp was only in the mid-fifties, probably to show off his muscles. Not the kind you got working out at a gym, I imagined, but the kind you got throwing around bales of hay. His jeans were tight and threadbare.

She looked about eight months pregnant and wore a frilly white cotton blouse, brown slacks, and a thick bright red sweater. Her mousy brown ponytail was tied up in a white bow and she looked happier than anyone I'd seen in years. Where did you go from there? Just lean back and enjoy the next sixty years? They would have a huge picnic table in the front yard of their farmhouse where the whole family, probably thirty people in all, came every Sunday to eat fried chicken piled high on a platter with mashed potatoes and gravy, corn on the cob, and chocolate cake for dessert.

He laced his fingers through hers and they stood side by side, smiling at one another. He kissed her cheek, and she punched him softly in the arm. They giggled and leaned against one another.

I could do that. How hard could that be? It was simple, natural, elemental like Spirit. That was how life was supposed to be lived. Nothing fancy. No earthshaking *samadhis* or electric encounters with *the bright*. Leave the Great and Powerful Gods alone, and just become part of the flow of life. Part of Spirit. I would find a man, have a baby, and stand on the porch of our cabin looking up into the mountains, soaking in Spirit. Finally, something I could do! Maybe we would even be part of a larger family. Maybe Sarah's family. It would be like Mollie had never died, like we'd just gone on to a better life together.

I paid my bill, left a big tip, and jumped in the car. Now I knew where I was going.

03

I slipped through Wyoming—Sundance, Buffalo, Sheridan—and was in Montana by late afternoon. Driving over the state line, I got a chill. Everything in my new home was huge, and went on forever. Big buttes. Big vistas. Big grasses. Big Sky. Anybody could come here and carve out a place for themselves. Be someone new, someone good. I was flying down the road at 90 miles per hour as the Rockies rose up before me, enormous and soul-filling.

They don't mark the Continental Divide, so you don't know you've crossed it until you're already there. At some point, I just realized that I was going more down than up, and that the water was flowing in the same direction I was driving. West! The air crackled with something unknown but familiar, something I knew instinctively was good for me. I had a blank canvas and was ready to paint.

At Missoula, I left Route 90 after almost eighteen hundred miles and turned north on 93 toward Flathead Lake, Kalispell, and Whitefish.

Whitefish was tucked up against Big Mountain, just west of the endless summits of Glacier National Park. It was drizzling when I drove into town, which made it seem even more like the set of a Western movie. Old brick and wooden buildings lined Main Street. I half expected to see hitching posts along the wooden sidewalks. Smoke curled up from little chimneys into low gray clouds, and the smell of wood fires hung in the air. At the very end of the street was a postcard view of Big Mountain.

I got a cozy room on the second floor of the square brick Whitefish Hotel, planning to hunker down, rest up, and get settled. When I was ready, I would find Sarah and see if this could be a place for me. Maybe the man on the porch with me and the baby would be a handsome cowboy, and we would run the ranch together when Sarah got too old. I would grow old there myself, and watch my children's children learn to ride and run the ranch. One day, I would sit on the porch where I'd stood with the cowboy and the first baby, and watch the sun start to set on my own life.

Not yet, though.

I unpacked and sat looking down on Main Street. Country music drifted up from the Bar None across the street as men in tight jeans began gathering for the evening. These Western guys seemed to have only two shapes—beefy or skeletal. Either they hoisted enormous beer bellies above their jeans, or their stomachs seemed almost concave and bony chins and cheekbones poked out from under their cowboy hats.

(There seemed to be two types of Western women, too—the frilly girl from the gas station and a rather manly style like some of Mollie's lesbian friends, which was confusing because they were all dripping with babies and wore wedding rings. They seemed to live on the cusp between changing a tire and breeding. I couldn't imagine being one of the frillies, but didn't want to look like a refugee from the Big Chicks Bar if I were going after a hunky Montana man, the porch, the baby, the picnic table, and the fried chicken.)

I saw several guys go into the Bar None who would have looked great on my porch, but I knew what would happen if I went over there. I never seemed to sit down and have just one drink anymore. Or even two. I kept drinking until I passed out, and lately I didn't always remember how I had gotten to wherever I woke up. I didn't want that to be Whitefish's first impression of me. Instead, I rummaged in my pack for the new bottle of Cutty Sark I'd picked up in Butte, turned off the lights so people couldn't see me, and sat in my window watching nightlife in Whitefish and thinking about the next few days.

I would need a new name here. I wasn't about to waltz into Big Sky with Sarah's dead daughter's name. Besides, I wanted to find out a bit about her before she knew who I was. She never wrote to Mollie, and Mollie refused to talk about her much. I guessed I could use Cathy Callahan, but I didn't want to go backward. My new name should be Western. I'd seen a billboard for a country singer outside Rapid City, a girl who looked kind of like me, except she wore a cowboy hat and smiled back over her shoulder. "Cat Abilene, Our Own South Dakota Songbird." That was a Western name. Cat. Cat Callahan! It was different, Western, and I could get a birth certificate for it if I ever needed one. Cat could be short for Cathy. Plus, it was kind of tough. You wouldn't want to mess with someone named Cat Callahan. You would want to be her friend.

By the fifth glass of Scotch, I could tell I was going to like Whitefish. It was sweet and simple. People looked nice. Anybody could fit in here.

ଓ

I woke up still dressed, with a foul mouth, and stood in the shower for a long time. I vowed to drink less now that I was in Montana, my true home.

I dressed and wandered out to Main Street. People were eating breakfast in cafes, going to work, and sitting around over coffee. They all seemed to know one another, and smiled pleasantly at me. I nodded back, but felt shy. I bought the *Whitefish Pilot* and read it over blueberry pancakes at a diner. At the general store, I got some food for the room— apples, salami, bread, crackers—plus some Coke and a fifth of Cutty. I wasn't going cold turkey with the Scotch, just cutting back.

I took a short hike on Big Mountain, picked up some brochures on Glacier National Park, and got back to the hotel around three o'clock. I had a drink and, after a nap, decided to check out the Bar None. I couldn't avoid it forever if I wanted to meet the people of Whitefish.

The crowd was raucous and noisy, with lots of yelling up and down the bar. My first Western bar. It was dark and woody, with a brick wall that ran the length of the place and Christmas lights everywhere. I sat at a corner table, but two couples quickly enveloped me in their group. They just invited themselves to sit down and started talking as if we'd known each other for years.

Jim and Ed were both beefy guys, about forty with big guts, cowboy hats, and boots. Ethel and Rena wore slacks and cowgirl blouses. Rena's blouse had sequins, which was strange because she definitely would have fit right in at the Big Chicks Bar. After two beers, she pulled out her wallet and showed me about 300 pictures of her children and grandchildren.

In an instant, the whole feel of the bar changed. A wave of electricity seemed to pass through the room, and I was on high alert. His presence beat like a drum deep in my chest. When I looked up, he was staring down at me. He had black hair and high cheekbones that made him look part Indian—except for his eyes. They were hard green slits. I couldn't look away. He had a tight, square jaw and ruddy skin, as if he rarely came indoors. Jeans and a tight red cowboy shirt. I guessed he was in his mid-twenties, although he could have been older or younger. He looked like he was carrying something inside him so rough that it made me seem like Snow White. I wanted to rub up against him, and then hit him really hard.

He was Porch Man.

He put one foot on the empty chair next to mine and leaned an elbow on his knee, holding his hat. "Mind if I join you?"

Nobody said anything, so I answered very casually, looking away, "Have a seat." He slid in, leaned back in the chair, and stared at me.

"What are you drinking?"

"Scotch."

He gestured to the bartender to bring us all another round, and introduced himself to Jim, Ethel, Ed, and Rena with a gruff, "I'm Tom." I couldn't tell whether or not they knew who he was, but they definitely didn't like the looks of him. Possibly because they could see that I did. The men couldn't not shake hands when he stuck his across the table, but Ethel and Rena pursed their lips and nodded without smiling. He held out his hand to me, and my hand melted into his. Our fingers trailed along each other's palms as we pulled away.

"Cat," I said. "Cat Callahan."

He nodded and looked from his bourbon, to me, back to his bourbon. He was a magnet, and I was iron filings. I wished the Bar None had dancing, or rooms to rent.

We drank and drank. The little lines of electricity between us became heavy, swelling into ropes of energy. Jim and Ethel and Ed and Rena faded from my focus, but each time I moved in closer to Tom, or he tried to talk only to me, they made a big deal about something in the bar ("Hey! There's Andy! Andy, c'mon over!") or asked me more about my trip. Tom leaned in. Jim boomed, "So Cat, you stop in Yellowstone?"

"No." I wasn't sure how to be both gracious and discouraging, so wound up frowning and smiling at the same time. The more I drank, the more I wanted to be alone with Tom. The more *they* drank, the more they wanted to be my long-lost protective aunts and uncles.

"Oh, you missed it! Right, Ethel? We were there last year. Took Jane and her husband, and the grandkids. Oh yeah, and Dan came along with his wife, but they left the baby with her mother. Right, hon? We saw Old Faithful. Boy, you oughtta..."

The devil on one shoulder turned my face back to Tom—but Jim, Ethel, Ed, and Rena joined forces with the angel on the other shoulder, who kept reminding me that I had had a lot to drink, that this was my first encounter with Whitefish society, that getting drunk in a bar and going home with someone like Tom would not be a good start, and that maybe there was a reason these nice people didn't like him.

I let the jolly foursome practically carry me across the street and put me in my room.

Chapter 12

The next morning, I woke up hungover and grateful to them, but eager to check out the Bar None again that night. Now that I was a regular, what could be the harm? I needed to keep up my relationship with the aunts and uncles, and also make some new friends.

He wasn't there. That night, or the next. Or the next. I stopped going and instead sat in the dark at my window, watching the door in case he showed up. I started buying Cutty at different stores, so nobody would think I was someone who bought a fifth every day or two. Once I made a run to Kalispell, fifteen miles back route 93, and laid in three fifths since nobody knew me there.

On Friday morning, I woke up and realized that if I didn't get out to meet Sarah soon, I never would. I'd driven by the ranch several times, past the big gate and huge wood arch with *Big Sky Ranch* burned into it. Under that, *Welcome. The Spencers*. I'd decided the best way to check out Sarah was to work at the Big Sky Ranch. At the very least, I'd get a look at her during the interview.

My heart pounded as I drove under the *Big Sky* sign for the first time and cruised up the long, winding driveway to the main house. Ahead, beyond the ranch, the Rockies soared up into the endless sky. To the sides of the unpaved road, hills and meadows stretched out until they met woods. There were little clusters of cabins—some large, some small—a big corral with about ten horses, a large barn, and more horses grazing in a pasture. The big house had a wood porch (my porch!) that ran its whole length with chairs every few feet, saddles resting on the railing, and my first actual hitching post. I parked over to the side of it all.

Before I even got out of the car, she was standing on the porch staring down at me, her hands on her hips and a stern look on her face. She was tall and big-boned like Mollie, but shaped by the Montana foothills rather than the Chicago Loop. Thick and lumbering, where Mollie had been fleshy and sensuous. Still, it made my heart leap to look at her. She wore jeans, a jean jacket, boots, and a cowboy hat. Her wild salt-and-pepper hair was pulled back into a low ponytail.

I smiled as I got out of the car, partly to get off to a good start, and partly because it was almost like running into Mollie out here in Montana.

"Mrs. Spencer?" I held out my hand as I walked toward her, but reached it up to her rather than coming up the porch steps. "I'm Cat Callahan. I'm looking for a job, and some folks in town suggested I talk to you." She reached out without a smile and gave my hand one cursory shake.

"They did, huh?" She shifted her weight to one hip and folded her arms. She was so different from Mollie, and so the same. I felt warm, just being around her—but had the feeling that for some reason, she didn't like me. She was treating me the way my four bodyguards had treated Tom. "Who told you that?"

"I don't remember their names. I can do just about anything. Cooking. Bookkeeping. Cleaning."

"You know anything about horses?"

"Uh, no."

"Where are you from?"

"Outside Chicago." I had the story in my back pocket. If pressed for details, I could at least give accurate geography and place names.

"I don't need any help just now."

"Mrs. Spencer, I need a job real bad. I work hard, and I'll do whatever you want done." She nodded by tipping her head back, then scanned the sky as if looking to see what the weather would be, pursed her lips, and shot a look back at me. I stayed smiling. Friendly and eager.

"Well, c'mon in a minute," she said grudgingly, turning toward the door. I jumped up onto the porch and followed her into the house. Just off the entry to the left was an enormous dining room with a long wood table like the one we'd had in the kitchen in Chicago, only it sat about twenty. A narrow hallway led to the back of the house, and Sarah's office was just to the right. She took off her jacket and wedged herself in behind the desk. I felt like I was back in our apartment, the night Stan first brought me to Mollie.

"Tell me about yourself," Sarah said, leaning back and folding her hands behind her head. I flushed. I felt like she could see right through me, but there was nothing to do except plunge in.

"I did bookkeeping in Chicago for a couple years after high school, but I got bored and wanted to come out here. I learned to cook at home. We had a big family, so I can cook for a lot of people. I was the oldest of seven kids. I'm good at cleaning. I want to live in Montana, Mrs. Spencer. I don't care what I do."

"Why don't you get yourself a job in town? Lots of bookkeeping there."

"I've lived in cities all my life. I want to be out someplace like this."

"All your life, huh?" She half smiled the way Mollie used to when she was amused but trying not to show it. I kept quiet. She would want someone who toed the line, didn't cause trouble, and wasn't a smart-aleck. The bookshelves were crammed with pictures, maybe thirty black-and-white and color photos. I yearned to look at them.

"How'd you wind up in Whitefish?"

"Just followed my nose. No reason."

She nodded, cocked her head and looked at me. Somebody plowed through the front door yelling, "Sarah!"

"Wait here. That's Cliff, my husband." She stalked out, and they disappeared into the dining room. I tried to sit still, but found myself standing in front of the pictures, drinking them in. There was the black and white one of Sarah and Mollie as children, out by the barn, that I'd seen in Mollie's album. Some of the real Mara, and a couple of...I flushed again, turned around, and saw her standing in the door. She had been watching me.

"Looking for something?"

"Are these your family?" I tried to sound casual, like I'd just been stretching my legs and noticing the decor.

"Yeah." She frowned. "Tell you what. You cook lunch for us, and we'll see about you. No pay, of course. We'll talk after. Call me Sarah."

She led me into the enormous white kitchen. It bristled with useful items—big pots, big frying pans, and about thirty large utensils hanging from hooks.

"Just figure something out from what we have. There'll be ten of us. Noon." With that, she was gone.

I looked around the kitchen and found a lot of good food. Even produce, which I guessed came from the garden I could see out the window. This was a practical kitchen, but warm and cozy—just as ours had been. It wasn't until I'd already started the meat loaf, double-baked potatoes, and green bean casserole that I realized I probably made everything just like Mollie had, and that Mollie and Sarah had probably learned to cook together. If Sarah had any suspicions about me, as I was sure she must, this might confirm them. Well, I'd deal with that if I had to. I didn't know how else to cook.

Sarah showed up in the kitchen for a taste at 11:50, just as I was putting the food on huge platters to serve it. She took one bite of the meat loaf and looked at me.

"Whadya put in this?" she asked slowly.

"Secret ingredient."

"Cinnamon?"

I nodded. Oh, boy. Her radar was just like Mollie's. I was toast. People were already ambling into the dining room, so I carried the food out to the big wood table. I met Cliff; the housekeeper, Juanita; her assistant, Angela; the foreman, Bill; and three hands. Everybody stared at me, but I only felt the pull from one direction. When I looked up, Tom was walking in the door and winding himself into a chair. When he saw me, he did a double-take, then acted as if he'd never met me.

After all the food was on the table, I cleared a space for myself way down at the end—a humble place, as far away from Tom as possible, from which I could keep an eye on both him and Sarah. She sat at the head, with Cliff to her right, Bill to her left, and Tom next to him. The rest of them filled in the other places, with Juanita and Angela down by me, speaking Spanish softly to one another.

My stomach was in knots. After a week alone in my room, there I was at the test lunch, sitting at the same table as Mollie's sister and the man I was going to marry. I wished the pitchers were filled with vodka instead of water and took a second double-baked potato.

Tom was too far away to say anything to me, but I got a lot of looks. Sarah saw it and, I could tell, didn't like it. That wasn't all that was wrong with her, though. Bill and Cliff kept trying to engage her in conversation, but she hunkered over her plate, looking alternately pissed off and distracted. Occasionally, she'd take a bite of green bean casserole and put down her fork. Stab a piece of meat loaf, and put it down. A couple times, she glared down the table at me.

I pretended not to notice and passed more casserole to Juanita, who gave me a big smile. I focused on her gleaming white teeth and smiled back, wishing I could return the second double-baked potato to the serving platter. I couldn't even finish the first.

A couple of the hands grunted things like, "Good meat loaf," and "Good potatoes. Gimme sommore, Sam." The food, at least, was a big hit. In twenty minutes, they ate everything except a few dabs of sauce at the bottom of the casserole dish.

Sarah disappeared after lunch. I cleared the table and was starting the dishes when the swinging door pushed open. I turned to see Tom leaning against the wall, his hands jammed into his pockets. He was dirtier than he had been in the Bar None and hadn't shaved, but was just as sumptuous. Instead of throwing myself on him, I just said, "Hey," and turned back to the dishes. He came around and leaned on the counter by the sink, where he could face me.

"Hey yourself. What are you doing out here?"

"Like Sarah said. Trying out to be the cook. Does she usually do the cooking?"

"Yeah. Her or Juanita, mostly her." He shifted his weight to the other foot. "Hope you get the job."

"Thanks." I gave him a big Juanita smile. The door pushed open again and Sarah bulldozed into the kitchen.

"You got nothing to do, Tom?"

He touched his forehead, which looked naked without his hat, and pushed himself away from the counter. "Sorry, Ms. Spencer." Then to me, "Seeya."

I nodded and turned to her, drying my hands for the verdict, forcing another smile into what felt like a black chasm.

"Good food...Cat!"

"Thanks."

She opened the freezer and took out a half-gallon of French Vanilla ice cream, pulled up a stool to the butcher block in the middle of the kitchen, and gestured for me to do the same. She started spooning the ice cream directly from the carton into her mouth and didn't offer me any.

"Do I look like a stupid woman?" she began, not taking her eyes from the ice cream.

"No, ma'am."

"Well, I'm going to take a wild guess here. If I'm wrong, it's no skin off my nose, or yours. I'm guessing you're that runaway kid Mollie helped out ten or twelve years back." I flushed and stared at the butcher block. "I'm guessing you've been using my daughter's name all these years, pretending to be her. I'm guessing you lied when you said you were Cat Callahan, just following your nose to Whitefish." I didn't say anything. She spooned an enormous clump of ice cream into her mouth and said through it, "Am I right?"

"Yes, but I can..."

"I bet you can explain. I bet you're just like Mollie that way. Maybe in your world, people can lie anytime they want, like you do. Not out here, though. Not to decent folks."

"I'm sorry. Cat Callahan is my real name. Cathy. I just wanted to get to know you before I..." She shoveled in more ice cream. "I wanted to know Mollie's family. I loved her." She glanced up at me for the first time, then back to the ice cream.

"You did, huh? Did you help her run that whorehouse?"

"We had a bakery..."

"Among other things. What made you think we'd want to see you?"

"I thought maybe, since I'd known Mollie..."

"Mollie left here a long time ago. We weren't exactly in touch. I just sent her Mara's things because she begged me so hard. I thought she'd die if she didn't get 'em. Knew it wasn't right. Regretted it ever since."

"Thank you for..."

"Yeah..." She returned the ice cream to the freezer and leaned back against it, her arms folded. "Look. I don't know you. You might be okay, but you don't belong here. I don't want to remember Mollie, or Mara—at least not through you. That's over and done. I don't want anybody around who's been living like she was my daughter. Or any liars. Or anybody who was around Mollie after she went bad."

"Mollie saved my life. She was the best person I ever met!" I saw myself moving toward Sarah and stopped, holding on to the butcher block to keep myself from moving any farther.

"You just try something with me, girl, and I'll have you picked up like that." She snapped her fingers in my face. I glared at her. "Don't think people around here won't take my word over yours." She pushed past me, saying over her shoulder, "Let's call it a draw. You get out of here and don't come back, and I'll leave you alone."

I moved out of the kitchen, down the hall and out the front door. Tom was lounging on the porch and stood when I came out. I scrambled down the stairs. He called after me, "You be at the bar tonight?"

"Yeah, sure." I slammed the car door and rumbled back over the driveway to the highway, tears stinging in my eyes. Instead of turning for Whitefish, I headed south toward Kalispell, looking for a bar I'd never been in. I would just stay a couple hours and be back to the Bar None in plenty of time for Tom. I had big plans for him.

ভ

The Wagon Wheel was another dark, friendly place almost identical to the Bar None except that it had neon beer ads instead of Christmas lights. By my third Scotch, I'd gathered around me a table of people who knew how to enjoy a drink or two. Waitresses, ranch hands, mechanics, store clerks and a heavyset woman with long, curly red hair who was, as she shouted to the whole bar at some point, standing on a chair with one boot planted on the table and glass held aloft, "Th'only woman CPA 'n Kalispell!" I wrote her name, Candy, on a cocktail napkin as a fallback job opportunity. "Cndy KPspel."

About seven o'clock, I figured I'd better get on the road to Whitefish to meet Tom at the Bar None. Didn't want to miss that! I stood up to say good-bye to everyone, but my chair tackled me and I landed back in it with a thump, spilling my drink. Big laugh. I tried again, and this time managed to get out of the chair and start weaving toward the door.

I was halfway there when he appeared, leaning in the doorway that led into the bar from the dark entryway—one hip slung over to the side, wearing a dark green cowboy shirt. I stopped in my tracks, thinking I must be seeing things. What was Tom doing here? He was supposed to be at the Bar None in Whitefish. He touched his hat and smiled like he was amused, or maybe like he thought I was drunk.

"Evening," he grinned. I'd only seen him smile once or twice. It was disarming. My knees went weak, either from him or from the Scotch.

"I thought you were going to the Bar None," he said. I just gave myself over to looking at him, steadying myself on the bar. He leaned on the bar, too, so that our forearms touched. I looked into his emerald eyes, but then it occurred to me that he had asked a question. What was it? Oh yeah, Whitefish.

"I was just going there," I said with a big smile. He smiled back.

"Well how 'bout I drive you?" That sounded good, but something was wrong with it.

"I have my car."

"You're not driving tonight. C'mon with me."

Okay. I linked my arm through his and we pushed out of the Wagon Wheel to the cheers of my new friends. Outside, the cold was brittle. I felt a little light-headed, but Tom helped me up into his truck. He fastened my seat belt, and we were off down the road to Whitefish.

"I guess you didn't get the job," he said.

"Nah." I didn't know how much to tell him, but did know enough to keep my mouth shut until I could think it through. "You work at the ranch?"

"Four days a week, in season, taking dudes out on rides. Slips back a bit now that winter's coming. Then odd jobs. Construction. Some ranch work. You gonna take off, or stay around?"

"I might stay around. Get a job in town." He smiled over at me. I had pinpricks all over. "Hey! How did you know I was at the Wagon Wheel?" He looked at me sideways.

"I saw you drive off the wrong way. When you weren't in the Bar, I figured you might be in Kalispell." After another mile, he looked over again. "Wanna see something?" He looked very pleased with whatever it was that he wanted to show me.

"What?"

"My cabin. Built it myself." He sounded so proud, maybe it really was about the cabin and not just about getting me back to his place. "Maybe you're too tired."

"No." I sat up straighter. "I'm not tired."

As we crunched into the cabin's long gravel driveway, he kept talking about all the great stuff that was out there in the night, just beyond where we could see. A barn, which we actually did see as we got closer to the tiny cabin. A pasture, two horses. Ten acres, all of it his. Bought with money from when his grandpa died. One day he'd have an even bigger spread. A real horse ranch, like Sarah's, with hundreds of head, the best in Northwest Montana. I strained to see if the cabin had a wooden porch. It did! This was the guy, and that was the porch. All we needed was the baby and a mountain view.

Tom pulled up almost to the cabin, jumped out, and said before he slammed his door, "Don't move!" He loped around the front of the truck, beating his hands together, opened my door and lifted me out. As my feet hit the ground, we were all over each other. His face looked like bronze granite, but his lips were soft. He was stronger than Jeff, and more urgent, rougher. I liked it. We clung together up the steps and into the cabin. It was a small living room, one bedroom, and the kitchen. I headed for the bedroom, but he pulled me back.

"Wait," he said, leaning down and kissing me again. He took me from one room to the other, showing me every little thing he had made—the bed, the dresser, the kitchen table, the table back in the living room. All the while, we were kissing and touching each other. I could have cared less about his carpentry, but the delay made everything sexier. He sat me on the green and brown plaid sofa, and faster than I could have imagined possible, got a roaring fire going and about ten blankets spread out in front of it like a nest. He came over and took my hand, pulled me up into his arms, and we fell down into the blankets.

It was all animal feeling, touching, smelling, tasting. I felt cared for, and at the same time pushed around. My mind went numb in a way it never had, even with Scotch. A buzzing stopped that I hadn't even known was there. Hours later, as I sank into unconsciousness, I had the fleeting thought that nothing I'd done so far had really mattered.

⌇

It was light when I woke up. Tom was buckling his belt, dressed for work at Big Sky. He brought me a dark red mug of steaming coffee and sat next to me on the blanket nest, sipping his.

"Hi," he said softly, brushing the hair out off my face.

"Hi." I felt a little shy. He kissed me lightly.

"You're beautiful." I stroked his face.

"So are you."

"You wanna stay here today? Hang out? Take a look around?"

I was dying to do just that, but said, "I better go back and change. Pull myself together."

"How 'bout if we go to the Bar tonight?"

"Okay."

"There's aspirin in the bathroom." He leaned down to kiss me and I smelled alcohol. Probably from last night. He'd been at least as drunk as I was. He pulled himself up and smiled over his shoulder at me as he left. I pulled a blanket around me like an Indian robe and crept into the kitchen for more coffee. The window looked out to a red barn and two sleek brown horses chasing one another around a pasture. Behind it, silent dark green forest—and in the distance, majestic snow-capped mountains. It was my postcard dream of Montana, and I was standing right in the middle of it. I was looking right at the porch where I would stand with Tom, holding our baby.

I started to wash our mugs and smelled booze again. I sniffed his, and the smell of bourbon made me wince. That wasn't from last night. Well, I'd been known to spike my coffee occasionally. It occurred to me that my car was still in Kalispell, but it didn't seem like the end of the world to spend the day breathing the same air he breathed, letting the sense of him sink into me, possibly learning things that might make me more attractive to him and speed up the day when we would stand together on the porch.

I padded into the bathroom, the blanket trailing behind me, and brushed my teeth with his toothbrush—which, strangely, seemed a little naughtier and more intimate than some of the things we'd done last night. In his medicine cabinet, next to the toothpaste, was the largest bottle of aspirin I'd ever seen. Pepto-Bismol, a razor, Noxzema shaving lotion for sensitive skin, and Mennen Speed Stick deodorant. That was it. No prescriptions, no nothing.

In the outdoor shower, I stood under a thick torrent of steaming water, staring out into the blue sky and the blanket of pines spreading up the mountain, breathing in the cleanness.

I pulled on a teal cowboy shirt from Tom's closet and realized that I was ravenous. In the fridge, I found a dozen eggs, some white bread, butter, a big chunk of cheddar cheese inexpertly wrapped in tinfoil, a pound of coffee, and thirty-seven beers stacked like sardines. In one cabinet, twelve cans of Hormel Chili, some dry spaghetti, a pack of filtered Winstons, matches, traces of what might have been flour, three Snickers bars, and some mouse droppings. In the other cabinet, enough booze to hold the gang at the Wagon Wheel for a week.

I wolfed down four scrambled eggs and three pieces of white toast, did the dishes, and wandered back into the bedroom. In the corner, books were stacked on shelves made of boards and cinderblocks. Mostly on woodworking, but two really filthy, oily ones on truck engines. *The Joy of Cooking* in mint condition, as if it had never been opened. I pulled it out slowly, noting exactly where it had been and being careful not to disturb anything around it. It was inscribed, "To my baby brother, so he won't starve!!!!! Amy." He had a sister. I wondered if there were any mementos from old girlfriends. Or wives. Not on this shelf, unless all those women had been auto mechanics or woodworkers.

As I started to replace *The Joy of Cooking*, I saw something dark stuffed in behind the books. I snaked my hand back between *Woodworking Basics* and *The Weekend Woodworker's Manual* and touched something soft. Even as I began pulling it from its hiding place, it felt oddly familiar. It was an old, old book, biodegrading into flat black, with soft gray cardboard pushing out where the cover had worn along the edges. Five disintegrating, twisted ribbons poked out the bottom. Their red, green, gold, blue, and black had faded to neutrals. The edges of the pages had been red, but were now a mottled pink.

The St. Joseph's Missal. I had followed the Mass with an exact duplicate of this book every morning from my first week at IC until the day I ran away. This one had been used even longer. The spine had peeled back, and the cover was cracked. The smell of mildew rose off it. I gently flipped a few pages and found what every Catholic child stuffs into his or her missal. A holy card! Holy cards were sappy, diaphanous renderings of scenes from the Bible and the saints' lives, about the size of playing cards. They were given as prizes in spelling bees, for good behavior, for special service like being an altar boy, and as acknowledgements of events like the feast day of the saint for whom you were named.

Tom's holy card had a picture of the Baby Jesus in the manger. A baffled St. Joseph stared down at the baby, who glowed in his own white light and hovered several inches above the straw—gazing out with huge blue eyes and the face of a twelve-year-old kid. Mary smiled down at him, holding her palms up in devotion and amazement, somehow beautifully coiffed and wearing a spanking clean blue-and-white outfit just moments after giving birth. Tiny finch-like birds circled above the crèche. Cattle and donkeys smiled knowingly. The Christ Child looked mildly disgruntled, as if he knew the birth canal was just the beginning of his troubles now that he was down on earth, but he gamely held up two pudgy fingers in blessing.

On the back, in perfect snaky Palmer Method penmanship, "Thomas Hannigan, make Mother Mary and our dear Baby Jesus proud of you! Sister Anne Marie." Hannigan. I had now slept with two men without knowing their last names, unless you counted "Baba." I carefully replaced the holy card.

I was holding a secret part of him. I knew him in a way that he absolutely could not be known by someone who had not used a duplicate of this missal. I placed it back exactly where it had been, using the outline not covered in dust as a guide, and then replaced *The Joy of Cooking*.

I took a long walk around the property, and even hiked a trail into the woods. It was exhausting, and I lay down for a short nap.

ଓଷ

The sound of screeching trucks woke me. I jumped out of bed and hurried to the window. Tom swung down from his truck, and another guy dismounted a red truck. What was this new guy doing here? I didn't like the look or feel of him. He was taller and skinnier than Tom, and wore just a dirty white T-shirt under his open jacket, despite the cold. His truck was beaten-up and had a big gash along the side of the bed.

He steadied himself against the hood, laughing and holding a beer up to Tom. As they both came weaving toward the cabin, I found myself making sure I had my pack close by and could get at my gun.

The wild guy, not Tom, pushed open the cabin door so hard it banged against the wall. They both fell in, laughing, bouncing off the wall and one another. Tom looked almost surprised when he saw me—then put on a big grin, lurched in my direction, and threw his arm around me. The other guy stumbled over my pack and fell back against the wall as if he'd been hit with a percussion bomb.

"This is Cat!" Tom beamed. "Jake, meet Cat."

Jake didn't pick himself up off the wall immediately, just tilted his head back and shot me a fleeting wolf smile. His black hair fell over his face and ears. I imagined him cutting it himself in the rearview mirror of his truck, maybe with a knife. He had a red mark—a birthmark or scar— just above his left cheekbone and small hazel eyes that darted from me, to Tom, to the kitchen, and back to me. With a little smirk, he made a big deal of pulling himself up and buttoning his jacket, as if I were some kind of uptight schoolteacher ruining their fun.

"Howdy, ma'am," he slurred, pretending to stand at attention. He grinned at Tom, like they were the bad boys who had been caught by this strict outsider. I wanted to haul back and hit him in the face as hard as I could. Instead I smiled, pulled gently out from under Tom's arm, took a step toward Jake, and put out my hand.

"Hey, Jake."

For a second, he didn't move. Then he gripped my hand, hard. I looked him right in the eye and saw a glitter that reminded me of something from way back that I couldn't quite name.

"Hey, Cat." He pumped my hand. Tom rocked on his heels, looking from Jake, to me, to Jake.

"Le's have a drink!" he said finally.

Jake went right to the cabinet, pulled down a fifth of bourbon, and drank from the bottle. He sank back against the kitchen counter. Tom poured a Scotch for me and bourbon from another bottle for himself. I leaned back against the counter opposite Jake and watched him lift the bottle again.

Tom leaned against the fridge and jerked his thumb at Jake, "He's got his own bottle." I nodded knowingly, like I was so gracious, so confident that I could be nice even to this rude trespasser because I had it all over anyone who might want to walk in here and try to mess this up for me. Jake seemed to see, much better than Tom did, exactly what I was thinking. His eyes narrowed. Tom stared into his drink.

"Hey, I recognize that shirt." Jake pointed the bottle at me. I flushed.

"Yeah, me too!" Tom said, holding out his drink, then stumbling over to Jake and bumping shoulders with him. They pushed each other back and forth, half wrestling.

"You movin' in? You got the U-Haul out back?" Jake laughed. I laughed along.

"No way!" I gave them a minute, then grabbed the conversation and threw it into the next yard. "You guys been friends for a long time?" Tom stopped the pushing, and slung an arm over Jake's shoulder.

"Jake works out at Sarah's, too. His day off, when you were there."

Jake's snaky little eyes bored into me. "You know Sarah?"

Tom stepped in and told the story of my test lunch. "She's a great cook!"

Jake opened the cabinet with all the Hormel Chili, picked up a can, pretended to inspect it, and turned back to me. "Oh yeah?"

I put on a flat smile. Tom came over and put his arm around me, kissed me. Jake made a big deal of taking a long swig, replacing the bottle, patting it, and closing the cabinet.

"Well, I better let you lovebirds alone."

"Yeah, see you in the morning," Tom said, now more interested in me. Jake pushed past us and stumbled over my pack near the door. He kicked it again, this time on purpose, and his foot hit something solid.

"Whatcha got in there?" The wolf grin again. He reached behind him and flicked open a switchblade. "One o' these?" He gave the pack another light kick and slammed the door on his way out. He revved the dented red truck, spewing gravel as he turned it around and roared out to the road.

Tom held me from behind and pointed his drink at my pack. "You goin' somewhere?" I turned around.

"No." We kissed. Hours later, we lay in bed exhausted. I stared at the bookshelf, but something told me not to say anything about the missal. I was getting the hang of being a Western woman, and a lot of it involved keeping your mouth shut. Thinking back over the encounter with Jake, that's when I'd had the upper hand.

Tom pulled me on top of him. "You wanna go get your car?"

"No." He kissed me again, and it was eleven by the time we pulled ourselves out of bed and started getting dressed for the half-hour drive to Kalispell.

"Hey," he said, pulling jeans over the thick muscles in his thighs. "Don't go to the hotel. Come back here." I went to him and held him. He wrapped his arms around me, gentle but with that urgent quality I loved.

"I have to go back sometime."

"No, you don't." I pulled away and looked at him. "Stay here. Go get your stuff and bring it back here."

"We don't even..."

"I know you. Better than you think."

"No, you don't." It sounded more angry than I'd intended. What was the matter with me? This was what I wanted, but it made me mad when he said he knew me. How could he know me? Who did he think he was?

He kissed me. A hard, long kiss. "Maybe not like you're talking about, but I know you," he whispered close to my ear. "We'll be all right." All the time, taking off the clothes I'd just put on and pushing me back to the bed. "You stay here with me. We'll be all right."

There was something in his hands, or his breath, or *something* that pulled me into him deeper and deeper. We'd be all right.

Chapter 13

We didn't get the car until morning. I drove to Whitefish and checked out of the hotel, then walked over to the Bar None and swung up onto a stool. Sonny, the owner, was wiping down the bar. Thick white hair and beard, round pink cheeks, and deep-set blue eyes made him look like a Santa Claus who had stopped in Montana for a drink and never left. I'd met him the first night I went to the bar, even talked to him for a while. At least, I thought I had.

"What can I do you for?" he asked without looking at me.

"Coffee, please!" Now he looked suspicious.

"You on the wagon?"

"Applying for a job. *Here*." I smiled my friendliest, most eager and responsible smile. "I can cook, wait tables, whatever you need." I knew they were short-handed and had even seen a cocktail waitress job advertised in the *Pilot*. He hesitated.

"I don't think so," he said slowly.

"Why not?" He picked up a broom and started sweeping behind the bar.

"I seen you drink. I don't want none o' that."

"Of *what*?" What did he mean? Sure, maybe I'd gotten a little tipsy. Everybody did that. It's why you went to a bar! He put down the broom and leaned his elbows on the bar, looking at me.

"You go on down to Lucia's. The Country Cupboard. She needs someone. Best you don't work in a bar. You don't wanna wind up like some o' these old gals in here—and you will, 'less you change your ways."

I grabbed my pack and pounded out of the bar, then walked up and down Main Street a couple of times to work off what he'd said. Who did he think he was? He had no idea about me! Finally, I pushed open the door to the Country Cupboard. The smell of baking bread and fried ham wafted over me. Lucia had a counter, five booths, and about ten tables with pale sage tablecloths and little bud vases with real flowers. Sage and yellow café curtains. It was eleven o'clock, and the place was empty except for two old boys drinking coffee in the corner.

A pretty, petite woman with black hair strode out of the kitchen, wiping her hands on a towel. She wore a yellow pantsuit with a dark red scarf tied tightly around her neck. Her smile was friendly, and her handshake was businesslike.

"I'm Lucia. You Cat?"

"How did you know that?"

"Sonny called. Said you might be headed this way." She sat down at one of the tables and pushed back a chair for me. I sat slowly, not liking that my introduction to this woman had been from Sonny. She didn't seem wary, though. In fact, quite the opposite.

"My cook's pregnant, leaving next week." She thrust the menu into my hands. "Can you do this, or learn it?" It looked easy enough. Plain comfort food, simple stuff. Chicken, gravy, steaks, big-time breakfasts.

"How much does it pay?" She took the menu back and smiled, leaning in and placing her black eyes close to my face.

"More than you'll make anywhere else in town."

Sonny! He was spreading lies about me, trying to make everybody in Whitefish think I was a drunk. I'd never lived in a small town before and, for an instant, considered getting in the car and driving back to Chicago, where at least you had some anonymity.

"How do you even know I can cook?"

"This is a small town, honey. We heard all about the lunch out at Big Sky. What we can't figure out is why Sarah didn't hire you." She smiled like she kind of wanted me to answer the question. I just smiled back. At least Sarah hadn't said anything more.

"When can I start?"

"Now. Come meet Lena so she can show you the ropes."

Lena could have been Lucia's twin—and, in fact, was her sister—except that she was almost as wide as she was tall and looked like she was about to drop a twenty-pound baby. She stood with her arm fully extended toward the griddle, expertly sliding eggs over easy and standing guard over two golden brown slices of ham. Since lunch hadn't started in the dining room, I figured she was cooking for herself.

Behind her, dreamily waiting for the toast to pop up, was the most beautiful woman I had ever seen. She was as tall as I was, with gold hair pulled back into a ponytail with a bright blue tie-back. Her skin was bronze, as if she'd gotten a little sunburned and then smoothed copper flecks all over herself. She wore a white polyester waitress uniform, nipped in at the waist, with a sage and yellow polka-dot apron. A small matching handkerchief peeked out of the breast pocket. Somehow, the uniform made her look lean, athletic, and self-assured. Muscles rippled in her arm as she flicked both toasts out of their slots with one deft pass and slathered them with butter.

"Lena, Abby, this is Cat. Our new cook."

Abby turned her dark blue eyes toward me and smiled as if we'd been best friends all our lives. Lena extended her free arm and squeezed my hand over and over. "Bless you!" she said, her eyes practically welling with tears. "You can start now to learn?" She nodded her head up and down, and I found myself nodding up and down with her. Lucia put her arm around Lena's shoulder.

"Lena is very anxious to go home and get ready for the baby."

"If I don't," Lena said, "I will have *here*—and you will have to *do*." She pointed at Lucia, then at Abby, then at me. Abby looked at me as she laughed.

It was decided that I would work lunch and dinner under Lena's supervision. I called Tom to let him know, but the phone rang and rang. He was out at Sarah's, of course, but he had no answering machine! What kind of a person had no answering machine? A ranch hand. A man of the land with a small footprint on the earth. Someone who stood on porches gazing into mountains with a wife and child.

⟨⟩

As the lunch crowd gathered, Lena turned into a martial arts master. She flung pots of soup and boiling potatoes around the stove, popped huge bubbling casseroles in and out of the enormous ovens—lasagna, baked beans, potatoes au gratin—stirred sizzling sauté pans full of caramelizing onions and bright green string beans with a flick of her wrist. She whirled around like eight-armed Shiva from Suk Bhavan, her dark curls swept back under a frayed white kerchief. Her English was short on vocabulary, long on intention.

"More brown!" she directed me. "Make hot! Put here!"

I did as I was told, and was deeply honored when she put me in charge of some pork chops. Abby glided while Lena swirled, but they worked as one. The plates Lena passed into the dining room were whisked onto enormous trays that were designed to hold six entrees, but were often stacked with eight or ten. By 2:35, eighty-three people had been served piping-hot meals, delivered with aplomb.

Jeb, the fifty-something busboy/dishwasher with only six visible teeth, swept everything away and I helped Abby set up for dinner. I was trying to match Lena's preternatural focus when I felt, then saw, Abby's golden brown hand on my arm.

"Want to get some coffee between lunch and dinner?"

I smiled and nodded.

"Yeah, yeah," Lucia waved from the kitchen. "Go ahead. Good job, Cat!" I hadn't been that thrilled since Sister Mary Celeste gave me my first holy card.

Abby pulled a red down vest over her uniform, and we ran across the street to the Coffee Corner. It was a cozy place suffused with the smell of roasting beans and baking cookies. Abby got a large coffee and not one, but two, giant peanut butter cookies. I got coffee and a chocolate chip cookie. We spread it all out on a tiny round table near the kitchen, away from the door.

"Do you hike?" she asked eagerly, dumping two sugars and a tiny plastic container of cream into her coffee.

"Uh, probably." Hiking was walking, right? Only on a trail, with trees around? I did that. Had done it many times since becoming a person of the West. "I just got to town. Where do you hike?"

"Glacier Park's just up the road." Her long golden arm pointed east. "Do you have hiking boots?" I had been hiking in a dirty old pair of tennis shoes. What would we be doing that required boots?

"I have sneakers."

"What size are you?" She stretched out her leg and put her foot next to mine. Her calf muscles bulged beneath the pantyhose, which had an inch-wide run in them. "Lucia makes me wear 'em. I tell her if she wants 'em without runs, she should pay me more."

"Nine."

"Me, too. You can use some of mine."

She leaned back and started nibbling around the edge of a cookie, staring out the window at downtown Whitefish. She ate down to a central disk about an inch in diameter, and held it up. "My fave. The chewy middle," she grinned and popped it in her mouth. She seemed to say whatever flew through her mind, which I found intriguing. What was someone like her doing in Whitefish, working at Lucia's, eating peanut butter cookies down to their middles and sharing hiking boots with someone like me? I noticed a small gold cross glinting at the hollow of her throat.

"That's pretty," I said. She caressed it.

"Thanks. I've accepted Jesus Christ as my personal savior."

She threw it out as if she were still talking about hiking boots and peanut butter cookies. I expected her to laugh, but she was absorbed in the second cookie, slowly working her way around its crispy periphery. I had no idea what she meant, or why a person would say such a thing, and steered the conversation to safer ground.

"Are you from around here?" I asked, focusing on my own cookie, eating around the chocolate bits, saving them for last.

It turned out that she had been born in Whitefish and gotten married when she was eighteen, but the guy had been killed in a horrible car crash. She had a two-year-old son, Rafe, and lived with her mother in the same house where she'd been born. They were all "Christians" and I would have to come to church with them sometime. She was only a little older than I was, but she had been married, had a baby, understood her God completely, and had her feet firmly planted exactly where they belonged. I wanted desperately to be her friend, and she acted as if we already *were* friends.

"What about you?" she asked, sipping her light, sugary coffee.

I gave her selected facts. Grew up in Chicago, out here for an adventure, to see the world. Nothing false, and nothing that would conflict with anything Sarah might say—although it appeared that Sarah wasn't saying much except that I was a good cook. All I really had to do was give everyone in Whitefish the same information, so Abby got what I'd given Tom.

Tom. Oh my God. He had no idea where I was! I started gathering up my things. "Hey, listen, I have an errand to run. I just moved in with this guy, and he doesn't know I'm working dinner tonight. We don't have an answering machine yet, so I'm gonna run out there and leave him a note." She looked aghast. I wasn't sure whether it was because I was living with someone, because I was rushing around so much between the two shifts, because we didn't have an answering machine, or because I was so worried about checking in with him.

"Who is he?"

"Tom Hannigan." Her eyebrows flew up, but other than that, nothing changed in her face.

"Okay. See you at dinner."

It was a ten-minute drive out to the cabin, and I gunned it. I grabbed a piece of paper from my pack and wrote, "Hi! Got a job. Have to work tonight. Back around nine, probably." How to sign it? Love? No, but something friendly, so he wouldn't be upset. Finally, I just wrote, "Cat" and dashed back to the restaurant.

Dinner was like lunch, but with different food and more people. Lena and Abby did their amazing dance, handling 107 guests over the three hours we were open. Lucia greeted each person like a long-lost friend. I helped where I could. We all high-fived at the end of the evening. Here, in a little restaurant in Whitefish, Montana, I belonged.

છ

Tom wasn't at the cabin when I got back, so I poured myself a nice big tumbler of neat Scotch. He had been there. I'd left my note propped up on the table. Now it was on the floor under the table, slightly crushed. Where was he? With Jake? At the Bar None? I had another Scotch, and another as I gingerly picked up the note and started making a shopping list on the back: romaine lettuce, butter, flour, decent bread, ground beef, veggies...

A truck crunched into the driveway. The door slammed, then the cabin door. He stood at the entry to the kitchen with his hands in his pockets. I went to hug him, but he sidestepped me, reached up into the cabinet, and poured some bourbon.

"How's the job?" he asked roughly. He wove back and forth a little and leaned against the counter. He seemed angry, but like he was holding himself in.

"Great. I'm the new cook at the Country Cupboard!" His eyes and face were red.

"So you just move in, and then come and go as you damn well please?" He came close to me. "*Huh*?" I took a step back, shocked and a little scared. He kept moving toward me, and I didn't like being backed up. I stopped, then leaned forward into his face.

"I got a *job*."

"*I got a job*," he mimicked.

What was he *doing*? I was furious and shoved him away. Hard. He shoved me back, on the shoulder, and I toppled backward. I reached to catch myself on the counter, and my glass shattered against it. Pain flew up my arm. A cut, then the burn of Scotch flowing into it. I looked down to see blood all over the heel of my hand. I felt lightheaded and suddenly Tom was holding me up, clutching me to him, then looking at my hand, wrapping it in a towel, and pulling me into the bathroom.

"I'm sorry. Honey, I'm so sorry. I was mad when I saw your note, and then Jake said..."

"Said what?!" I was furious, scared, and a little shocky.

"He saw you go into the Bar None this morning. Figured you might have stayed there all day. Let me see this." He started to unwrap the towel, now sopping with blood.

"No!" I tried to pull back my hand, but that just made it hurt more. "*Obviously*, I wasn't in the Bar!"

He slowly pried the towel away, which made it bleed again.

"We're going to the hospital," he said in a low voice.

"No, we're not." I cowered against the bathroom wall.

"Then here, let me fix it." He carefully cleaned the cut and dabbed it with antiseptic, which really hurt. Then he took some little band-aid-like sutures and, with his tongue between his teeth, delicately closed the wound. He put a gauze pad over the whole thing, wrapped it up with more gauze, and handed me four aspirin. "Take these." I calmed down as he worked, and I saw how gentle he was.

He drew a deep, warm, sudsy bubble bath in the big copper claw-footed tub. I sat on the bed, numb and still a little scared. He very tenderly removed all my clothes, gently stroking me like a child, and led me back into the bathroom. "Now hold your hand out, like this, so you don't get it wet." I leaned on him as I stepped in and eased myself down into the white cloud. I let it soothe my body and feelings, and closed my eyes to anything outside my own skin. He knelt by the tub and stroked my shoulders.

"Honey, I'm so sorry. Does it hurt?"

"Yes." I wouldn't open my eyes.

"I have a temper. I'll never do that again. I'll be so careful. Please open your eyes."

I did. His nose was red and he had tears in his eyes.

"I promise. I'll never do that again. I promise. Please say it's okay." Tears came to my eyes. "Please."

"Okay."

We had not made love that gently before. The slightest caress seemed to touch every cell in my body and left me knowing that, whatever happened, we belonged together. I cried myself to sleep because my hand hurt, but softly, and with his arms around me.

Lucia frowned when I told her I'd cut my hand on a broken glass doing the dishes. She made me go over to the hospital, where a young doctor with pimples frowned as he cleaned it again and took five stitches. Lena frowned when she heard I would be reduced to observing for the next few days, and that my training would be extended accordingly. Abby frowned, probably because she didn't like being lied to, and looked at me sharply.

"It'll be fine by Monday," she said. We had made plans hike to Avalanche Lake in Glacier National Park.

⚃

I met Abby at the restaurant at eight o'clock Monday morning, and we drove east in her pickup over Going-to-the-Sun Highway toward the Avalanche Lake trailhead. Right away, I saw why my sneakers would not work here and was grateful for Abby's loaner boots. The sheer size of these mountains took my breath away. They were nothing like the tennis shoe mountains where I'd hiked on the way out. These were hiking boot mountains, immense cathedrals of granite and ice that spread out into the distance as far as I could see, soared up into the clouds, and plunged down into valleys that cradled mile after mile of dark green trees with no roads or human trails. I had never encountered anything so large, or so wild.

Signs and park brochures warned against grizzlies, crevasses in the glaciers, bull moose, and many other dangers—but when I looked up into the face of the mountains from the trailhead, it felt like they were holding me in a warm, intimate embrace. Spirit reached down into me from the vastness, steady and powerful. I held my arms out to the side as if to hug it all and smiled at Abby. She smiled back as if she knew exactly what I was feeling and felt it, too.

The trail wound up three miles through a dense pine and cedar forest, with Avalanche Creek thundering beside us the whole way. Bright, clear water from the snowcaps and glaciers crashed over rocks and foamed around broken logs, roaring toward the Pacific. The air was crisp and sunny, spreading out over yawning distances into endless vistas of mountains and valleys.

We climbed out on a rock by Avalanche Creek to eat the chicken sandwiches and potato chips Abby had brought, and watched the sun sparkle in the churning water below.

"Pretty, huh?" she said softly. I turned and looked at my new friend. Her golden ponytail glinted in the sunlight. She seemed utterly serene, at one with this world of mountains and sunshine and roaring water—and with herself. Wherever she was going, she was already there. She seemed like the gatekeeper to a world of peace.

"I want to go on every trail in Glacier. I need hiking boots."

"Yes, you do. We'll get 'em for you." She bit into her sandwich and I unwrapped mine. Homemade cracked wheat bread.

"Did you make this bread?"

"My mom." She looked up into craggy peaks soaring all around us and smiled. "Tell me about Tom." Whatever she knew, or thought she knew, I tried to trump it with the story of our whirlwind romance, how I was swept off my feet, and how wonderful he was. She didn't seem convinced.

"How's the cut?"

"Better! Get the stitches out next week."

"Did he do it?" I stared at her. I knew she hadn't believed the dishwashing story, but why did she have to blame Tom? I didn't want to be on the outs with her, so I smoothed it over.

"Not really. We were scuffling, I guess, and I slipped. My glass broke on the counter." She nodded and didn't say anything else. I waited for her to lecture me, but she just looked back up into the mountains. I wanted to be a better person, to make her like me and help me get that solid peace she had. I didn't like the energy between us when we talked about Tom.

"Are you dating anybody?" I asked.

"No," she smiled enigmatically, looking a tiny bit like one of the smug saint statues lounging around our first-grade classroom. She almost seemed proud of it. I waited and smiled. "If I'm supposed to get married again, the Lord will send him to me." The what? Who was she talking about? Jesus? Baby Jesus would send her a boyfriend? "I'd only be interested in a good Christian man, and there aren't many of those in Whitefish." I must have looked as stunned as I felt, because she said, "I thought I told you, I've accepted Jesus Christ as my personal savior."

Yeah, she had, but I wasn't sure what it actually meant—other than being, I supposed, some sort of grown-up *little Protestant child.* I wanted to be like Abby, but I didn't see how she got all that peace just from being a little Protestant child, and couldn't imagine becoming one myself. I couldn't think of anything to say, so I kept chewing my chicken sandwich.

"Come with Mom and me to church next Sunday. Del and Barb will be working." Del and Barb were the other waitress and cook. I pictured myself in a revival tent, shaking my hands above my head, waving snakes in the air, shouting "Hallelujah!" and going forward to "accept Jesus Christ as my personal savior."

"Maybe."

Avalanche Creek thundered below us. We lay on the big rock like lizards for another half hour, then hiked on up to the lake. It was glorious, round and sapphire blue, rimmed with dark green forest. High above us, waterfalls gushed out over granite slabs into freefall, floating slowly down until they disappeared into the rolling blankets of green. We looked out across miles of valley wrapped in trees and dotted with more waterfalls, and beyond them to the white-peaked mountains in the distance—all throbbing with the slow, ancient, languorous power of Spirit.

On the hike down, we talked about Lucia and the restaurant, Lena, Abby's mother and son, a little about her pastor, Rev. Diamond, and his Jesus Our Good Shepherd Hallelujah Church just outside town. I kept pretty quiet.

"Do you love him?" she said as we switched over to the Trail of the Cedars near the parking lot.

"Huh?" I wasn't sure whether she meant Tom or Jesus.

"Tom. Do you love him?"

"Of course I do. I wouldn't be living with him if I didn't."

Would I? Of course, I loved him. He was perfect for the porch and baby. I guess a lot of guys were, but Tom was raw, sexy, and masculine in a Montana cowboy way. Of course, I loved him.

৪৩

Not to be outdone by Abby as my personal wilderness guide, Tom took me for my first horse trip into Glacier that same week. His two quarter horses were Chase and Brownie. Brownie was older and gentler, so I rode her. She had big brown eyes and a sweet way of bumping her soft muzzle against my chest. Chase was a gelding who only behaved when he was around Brownie.

Tom had more time off now that there weren't many guests at Big Sky, and I spent all my time off with him except when he and Jake were camping, hunting, or fishing. They went off for days or weeks at a time, at least once a month.

When they were gone, I hiked and backpacked with Abby. My time with her was quiet. I was more relaxed with her than I had ever been with anyone except Mollie. Sometimes we went for hours without talking. She didn't drink, so I didn't either on those trips. I would come back feeling so alive I could hardly stand to be in my own skin. I would vow never to drink again—but then I'd get anxious or bored, or Tom would come home and we'd want to celebrate, and I'd overdo it. Or he'd come home days late and I'd be pissed off, so we'd both drink too much and have a horrible fight.

Sometimes we had long, slow evenings at home. He made beautiful oak bookshelves. I read novels and cooked. I loved being with him when he was calm, and reaching over while I was reading to feel the muscles in his shoulders. He would nestle in against me, smile at me with his bright green eyes and then stare into the fire. We lay on the couch or in the nest of blankets in front of the fire, sipping our drinks, just being quiet or talking about the horse ranch we'd have one day. Sometimes he'd kiss the little scar on my hand.

Other times, he would get furious for no reason other than having drunk too much. He'd slam the door, turn on the light over the barn door, and split wood in the blowing snow. Or else go off on a bender.

One time early that spring, he took off in a rage and slunk back in the door three days later, just as I was leaving for work. He looked like he hadn't shaved, eaten, showered, or combed his hair the whole time he was away. He just stood there in the doorway, all hunched over, and held out a little box with a pink bow three times its width. I wanted to scream at him, to hit him, but the shape of the box stopped me. I gave him what I hoped was a blank look, and opened it. Inside was a half-carat diamond ring.

I had made it. Finally, everything was going to be all right. The porch. The baby. Tom. I slipped it on and threw my arms around his neck, but he just gave me a sheepish look and pulled away to get coffee. I didn't trust myself to do or say anything more, so just left quietly for work. That night, I did something I'd wanted to do for months, but hadn't let myself. Tears welled in my eyes when I heard Julie say hello.

"How soon can you buy a bridesmaid dress and get to Montana?" Talking to Julie was like being in the soft yellow glow of our kitchen late at night, eating hot apple-rhubarb pie with rich vanilla ice cream melting slowly down the sides. We had an initial round of squealing about the wedding, then neighborhood gossip, and then she got down to business.

"So who is this guy?"

"He is so good-looking. You'll die. Very hot. He taught me to ride a horse, and we camped in the Rocky Mountains. He wears cowboy boots, even to a bar, and a cowboy hat."

"Does he love you, hon?"

"Of course he does. We're getting married!" I could hardly blame her for not trusting my judgment.

"You just tell me when, and I'll get myself there," she said finally.

Chapter 14

We had to postpone the wedding. Jake came into some money—I never really understood how—and bought a little plot of land a few miles down the road. Tom and some other guys had to help him build a cabin. Then he and Tom had to take one last big trip together, fishing in Alberta, before Tom got his "ball and chain."

Jake and I played tug-of-war with Tom that whole spring and into the summer. When Jake pulled him one way, I grabbed his other arm and pulled my way. Hard. Sometimes Tom came with me, and sometimes he pushed back so hard I sprained my wrist or even cracked a rib. Other times, he just got sullen and drank. He would go off somewhere—to Jake's, to a bar, splitting wood, or just driving his truck around Flathead Valley—and I wouldn't know where he was unless somebody saw him and called me. To my chagrin, it was often Sonny who spotted him. "Saw your guy tearin' down 93 like a bat outta hell!" "Big fight at the Wagon Wheel last night. Heard Tom was there."

I wanted Tom to step up, set a date, stand on the porch with me, and be in my picture. I never exactly told him what the picture was, because I didn't think he'd like seeing himself that way. I certainly didn't want him talking to Jake about it, so I didn't give him the words to do so. I figured that once we got everything in place, when we had the baby and were actually standing on the porch, he would settle down and like it. He was Thomas Hannigan, for God's sake, with the missal and holy card.

When I lost the tug-of-war and he took off hunting with Jake in Idaho or Alberta, I sometimes sat at the kitchen table until midnight, sipping Scotch and plotting how to trap or force him into being Porch Man, married man, stay-put-and-don't-go-hunting father. I began to feel pathetic, out of control, and only another drink took the edge off.

If I didn't let myself have the drink right away, I got confused and annoyed. I wanted to kick Tom in the teeth for how he treated me. What was I doing out here in the middle of nowhere, trying to have a baby with someone who kept dragging his feet about marrying me? So I'd have another drink, and another and another—and I'd press even harder for the porch tableau.

In the morning, just as I was waking up, I began to feel *the dark* moving inside me again, slimy and venomous. Oozing inside it was a picture of me bullying Tom, and of him hurting me. That picture faded into all the old ones—Mother, running away, the disaster with Jeff, killing the baby—and then a new picture rose up. This one was of me, sitting drunk and sloppy at the kitchen table. The bigger and stronger *the dark* got, the more mysterious and obscure it became. I felt it as a throbbing, creeping miasma, vicious and sadistic, that lived somewhere in my primal lizard brain. I tried to tell myself it was like having a foreign body inside me, but my worst fear was that *the dark* was the real me.

When it took hold of me like that, I was afraid to look in the mirror for fear it would leap out of my chest, a horrible, charred monster that lashed out to kill—violent, furious, guilty—then coiled back on itself to strike again. Those mornings, I had to have a drink or two before working breakfast, just to keep *the dark* down so I could get through the day. I would brush my teeth really hard before leaving for the restaurant, so Lucia wouldn't smell the Scotch on my breath.

It seemed like the only ways to keep *the dark* at bay were to work really long hours, to be out in nature with Spirit, or to drink Scotch—so I made sure I always had at least one of those things handy. Scotch was the quickest and the surest, but everything was in the mix. Sometimes it seemed like *the dark*, Spirit, Scotch, Jake, Tom, and I were all chasing each other around in circles. Nobody was winning, and we were all getting exhausted. Only the baby would stop it. With the baby, I wouldn't have to drink so much. Spirit and the porch would be enough, and I would finally be happy. In the right place, doing the right thing.

In late July, I got smart. Tom had just gotten back from fishing in Idaho with Jake, and I had spent four days in Glacier with Abby, not drinking. I made him a pot roast dinner, his favorite, and told him that if we weren't married by September 1, I would be moving on. Probably go to Reno, or even San Francisco. The next day, we got our blood tests.

I called Julie and told her the wedding was on again. A week later, a box arrived containing two dresses—a pink organza for her, and a white silk for me. She was leaving nothing to chance, fashion-wise. The white silk dress was strangely simple, for something she had chosen. No flounces, layering, or pastel trim. It was a floor-length fitted sheath, with a ballerina neck and three-quarter sleeves. It was gorgeous, even comfortable, and I felt beautiful when I put it on. Still, the dress wasn't right for City Hall, which was where we'd planned to get married. I would not hurt Julie's feelings by not wearing it, so we moved the whole wedding back to our cabin.

Lucia was in charge of food and logistics, but the extra work was "no problem" when I explained about Julie. Nothing was a problem for Lucia.

She always just smiled, adjusted, and made everything around her work. One day soon, I would be like that.

☙

Julie arrived the day before the wedding, emerging from her car in turquoise Capris with a pink blouse, bright yellow jacket, and strappy white sandals with heels that were not made for gravel driveways—or really, anywhere in Montana. I could tell she'd bought the outfit especially for her arrival.

"What's she got up as?" Tom asked as we watched her climb out of the car, and I ran out to give her a hug. Her face was more lined, and there were dark circles under her eyes—but that could have been from the drive. I hugged her again, soaking in her presence. Tom ambled out and joined us in the driveway.

"Whoa! Guess you wanted us to see you comin'!" he joked, shading his eyes. I saw hurt flicker in hers, then a second of being pissed, and then her company smile.

"You're Tom!" She put her hands on his arms, kind of waiting for a hug, but he pulled away and stuck out his hand, smiling stiffly.

"You're Julie." They shook hands and smiled at one another with lots of teeth. I found myself talking loudly, looking back and forth between them.

"Hey, come on in and see the place. How was the drive? Are you hungry? Tom, let's have drinks to celebrate." I linked one arm through Julie's, and the other through Tom's, and propelled us all into the cabin.

Sonny could have sent a child to college on the money we spent that night at the Bar None. Our party included Julie, Lucia, Lena and her husband, Abby and her mother, Jake, and Tom's sister Amy, who had driven up from Butte and was staying with a friend in town. Abby and her mother had Diet Cokes and were gone by eight thirty. The restaurant gang left early, too, but the rest of us were just getting started.

I had decided it would be better if I didn't drink at all that night. I could be a gracious hostess, impress Tom's sister, and feel much, much better for my wedding in the morning. The only problem was, I wouldn't have any fun. I made a big show of having a Diet Coke the first round, which worked nicely because that's what Abby and her mom saw me drink. After they left, though, the whole feeling around the table changed. Everybody relaxed a little and I decided not to be such a wet blanket, to order just one Scotch—on the rocks, so it would be very diluted.

An hour later, I threw up in the bathroom. When I came out of the stall, Julie was leaning against the sink, waiting for me. I rinsed out my mouth, splashed a little water on my face, and combed my hair.

"Hon, are you all right?"

"Sure! Just a little nervous."

"You don't have to go through with this. You can come home with me."

"I want this."

"Want what?"

"Him. A home."

"Yeah, but..."

I swung my arm widely. "The outdoors!" She looked puzzled. "Nature...horses. You know, the mountains!" I wasn't communicating very well, but I wasn't about to talk about Spirit, the porch, and the simple life while standing in a bathroom at the Bar None with a foul mouth. "*Babies!*"

"You're *pregnant*?" She looked thrilled.

"No, but I will be soon." In the mirror, I looked thirty-five years old instead of twenty, disheveled, and even a little crazy. Julie held my shoulders and looked right into my eyes, her face about two inches from mine.

"Listen to me." She shook me a little. "Listen to me. You call me if you need me. Promise?"

"I'm fine, Jules. I'm gonna be just fine."

"Promise."

"Okay, okay. C'mon." I dragged her back to the table.

When we got home, Tom and I had a terrible fight.

"Man, after all you did to make me marry you, you don't pay much attention to me!" He was practically shouting. I closed the bedroom door, hoping Julie hadn't heard. It pissed me off, though, and *the dark* rose up in me. I shoved him.

"Shut up. She can hear you," I hissed. I shoved him again, just to make sure he knew I meant it. He shoved me back. I tried to catch myself against the closet, but the door slammed me in the side of my face with a CRACK. The bedroom door flew open and Julie stood there for an instant, then came toward me.

"I'm fine. I just slipped." Tom put his arm around me, and Julie backed into the living room. He closed our door. I went into the bathroom, took five aspirin, and drank about a quart of water against how I would feel in the morning. My cheek and eye hurt, but looked okay. A little flushed from having had a drink, maybe—but okay.

When I opened the bathroom door, he was kneeling on the other side, holding up a wildflower from the bouquet I'd picked earlier for our nightstand.

"I'm sorry." He looked up. "I'm a shit." He held up the flower. "Will you marry me?"That was the first time we made up without making love. Maybe we were both too drunk. We spooned, and I had a hard time getting to sleep. I thought about my dad, and what it would be like if he were giving me away instead of Julie. I pictured him in his dark gray suit and maroon tie. "This suit makes me feel like a winner, sweetheart," he would say when I told him how great he looked. "Like a winner," he repeated, adjusting his tie in the hall mirror and smiling down at me.

I was glad he wasn't here, glad he wouldn't see me. Looking at myself through his eyes, I felt ashamed. If I hadn't run away, maybe I would have married a lawyer and lived on the North Shore of Chicago, been in some ladies' club and drunk one glass of wine a year. The tears started, but I didn't let Tom see them.

؃

The sunlight hurt my eyes, even before I opened them. I tried sinking back to sleep, but my face throbbed from a dark point of pain that sent jagged waves of queasiness along every nerve. Even my hair hurt.

I turned my neck slowly, centimeter by centimeter, toward Tom, rubbing the gunk from my eyes and forcing them open. He was out cold. Lucia was moving around in the living room, chatting with Julie in low voices. The clock said 9:45. Tom was supposed to pick up Amy in town at nine thirty, buy her breakfast and bring her out to the cabin. Last night, I'd thought that was a brilliant idea. It would give them time together, which I thought would make me seem like a generous sister-in-law who was willing to share Tom with her—and also get him out of the house while I dressed and Lucia worked her magic. I stroked his shoulder. He groaned. I spooned him from behind and he turned toward me.

"Happy wedding day," I said. He smiled with his eyes closed.

"Happy wedding day, yourself." He held me tight. "I love you."

"I love you, too." He pulled away and looked at me.

"Jesus!" He stared at my cheek, his hand hovering over it as if he wanted to stroke it, but didn't dare.

"What?"

"Sweetheart..." The dull throb spread heavily across my right eye and cheek. I touched the temple gingerly. A flash of pain. "Jesus...What happened?" I pulled myself out of bed and made my way stiffly to the bathroom mirror. A black eye, dark gray rimmed in crimson, and a bruise right across the right cheekbone. All of it puffy and swollen. My whole face was lopsided. Tom stood behind me, looking over my shoulder into the mirror. "Did I do that?" He was aghast, and clearly had no memory. I vaguely recalled falling against the closet door.

"I don't think so. I think I fell against the closet."

"Oh, my God." He put his arms around me, but I pulled away and leaned into the mirror again. He looked over my shoulder. "Do you have any, you know...makeup?" he asked.

"No, but Julie will." He looked pained. "I have to tell her. I'll say I fell. You need to get out of here. You're late for Amy."

"Amy?"

"You're taking her to breakfast and bringing her back here." He looked dumbfounded, but eager to do as he was told. "You have to be back by eleven o'clock."

He showered and left quickly. I showered, put on my red chenille bathrobe, and called into the living room for Julie. She walked in hesitantly and put her hand to her mouth when she saw my face. I had felt pretty okay until that moment, but seeing myself through her eyes made me want to grab my pack, jump in the car, drive west, and never talk to another human being again. She held up one finger, disappeared, and came back with a baby blue plastic case with bright yellow flowers all over it. She made me sit in a chair by the window and talked as she worked.

"Baby, I want you to come home with me."

"No."

She frowned, then focused on the task at hand, laying on cover-up and foundation in sheets. "Yeah, yeah. Good," she said to herself. I decided to speak only when spoken to. "Mmm, hmm." She worked quickly, deftly, moving on to the eye shadow and mascara.

"Go easy," I said, imagining what I would look like if she had her way with my eye makeup.

"Yeah? I could say the same to you." More silence, while she lined my lips.

She led me to the bathroom mirror, standing behind me as Tom had a half hour earlier. I couldn't believe how much better it looked. You could tell a little, but maybe not if you didn't already know. I tried smiling. It hurt a little, but not much. It was more makeup than I'd ever worn, but I wasn't about to complain. Instead, I turned and held her close, talking in her ear.

"Jules, I have to do this. I want you with me. Please be with me."

She held my shoulders. Tears had welled in her eyes, but she pushed them down and forced the words out.

"I'm with you."

"Let's have a happy day, okay?" It was something Mollie often said to us at breakfast.

"Okay, we'll have a happy day." That was our response, hers and Loreen's and mine. She poked at my hair. "We'll have to fix this."

I held her hand tight, and we went into the living room to help Lucia.

༄

Abby's Pastor Diamond had been recruited when we switched the wedding from City Hall to the cabin. I had my doubts about using a culty, hellfire, snake-waving "pastor"—but Abby said he would be perfect. She assured me that he did not, in fact, wave snakes, and that it would be extremely difficult to get anybody else on such short notice, especially with no connections to any church. I wasn't going to bite on that.

He arrived at exactly eleven, fifteen minutes early, peeking around the door as if he expected to find Santa's workshop inside. He did look a little like an elf and exuded a soft, kind ebullience that washed over everything and everyone in his presence. He had the roundest head I had ever seen, and a face that glowed pink and was unlined except around his little sapphire eyes. Only thin puffs of gray hair made him look over forty.

My instinct was to pull him into the bedroom, throw myself on his round little shoulder, pour my heart out to him, tell him I was scared to marry Tom but *had* to, and make him promise that everything would be okay. Instead, I walked toward him with my hand extended. He took it very gently and placed his left hand over it. We smiled into one another's eyes and he managed to convey without words that meeting me was the high point of his life.

"Cat?" he asked conspiratorially. I nodded.

"Pastor Diamond?" He nodded.

"I hope you'll be very, very happy," he beamed. "I'm sure God will bless you and Tom." He glowed with the same quiet peace and certainty that Abby did. How did they *do* that, on no more than little Protestant child dogma? I squeezed his hand, not knowing what to say.

"Is Mrs. Hernandez here?" I pointed toward the kitchen, and he wafted off to find Lucia with an innocent, ethereal air that made me want to follow him.

A few minutes later, the cabin flooded with "Here Comes the Bride." I panicked. I was still in my bathrobe, and Tom and Amy were still in Whitefish. In the corner, Pastor Diamond and Lucia were bent over her boom box, dissolved into giggles.

"No problem, no problem," she called across the room, more giddy than I'd ever seen her. "Just testing." Now *she* was his best friend. "Testing, testing..." Lucia shouted, and giggled again. What was *wrong* with her?

Julie grabbed me and dragged me into the bedroom to get dressed. When Tom came back, she made me hide in the bathroom while he put on his suit so he wouldn't see me, then shooed him out into the living room. She darted out for a moment to consult with Lucia, dashed back in, and "Here Comes the Bride" started again. I just stared at her, thinking they were still testing.

"You ready?" She smiled, and touched my shoulder.

"Is it now?" I felt stupid, confused, as if I were hovering above myself.

"Yes! You're so pretty. I'm so proud of you, hon. I know Mollie's looking down on us, and she's proud, too."

I couldn't speak, only nod. She touched my cheek again, turned, and marched out of the bedroom in time to the music. I watched the pink organza disappear around the corner, watched myself step into the living room and start down the little aisle between the folding chairs. The restaurant gang sat in back, where they could fly up to attend to anything in the kitchen that might need tucking in. Jake was right in front of them, pale and smirky in black jeans, black shirt and black string tie, sprawled sideways with his boot on a chair in the next row up. Abby's mother sat primly across the aisle from him in her pale lavender suit and hat. Abby was beside her in a simple blue dress, holding her mother's white-gloved hand and smiling at me. Julie stood to Pastor Diamond's right, and Amy next to Tom. She looked solemn and austere in her navy blue dress. I hadn't seen so many women in dresses since I'd left Chicago.

Everybody seemed to have found their places except me.

We faced Pastor Diamond, but Tom kept sneaking peeks at me and puffing up each time he did—or maybe he was just looking to see if Julie's makeup had covered the bruise. Pastor Diamond beamed at us and started talking. I have no idea what he said, but at some point I said "I do" and Tom said "I do" and he said to Tom, "You may kiss the bride" and Tom did, just like in the movies.

We turned around and everybody clapped. Tom looked confused, and he started clapping too. I hugged Julie, then Abby, and everybody kind of drifted around us and I hugged everybody except Jake, who was pouring himself a drink in the corner of the kitchen.

I didn't have anything to drink at the wedding, so the whole event was in Technicolor and very intense. After an hour of eating, dancing, being on my best behavior, and watching other people drink, I escaped into the bedroom. I soaked up the quiet and found myself staring into the back corner of the closet at my secret getaway pack. Hidden inside it were a change of clothes, basic toiletries, a stash of money, some trail bars, and my gun. I thought I should probably unpack it now that I was a married woman, but instead just went back into the living room.

A few people were still milling around, but most had left and things were winding down. Julie lugged her suitcase toward the front door.

"Don't come outside in your dress, hon."

I hugged her for a long time. I wanted her to stay, and wanted her to go.

"Drive safe."

"Hey, don't forget my number again. Okay?"

"Okay."

I watched her pull her little red suitcase over the gravel and load it into the trunk of her blue Chevy. She wore the same outfit she'd had on when she arrived, but with a bright yellow kerchief tied beneath her chin. She turned and waved, and I waved back. Tears burned in my eyes.

Chapter 15

Tom and I went to Glacier for a weekend honeymoon. We drove the full length of Going-to-the-Sun Highway to Many Glacier, a sprawling, Swiss-style hotel built by the Great Northern Railroad in 1915. We stood on our rustic little balcony, our arms around one another, looking out over the blue glass of Swiftcurrent Lake and the afternoon sun on craggy granite mountains all around us. It was almost perfect, a once-removed version of the porch tableau, minus the baby. We were on different wave lengths, though. I wanted to hike, and he wanted to sit in the Interlaken Lounge sipping booze and feeding one another fondue. I was crabby and resentful, but pretended to be nice. I think he was relieved on Sunday afternoon, when it started to spit rain and I suggested we start home early.

I thought everything would be different once we were married, but nothing changed. The minute we got back to the cabin from our "honeymoon," Tom was on the phone with Jake. Two days later, they left on a two-week fishing trip to Alberta. I felt abandoned, but was just as glad to have a break from being married. I worked double shifts while he was gone, which delighted Barb. She had a new grandson and her life was now about looking into his eyes. Most nights, I came home exhausted, had a couple of Scotches, and fell into bed. Still, I was glad to see him when he got back.

That became our pattern. Things were great, but then we drank and fought and he left. Everything was better when he got back, but then we drank and fought...over and over. It was like having one foot on the brake and the other on the accelerator, revving my engine without really knowing where I was headed—or even if I wanted to go.

One night about six months after we were married and he was off hunting with Jake, I sat out back behind the cabin in a frayed green-and-blue plastic chaise lounge, letting Spirit and Cutty Sark flow over me. I stared up at the mountains, black against a streaky purple-peach sky and a pale, milky half moon. I could almost see a golden field, like the northern lights, streaming up from the highest peaks into the soft dark sky and beyond. Those glimpses of Spirit kept me going—but then I turned my head and looked back at the cabin, with its little porch and white railing, ghostly in the moonlight. I stared at the blank space where Tom and I should be standing with the baby.

Over a year of no birth control, and nothing. The nuns had assured us that just *looking* at a boy the wrong way could result in pregnancy—and in my case, they had not been far off. Now that I wanted it, though, nothing! The sooner we got that baby in the works, the better. *The dark* was living closer and closer to the surface. It liked Scotch. Scotch made it bigger, even as it numbed me temporarily. It also liked fighting with Tom. That made it bigger, too. When we had the baby, I wouldn't drink or fight with Tom as much. *The dark* would ease off. Spirit would be enough for me, and I would be more a part of it. I just needed the booze now to soften the edges.

I tried to imagine a little person who was half me and half Tom, to morph our two faces into one and shrink it down to the size of a baby's face. Then it struck me. That little person could be living inside me at this very moment! I pulled myself out of the chaise and wove unsteadily back toward the porch and up the stairs into the kitchen to check the calendar. Thirteen days late. I could be pregnant!

The phone rang. I wasn't in a mood to answer it, but anyone calling at eleven at night...

"Hullo," I mumbled.

"Cat? Is that you? *Cat?*" The voice sounded familiar, but I couldn't place it.

"Yeah."

"It's Amy." My God, his sister. Was he dead? I pictured him and Jake driving drunk and careening off the road. "Tom's here. I'm taking care of him." What was he doing in Butte? Why was she taking care of him?

"I thought he and Jake were in Idaho. Is he okay?"

"He's *here*. He's okay. They were drinking some, though." It turned out that they had never even gone to Idaho. They'd been on a bender and found their way to Butte four days earlier. "They're okay now. Just a little hungover. They're starting home tomorrow. Tom wanted me to let you know..."

"Let me talk to him," I said.

"Uh, he's not here now. They went to get some groceries."

Right.

"Well, tell him to call me."

"Sure." I didn't like the sound of her. I wondered how long they'd really been there, and if she'd been drinking with them. At work the next morning, I got my period.

When I got home, Tom was flung out on the couch, snoring in deep rhythmic rattles, his mouth wide open to the ceiling. A basketball game blared on the television. I wanted to grab the fireplace poker and slam it into his stomach, but instead I just stood looking down at him, trying to muster some wifely compassion.

Even gray-skinned, smelly, and rumpled, he was handsome. A week of not shaving made him look rugged. The long, delicate black eyelashes made him seem almost vulnerable. A jagged red gash cut across his forehead. It looked a couple of days old, and like it was starting to get infected. I wanted to pull him into my arms and fix it, then pummel him with my fists.

I kicked the front of the couch, harder than I meant to. He jumped a little, then settled back into a fetal position, snoring into his forearm.

"Hey!" I said.

The velvet eyelashes twitched. His eyes moved back and forth behind the lids. One green eye slit open, then shut again.

"Hey!" I kicked the couch again, really hard. His arm flew out and snatched my calf. His mouth smiled, but his eyes were hard. I couldn't tell whether he was angry pretending to be playful, or playful pretending to be angry. He twisted my leg and I landed hard on the floor—but that broke his grip. I jumped up quickly, feeling *the dark* rise in me, and pinned his shoulders back against the couch with my full weight, half shaking him and half trying to hug him.

"What's the *matter* with you?" I screamed.

"What's the matter with *you*? Get the fuck off me." He pushed me off. I caught my balance and stood looking down at him. He closed his eyes again and turned away.

"What happened to your forehead? Where have you been? What happened to your face?" *the dark* yelled, hammering his back with my fists.

He turned around, stared, and slowly stood up. He swayed a little and started toward me. I planted my feet and looked him in the eye. If he messed with me, I would let *the dark* loose. He got to within a foot and stopped. He lifted his hand and jabbed his index finger an inch from my nose. His face was contorted, furious. A vein bulged at his temple, and his skin was splotchy red.

"You...get out of my face." The words were murderous and final. He turned, walked unsteadily into the bedroom, and slammed the door. I hadn't given way, but my heart was pounding. I flicked off the television, then walked to the kitchen and poured myself a double.

I got my period the next three months.

03

Every fourth Monday night when the restaurant was closed, Lucia made dinner for all of us. We pushed together a couple of tables, ate a delicious meal, and then sat around talking and drinking wine. I liked getting to know these women. Del and Barb had been rodeo girls thirty years earlier, before finding two good old boys, "pardners" themselves, to marry. Lena was a master seamstress as well as a master cook, and had even tailored jackets for her husband. Lucia had actually spent time in a convent before she realized "I didn't have that kind of vocation" and met her late husband at a Jesuit retreat.

One Monday night as we were eating dessert—my devil's food cake with buttercream frosting—Lucia said, "If you're so set on having a baby and it's not happening, why don't you go see a doctor?"

It had never occurred to me, but it was a great idea. Plus, I was delighted to do something she had suggested and approved.

"You're right," I smiled. "I will."

The next week, I went to see a doctor in Kalispell. A young dark-haired woman with pasty skin and Cleopatra eyeliner had me fill out a medical history, showed me to an exam room, and handed me a light blue paper gown. She told me to take off all my clothes and left without a smile. The room was cold. Everything in it was black, white, or chrome—all tinged with blue-gray from the fluorescent lights. A small, hidden motor sent a low whirring sound through the antiseptic air.

I changed and gingerly pulled myself up onto the exam table, trying not to split the white paper that covered it. My hands looked bloodless and ghostly against the blue gown when I folded them in my lap. They trembled when I wiped them on the gown. The whole thing reminded me of killing the little baby in Chicago.

A knock. A very tall, thin man in a white coat poked his head around the door, then drew the rest of his long, angular body in after it. He must have been about sixty, with skin like fragile parchment. Sparse, curly gray hair covered the back half of his head and stood straight on end, like Einstein's. Alarming gray hairs protruded from his nose and ears, but his eyes were kind and his smile was soft. He held out a hand with fingers so long and bony they seemed alien.

"Jim Cravens," he said with a friendly smile. His voice was deep, modulated like a radio announcer's. I took his hand lightly, careful not to break the skin.

He scanned my history, asked some questions about how long I'd been trying to get pregnant, how often we had sex, what kind of birth control I'd used.

"Well, Cat," he said finally, "we're going to find out what's going on." He patted my shoulder, got me into the stirrups, and started the pelvic.

We sat in his office after the exam, and he asked me more questions about the abortion. I was amazed at how little I remembered. Obvious things like what procedure they had used and how long it had taken for me to feel okay after I got home. I could hardly recall any of it. I had felt really bad for a couple of weeks—but couldn't remember whether the pain had been physical or just emotional. He asked if I'd gone back to the clinic when I didn't feel well, and I didn't think I had. No, I hadn't.

"I'm sorry," I said. "I should remember." He looked up, closed his file, laid his long fingers flat on the desk, and leaned toward me.

"That must have been a terrible time for you," he said softly. "Now, I want you to get some tests…" He gave me a sheaf of papers for blood tests and X-rays and told me how to get to all the places I needed to go. "Why don't you come back about four o'clock and we'll talk. Go have a nice lunch, do some shopping." He said this as if the shopping were a prescription he wrote often, and with surefire results.

Cleo gave me a wan smile when I appeared in her reception area. I had already forgotten how to get to the lab and radiology. She must have been used to trembling, undone women, and gave me surprisingly clear directions.

"He said to come back at four," I told her. She marked it in her book, then gave me the once-over.

"You should go shopping," she said professionally. "Try Taylor's. They have a sale this week."

ℭ

By noon, I was out on the street. A light snow was falling, but the sun was out—which made everything seem crystalline and surreal. A faint static whirred around my brain. Not actually a sound, just a sense that there might not be enough oil in the engine.

I found a diner and wolfed down a toasted cheese sandwich with a big bowl of tomato soup—comforting and filling. Out in the cold air again, I walked and walked. Up and down the streets of Kalispell. Past small appliance repair shops, dry cleaners, grocery stores. Up side streets into neighborhoods where tiny wood houses huddled together. I couldn't stop walking, and couldn't seem to pull my thoughts together.

Finally, I found myself in front of a big stone church with flying buttresses and a yellow sign with red letters: *St. Matthew's Catholic Church. All are welcome.* I peeked inside and inhaled the thick smell of incense, let myself be pulled into the dark silence. I stood in the shadows at the back of the church, completely still for the first time in hours, and realized I'd been walking so fast I was sweating despite the cold.

The altar was lit softly from above, draped in shimmering red altar linens and overhung with an ornate canopy. I slunk into a pew near the back where I wouldn't be seen by the devout old women making Visits to the Blessed Sacrament or doing the Stations of the Cross, shuffling from one Purgatory-reducing spot to the next. I leaned back and let the darkness and silence seep into me. I did not believe in this God, with his Purgatory ledger and his nuns with red plastic rulers, but something deep in my cells yearned for him. I was beyond bankruptcy in this system, a multiple offender with back-to-back eternal damnation sentences. Still, those infinitesimal buzzing strings of energy I used to call *the bright* hung in the air—and I felt strangely like I was in the right place.

It wasn't exactly the IC god I was feeling, but some amalgam of that, the infinite I AM Oneness, Spirit, and even Pastor Diamond's god of certainty. That amalgam god was made up of all my best hopes for what God might be, if I were good or strong enough to overcome *the dark* one day and get back into the fold, wherever that was.

I pulled myself up from the pew onto the kneeler, closed my eyes, fused all those gods together in my mind, and prayed in a desperate way that had to work. *Give me that baby.* I had done my absolute best, all my life, when it came to God. Now it was time for him to deliver.

Please... Then I started sobbing and didn't stop for an hour.

ℤ

Dr. Cravens leapt up when Cleo opened the door to let me into his office. He cupped a hand under my elbow, led me over to the two upholstered visitors' chairs, and sat down beside me.

"I'm afraid we didn't get the result we wanted, Cat," he said, leaning his elbows on his knees and clutching the file with one hand. I couldn't move. My feet felt leaden, my face frozen, my hands limp on the arms of the chair. He explained how it looked like I'd gotten an infection in my Fallopian tubes while killing the baby and now they were all scarred and blocked, so it was very, very unlikely that I could ever get pregnant and of course there was adoption and maybe artificial insemination and all kinds of things we could...

I just stared at him. Mostly, I looked at his nose hairs and wondered why one of the people in the family pictures all over his office hadn't given him one of those whirling clipper things for Father's Day or his birthday.

"Why don't you and your husband talk this over and..."

My husband? Was he even home this week? No, in Alberta, hunting. He didn't even know I was here. I wanted *my* baby, not somebody else's. I wanted the elemental part, the Spirit part...

"Let's make an appointment for next month and talk about your options. You can bring him if..."

I stood up. What had he just said?

"So, I can't get pregnant because of the scar tissue?"

"Probably not, but they may be able to harvest your eggs, and if your husband would..." Maybe they could dig around in my ovaries and yank out some eggs, and Tom could jack off and then, in a test tube...that wasn't what I wanted. I pushed past him. He stepped back and looked a little stunned. I was out the door, following the green-and-white exit signs.

"Don't forget to make an appointment," he called after me. I kept moving, trying to breathe.

I rushed past Cleo and into the street. My mind was in whiteout. I couldn't think, couldn't feel. All I could do was walk. Up and down the same streets I'd walked earlier, into the residential areas, but nowhere near that church.

I paused at Taylor's, where they were having the sale, and stood staring into the window. Dresses. Skirts. Slacks. Jackets.

A sharp, menacing whistle broke the cold air.

"Hey, mama! Wanna suck my dick?" Gales of high-pitched drunken laughter. I turned to see five guys bouncing around the back of a beat-up black pickup, all maybe fifteen years old and smashed. One of them stood up and mooned me. I kept my face blank, then felt a flush and dropped my eyes. Disengage, Mollie's cop friends had taught me. Boy, had they picked the wrong girl, on the wrong day. *The dark* snapped to life. If I'd had my gun, I would have walked right over to them, put it in one kid's face, watched him freak out, and pulled the trigger. They honked, and another one grabbed his crotch.

I ducked into Taylor's until they drove off, then slipped back onto the street, melting into the buildings so they wouldn't see me, and watched where they went. After a few blocks, they pulled in and stopped, piled out of the truck and staggered noisily into one of the tiny houses. It was almost dark, and getting colder.

I ran the six blocks back to my car, drove to where I had left them, and parked across the street from their truck. *The dark* had me. I could feel the blood pounding in my temples. I would show them mean. I reached into the glove box for my multi-tool and fixed it to the serrated knife, then slid out of the car and moved toward their truck. It was already beaten up and gouged, but I took the knife and raked it along the driver's door. Paint splayed out of the crevasses and floated to the ground like black snow. I raked back the other way. It felt good. I took the needle-nose pliers and stabbed into the hood as hard as I could. It made a pointy dent. I did that a couple more times. The truck was already a mess, but it made me feel good to make it worse.

Lights turned off in the house where they'd gone, and I thought they might be watching me. I dashed to my car, gunned it, and was back on the highway in five minutes—heading south toward Flathead Lake, away from Kalispell and Whitefish.

I drove fast until I was well away from anybody who might be chasing me—the cops or the guys. I veered left on 82 and stopped in Bigfork for a fifth of Scotch, then drove slowly along the east shore, looking for a place to stop.

I pulled into a turnout and nudged the car close up against the trees, grabbed an extra jacket and a flashlight from the trunk, and moved carefully down the narrow switchbacks toward the water. A battered little pier jutted out over the lake. I walked carefully to the end and sat with my feet dangling over the black water. The first long pull of Scotch felt warm and familiar. Comforting.

The moon shimmered on the dark water. Black mountains loomed up against an indigo sky. Big stars, everywhere. Spirit had its work cut out for it tonight. *The dark* rose into my throat, black with rage and bitterness, dragging me along. I gave it more Scotch. It receded for a minute, then swelled. I looked into the black lake, listened to it lap against the creaky pier. I could jump down there, hold on to something on the bottom until I passed out and drowned—but I was too tired. No more Scotch left. I threw the bottle into the lake.

I just needed a little rest, and stretched out on the pier with my head resting on my arms. One minute it seemed like thick, solid walls of coal were slowly closing in on me from all sides like a vice. The next, it felt like there was nothing solid to hang on to, not even my own body, and I was in free fall.

જી

The yelling came from far away.

"You okay?" It was a man's voice—concerned, even frantic. The splash of oars in the lake. "Hey! You okay?" I slit open an eye and saw two fishermen rowing furiously toward me. "Lady, you okay?"

I lifted myself up on one elbow, fought through the cobwebs and throbbing in my head, waved, and yelled back.

"Yeah! Thanks! I'm fine. Just fell asleep." They looked skeptical. To convince them and myself, I struggled to my feet, waving and smiling. I felt for my keys in the pocket of my jeans, jangled them at the fishermen, and pointed up to the road. Waving and smiling. They waved back, but looked unconvinced and sat motionless in the boat, watching me climb painfully up the trail to my car.

Where was I? Flathead Lake. No baby. The Scotch. I wasn't at work. Hadn't called Lucia. Hadn't called Abby, who was out at the cabin. She'd said she would stay until I got back yesterday afternoon and feed the horses. Tom and Jake were off in Alberta, or somewhere. I was freezing.

My clothes were damp. I felt like I'd been run over by a truck. Oh yeah, the truck. The Kalispell guys. Well, I wouldn't be going back there for a while. I'd drive around the lake and figure out what to do. Stop for coffee and something to eat.

I revved out of the turnout and was just getting my bearings on the road, fiddling with the heater, when I felt and heard a dull THUD. I swerved onto the shoulder and looked back. A raccoon lay dead in the road, cut almost in half by my tire, lying in a pool of dark red. I made myself not think about it and just pulled back onto the road, looking for food. Coffee, too, with something in it so I wouldn't feel so jumpy.

Up ahead, a worn wooden sign with faded letters: *Salish Food Mart*. It was a rough square building with a small gravel parking lot. I got some white bread, salami, hot black coffee, and a fifth of Cutty. Actually, two fifths. At the pay phone outside, I left messages asking Barb to work for me the next few days and Abby to stay at the cabin. I knew they'd be at work, so I called them at home. I didn't want to talk to them.

ଔ

The next morning I woke up in a tiny room, half covered with a purple quilt that reeked of disinfectant and stale cigarette smoke. When I hauled myself up to pee and throw up (again, apparently), I found a key on the grimy Formica table. Attached to it with a flimsy metal chain was a wood cutout of a pine tree with black letters: *Lone Pine Motor Inn, Polson, Mt.* I was at the southern end of Flathead Lake, with no idea how I'd gotten there.

I flicked on the overhead light, and the room filled with fluorescent glare. Just like Dr. Cravens' exam room. I flicked it off and peeked through the slit where the gray plastic blackout curtains met. The sun was just coming up. In the parking lot, a tired-looking woman with a red-and-blue scarf wound loosely around huge pink hair rollers heaved an ice chest into the back of a maroon station wagon. A little blonde girl about four years old burst out of the room next door and ran to her with her arms up. The woman smiled and suddenly looked ten years younger, swept up the little girl and hugged her. A man came out carrying a heavy suitcase and a baby.

Another door opened across the parking lot. Two guys in their forties with beer guts and baseball caps loaded fishing gear into their truck, laughing and shouting at one another. They waved at the family and sped off.

I closed the curtains and took a long shower.

ଔ

I woke up to deep, heavy throbbing in my leg. Each time blood pumped, pain knifed through the inside of my left calf, down low by the ankle. When I reached down, my finger touched something soft and sticky. I pulled myself up and hobbled to the bathroom.

Under the hissing fluorescent light, a deep, ragged cut gouged out six inches along my calf. It was reddish, with little streaks of yellowish pus. Dirty, too, filled with dark gobs of something I hoped was just mud. I ran it under the shower to get off the surface dirt and dried blood, and thought I would pass out from the pain. It felt very deep, aching in the middle and stinging near the edges. I thought about the emergency room in Kalispell, but I wasn't even sure I could make it to the car, let alone drive when I got there.

I propped the calf up on the sink to get a better look, and saw red muscle. I just made it to the toilet to throw up, then slumped on the linoleum floor. I stared at the mildew in the far corner of the ceiling, at the brown ring in the tub, at the greasy film on the pipes coming down from the sink, anywhere but at my calf. The throbbing got worse. How had this happened? I must have gone outside, but had no memory of doing so.

I got one hand on the toilet and one on the sink, then pulled myself up so I was balancing unsteadily on one leg with the calf hooked up on the sink. There was red flesh, skin pushed around where it shouldn't be, dirt and dried blood even after the rinse in the shower, and edges that were too far apart. I had never been hurt this badly.

I reached behind me to the towel rack over the toilet and grabbed the thin white washcloth. It was torn on the corner, scratchy, and didn't look real clean. I ran it under hot water for a few minutes. The small soap on the sink had brownish ruts in it, so I ran that under the hot water, too. I rubbed some soap on the cloth. Then, very gently, I started cleaning. First to the sides where there was still dried blood. It hurt more, bled more. I watched my shaking fingers move along the cut, slowly and carefully wiping away anything didn't seem to belong there. Trying not to make it worse. Not really knowing where to put the soap, and where not to touch it at all.

The cut looked almost like a bear had clawed me, but that couldn't be. I would be mauled in other places, and in much worse shape. My only other injury was a bruised hip. Had it been something metal? That would account for how deep it was, but it was so dirty it looked more like I'd been out on a trail somewhere and fallen into something—maybe a branch—at just the wrong angle. That would also account for the hip. Where had I gone? How had I gotten there and back without remembering?

I swore I would not have anything to drink for a week. This time, I meant it.

The washcloth was dark red. I rinsed it out and started again. I needed something to close this gash. There must be a drugstore in town. The pain drew lines from my ankle all the way up to my left shoulder. I pushed the edges together a little, then plastered the washcloth over the cut and wrapped the whole thing as tight as I could in the face towel. I must have done a pretty good job because it hadn't bled through by the time I got to the car.

At the store in Polson, I checked again and it had only bled through a little. I got some antibacterial spray, some big bandages, some gauze, and little wing-like bandages to hold the edges together. Also aspirin, instant coffee, a loaf of bread, a box of chocolate-covered doughnuts, peanut butter, and some Scotch. I wasn't going cold turkey, not while I had to deal with this leg.

I spent the next hour getting back to the Lone Pine, cleaning the cut again, spraying it, suturing it with the little wing bandages, and getting the big bandages on. Then I took five aspirin and lay down to rest with the leg propped up on a pillow.

I woke up and ate a huge peanut butter sandwich, then poured a drink and lay down again. It still hurt, but a little less. There was some war on TV. I had some doughnuts and a little more Scotch. I looked down at my leg, bandaged and still propped up on the other pillow. No red. Good job. No more blood.

ᚙ

I woke up in the car, parked just off the road. Slumped over the steering wheel, drooling, with a crushing headache, my eyes swollen and crusty. I pushed myself slowly back into the seat and looked around. My pack was on the floor of the passenger seat, along with the plastic bag of groceries and medical supplies. I had no memory of putting them there, or of driving. The vise around my head tightened when I bent down to pick up my pack, but I needed aspirin. I threw them back and shuffled through the rest of the pack. Everything was intact, and there was a receipt from the Lone Pine.

I dragged my throbbing leg out from under the dash. It had bled through. Slowly, I took off all the bandages and cleaned it with water from the bottle in the glove box. It looked awful, and was getting red again. The rustling of the plastic was deafening when I rummaged around in the bag for new dressing. My head, and every muscle in my body, hurt whenever I moved.

I looked around the car for the Scotch. Not in the plastic bag. Not in the backseat. I got out and grubbed around under the seats, but found nothing. I splashed some of the water on my face, got my bearings from the sun and lake, and began winding slowly back toward Whitefish.

Up ahead, a gas station with a diner attached. *Sheila's Place Breakfast All Hours.* I pulled in and was suddenly ravenous. Outside Sheila's door, a rack of newspapers ruffled in the dry wind. I held back the corner of one and looked at the date. Four days since Dr. Cravens. Three days since calling Barb and Abby. Shame surged through me. *The dark* wanted more Scotch, but I knew if I gave it any, I would never get back to Whitefish.

I sat at the sticky tan counter and devoured three eggs, home fries, toast with orange marmalade, bacon, and three cups of coffee. Sheila had loud red hair and flat blue eyes. Her name tag nested in a large purple fake flower that clung to the front of her uniform. When she leaned on the counter, a mass of wrinkles appeared around her cleavage.

"Getcha something a little stronger for your coffee, doll?" A kindred spirit. I hesitated, then thought of Lucia and Abby—and strangely, of Mollie. I hoped she didn't "have her eye on me," as she had promised. I didn't want her to see me like this. If I didn't go back now, I never would.

"No, thanks." Sheila shrugged and wandered off into the kitchen. I laid a twenty-dollar bill on the counter and left quietly. The whole way back to Whitefish, I let the gray static fill my mind. I didn't want to think about where I'd been or where I was going.

Pulling into our driveway, I looked for signs of life in the cabin. It felt like somebody else's house now. I pushed open the door and called out, "Abby?" Silence. Everything had been cleaned and straightened up. The bed was made and there were fresh flowers on the nightstand. Abby's suitcase was at the foot of the bed. She had stayed out here when I didn't show up, and had taken care of the place and the horses. I showered, put on clean clothes, and drove into town.

☙

As I inched in the back door of the kitchen, Lucia spotted me from the dining room. She finished with some customers and bore down on me as I leaned against the big refrigerator, staring up at me with fists on her hips.

"Go home," she said.

"I'm sorry, Lucia, I…"

"You reek of the stuff. Go home. If you can stay sober for two days, come back and we'll talk." She turned on her heel and left. Lena scurried over from the grill and gave me a quick hug.

"I am glad you are back," she said, and smiling sheepishly. "And not just because I want to go home." She looked me up and down. "You don't look so good. You are okay? You are limping?" She led me over to a chair by the freezer and made me sit.

I looked down and saw blood on my jeans. In my hurry to get to work, I'd just slapped a big bandage on without the winged sutures. Lena's eyes followed mine. She rolled up my jeans and put her hands to her mouth, in the air, back to her mouth. She flew off into the dining room. In seconds, she was back with Lucia, who looked at me darkly and made Abby take me over to the clinic.

"I'm so sorry," I said to Abby on the way across town.

"Cat, I have a little boy..."

"I know, I know. I'm sorry." She didn't say any more, but treated me like a stupid child, or an impaired person, like she couldn't tell me how disgusted and frustrated she was because I couldn't take it. I slumped in the passenger seat, feeling guilty and resentful.

At the clinic, they gave me a local anesthetic, cleaned up the wound, took some stitches, and redressed it. Then a tetanus shot, which really hurt.

"What can I do to make this better?" I asked Abby on the way back to the restaurant. She looked at me as if I should know, but didn't.

"I just don't understand, Cat."

"I don't either." I really didn't.

Chapter 16

At home, I poured out all the booze. It seemed a terrible waste—a sin, really—but it had to be done, so I just shut my eyes and did it. I spent the two days of exile watching TV, hobbling around, reading, doing crossword puzzles, and hanging out with the horses.

Tom came home the second night, drunk, and went straight to the kitchen cupboard for his bourbon. When I told him what I'd done, he bellowed, "You *what?*"

"I knew I'd drink it if it was here, so I poured it out." He looked dumbfounded, then enraged.

"Fuck you!" He started toward me, but I didn't move. Just glared back at him and kept quiet. He turned abruptly, slammed out of the cabin, and came back an hour later with three fifths of bourbon and a case of beer. As he was putting away the booze, he yelled over his shoulder, "I talked to Sarah." He worked for Sarah. Of course he talked to her. "Yeah, we had a good long talk. She told me all about her sister. All about you, too."

I felt the flush up to my hairline. I had thought I was safely past all that, that Sarah was keeping quiet about giving Mara's IDs to Mollie for me.

"I get home from the trip and go straight to work. Turns out Lucia had called out there, looking for me to find you. Nobody knew where you were. They got some weird messages from you, said you sounded drunk. So Sarah tells me all about you, and I look like an idiot!" He slammed the cupboard shut and turned to face me. "How come you lied to me!?" I couldn't say anything. "How come you made me look like an idiot?"

"I didn't mean to. I just didn't..."

"Cat's not even your real name, and people from Chicago are after you. Cops, maybe."

"Nobody's after me!"

"Says you."

He pulled on his jacket and walked out, throwing me a nasty look over his shoulder. I went to bed. My meeting with Lucia was the next morning.

ᏣᏍ

"What are you doing?" Lucia asked in a low voice that was almost sad. We sat at a corner table, between the breakfast and lunch crowds. She leaned back in the chair and folded her arms.

"Lucia, I haven't had a drink in..."

"Yeah, yeah. You can bullshit me all you want about your drinking. Just don't show up drunk, don't show up late, or you're fired. Got that?"

"Yes."

"I'm talking about the other thing." Oh God, Sarah didn't... "I tried calling Tom out at Big Sky when you didn't show up, and Sarah acted real funny. Then yesterday, she calls me back. She says that since she told Tom, she's telling me. The whole story. All about her sister, that you ran away from your parents, used Mara's IDs. Now you show up here, someone different again." She paused. I didn't know what to say. She looked not just angry, but hurt. Her eyes shot back and forth between my face and the tablecloth. "I thought you were a nice kid. That's why I helped you. What are you doing?"

"Lucia, I didn't mean to hurt you. I just...when I went to see Sarah, she...I didn't mean any harm." She nodded as if she didn't believe me.

"I should fire you." I just looked down at the table. "But whatever else you are, you're a good cook. I will give you one more chance." Relief washed over me, and gratitude.

"Thank you, Lucia. You won't be sorry. You'll see. I'll work so hard. I won't drink."

She stood up. The meeting was over. "What do we call you now?"

"Let's stick with Cat." She shrugged and headed for the cash register.

I did work hard. Over the next few weeks, I didn't show up drunk or late. I worked extra shifts. I was quiet and humble and nice to everyone. When *the dark* rose up, sometimes it got Scotch, sometimes Spirit, and sometimes I just bullied it down. When I got home from work, I relaxed with a drink—but always got to bed early, so I'd be okay in the morning.

Tom acted like I was some girl he'd picked up off the streets, didn't know very well, and didn't like much. He grunted logistics at me—"Goin' to Alberta next week. Back Sunday," "We're outta bread," "I'll get more wood in tonight"—but when he drank, all the rage came pouring out. When he chopped wood out by the barn, sometimes I thought he would start moving toward the cabin, still swinging the ax, until he leveled it. Twice since I'd come back from Polson, he'd started toward me and I'd been truly afraid. Something held him back, though, some internal braking system. He would stop, slam out, and come back a day or two later. I found myself watching him, making sure I was on the balls of my feet.

I thought about leaving, but didn't. I thought he might kick me out, but he didn't. Sarah's revelations put us on new ground. I think we were both in shock.

It was like living with a stranger, but one with whom I had sex. We would look at one another across the cabin, and it would start. He was no longer Porch Man, but a guy with whom I could have the kind of hot, increasingly rough sex that tore me out of my well-behaved, toned-down, scared-rabbit way of living. *The dark* liked that, too.

ᘐ

"You tell them tonight," Lucia said the morning of our next Monday staff dinner. "All about you. They know something is up, but not what it is. If Sarah talks to me, she might talk to other people. You tell them." I hated it, but Lucia was right. The more I lied, or didn't tell the truth, the worse it would get.

As everybody gathered around the table, Lucia said, "Cat has something to tell you." They looked expectant, but wary. Then shocked as I reeled out the whole story of how I got to Whitefish, starting with running away from Elmhurst. I left out the part about Jeff and the abortion. Even Sarah didn't know that.

Del and Barb looked intrigued, as if I were talking about someone on one of their soap operas. Abby looked shocked and hurt. Lucia looked like a habit-less nun on a grumpy day. Lena looked as if she might cry and wrung my hand.

"You were so sad!" she said. The rest of them stared at her, then at me. "Your parents, they beat you?"

"No." She just wrung my hand harder and actually started to cry.

"So!" Lucia said. "Anybody got any more questions?"

Silence. They glanced around at one another, at Lucia, at me.

"Okay," she said. "Who wants enchiladas?"

Everybody dug in and focused on the delicious food. We had never had such a quiet dinner. I wanted desperately for everything to be okay between Abby and me.

"Hey, Tom's going out of town next week. Wanna hike Iceberg?" I asked. She glanced up, then back at her plate.

"Sorry, we have church stuff." That was it.

"Okay. Maybe some other time." She smiled a little and started talking to Del about her schedule.

Barb brought out the wine and I made a big point of not wanting any. Actually, I didn't want any. I wanted a big beer stein full of neat Scotch, and I sure wasn't going to get it here. Nobody talked to me. Even Lena was oddly silent. I couldn't stand it.

We usually hung out until about ten o'clock, talking and drinking—but by seven thirty, I was through. I finished my enchiladas, gulped down Lucia's flan, and told them I was coming down with a cold and better get home to bed. I'd see them in the morning. They all kind of nodded and murmured goodnight. Lena took my hand and said, "Get better. Be well."

I don't ever recall feeling as lonely as I did driving from the restaurant to the cabin that night. It was cool and crisp out, with bright stars and a full moon. Tom's truck glinted in the moonlight—but the lights in the kitchen were off and something felt out of kilter. I eased in next to the truck and didn't make a lot of noise as I opened the door.

The living room was flooded with candlelight. Two highball glasses and a half bowl of pretzels sat on the table. On the floor in front of the roaring fire, half-covered with the green comforter from our bed, were Tom and Janice Shoddenheimer, the pouty blonde waitress at the Wagon Wheel.

I froze. They turned to me in slow motion. We stared at one another as if we'd all suddenly run into a bear on the trail. Then a wild scramble of limbs and pillows and comforter. Tom spat, "Shit!" What did he think, that I wouldn't come home? I was hours early, but what was he doing, bringing her here? I felt like I was back at Suk Bhavan, walking in on Jeff and Sally. Was this how all men ended relationships? Did they think it was the only way to get rid of me?

The dark took over, furious, spreading out through my whole body. I strode to the closet and pulled out my getaway pack. My hand moved into it and curled around the gun. Pulled it out of the pack. It felt hard and powerful against my palm. I walked back into the living room with the pack slung over one shoulder. Tom was pulling on his jeans. She was on the couch with the comforter clutched up to her chin, her wide eyes darting from him to me.

Slowly, I raised the gun and pointed it at Tom. I wanted to scare him, to show him who had the power.

"Whoa!" he said under his breath, jumping back. Janice screamed and pulled the comforter up over her head. Tom stumbled toward the door where his enormous hunting knife hung in its sheath. Even drunk, he was fast. He grabbed the knife and turned on me, arms spread out to either side, slightly crouched, blocking the door so I couldn't just run for it.

"Gimme the gun," he slurred. "Give it here, or I'll cut you." His voice was low and unsteady. "I will!" He moved in on me slowly, holding the knife at chest level and making little flicks with it in the air as I backed into the kitchen. I took the safety off the gun. His bright green eyes shot hatred. I couldn't look away from them. He didn't think I would shoot, or he wouldn't come at me like that.

His knife cut through the air with a whooshing sound that was more frightening than the sight of it slicing an inch from my arm. If I'd jumped more slowly, if he'd had less bourbon, or if I'd had any Scotch, it would have slashed through to the bone. The thrust threw him off balance, and he staggered against the wall. Janice's screams gave way to sobs and moaning under the comforter. He righted himself, his face red and mouth curled into a snarl, his teeth bared and clenched. He might have been trying to scare me before, but now he meant to do real harm.

I felt the kitchen wall against my back. There was nowhere to jump or run. He curled back to strike again, a ball of rage. The knife glinted in the candlelight.

The dark surged through me, strong and composed, deadly. Calmly, as if I did it every day, I pointed the gun at his right upper arm. Hard muscles rippled under white skin. His biceps and triceps, and all the little muscles around them, stood out in high relief, trembling slightly from the adrenaline. Beautiful. I pulled the trigger. A patch of skin exploded into bloody meat. Flecks of blood spattered on my blue denim shirt. The knife flew through the air and clattered to the kitchen floor. He roared in pain and dropped to the floor, curled into a ball.

I moved around him slowly, backing toward the door, still pointing the gun at him. Janice shrieked again, but stayed buried under the comforter. Blood spread out across his skin. He tried to get up, but stumbled and sank again to the floor. The last thing I saw on his face was raw hatred. I backed out the door and ran to my car. My hands shook. I revved out to the road, spewing gravel in my wake, and floored it south. Away.

I pushed the speedometer up to 90, got some distance, then pulled out onto the back roads. Had I killed him? What was the artery in the upper arm? Could he bleed out from it? What if he were lying on the cabin floor at this moment, dying? Was shooting a felony? Assault? Battery? Attempt to kill? I could go to jail.

I drove all through the night, fast, on two-lane roads lit only by my headlights and the moon. I needed a drink, but I didn't dare do that. I had to get out of Montana. That would make it better. I stopped for gas in small, out-of-the-way places, covering my head with a dark green scarf. By mid-morning, I couldn't stay awake. I followed faint tracks off a side road and backed the car into a derelict barn somewhere in southern Idaho.

CB

I pulled through the dark water, swimming frantically *up*, struggling for a surface I couldn't see…and finally broke through it, rasped in air, and banged my arm on the steering wheel as I jolted awake. I was alive and in my own car. Not in the water. I had slept sitting up, leaning back. My face felt crusty and my mouth was foul. I had a slamming headache. The wheat field outside was golden and rosy, broken only by the long, dark gray shadows of telephone poles stretching out across it.

I saw it first out of the corner of my eye. Very slowly, starting from the right side of the car, a dark brown shape slid across the windshield toward me, sinuous and flexy, twisting over the glass. A snake! Adrenaline shot out from my core into my fingers and hips, thick and achy. The windows were up, thank God. Could it slide down under the car and get in through the bottom? Through the motor, somehow? I reached for the key with shaking fingers. The engine turned over slowly, loudly, shaking the rotting wood of my hideout. I could not take my eyes off the snake, even when I shot out of the barn and floored it across the field to the road.

The horrible thing clung to the window. With what? It was about two feet long, thick and fat. Slowly, as I gathered speed, it got pushed sideways up the windshield and disappeared over the top of the car. In the rearview, I saw it bounce on the road and slither away into the golden field.

I drove for two days through Idaho and Wyoming, in a bubble where I could see out but people couldn't see in, eating at fast food drive-throughs, hiding the car at night and sleeping in it. I drank only once, in Cody, Wyoming, but nothing bad happened.

I needed another car in case Tom and Janice had called the cops, and Wyoming was a great place to buy one without a lot of red tape. Ed, of Ed's Lot, leaned one fist on the fender of an old blue Ford. He slit his eyes at me and took a drag on his Lucky, tossed it away, and adjusted his cap.

"Not much to look at, but it runs good." I said nothing and stared at him from behind my scarf and sunglasses. "Tell you what. I'll take that old red one off your hands, give you this one here for a grand." He heaved his weight off the fender and folded his arms. "Cash."

I pointed the blue car toward the Tetons, just south of Yellowstone, and drove through a sagebrush valley surrounded by granite mountains with rushing streams, alpine lakes, carpets of deep green forests, and the Snake River winding through it all. I opened up to Spirit, let it lift me just enough above *the dark* that I could keep driving. It was like listening to two radio stations at the same time. The only way to get some quiet was to drive faster and faster.

The road ahead was two lanes in rolling hills with big, winding curves. I cruised at 90 miles an hour until a slow-moving station wagon appeared out of nowhere in front of me and I had to slam on the brakes. Two kids, about six and eight, stuck out their tongues and made faces at me through the back window. I honked, pissed off that this little family was in my way, wanting them to pull over so I could go around without having to weave into the left lane with all the blind turns.

They ignored me. I gunned the blue car into the left lane. Just then, a big green-and-silver semi rounded the curve ahead. It bore down on me, horn blaring low and slow. I pressed harder, but the accelerator was already on the floor. He was coming right at me. If I swerved hard back into the right lane, I would hit the station wagon—but that seemed better than a head on. I pulled the wheel right. The wagon had slowed down, giving me just enough room to slide in front of it. The semi's horn was still moaning as he whooshed by in the other direction.

My heart pounded for miles. I gripped the wheel hard and felt sweat rolling down my neck. I was just starting to calm down when a large brown mass rose up on the road just ahead of me. Garbage, or something from the back of a truck? No, a deer! Lying in the road. I screeched onto the right shoulder to avoid it and sat with my forehead on the wheel, my breath heaving in and out.

The smell of burning rubber hung in the air. I looked slowly to my left, into the deer's eyes. They were desperate and peaceful at the same time, straining toward something I couldn't fathom. A bloody red cavity was ripped out of her chest, about eighteen inches across and six inches deep. Her legs splayed at odd angles and were a mass of cuts. Blood splattered away from her over the road in a V shape, like spray paint. It hadn't been long since she had been hit. I couldn't breathe. I either had to get away quickly, or get very close.

One leg was still twitching as I knelt down. Flies and fleas massed over her brown coat and the soft white fur around her muzzle. I waved them away and put my hand on her flank. Her eyes faded, then fixed. There was an intake of breath, a holding, and I felt her life collapse under my hand. Blood still oozed around the cavity, dark red and mushy. I could see the remnants of veins and arteries, and imagined that I saw the shattered heart still trying to pump. Her mouth was open. She looked sweet, almost surprised. Fleas jumped all around. Five minutes ago, she had been alive, vital, wild. Now she was meat. When I took my hand away, its imprint stayed on her coat.

I took the hind legs and pulled her off the road. Her neck and forelegs stretched out, dragging behind the body. She was lighter than I'd expected, or maybe I just had so much adrenaline coursing through me that it seemed that way. The station wagon passed by slowly, the kids' horror-stricken faces plastered to the window. I crept into the ditch and threw up. Went back to the car and took a swig of water. Threw up again.

I sat sideways in the driver's seat with my feet on the ground, leaning my elbows on my knees, and looked up into the soaring mountains, the bright blue sky. I could go home to Chicago and stay with Julie. She would take care of me until *the dark* eased off. I knew that wouldn't happen, though. *The dark* was just getting its teeth into me. It wouldn't let go now. If I went home, I would act even worse—only in a place where life was real. Not this wild, made-up place. I would find a way to hurt Julie, probably burn down the bakery, especially without Spirit around to help. I looked up into the Wyoming mountains, half hoping that Spirit would reach down, scoop me up, and take me somewhere—but it didn't.

I felt lost, ashamed, and very, very tired. Even as I reached out to Spirit with one hand, I felt myself reaching out with the other for *the dark*'s strength. I needed it to keep moving. In the end, I was no better than *the dark* was—and it had a lot more energy than I did.

I took one more look at the deer, now buzzing with flies, and pulled the car door shut. *The dark* slid its arms and hands down into mine, gripped the wheel, and gunned the engine for Reno, the Biggest Little City in the World. I stopped for Scotch in Elko, and flew over the desert through the mesas, hills, and scrub. The sun cut sharp shadows as it got lower in the sky. The air was flinty and crisp. Winnemucca, Mustang, Sparks. Reno.

☘

The next few weeks or months—I don't know which—in Reno were a patchwork of images and sensations, like a movie trailer. Even as it was happening, I could hardly recall events from day to day.

I remember standing in a casino the day I arrived, encased in what seemed like miles of running, flashing lights. Bright reds and blues, oranges and greens, yellows, silver and gold—all racing up and down, over and around, faster and faster. The air was alive with excitement, compulsion, and the electronic trilling of the slots, pieces of melody repeating over and over, competing with one another.

Grounding it all, holding it together, at the center of everything, were the blackjack dealers. I stood for hours, sipping Scotch and watching them. Many were older gals, deeply tanned blondes with lots of makeup and perfect manicures. They stood very straight and wore spiffy outfits—usually black slacks, crisp white shirts, black bow ties, and sometimes dark-colored vests that conveyed authority. They seemed to know stuff I didn't—stuff about evil and power. I felt like I'd be better off if I were one of them.

I imagined them as former seventh-grade math teachers, or smart former showgirls, or blowsy women with aspirations beyond cosmetology school, or retired accountants with sharp, steely eyes who now wore glittering eyeshadow behind their wire-rimmed glasses. They were all business, in command, supremely confident, dealing out terse smiles when necessary to keep the game running quickly and smoothly. The decks rested gently in their hands until the moment they flicked out the first card and set in motion the world that existed within that green semicircle of felt.

One of them, Shirley, taught me to deal and set me up to work private parties. I liked that and was good at it—but didn't do it too often because I couldn't drink when I was dealing. Wasn't supposed to, anyway.

ᚼ

I remember the wall of heat baking my skin and a metallic scent in the air. My mind and body succumbed to the haze and heat. Breakfast 24/7 at the Cal Neva for $3.25. The arched sign with *Biggest Little City in the World* in huge red-and-white letters. The famous spiked silver ball turning slowly, glinting dully in the afternoon sunlight. The Foxy Olive Bar. Juicy's Giant Hamburgers. The Holiday Apartments on Mill with fake red bricks and turquoise trim, where I lived. I stayed in that room for days or weeks without sobering up, then staggered out into the bright sunlight to buy food and booze.

ᚼ

I remember seeing a woman cop in front of the Victory Outreach Church ("Creating a Legacy of Hope"), bending over a homeless guy with no shirt and an enormous belt buckle that dwarfed his frail body.

"Won this in a rodeo!" he yelled at her from the sidewalk where he lay. "A rodeo!" He was a deep red-brown, with no shoes and filthy jeans. His hair looked like it hadn't been washed or combed in months.

"Good for you," the cop said calmly with a tight smile. A few minutes later she and four male cops loaded him gently into a paddy wagon. She was still smiling, all business, just like the blackjack dealers.

ᚼ

I remember sitting on a bench one afternoon, looking up from the street, the people, the gambling, and the glitz into glorious mountains, dark green with shining crystal patches of snow. The sky was wide and clean and blue. Fat white clouds with wispy tails looked like swirling ice cream cones. I felt Spirit for a minute, but then felt ashamed and went to get a drink at the bar on the corner. Later, I stole a candy bar from the mom-and-pop. Saw a cigarette butt on the floor at the laundromat and was so drunk that I picked it up and smoked it.

୧ଓ

I remember getting myself cleaned up, dressed in my black slacks and dark green vest, crisp white shirt and black bow tie to work a private party. I needed money and took some extra "tips" off the top. A fist came toward my face and I woke up on the thin, scratchy carpet at the Golden Phoenix, a security guard under each arm moving me toward the door. I spent that night in jail.

୧ଓ

I remember the alley, at least parts of it, somewhere near the Eldorado. I do not remember how I got there, only waking up. I came from far away, from the blackness, and was still half there when my eyes opened. I thought I might be dead, except that my face, left arm, side, and left ankle pounded with dull, radiating pain.

High above me were loading docks, garbage cans, and narrow slits of sun. Beneath my cheek, scratchy bricks and wet, slimy dirt. Sticky. Very slowly, I moved my right hand to my face. It was smashed, and cut in two places. My side was slashed open. Each time I took a breath, pain shot through my ribs. There was blood all over. I knew my left ankle and left forearm were broken. I was still drunk, and couldn't move. It was like dreaming, being chased but unable to move my legs. I let go into the blackness.

When I woke up again, it was light. Blood was crusted on my face and still oozing from my side. The ankle and arm were swollen and useless. I thought about calling out, but that might bring the cops, or somebody scavenging for money or clothes—or whoever did this. Maybe it had been a customer from the party. I must have been drunk for a long time, because I couldn't think or talk. I didn't know if I wanted anybody to help me.

The light and noise woke me up again. A few tourists staggered by on the sidewalk. I lifted my head up slowly, every bruise and break screaming, and fell back down. If I stayed there, I would die. That seemed okay. Maybe better. A quiet peace settled over me. It was okay to die.

Then, from nowhere, I felt something raw and silver rise up inside me—not *the bright* or *the dark*, but something I hadn't called and didn't know. It was sinuous and ephemeral, strong and clean and gentle. Much stronger than I was, and it was helping me. I pushed myself up on my good elbow and looked around. Started pulling myself slowly over the rough bricks toward the street, scraping open cuts and bumping my bad ankle and arm. I pulled with my right arm, pushed with my right leg. It made everything hurt more, and bleed more—but the more I moved, the more I wanted to be found.

When I got almost to the sidewalk, two couples who had been walking along arm in arm, laughing, saw me. The women screamed. I saw myself through their eyes, bloody and broken, half dead, covered with vomit and filth from the alley. Meat.

Then I heard the siren, and people picked me up off the alley—and that's all I remember.

Chapter 17

I woke up into blinding white, and thought again that I might be dead. Then the pain washed over me, heavy and sluggish, moving out from my ankle, arm, side, and face. I opened my eyes slowly. White flashed off the walls, the ceiling, the sheets. A nurse leaned over me in a bright white uniform, nodded and smiled. She said something, adjusted my IV, and faded away.

When I woke up again, my skin was scratchy and raw. Brown lines ached up my arm and leg. I felt my face with my good hand. It was all bandaged. My tongue was dry and swollen. Muscles screamed when I tried to move them, but I had been cleaned up and somebody seemed to be taking care of me. I ran a shaking hand over the sheet. Rough and thick, but clean.

More people in white poked and prodded, changed dressings, gave me shots and pills that made me sleepy. I felt confused and nervous, but didn't want them to kick me out so didn't complain. Even when I felt bugs crawling over my legs, I kept quiet.

A very large woman in a pink-and-green striped blouse held my hand. She smelled like pungent sweat and had frizzy gray hair. "You'll feel better soon," she said soothingly. "It's just the detox." When the bugs crawled, or when my veins and muscles felt like fire, I went up into the cracks in the ceiling like I used to with my mother. I couldn't think and couldn't have talked if I'd wanted to. Each morning, the shock and pain of waking up. Then realizing I was in the hospital. Then drugs and sleeping until afternoon, hanging on until evening. More drugs, sleeping.

One day, I could talk. Not think too well, but talk. The nurse told me I'd been "out" for a week after the ambulance brought me in. I wanted Scotch in the way animals want water, but was glad I couldn't get any. There was no doubt in my mind that if I ever drank again, I would die.

"That's for sure," said the large woman who had talked about "the detox." Her name was Betty. She came to see me every day, and acted like she knew a whole lot more about me than I did.

My roommate in the hospital was Annie. She must have been 115, and she'd had a stroke. Her son Ronny, a retired casino worker, shuffled in on his walker every day to see her. I would have thought he was a patient, too, but for his snappy red vest and his entourage, which included Annie's middle-aged grandchildren, *their* children, and one infant great-great-grandchild. They all sat or stood in a loop around her bed and told her all about everything: work, school, vacations, who was doing what, and seemingly every thought that had crossed anybody's mind in the twenty-four hours since they had last seen her. She beamed and nodded.

After they left each day, she turned to me and smiled beatifically, then fell into a deep sleep. I smiled back and nodded, as if to confirm the goodness of it all—but I had no idea if things were good.

Annie got the whole family package that I had wanted with Tom. I got *the dark*. It seemed to have disappeared again, though. I didn't know where it was at that point. I hoped that maybe I'd finally outrun it. More likely, it had just gone underground, like it did sometimes. Or else it had me so completely that I wasn't even aware of it.

Betty wanted to know all about me, and I pretended to be more out of it than I actually was. To get her off my back one day, I told her I'd tried to have a family like Annie, but that it hadn't worked out. She said that was probably because I was a drunk. I glared at her and thought, "Yeah, asshole, not to mention that I can't have kids and Tom's a drunk, too, and the Suk baby, and..." I rang my call button and told the nurse I was in a whole lot of pain and needed more morphine.

I don't know why I put up with Betty. I guess because talking to anyone, even her, seemed to bring me back from wherever I'd been— and that had to be good. Plus, I could tell Betty had pull at the hospital in the same way that Mollie had had pull in the old neighborhood. It couldn't hurt to have an ally.

When I could get into a wheelchair, Betty dragged me to some Alcoholics Anonymous meetings in the hospital. They were incredibly boring, but it was better than sitting in bed all day. Plus, the AA people did seem to have a handle on how to stop drinking. I decided to use their tricks and rules until I no longer wanted to drink. It was a lot like the IC purgatory yoyo system, complete with little sayings like "One day at a time" and "Easy does it." I hated their slow, stupid, humble approach. It seemed like everything about AA was just the opposite of how I liked to do things, which kind of explained why I drank so much.

At some point, a nurse brought me a plastic bag containing the clothes I'd been wearing when they picked me up and the key to my apartment. The clothes were all bloody and torn. I threw them away and put the key in the drawer of my nightstand. My pack was back at the apartment. At least, I thought it was. That key felt like the only thing that tethered me to a life outside the floating white world of the hospital.

I didn't want to leave. The routine, the drugs, the gauzy limbo-like pace, Annie and her family, even the boring routine of the AA meetings— it was all comforting and stable. I could not imagine being on the outside and actually wound up staying longer than anybody had anticipated. The wound on my side got infected and wouldn't heal, despite IV antibiotics. Finally my body got stronger and Betty got me into a halfway house that was part of the hospital. I must have been in the hospital and the halfway house about six weeks altogether, because they took my casts off the day I left.

I sat in an exam room flooded with glaring fluorescent light, my arm propped up on a table. A kid in light green scrubs who looked about thirteen came at me with a huge circular saw that I was sure would cut my arm in two, but I had learned just to let people do their jobs. Everything I knew had gotten me exactly where I was. That's what they said in AA, anyway, and it seemed true. When the kid pulled the cast away, my arm was about two-thirds its normal width, wizened and ghostly white, with thick black hairs lying limply all over it. I looked up at him in horror.

"They always look like that." He laughed and handed me a tennis ball. "Squeeze this, exercise it, and you'll be good as new in a week or so." I didn't believe him, but took the tennis ball and put it in the grocery bag that Betty had brought me since I didn't have my pack or a purse.

"Good as new," he repeated. What was that? Good as what? The kid sawed off my leg cast, helped me put on my shoe, and smiled reassuringly. Then he put his hand under my elbow and lifted me up, out of his exam room so he could get to his next patient. An orderly took me to sign papers, and pointed to the large hospital doors. I was free, white, and twenty-one.

Walking out into the sunlight, I felt lost and blinded. My mind moved very slowly, and mostly without words. That was scary. I didn't like being that vulnerable, but there wasn't much I could do about it. The sun burned my eyes and skin. The air felt thin and sharp. I couldn't stay in Reno, that was for sure. I took the bus to my apartment and was astonished to find my car parked out front. Nobody had stolen or stripped it. I went into the apartment for my pack, stuffed in some extra clothes, and walked numbly back to the car. I tried the key, and it turned over.

I drove west over the Sierra Nevada on Route 80 through Truckee, Soda Springs, and Emigrant Gap—and finally stopped at Auburn, California, because I liked the name. I wanted a small, quiet town where I could just be still and rest. Auburn looked like that kind of place. I ate at a diner, looked around, and decided to stay. I got a tiny studio apartment with a futon and, in a few weeks, a job cooking in a place much like Lucia's. For two years, I went to work, to AA meetings, then home. Rested and healed. Laid low, wrote in a journal, hiked and camped in the foothills. I went numb, and cauterized big sections of my brain and heart.

I didn't pay much attention to God in those years. AA insisted that we have a "higher power," so I dusted off the old Immaculate Conception God and used him. They liked that, and it made as much sense as anything.

ಅ

When I felt stronger, I got restless and moved to San Francisco. I wanted to live in a bigger, more exciting place, and by the ocean. I was tired of cooking, so I got a job as an assistant office manager at a real estate firm. I'd never done anything like that, but I knew how to follow instructions. The Office Procedures document was just like a recipe. My boss, Deborah, had been there since the Paleolithic and ran the place with an iron hand. All the agents were terrified of her. I wasn't, and I think that's why she liked me.

Everybody in the office had taken Werner Erhard's human potential seminar, the four-day "est training." They insisted I come with them to a "guest seminar" at the Masonic Auditorium one night after work. We sat up front, all seven of us. The rest of them kept clutching one another's hands and stealing glances at me, as if I were an innocent about to be initiated into something wonderful. It reminded me of the night Mollie, Julie, and Loreen had stood outside our bathroom drinking champagne, shouting instructions, and urging me on as I wrestled with my first Tampax. All 3,000 people at the Masonic seemed to be engrossed in deep, soul-level conversations and beamed at one another for no reason that I could see, which was both creepy and intriguing.

Suddenly the lights dimmed to black, then flared up and flooded the auditorium. The buzz exploded into wild applause and people leapt to their feet. Tiny spotlights danced and circled around the audience, finally converging on the stage and a slim, good-looking man in his forties with dark hair and hazel eyes, wearing a navy sport coat and light blue shirt open at the collar. Werner Erhard himself! He perched casually on a barstool as one might in one's own kitchen. The crowd roared! He rose slowly to his feet and waved, as if he'd simply been sitting there contemplating Truth and was surprised by the presence of all these people and their frantic ovation.

I have no recollection of what he said, but the purpose of the evening became clear at the break. It was a guerrilla recruiting event. "Assistants" carrying stacks of cards and pens prowled through the crowd, signing people up for the four-day course. A woman with curly red hair, freckles, and an urgent smile cornered me and asked if I would be "willing to change my life forever." I was so stunned, and so intrigued by all the smiling and enthusiasm, that I signed up. That was the start of my new addiction, personal growth and human potential seminars.

I wasn't quite sure what happened at est—still am not—but I was attracted to those people. I found out that they smiled because they had hope. For a better world, for being better people, for something. Plus, they were a gang. They were learning to be better people and trying to save the world *together*. Hanging out with them was more fun than just going back and forth between the real estate office and my apartment, healthier than drinking, and much, much more interesting than AA.

Everybody who took est back in the 1970s wanted to be Werner Erhard, and about half of them went out and started their own human potential seminar businesses. We seminar aficionados called it the California Consciousness Circuit. Self-proclaimed gurus popped up on every street corner, hawking spiritual baubles with veiled promises of better sex or more money. (The promises had to be veiled because nobody would admit to wanting more sex or more money. Life on the Circuit was all about "making a contribution" and "evolving the species.")

I wasn't real interested in sex—I was good at throwing internal switches, and that seemed like a good one to turn off—and I had seen early on that with a few more years in real estate under my belt, I wouldn't have to worry about money. I took those workshops for other reasons. First, to hang out with the hopeful people. Second, on the off chance that, rooting around beneath the surface of my mind and heart, I might find out what was wrong with me and maybe even discover a way to kill *the dark* when it showed up again—as I knew it would.

To those ends, I did most of what was out there. Shiatsu, rolfing, acupuncture, Fendenkrais, and massages of all kinds. Inner child work, hypnotherapy, and Sun Process for a better disposition. Psychic, tarot, and aura readings. Marathon psychodrama, vision quests, and "clarity" intensives. Long, long days and weeks of meditation. Astral travel, mining the subconscious for "barriers" to success, hot tubs at Esalen in Big Sur, women's circles in the Sonoma woods under a full moon. Most of the teachers and gurus had something I thought or hoped might make me better—a new slant on life, a generosity of spirit that I lacked, sometimes just a nice smile.

Nobody knew much about *the dark*. Or if they did, they weren't talking. On those rare occasions when I brought it up, they just stared at me skeptically for a minute, then turned the discussion to safer ground. Still, I began piecing together bits of information about *the dark*, just as I had pieced together bits of information about life when I first lived with Mollie.

People on the Consciousness Circuit talked a lot about our "shadow," the part of ourselves that gossiped, smoked, hated people we were supposed to like, and did other less than perfect things. The "shadow" seemed like a rather benign, kiddy version of *the dark*. Since many of the post-Werner gurus fancied themselves so wise that, in their own minds, they were actually quasi-therapists, I also stumbled across a lot of psychological information. Eventually, I came to see that *the dark* wasn't a black snake or a creepy, amorphous ball of evil in my gut. It was shame from when Mother had sex with me, being seen as evil for all those years that I lived with her, and anger about just about everything. All of that made for more bad behavior and shame, which snowballed over and over on top of itself to produce what I called *the dark*. It had all started in the closet in Chicago, but I had brought it with me wherever I went—to Immaculate Conception, to Jeff, to Tom, and to Reno. In saner moments, I remembered what *the dark* was and how it came to be. When it was actually in my face, as it often was in dreams, I completely forgot about that process and just cowered in terror.

Over nearly twenty years on the Consciousness Circuit and in AA, I worked through a lot of "baggage." I screamed at Mother and beat a big red pillow with a large rubber bat in psychodrama marathons. I "took responsibility" for my part in the Suk debacle. (I had been needy and, however much of a jerk he may have been, I had driven him to a lot of what he did.) I "owned" my side of the Tom debacle. (However much of a jerk *he* may have been, I had been, as Betty pointed out in the hospital, a drunk. Worse, a drunk with a hidden agenda—since I had never actually clued him in on what he was doing in my life or let him vote about whether or not he wanted to be Porch Man.)

When I looked back on my time in Montana, and even in Chicago, from an older and more sober perspective, my jaw dropped. I could not believe I had been as crazy as I was and not even known it.

È

In those years after moving to San Francisco, I also got back on my feet financially. My boss, Deborah, took me under her wing. I got my real estate license and discovered I was as good at selling million-dollar homes as I had been at selling pastries in the bakery. For the real estate background check, I went back to my real name, for which I could get a legitimate birth certificate with nothing potentially illegal attached to it. I became a player in the real estate boom, which was a good thing because all those seminars were *expensive*.

However, I had no idea what "expensive" meant until I started "soul retrieval therapy" with Joy Lupa. Joy was a real, licensed therapist—but she had also studied with a Native American shaman who was into retrieving the souls of people who had gone way, way off track. People like me. In addition, she belonged to a Women Who Run with Wolves support group for girl therapists, and they were always coming up with harebrained schemes to try out on their patients. One was the "Return Ticket," in which you physically retraced your steps through the most awful moments in your life and healed them. It partnered nicely with her soul retrieval business.

"You need this Return Ticket," Joy croaked, waving her bony hand in the air and bringing it to rest on maps of *The Western States* and *Iowa, Illinois, and Indiana* that lay spread out on the little therapy table between us. She had "suggested" that I order them up from AAA and bring them to our session.

Joy weighed about ninety-seven pounds and wore the huge tortoiseshell glasses favored by book editors in the 1970s. Her office dripped with Tibetan throw fabrics. Deep blues, bright reds, orangey golds. You couldn't see the surface of her desk for all the deep-green and purple candles, the incense holders and Shiva statues. Brightly colored prayer flags marched across one wall. It felt like we were in Kathmandu—or Suk Bhavan.

"A backward journey that retraces your life, recontextualizes everything. Helps you see the big picture," she explained.

"For $150 an hour, Joy, I'd like to fix it here."

She slumped down in her chair, almost disappearing into her big black turtleneck.

"You need to unwind this thing," she said darkly.

"But then I'll be unwound."

"Yes."

When we came to that impasse, as we always did, I would take a break from soul retrieval therapy for a year or two.

⋆

Twenty years after Reno, I had enough money, enough friends, enough health, enough sobriety. Life was okay. Between real estate and the Consciousness Circuit, I was busy—but not particularly engaged.

I went to the office, showed people homes, and closed deals. I went out to trendy restaurants with friends and talked about our other friends, about movies, about the latest Consciousness Circuit offerings. I played tennis and surfed, took a vacation in Bali, even got an M.A. in Economics at the University of San Francisco. I went back to the office, did more seminars, went to the *new* trendy restaurant.

It occurred to me one morning, having coffee on the deck of my condo overlooking the Pacific Ocean, that my life was that of a highly intelligent, well-adapted animal. The differences between my life and the life of a cow were minimal. Instead of going out to the pasture every morning, I went to the real estate office. I could read magazines and do math, which cows could not. I made a living and took care of myself, which most cows did not. I was a lot smarter than a cow, but we both operated pretty much on the surface of things.

For some reason, realizing that I was just going through the motions of life made me very angry.

Plus, I had begun to feel a slow, poisonous movement inside me. *The dark* was waking up again and starting to hunt. Its heavy breath rasped in the back of my mind as it inched closer to the surface...the night a cop stopped me for going 103 over the back roads of Sonoma County in my new red Mercedes convertible...the week I surfed the North Shore of Oahu, which no woman my age, who had learned to surf as an adult, had any business doing...the day I picked a fight with a client and blew a two-million-dollar million deal.

That was the worst. The minute he began talking about backing out of the deal—"Ya know, I talked to the wife and I'm having some second thoughts"—*the dark*'s ragged energy surged up. We were standing next to my desk. In my mind, I leapt across the space between us and wrapped my hands around his throat. I knew the best strategy was to hear him out, feel his pain, let him get the grumpiness out of his system, and then work him back around to his original enthusiasm. I'd done it a million times—but this time, the edginess skidded quickly into red rage. I could not believe he had led me down the garden path and was making a fool of me.

"Don't give me that shit!" I said in a voice that carried throughout the office. He jumped back, then took a step toward me.

"Who the fuck do you think you are?" he shouted. All I could see was the left lapel of his blue jacket. *The dark* shot out through my hands, and I shoved him. It felt like I was back in the cabin with Tom. For a second, he looked like he might come at me. Instead, he grabbed his briefcase and yelled over his shoulder as he strode out, "You're a crazy bitch, you know that?"

I looked around to see sixteen horrified stares. Everybody returned quickly to their work, and nobody spoke to me. I huffed out of the office, went home, put on my wet suit, and went surfing at Ocean Beach so I wouldn't drink.

I knew *the dark* could smell my fear. To calm and center myself in the weeks following the "crazy bitch" incident, I made lists of all the things that were good about my life, things that made me no longer susceptible to *the dark*: my condo and bank account, friends, all the good work and healing I'd done on the Consciousness Circuit. It didn't work. No matter how many lists I made, I could feel that dark head slithering closer and closer to the surface. It didn't matter that I was sober, that I had twenty years of "looking at my stuff" and beating big red pillows with rubber bats to "Get it out! Get it out!" It didn't matter that I knew my enneagram and Meyers-Briggs types, that I had years of black belt therapy with Joy. *The dark* was stronger.

Even as *the dark* was skulking around the edges of my soul, I started having vague, objectless yearnings for the sacred. The two seemed to come together. Not the Catholic God, although I would find myself sitting in the back of old St. Dominic's church, staring into the banks of shimmering red votive lights. Not the Eastern mystics, although I would find myself driving far out of my way to go by Spirit Rock, the beautiful Buddhist retreat in Marin County. Not even Spirit, although I would find myself stopped dead in my tracks amid the redwoods in Muir Woods, staring up into the tops of the trees and beyond them to the sparkling, limitless sky.

One night I stood out on my deck at dusk, watching the dark orange sun sink into a teal ocean, throwing salmon pink and burnished gold streaks up into the pale blue sky. What to do? *The dark* had beaten me in Reno, and it was coming for me again. It would kill me this time—and I sensed that whatever came after that kind of death would not be good.

The two things I'd tried against it, booze and gods, hadn't worked. Booze was out of the question; it only made *the dark* stronger, and drinking again would surely kill me. The gods were all fine when everything was going well, when the sun was out and life was shiny— but they turned frivolous, inept, or chicken when asked to go up against *the dark*. The Immaculate Conception Graybeard turned mean and vengeful. I AM Oneness just hung quivering in the air—so transported, detached, and self-absorbed that it was useless if you wanted to get anything *done*. Besides, my perception of it had probably had a lot to do with Jeff's pecs. In any case, it had horrible judgment for choosing him as its earthly rep. Spirit wafted sublimely around the Rocky Mountain summits, but was not available in urban environments—and it sure hadn't been much help on the runaway road from Montana to Reno.

The ocean turned dark blue. It got cold on the deck, but I didn't go inside. Something out over the water was calling to me as I leaned against the railing, bundled in fleece against the chill and salty wind, listening to the surf and watching the fat bright moon play in the dark waves. Something like what I had called *the bright* was still out there—and I still wanted it.

It wasn't exactly a god, but it was sacred. I didn't have words for it. It was the nameless impulse that had pulled me up off the mattress in my closet and away from Mother when I was six. It was the raw silver energy that had dragged me out of the Reno alley when I wasn't even sure I wanted to live. It was powerful beyond what I could fathom or control. It had been kind to me when I could not help myself. It was content to stand offstage, without praise or worship—but when nothing else worked and I had no strength left, it was there. When I tried to wrap my mind around what it was, I got embarrassed and had to think about something else. If I dwelled on what it had done for me, or how it seemed to care for me, I started to cry.

Opening the divine can of worms was dangerous. It would bring *the dark* to the surface for sure and make it even wilder—but *the dark* was coming for me anyway, and I was no longer willing to live like a cow. That raw, sacred silver energy was all I wanted in life. Anything less was "small potatoes," as Sister Mary Celeste had said. If I wound up living without it, then I might as well have stayed in Elmhurst. Also, it was the one thing that had proven stronger than *the dark*.

Suddenly, I knew exactly what to do, just as I had the day I ran away from Elmhurst. Then, the message had been: *Run!* Now, the answer was: *Turn around.* I had to retrace my steps to Chicago. I had to turn and face *the dark* in the place it had begun—my mother. If I could stand in front of her without fear or shame or anger, then I would have beaten *the dark* or at least found a way to live with it. That would make me good, whole, and healed. I knew I couldn't stand before Mother and *the dark* without the raw silver energy, so I would have to find that somewhere along the way as well. Either I would find it, or *the dark* would get me. Either way, the struggle would be over.

The words floated up: *Change or die.* It was the rule I had first learned in *Our Oceans* when I was ten, and one of the few things I knew to be true about life. I had been standing out at the end of the high dive for twenty years, ever since coming to San Francisco—not willing to jump, but not willing to climb back down the ladder in defeat.

Time to jump. I'd find out soon enough whether or not there was any water in the pool.

Chapter 18

At nine the next morning, I sat on the off-white sofa in my condo, staring out at the ocean again, sipping rich black coffee. Packed and ready for Reno, my first stop. Well, not exactly ready—but willing, and maybe able. Running away from Elmhurst at ten was a snap compared to this. It felt like I was playing Russian roulette, with *the dark* loaded into five chambers and the raw silver energy into one.

In the light of day, the trip seemed hopeless, ridiculous. I was probably too broken to defeat *the dark*—too "ruined," like Black Beauty. Going after the divine again was like hitting on a 16 in blackjack. Maybe a 15, or even a 14—but it was my only shot. I had to put my money there and just keep playing until I either won or ran out of chips, and *the dark* hauled me off into the night.

Joy was delighted when I called for last-minute pointers. (I told her I was doing a Return Ticket, which I kind of was.) Instead of practical advice, she gushed a lot of unsolicited information like, "You were never really chasing God, darling, just running from yourself. Running so fast you forgot why you even left home, and…"

"Yeah, but what should I *do*?"

"Just go to the places where significant events happened. Feel the feelings. Release the shame. Ask the Goddess's intercession. Open your heart to the universal flow. Take a notebook…"

As she spoke, I fingered the little box of éclairs I'd made for the trip, sorely tempted to pop one in my mouth so that her words might sound a little more practical and reasonable, a little less crackpot and wolfy.

"Okay, Joy. Thanks. See ya."

"Call me when…"

I hung up, unable to take any more, and checked my old Montana pack one last time. My hand brushed against the gun. It struck me that taking a gun to Reno was a really bad idea. I pulled it out and laid it on the kitchen counter. That didn't seem right, either. It was stupid, but the gun made me feel reckless and brave, which was a lot better than feeling scared and foolish. I shoved it back into a deep inner pocket, slung the pack over my shoulder, grabbed the éclairs, and locked the door behind me.

Flying across the Bay Bridge with the top down and sea air whipping all around me, I felt like the Buddha with a mouth full of éclair. I let the flavors ooze together and slide over my tongue—rich custard filling melting into fluffy pastry and double dark chocolate icing. It felt great to be on the road, out of Dodge, with the wind flying through my hair. Free and easy. Five hours to Reno. That was .8 éclairs per hour, but I reached for another as soon as I came off the bridge in Berkeley.

Two hours later, I sped past Auburn but didn't stop. All the éclairs were gone, and I was only about halfway to Reno. I revved up into the Sierra Nevada, then dropped down and roared east on Route 80 along the Truckee River and the old railroad tracks. Dust swirled around the tiny casino shacks tucked in among the dry tan mesas and buff desert.

Finally, Reno rose on the horizon. I hadn't been there since the day I left the hospital, raw and weak. The skyline was bigger and thicker than I remembered, with oddly angled mega-casinos rising up all flashy and surreal against the wide blue sky and clean white clouds. The Silver Legacy's giant silver sphere hunkered solidly in the lap of it all.

So there I was in Reno, different but the same. Older, wiser, richer, sober, and more focused—but still carrying *the dark* in a place I couldn't look.

I pulled off at Exit 13 and wound through town toward the Eldorado. Glitzy new casinos towered over the Old Reno derelicts that squatted beside them, their marquees broken and rusty, chain-link fences thrown up around them, doors and windows boarded up. As I passed the Golden Phoenix, where I had passed out on the floor, a putrid taste rose in my mouth. The muscles in my neck and back felt like rocks.

I parked, slid the gun in with the spare tire, and walked through what felt like miles of slots and tables toward the Eldorado's reception desk. It was as if I had never left. The streaming electronic noises, all playing on top of one another. The dealers with their commanding presence and crisp white shirts. The naked craving in the air—for more chips, more free drinks, more of something, anything. I wanted a drink for the first time in years, so I walked more quickly, got a Diet Coke, and went upstairs.

The room was okay—small, dark, and bare. I drew the blinds against the afternoon sun. I wanted three large bags of potato chips, a six-pack of something, and hour after hour of mindless television—but the sooner I started, the sooner I would get whatever I was supposed to get in the Biggest Little City in the World. Joy said just walk around, see what comes up. I couldn't imagine a god of any consequence, let alone the raw silver energy, popping out from behind a slot machine or up from under a blackjack table—but I sensed it would be a good idea to look Reno in the eye.

I walked down Wells Street past tattoo parlors, wedding chapels, pawnbrokers, and a run-down motel with rooms for $29 and plastic sheeting covering a third of the facade. Images flashed up and receded in fits and starts, snatches of scenes here and there. Drinking in a corner bar. It could have been the one I was passing right then, or a hundred others. The Holiday Apartments, where my car sat for six weeks while I was in the hospital.

Suddenly, I was in front of the Triangle Club, the AA meeting place—a squat little red brick building with cement trim. It looked vaguely like a shrunken, flattened version of Immaculate Conception Grammar School. Somebody had rolled me out of a car there one night, and I was so drunk that I had gone in. The AA people had grabbed me, made me go into a meeting, and only let me out when I started screaming at the top of my lungs. I felt nauseous, just thinking about it.

How did I deal blackjack, that drunk all the time? Poorly, I guess. That was probably how I got into the alley where I almost died.

Before I realized where I was going, I was staring into it. The alley off Second between Sierra and Virginia. It was dark and filthy, studded with loading platforms, littered with garbage cans, so narrow that the sun could barely squeeze in. Phantom pain seeped into my arm and ankle, my ribs and face. I walked in, my heart pounding, chilled as I moved from bright sunlight into shadow that closed in on all sides. I went all the way to the end of the alley, then turned back toward the street. I picked a spot on the ground and imagined myself lying there, slipping in and out of consciousness, wincing as the pain surged through me, then falling motionless again.

I dropped to my haunches. It felt like I was both watching a movie, and in it. The pain was only partly physical, a low ache that gripped my bones and muscles, oozed into my cells and held them tight. My head pounded as I watched that broken woman lie twisted and bleeding. Shame and guilt washed over me in waves until I was sobbing. I crouched there and let it take me over, crying and sobbing, clutching my arms around my knees. I lost track of why I was crying and slid down into a dark well of tears without knowing what they were about or how long they had been there.

At some point, I found myself standing up and not sobbing anymore. I felt blank inside. Empty, and oddly light. Still shocked by that person in the alley, but also kind of astonished that she had survived. I thought about the raw silver energy—but it was only a thought, not a presence there with me in the alley. I didn't know what else to do, so I swatted the dirt from my jeans and walked back to the Eldorado.

In the silence of the small dark room, I felt strangely peaceful. I stood at the window and watched running lights dance around the facades of casinos across the street—bright oranges and blues, reds, silver, greens and yellows, all sweeping around the buildings faster than my eyes could follow, chasing one another.

Above it all, hanging quiet and still in the purple-black sky, a full butter moon.

∾

At sunrise, I sped east on Route 80 toward Sparks, Mustang, Winnemucca, and Elko. The desert was rolling hills, mesas, and gentle passes covered with khaki and dark-olive sagebrush. I wanted to make Polson, at the foot of Flathead Lake, by nightfall. It was a long drive, but I had a fast car.

What did all that sobbing in the alley mean? Was I just supposed to wallow in the misery, like Joy and her wolfy pals suggested? I didn't think so, but it did take the edge off *the dark* to face it down like that. Or at least, face down the memory of it. I knew it must be in the car with me as I pushed toward Montana—quiet, coiled, and waiting to strike—but I couldn't feel it. That was scary.

I hadn't been anywhere near Montana since the night I'd shot Tom and run. Energy curled up my spine as I headed north from Missoula on Route 93 toward Flathead Lake and Polson. Soon I started passing rustic wooden signs for the Lone Pine Motel, my base camp for the four-day bender.

The Lone Pine was new and improved, like me. Neat rows of small motel rooms, all spiffed up with fresh white paint and dark green trim, looking as prosperous and resort-like as the rest of Polson had become. Peering through the trees toward Flathead Lake, I saw a little pier and wondered if it might be the one where I'd passed out all night. I walked down the tree-lined path to the water, but discovered only a small beach and a different pier. The late fall breeze whipped up tiny whitecaps on the lake. Pretty. Dark green mountains rose up around the sparkling blue water. I felt a bit of Spirit whistling around in the pines, but no earthshaking memories. I had talked about the bender in AA, so it had lost a lot of its charge. The Lone Pine offered no big catharsis. I felt like a tourist at a lakeside motel, exactly what I was.

I took a room, dumped my pack on the bed, and sat at the little table overlooking the lake. It could have been the room I'd stayed in twenty years earlier, except it seemed a lot cleaner. Red-and-brown plaid bedspread, table and chair, TV, tiny bathroom. I remembered waking up that first morning of the bender and finding the wooden cutout of a pine tree with the key attached, and the sinking feeling that I'd crossed some line to wake up in a place so far from home, with no idea how I'd gotten there. Knowing that I must have talked to someone and given them money in order to get that key, and yet my last memory being of Kalispell, an hour away, and scraping the paint off those kids' truck. It was chilling to think that the person who did that had been living inside me all these years. Was still living there.

I unwrapped the tuna sandwich I'd picked up in town and watched the sun go down. Where was *the dark* hiding? I had half expected it to come clawing out of me the minute I set out across the Bay Bridge, making me speed and drink and leave people for dead. Instead, it seemed to have slunk away somewhere. Maybe I could outrun it after all, if I just kept moving. Right! I grabbed my notebook and wrote across the first page: *What is the raw sacred silver energy*? I pulled open a bag of Lay's Potato Chips—something I never, ever permitted myself at home— and rummaged around for a really curly one, maybe even a double chip. I picked up my pen, put it down again, and took another bite of tuna.

What had I liked about all those gods? Was the raw silver energy just another one of them, one that hadn't failed yet? What did *the bright* of the kite, the Immaculate Conception purgatory yoyo God, Suk Baba and eight-armed Shiva's I AM Oneness, and Spirit of the mountains have in common? I stared out the window. Fishermen docked their boats and trudged up from the lake with their catches. Lights flickered on in other Lone Pine units.

Powerful, I wrote. *Makes me high. Mysterious. Loving? Not the yoyo God. He could be a prick. I AM Oneness wasn't mean, but it was inscrutable and very Indian. Sparkly. Luminous. Glow-y. Mostly, relieve the pain and make me high.*

Except for "powerful," a quality that none of these gods had seen fit to share with me, most of what I'd just written could be had by dropping acid. I snapped the notebook shut. Did I really just want to get loaded? Suddenly, I recalled playing Mr. Potato Head with my babysitter in Chicago, Mrs. Strohm. You took a potato and stuck in little plastic ears, eyes, and mouth to create different faces. I was reduced to that, when it came to the divine. I would try this again later.

Brushing my teeth before turning in, I remembered the last time I had been in a bathroom like this one—maybe this very one—collapsed on the floor and trying to suture a dangerous, gory wound on my leg. The woman in the mirror today was sober, but not particularly healed. Or open. Or at peace. She looked a whole lot better than the one on the floor with the gaping wound, but that was just on the surface. Inside, she wasn't much different. She just hid it better. What the hell was I thinking, going back to Chicago and even contemplating seeing my mother? What was I doing outside San Francisco? What if I had killed Tom? Who did I think I was, even to think about the divine? I was just as crazy as I'd always thought I was, and maybe just as evil.

I wondered if the liquor store a few miles back was still open. To make sure I didn't leave the room, I took two Ambien and slept for nine hours.

ଔ

The sun slivered in and woke me up. I made coffee, sat down at the table with some trail mix, and reread what I'd written over my tuna sandwich and potato chips dinner. Hopeless!

Plus, I had a headache from the Ambien. Only then did I realize that I'd been visited by *the dark* the night before, whispering in my ear as I brushed my teeth. It was a quieter, more subtle version, one that spoke to me where I was today. I had not thought seriously about a drink in at least fifteen years, yet there it was. So now I was on the road, headed toward Mother, with the search for the raw silver energy going nowhere and *the dark* slinking around in disguise.

I thought about hightailing it back to San Francisco, but I already knew what was waiting back there. I stashed away my Mr. Potato Head scribbling and hit the road for Kalispell.

Main Street looked much as it had twenty years earlier, except for the gentrified tourist shops and coffeehouses that fanned out into tree-lined streets, quaint little houses, and beautiful gardens with terra-cotta bunnies, birdbaths, American flags, gazebos and, literally, white picket fences. Farther out, the houses got older and more precarious. The yards turned into dirt lots surrounded by chain-link fences, with worn plastic push-cars and baseball bats strewn around and barking dogs straining against chains that bound them to steel posts.

That was the kind of neighborhood where I had keyed the truck, then made my getaway to the bender in Polson. I had been a ball of fury that night, angry at Dr. Cravens for ruining my last shot at being regular, angry at the kids in the truck for taunting me, angry at myself for having had the abortion that made it so I couldn't have kids and find peace. Most of all, angry at God for not giving me what I wanted, even when I begged.

I drove to Dr. Cravens' office, but found only a low-slung tan brick building housing an insurance agency. I parked in front and leaned my temple on the steering wheel, staring at it. Dr. Cravens was probably dead, but he had never been the problem. He had just been a nice old man who gave me the science of what I'd done.

I pulled away from the curb and headed for St. Matthew's, where I had prayed so hard to the amalgam god I'd cobbled together that day. The god who had just glanced at me, looked away, and kept filing his nails. The church was much smaller than I remembered. I walked up the stone stairs and pushed open the wood door. Rose and violet fabrics hung from the walls and over the altar. The smell of frankincense was heavy in the air, and the late afternoon sun pushed colors through the stained glass windows—gold, peacock, indigo, jade. The hush was broken only by muffled footsteps on the hardwood floors. It was a Saturday afternoon and people were milling around, doing the Vatican II version of Confession. They called it Reconciliation. Confession lite.

I sat way over to the side, in the back of the church, breathing in the incense, the calm, the feeling of peace and the sacred. This mean old ledger-wielding God would never work for me and I would never make it in his system, but it felt good to be enveloped in the shadows and the quiet, the incense and candles. Tendrils of guilt and remorse played around the edges of that cocoon, but for a moment I let it warm and hold me.

I wondered what might have happened if the amalgam god, the Great and Powerful Goz to whom I had prayed that afternoon, had answered my prayer and given Tom and me a baby. For the first time, I saw clearly that *the dark* would have gotten the baby, too. Maybe through me. I might have killed it, or done something worse. I might have done to it what Mother did to me.

I said a prayer of thanks to Goz, breathed one last frankincense breath, and walked slowly back to the car.

CB

Whitefish was just up the road. I remembered driving into town that first time over this same road, high on my first encounter with Spirit, the god of the mountains and wild rivers and windblown vastness of the West. Full of anticipation and absolutely certain that I would be happy there.

The main drags, Central and Spokane Avenues, hadn't changed much. Whitefish still had an Old West feel, with roofs that overhung the sidewalks, small town bars and restaurants. Big Mountain had become a huge ski attraction that drew lots of tourists, but the fancy lodges were all up closer to the action, outside town.

The old brick hotel where I had stayed those first few nights was still there, and so was the Bar None. I poked my head in. It looked exactly the same. Low and dark, lit with Christmas lights, neon orange and blue beer ads, people scattered along the bar and at tables lining the long brick wall all the way back to the kitchen. Music, laughing, yelling, the occasional pounding on a table. It might have been twenty years ago. I smiled and let the door fall shut.

The highway out to Sarah's place was flanked by low mountains, prairie, small spreads—and now by fast food places, stands selling huckleberry products and other tourist items, and antique shops. Sarah's place still looked like a dude ranch from the road, but the huge wooden *Big Sky Ranch* sign was gone. In its place was a large white sign with contemporary lettering and a brand.

Triple T Guest Ranch

TTT

Did Sarah die? Go out of business because she lost her temper with complete strangers who only meant well? I parked right where I had twenty years earlier, to the side of the large porch that surrounded the big house, and remembered how excited I had been to meet people who might become my family and connect me forever with Mollie.

The little lobby had been repainted a cheery peach color, and there was a new, polished oak reception counter. Behind it stood a woman who could have been Dale Evans, Queen of the West—wife of Roy Rogers, King of the Cowboys. She was about thirty, with Dale's plucky demeanor, sausage curls, and pressed cowgirl outfit. She looked up and smiled brightly.

"Hi there. I'm Martha Mobley. Welcome to the Triple T," she said earnestly with an odd accent that was part Southern, part cowboy. She reached her hand over the counter. White buckskin fringe danced on her sleeves and across the bodice of her bright blue cowgirl blouse. I took the hand.

"Cat Callahan." No reaction. I hadn't used that name in twenty years, but I wanted to see if there were stories. At least I hadn't become a dark legend. "Uh, does Sarah Spencer still run the ranch?" I smiled as if Sarah were a long-lost relative who would be thrilled to see me. This got Martha's attention. She leaned forward conspiratorially on the counter, as if we had known one another all our lives and were accustomed to sharing gossip.

"Why no, Cat. When Cliff passed on about ten years ago, she moved down to Pocatello to be near her grandchildren. My folks bought the place from her. They're retired now, and I'm in charge. Are you related?" Now we were clearly in South Georgia.

"Distantly. I came here when I was very young. Would you mind if I took a look around, just a little, for old time's sake?" I found myself mirroring her accent and manner, which was unpleasant to observe but did produce a good result.

"Oh please!" Martha reared back and threw up her hands, making the buckskin fringe shimmy again. "Please, make yourself to home!"

"Oh, thank you so much. Appreciate it. All sorts of memories..." I smiled and backed into the big dining room, giving her a little wave as I rounded the corner. The same huge wood table where I served that first meat loaf lunch. I ran my hand along its rough edge. I had been so nervous that day. Everything seemed smaller now. I stepped into the kitchen where Sarah told me never to show my face at the ranch again. It had been renovated. New appliances, new counters, everything spanking clean.

I closed my eyes and pulled back through time to that afternoon, letting all of that hope, confusion, anger, and frustration wash over me again. I felt the humiliation of being called a fake, the anger at her put-downs of Mollie, the shame of not being wanted by someone I wanted so desperately to embrace me. Strangely, it wasn't nearly as bad as the story I had been telling myself for decades about Sarah—the horrible, cruel attack that had completely decimated me. It was more like a client not being able to get a loan approved. Not terrific, but definitely something I could handle. Odd. Maybe I was making it *all* up. Maybe things with Mother hadn't been as bad as I'd thought they were, either, and I was just crazy.

Sarah's old office, where I had stared hungrily at all the family pictures, was just across the hall. All the framed photos were gone. The little room was lined with gray metal file cabinets, computers, printers, and steel supply cabinets—as if the old office had never existed.

I decided make the Triple T my staging area for Whitefish. If I needed information, Martha probably either had it or could get it. I took a cozy room upstairs in the big house with a rocking chair, pine armoire, dark red quilt, calico scatter pillows, and an extra blanket on the bed.

I sat in the rocking chair and watched the sun fade on the mountains, let myself imagine that this room would have been mine if things had gone differently with Sarah. I might have become like her daughter, one of the Spencers of Big Sky. Cat, out at Big Sky, Sarah's girl. Nestled at the core of a family, important to the ranch, someone with people and a place of her own, who never questioned where she belonged, or what or who she loved. I imagined a photo of me at forty in that life, turning from saddling a horse to grin into the camera, a grown-up version of the real Mara with her tousled short hair blowing in the Montana wind. Someone who had a husband and family, who took over the ranch when Sarah retired, and who passed it on to her children. Someone with her finger on the pulse of the mountains and rivers, who loved and was loved, who lived a life that was simple, clear, clean, rich, deep, and certain—and when she died, was remembered for her kindness and joy. Someone suffused with Spirit, who lived in it and let it live in her without even thinking about it. I let that life settle around me like a quilt on my shoulders, and fell asleep in the rocker.

When I jerked awake, it was completely dark except for the moon hanging bright over the barn and flooding into the room. I grabbed my jacket and tiptoed through the big house to the porch. Leaning up against the railing, I listened to the wind in the pines and smelled the crisp, pungent air. The vastness of the High Rockies, their power and wildness, swept into me. I forgot about the raw silver energy, the god quest, *the dark*—and just let myself be.

Ë

In the morning, Martha knocked on my door with hot, freshly baked huckleberry muffins. She plopped right down in the rocker and wanted to chat about the tourist season being over, news of the ranch, and how exactly I was related to Sarah. It was time to hit the road. If I needed a place that night, I could stay at the hotel in town.

Next stop, Tom's cabin. Before pulling out of the long Triple T driveway, I popped the trunk, grabbed my gun, and slipped it back into my pack. What was I doing? One thing I was pretty sure would *not* happen there was an armed confrontation—but logical function seemed to have been suspended where Tom was concerned. My body and lizard brain were in charge, as they often had been around him. That didn't bode well, but there wasn't much I could do about it. I was scared and wanted my gun nearby, even if I had no intention of using it.

I had run all the scenarios in my mind, everything from finding him with Janice Shoddenheimer and nine children, all standing together by the railing gazing into the mountains as I had wanted to do—to finding out that some crazy, drunken woman had shot him dead twenty years earlier and hey, come to think of it, she looked a lot like me. On the road over to the cabin, I tried to picture Tom as he would be today. In my mind, he looked the same—only his green cowboy shirt was frayed at the collar and his hair had gray in it. Plus, he had lots and lots of lines on his face. More than I had—and deeper. His boots were scruffy, too. I tried not to find the picture sexy and prepared myself once more to see him with Janice and a brace of children.

There it was, nestled just off the highway. The last time I drove over that road, I had just blown a hole in Tom's shoulder and felt like I was running for my life.

A tan Volvo squatted in front of the cabin. Not exactly Tom's kind of car. My God, two kiddy seats in the back. I took a deep breath, draped my pack casually over my shoulder, and knocked on the screen door. A young woman appeared with a toddler on her hip. Applesauce dribbled from the little boy's mouth. He frowned at me and started to cry.

"Hi," the woman said, her eyes darting from me to the howling kid and back to me. She was twenty pounds overweight with long, unkempt dishwater-blonde hair—but she was not Janice Shoddenheimer. Relief swept through me.

"Is Tom Hannigan here?" I asked. I hadn't planned on having to talk over a screaming kid. The woman frowned and looked confused. A good-looking man, very skinny and tall, came up behind her.

"Hi," I smiled up at him, relief coursing through me again. The Volvo and the car seats and the young wife belonged to *this* guy, not Tom. He held the door open and I walked in.

"Tom Hannigan?" he said, shaking his head. "We don't know anybody by that name." He looked to the woman for confirmation, but she was heading into the bedroom, where another kid was wailing. "We're renters. Come here every summer. Lady who owns this place is Jenny Ashcroft." I had never heard that name. I nodded and looked around. It had been painted a soothing beige. All new furniture, including a high chair dripping with applesauce and what appeared to be smashed baby carrots. I had been married in this room, maybe killed Tom in this room.

I stood on the exact spot where I had aimed my gun and pulled the trigger, imagined watching the blood splatter everywhere. A rush of heat and sweat spread across my body. I caught myself against the wall.

"You okay?" the guy asked, putting his hand under my elbow. "Want some water?"

"I'm fine. Thank you. Sorry to have bothered you. I used to know someone who lived here. I know people in town who can help me find him." I nodded and smiled, easing toward the door. "Thanks again."

"Okay." Both kids were screaming now. He glanced toward the bedroom. I waved good-bye and pushed out the door. He hesitated, then went to help the woman with the kids.

I stood on the porch for a moment as I had dreamed of doing with Tom and the baby, looking up into the mountains. The barn and horses were gone, but the mountains were steadfast. They were the only things that seemed bigger than they had been two decades earlier. Everything else seemed smaller.

What I did in this cabin was really, really bad. I'd had no idea how bad until that minute. I had let him hit me, hurt me. I had blown a hole in his body and splattered his blood all over the place. On purpose. I'd had no way of knowing that he wouldn't die, and hadn't waited to find out. I'd just run and let *the dark* take me. Jesus.

The kids were crying louder, as if they wanted me to go away. If I'd had a kid, I would have stayed here. If I'd stayed here, there was no doubt in my mind that, one way or another, I would be dead by now along with Tom and probably the kid.

I had been much, much crazier than I'd thought, and it wasn't just the boozy fog. Even without the Scotch, I hadn't really been present in my own life for a long time. I had watched myself sleepwalk from the apartment to Elmhurst, to Chicago, to Montana, to Reno, and even to San Francisco. It was as if I'd never come down from the cracks in the closet ceiling. Maybe I still hadn't come down. Maybe I'd only hoped or pretended that there was some divine, transcendent presence out there—and that I was special enough to find it—because I couldn't tolerate my life as it really was, or myself as I really was.

Looking up into the high granite peaks, something felt *off*. I had never had evil thoughts like that when I was in the mountains, close to nature. *The dark* again! The new, more subtle version. I jumped off the porch and practically ran to the car. The black thoughts fell off me as I moved, but my hand shook as I put the key in the ignition. I crunched out the driveway and sped toward town with all the windows down, my hair blowing in the mountain wind, feeling punched in the stomach.

Where was he? Lucia would know.

ᴄȣ

Back in Whitefish, I parked on Central and walked up and down the street a few times, working up the nerve to go into the restaurant. When I peeked in the window, Abby was at the cash register. I had forgotten how beautiful she was, how tall and straight she stood, and caught my breath. She was still slim, with the muscular legs and long blonde hair, but it was swept up into a gold mass at the back of her head. She was wearing a simple navy blue dress instead of her waitress uniform. She grabbed some menus and seated three people who looked like tourists. A young guy was taking an order at the only other occupied table.

I walked in slowly, wondering if she would recognize me. She did a double-take and froze for a second, then looked like she wanted to run, but knew she couldn't. She put on a stiff little smile and moved toward me. Streaks of gray cut through her hair, but it made her even more striking. The small sags and wrinkles somehow made her sexier. She still wore that little golden cross at her neck.

"Cat," she said, extending her hand formally, as if I were the mayor coming to eat at the restaurant.

"Hi, Abby." I reached out shyly and hugged her, but she was stiff in my arms.

"Let's go back here." She signaled to the kid to take over and led me to Lucia's old office in the back, which seemed to be hers now. "We never thought we'd see you again after you...left town." She motioned to a chair and I sat, frustrated that I couldn't seem to punch through her invisible shield.

"I'm so sorry, Abby," I said and launched into an abbreviated, laundered version of the last twenty years. I went easy on the Consciousness Circuit info and stressed AA and my higher power. "I wish I hadn't run like that, but I was sure he'd be okay," I lied. What kind of a person lied about something like that? Abby nodded and looked at the floor. I couldn't believe it hurt so much to have her shut me out. "I went by the cabin, but I guess somebody else owns it now?"

She nodded and looked up at me. "Cat, Tom died in a car accident about a year after you left." My chest felt like a rock, but little fingers of relief crept along its edges. At least I hadn't killed him. "Down on that bad stretch of two-lane on the east shore of Flathead Lake? It was a head-on." I stared into the grain of her wood desk, trying to take this in.

"Can I get you something?" Abby asked. She added quickly, "A soft drink? Water?" I could tell she hadn't believed a word of what I'd said about AA. I shook my head, and she looked relieved. "There was a family in the other car, a couple with two kids. Nobody survived. Four of them, plus him and Janice. He was drunk. Amy came up from Butte and sold the place."

I could not get my mind around Tom not being somewhere, and imagined him lying twisted in the wreck, his chest ripped out like the deer I had seen on the road right before Reno. I felt like I might throw up. Put my hand over my mouth and closed my eyes, then felt dizzy and opened them.

Abby was staring at me. "I'm sorry. I didn't realize it would upset you so much. I mean..."

"I shot him."

"Yes."

We sat in silence. She still seemed wary, but just sat quietly and let me digest. I wanted so much to connect with her.

"What about you?" I asked. She seemed glad to talk about something else and gave me a neatly organized account of her last twenty years. The kid up front was her son Rafe, home for the summer from grad school at the University of Montana, which made me feel about eighty-seven years old. She still went to the same church with Pastor Diamond, who was old but as active as ever. Her life was much the same, except now she owned the restaurant. I smiled and asked what Lucia was up to, expecting to hear that in retirement she was a state legislator or skydiver.

"Lucia passed away six years ago. Cancer." No. That could not be.

"She wasn't that old!"

"She was sixty-six. She willed the place to me." The floor felt like it was giving way beneath me, and I was in free fall. Rafe stuck his head around the corner.

"Mom?"

"Yes, honey."

"They won't take this guy's credit card."

She left without asking if he remembered me. He looked at me with wide eyes, as if he either remembered or had heard stories and figured out who I was. Aunt Cat who gunned down her husband and skipped town. He disappeared quickly, and I sat staring at a wall calendar with photos of Glacier National Park. September was Two Medicine Lake at sunset.

"I'm sorry," Abby said when she returned, lowering herself into the chair.

"What about Lena?" I asked.

"She's over at North Valley with pneumonia. She's been going downhill ever since Lucia died. One thing after another. Robert—her husband?—died the year after Lucia."

"Why is everybody dying? Why are they all dead?" Tears welled in my eyes. She leaned back, crossed her arms and looked distressed, as if she just wanted to be rid of me. I made the tears go away. "I'd love to go see Lena. Do you think it would be okay?"

"Uh, sure." She wasn't so sure, though. She was seeing someone whose life had always looked out of control, dangerous, illegal, immoral, and wrong in some visceral way—just the opposite of hers.

I didn't have the heart to hug her again when I left. The stiffness in the air was bad enough. Abby was someone who knew goodness when she saw it, and she wanted nothing to do with me.

CB

I walked past the Bar None again on the way back to the car and thought about going in—but truly, I had been there and done that. Booze was *the dark*'s first line of attack. I slumped behind the wheel of the car, feeling sad and numb. Tom was dead. Lucia was dead. Abby hated me. Very likely, this trip was just poking at a hornets' nest and I would wind up in worse shape than I had been in San Francisco. I was tempted again to turn back, but couldn't. Something drove me forward. I told myself that there were still fifteen hundred miles ahead, and anything could happen.

The road out of town was thick with tourist shops and huckleberry stands. I didn't remember the huckleberry being such a linchpin of Flathead Valley's economy—but my attention had been on other things. Maybe the huckleberry was just a lure for the real linchpin now, tourists.

One shop was actually shaped like an enormous red-purple huckleberry, morphed into a cartoon character with large, dilated black-and-white eyes and a vague, cherry-pink grin. He looked like he was on Ecstasy. I had to see this and swung into the gravel parking lot. Even the interior walls of the Huckleberry Shop were painted purple. It was dizzying. Track lights glistened down on huckleberry jams, syrups, honey, candy, preserves, muffins, muffin mix, bark, coffee, ice cream, and even huckleberry horseradish. There were no men in the shop, only tired-looking women and their pale, thin, lank-haired teenage daughters, who skulked around the periphery looking world-weary and far, far above it all.

I bought a muffin and sat outside on the wooden steps, which were painted green to simulate the vine. The muffin was good—almost as good as Martha's had been. Crisp on top, fresh and chewy inside. Huckleberries have a strong, wild taste. How could both Tom and Lucia be dead?

People crunched around the parking lot, in and out of the Huckleberry Shop and the Tastee Freez across the street. Next to the Tastee Freez, a bit back from the road, dust rose from a small crowd spilling out of a square white clapboard building with a steeple. Looming high above the little church, craning out toward the road as if reaching over the shoulder of the Tastee Freez ice cream cone sculpture, was a sign in the shape of an enormous burnt-orange heart. A metallic gold crown perched atop it, and a vermilion shepherd's crook pointed jauntily off to the side. White letters on the sign read:

Jesus Our Good Shepherd
Hallelujah Church
Rev. Kenny Diamond, Pastor

Pastor Diamond! When the crowd outside was down to the last stragglers, I skittered across the road and walked up the church's wooden steps. Just inside, on the wall of the dimly lit vestibule, was a six-foot bronze plaque with raised black letters:

The Lord is my Shepherd; I shall not want.
He maketh me to lie down in green pastures:
He leadeth me beside the still waters.
He restoreth my soul.
He leadeth me in the paths of righteousness for His name's sake.
Yea, though I walk through the valley of the shadow of death,

I will fear no evil: For thou art with me.
Psalm 23

Boy, wouldn't *that* be nice. Just sit down, lean back, open up your fried chicken church supper, and God would keep the flies away. The Lord might be other people's Shepherd, but he wasn't mine. He might lead people like Abby in the "paths of righteousness," but not me. I *didn't* lie down in green pastures or walk beside still water. I *did* want. I *did* fear. My soul was not restored, for all the "soul retrieval therapy" I'd done with Joy. Resting back into the arms of God the way Abby and Pastor Diamond did, trusting that I was cherished and watched over, felt like coming home from a month in the Burn Unit and sticking my hand over an open flame on the stove.

Still, the absolute certainty of those words fascinated me. They were cast in metal and hung on a wall. A person as good as Pastor Diamond was trusted them that much. I wanted that kind of certainty.

Suddenly, Pastor Diamond himself was standing in the vestibule with me. He was as round and elfin as ever, but his pink cheeks had faded to chalk. He stooped and was completely bald. His dancing sapphire eyes were barely visible behind Coke-bottle glasses, but he still carried that odd, irresistible radiance that scooped me up, filled my heart to overflowing with something I couldn't quite understand, and made me want more of whatever he had. I smiled, just seeing him, the same way I had at our wedding, but he clearly didn't recognize me. Maybe he just couldn't see me.

"Pastor Diamond?" I said, moving closer to him.

"Yes?" He seemed delighted, but in a general way. I could have been anyone.

"Cat Callahan!" He stared just above my face and squinted. "You married me about twenty years ago? To a guy named Tom, who died in a car crash?"

He smiled beatifically, as if we were best friends, but obviously had no clue who I was. He shuffled toward me and looked up into my eyes. Before, he had been charismatic. Now, he was luminous.

"The Psalm is about you, you know," he said, gesturing toward the plaque as if he had been watching me and reading my mind.

"It is *not*!" I heard myself say, shocked at how loud and defensive it sounded. He smiled, as if he got this reaction a lot.

"Of course it is," he said quietly. He took my hands in his soft little ones and filled the vestibule with his presence. He glowed with an absolute clarity that, whatever the problem, we would take care of it right here and now! Because all problems had the same solution—God's love—and not to worry, the world was awash in it.

I felt nervous, awkward, and didn't know what to do or say. What the hell.

"I'm on a quest to find the raw silver energy and kill *the dark*—and it's not going very well!" Pastor Diamond nodded as if he understood everything. I sensed that on some level, he actually did.

"Good for you!" he exclaimed, still nodding and smiling. "Just remember," he said, leaning in close, "the most important thing is to remember that God loves you."

I frowned. He looked up at the ceiling, as if all the answers were there and God's infinite love might come tumbling down through a trapdoor. I glanced up, but saw only drywall. He suddenly turned canny, leaned in and asked as if he were offering me a plate of pecan sandies, "Would you like to be healed and know that you are God's child?"

I slumped down like one of the teenagers in the Huckleberry Shop.

"Uh...sure."

He reached up and tapped my forehead three times with his index finger.

"The Lord is your shepherd," he said. I closed my eyes. The words throbbed faintly like a second heart, radiating through me a force that shimmered inside a vast silence, full of acceptance, forgiveness, and deep love. It pinged on the same frequency as *the bright* and turned me in that direction like a plant to the sun, took me to where I felt at peace, whole, even joyful. When I slowly opened my eyes, everything seemed suffused with golden light. The walls, the plaque, even Pastor Diamond. We were all in the Gold Zone.

"See?" he said exuberantly. I panicked as my regular mind began to return and fill with paranoia. What was I doing in a Protestant church, with a "pastor" tapping my forehead? The Gold Zone still pulsed around us, but for how long?

"What about *the dark*?!" I practically yelled, jarring the golden light.

"Oh, that's just a figment of your imagination," he scoffed. "A Fig Newton," he said in a hushed, amused voice, pleased with his little joke.

He slipped his hands from mine, patted my arm, and sidled through dark wooden doors into the sanctuary. I stared after him, much as I often stared at one of my tax guy Ray's spreadsheets when they pointed to the absolute wisdom and inevitability of doing something that I hadn't thought I'd wanted to do.

When I finally uprooted myself and went after him, Pastor Diamond was already halfway down the aisle of the church. An old woman in a dark red kerchief sat in the front pew. She turned, stood, and threw herself into his arms sobbing. She was taller than he was and looked like she might bowl him over, but he held her up. Soon they were both standing in his glow. They sat together in a pew with their hands clasped and their heads close.

I backed into the vestibule, thinking I might wait for him, but felt suddenly exhausted. On the wall beside the plaque was a plastic holder full of little prayer cards with the Psalm printed on them. I took one, stuffed it into the back pocket of my jeans, and stepped out into the sunlight.

It could not be that simple. If it were, I could go around tapping myself on the forehead and never leave the Gold Zone. Turning my head toward the church so that nobody could see, I surreptitiously tapped my forehead.

Nothing!

೧೩

I headed east across Montana. The high sun glinted off other cars in what seemed like tiny sunbursts of gold, orange, and tangerine, turning them into kaleidoscopes of shining metal and glass. The Gold Zone still shimmered around me, but I could sense it fading with every mile I put between me and the Jesus Our Good Shepherd Hallelujah Church. So much for Pastor Diamond's god, if you needed line of sight to make it work.

The High Rockies subsided into lower, sprawling hills and finally gave way to buttes, rivers, and endless ocher prairie dotted with purple grasses and dark green trees. In the long drive across Big Sky Country, the gold faded entirely. I drove fast and let my mind spread out into the vastness and silence. I didn't even try to think, just breathed it all in and forgot about conjuring up a god on a deadline. If some god out there wanted to connect, then let *it* find *me*.

At the Custer Battlefield, I hiked up from the Visitor Center to the point that overlooked Last Stand Hill. Mile after mile of undulating prairie grass grew high and wild, nearly covering the crumbling little gravestones. The only sound was the wind rushing down off the low mountains and pushing through the grass.

A sleek purple bus edged into the parking lot below. Tourists in pastels lowered themselves out slowly and moved toward the Visitor Center. Three of them—a mother with a boy and girl who look about eleven and thirteen—started up the trail toward my overlook. The kids were literally dragging their feet. The mom had her arm around the boy's shoulder. His taller, overweight sister followed behind them, looking at the ground. The mother nodded curtly to me as they arrived, and I nodded back.

"Tell the story, Jason. What happened to General Custer?"

The kid started a recitation. His nails were manicured, his hair neatly clipped—a younger, male version of his mother. The girl was at that horrible moment of adolescence when everything was in the wrong place, there was too much of it, and it was hard to imagine that any of it would ever sort itself out. She was puffy and shapeless, too old for the boyish shorts and T-shirt she was wearing—but I couldn't think of anything that would actually look good on her. It was hard to tell whether her dull brown hair was greasy or just soaked in sweat. She had pimples.

"Stand up straight, Pamela!" the mother hissed. The girl unfolded a little and leaned awkwardly against the little fence that surrounded the overlook. "Well, now you look like a weight lifter!" The girl turned toward the battlefield, away from the mother.

I literally saw red. From nowhere, my mind filled with the image of walking out the door to Terry O'Hara's boy-girl party and Mother telling me I looked like a basketball player. *The dark* surged up and let loose before I even knew it was there. I walked over to the girl, gripped the wood railing, and said so low that only she could hear, "Your mother is a piece of shit. I know things are terrible now—but trust me, one day you're going to be gorgeous and rich, and she's going to get a terrible disease, suffer, and die." I could not believe I was saying this. The girl looked me squarely in the eye and burst into a radiant smile. I didn't dare look at her again, or I would laugh.

Then I walked over to the mother and said so that only she could hear, "You fucking bitch. Don't hurt that girl again." She froze in place, her mouth hanging open, and stared at me. I didn't know which of us was more surprised.

I turned quickly, before anything else could happen, and sprinted down the little trail to the parking lot. Many of the old people had never even gotten off the bus. Others were winding their way back from the Visitor Center, clutching little paper bags the size of postcards. I stood by my car and waved to them over and over, until the whole bus was waving back, nodding and smiling.

I slipped back onto 90 for the jump to Rapid City and checked into a Holiday Inn just off the freeway. I soaked in the tub, thinking about my behavior at the Custer Battlefield. Not good. Not anticipated. Odd and capricious. *Angry*. Way out of control. *The dark* had me again! I felt crazed and unhealed, dangerous, and terrified to be heading into the vortex.

Mother. I tried to conjure up a picture of her, but wound up imagining a huge black crow, twenty feet long with razor-sharp talons, falling from the sky and pinning me to the ground while she picked out my guts. Then I became huge—and she wasn't the crow, but her old self with the yellow hair and white skin. I pushed her against the wall and pounded her face with my fist until the head was bloody pulp. Bad, bad. Short-term gains. A sugar high. I tried forcing myself to see her in a good way, a kind way—but fuzzed out. Could not stand to look. Visualization was a mainstay of the Consciousness Circuit, but it went haywire in *the dark*'s grasp.

I wanted desperately to be good enough that all was forgiven, strong enough that all was healed—but the shifting, ominous shapes that half-surfaced when I tried to think about her still paralyzed me. I didn't even want to imagine how much room they had been taking up inside me all these years. Then something Joy once said floated to the surface. She had looked over her tortoiseshell glasses at me during a rather slow session one rainy afternoon, leaned in, and asked, "You know, don't you, that your mother was crazy as a loon?" If that were true, then maybe I wasn't as bad as my lizard brain and *the dark* kept telling me I was.

Joy was also a big fan of the Gnostic Gospel of St. Thomas. She quoted it so much that most of her clients were able to recite long passages from memory. In her group workshops, we could always tell when she was about to launch into one of her Gospel of St. Thomas riffs, and would start mouthing along with her phrases like, "If you bring forth what is within you, what is within you will save you. If you do not bring forth what is within you, what is within you will kill you." I was bringing forth what was within me, all right, but it didn't seem to be getting me anywhere.

I did not sleep well.

At five thirty the next morning, I was racing east again toward Chicago across South Dakota, the bottom of Minnesota and Wisconsin. I hardly noticed the beauty outside the car. I was panicked at not having nailed down the raw silver energy and having no weapons against Mother or *the dark*. What was I thinking? I scrambled for some Goz-y, Potato Head-y god with the heart-thumping grandeur of Spirit, the certainty of the Pastor Diamond and Immaculate Conception gods, the pervasiveness of I AM Oneness, the comfort and wholeness of *the bright*. Maybe if I just memorized that list and used it as a mantra, something good would happen. I tried to repeat it to myself, but all I could think of was that huge, ravenous black crow.

I reached the Hilton O'Hare at ten that night, after driving 900 miles. The hotel was slightly removed from everybody, but central to Elmhurst, the North Side, and the Loop. In the room, I stared east toward Lake Michigan and the glow of downtown. Tired and discouraged as I was, just being in Chicago made me feel better. This was home. You could still put me down on any street corner in this city and I would feel more at home than I did outside the San Francisco condo I had owned for ten years.

When things happened here, they counted more than they did in the West, with all that space and all those strangers.

Chapter 19

In the morning I drank a pot of coffee, but still couldn't remember anything from the Goz mantra I'd made up on the road. I chucked my notebook in the wastebasket and decided that if *the dark* got me, it got me. At least it would all be over. I had no idea where the raw silver energy lived, how to get at it, or even if it would work again against Mother.

Elmhurst was only five minutes from the airport. The red brick house with the careful white trim at 221 Fairgrove was so tiny that it almost looked like a dollhouse. It didn't feel evil or ominous, just empty. Small and weak. Flat. I parked across the street and slumped down behind the wheel, tried to imagine myself at ten, getting on my bike and pedaling *away*, forever. Scared and desperate, but somewhere near my core, also relieved and excited. I had known from the moment I put my foot on that pedal and headed for the quarry that I would never get caught, and never go back. A young woman with short black hair came out of the house, picked up the newspaper in the front yard, waved to a neighbor, and walked back in. This was her place now.

I inched away from the curb and slowly drove the route I had walked each morning to escape into the glory of Immaculate Conception Grammar School.

The huge parking lot looked almost exactly as it had on my first morning at IC—masses of kids swarming around in navy jumpers or slacks, with crisp white shirts. Except, *the nuns were not wearing habits!* They seemed stuck somewhere between the real-deal habit that they had worn when I was there, and dorky 1950s clothes. Cropped hair with long dark skirts, shapeless light-colored blouses and, even in Indian summer heat, sweaters or cotton blazers—probably to hide their breasts! A few of the older ones wore short, flimsy veils bobby-pinned into their gray hair.

They looked *God-awful!* No longer mysterious creatures trailing yards of luscious black fabric, they seemed like frumpy regular women who had been locked in a K-Mart for an hour and told to pick out unobtrusive, modest wardrobes. They hadn't known where to begin after thirty years in black, so they just closed their eyes and started tossing items over their shoulders into shopping carts.

I hopped out of the car and scanned for Sister Mary Celeste, the first-grade nun who had introduced us to the cavalcade of saints and the Purgatory accounting system. No one looked like I imagined she would look at about fifty, without a habit—kind of like Katharine Hepburn in *The Lion in Winter*. Then, out of the corner of my eye, I did spot a familiar face. Sister Agatha, the red plastic ruler nun! She looked oddly the same as she had back then, only older and tougher. Her head was covered with gray curls. I made a beeline for her—trying to look like a parent, or some other legitimate adult Catholic.

"Sister Agatha?" I called. She turned and gave me a friendly smile.

"Why yes!" I swam through the sea of kids to her side and was amazed at how tiny she was. In my memory, she loomed above me at about six feet. In fact, she was about five-foot-two to my five-foot-eight. I didn't have any particular agenda with Sister Agatha, but suddenly the strange, awful truth serum of the Custer Battlefield washed over me again.

"You probably don't remember this, but I had you in fourth grade. You hit me with a ruler and I ran away from home." Whoa! She *did* remember, and she looked scared! I bet my disappearance somehow got to be this woman's fault. It would have been convenient for my mother if Immaculate Conception and the Church were to blame.

Sister Agatha actually started to back away from me into the mass of screaming kids. As much as I rather enjoyed the experience of striking fear into the red plastic ruler nun, curiosity trumped power-mongering. I caught her shoulder gently.

"Wait, I'm not here to cause trouble. You had almost nothing to do with my running away." She paused, looking a bit more like her old self, as if there might be something here for her. She tilted her head back and looked up at me, holding my eye for the first time. "Was there some trouble after I left?" I asked innocently.

Fifteen minutes later, Sister Agatha and I were sitting in "the office" with the current principal, Sister Alice McDermott. Sister Alice was about forty and, except for her black nun shoes and bowl haircut, looked like a non-litigating partner at a downtown law firm in her navy suit, pale pink poly blouse, and fake pearls. Her first call was to IC's pastor, Monsignor Gallagher, and his was to the archdiocese's legal counsel.

Within an hour, the two nuns had been sent away and the portly, officious Monsignor Gallagher had squeezed himself, his black-and-crimson cassock, and the regalia of crucifixes and golden chains that dripped from him behind Sister Alice's desk. Kevin Donnelly, the legal counsel, and I sat in the two smaller chairs opposite him. Donnelly was whip-thin, about my father's age, red-faced and scrubbed in the way of older Irish men who are the first in their family to make it big. He emitted an aura of money and toughness, gave me a thin smile, and asked what brought me to Chicago.

I was still my father's daughter, and I knew just how to handle men like Kevin Donnelly. It was something every Irish girl learned long before she was ten years old. These men were brutal at work, but they melted before the adoring, conspiratorial, oldest-Irish-daughter kind of grin I gave him. Every line in him softened when I leaned forward and said, as if the sun and moon set in him, "Mr. Donnelly, I have no idea what happened after I left, but I do know that no one at IC was to blame. If there was any trouble, I'd like to remedy that." Another smile, as if only he were strong enough or wonderful enough to give me my heart's desire. "Could you tell me what happened?"

Sure enough, my parents had threatened a lawsuit. Listening behind Donnelly's words, as he intended for me to do, I saw that my mother had been the prime mover and had dragged Dad reluctantly through the process. Eventually, Donnelly and Dad sat down and put together something that saved the archdiocese embarrassment and money, saved Dad from bringing this humiliating (and probably unwinnable) suit, and saved Mother's face so he could live with her. The only person who hadn't been happy about the outcome was Sister Agatha, who had spent ten years ministering to Pagan Babies in a remote area of Honduras.

Donnelly mentioned casually, smiling fondly and paternally at me, that of course the statute of limitations had expired and so it was all moot at this point—but perhaps I might drop by his office later in the week and sign a waiver, and he would take me to lunch. I smiled and nodded, but said nothing as I pocketed the card he handed me.

We both thanked Monsignor Gallagher (for nothing) and walked out to the parking lot together. It was empty now. The kids were all in their classrooms, doing the phonics mantra or learning about the saints. I wanted one more thing from Donnelly.

"Can you tell me the extent of the search they did?"

"Uh, local law enforcement..."

"Anything beyond that?" Our eyes met.

"I don't believe so." He knew he was telling me worlds.

I watched him stride to his car and realized that I was standing on almost the exact spot where Terry O'Hara had gotten hauled out of line for scuffing his feet right before our first Visit to the Blessed Sacrament. I remembered the *squish, squish* of liquefying blacktop under our saddle shoes when we were forced to stand on the playground for hours in the heat for the Living Rosary, huddled together in little groups that represented the various beads.

I had been extraordinarily happy in this place. In truth, my running away really did have very little to do with Sister Agatha hitting me. That had just been an excuse. I had needed a way to get out from under Mother and to put some distance between me and Ghost Girl before she sank back into Dead Girl.

A smile spread across my face as I took a few steps in place and felt the familiar stickiness beneath my shoes.

ભ

I took Route 83 from Elmhurst to the North Side of Chicago, just as Stan had thirty years earlier. I was a little nervous about seeing Julie, because we had lost touch. That is to say, I hadn't called her after I got to San Francisco. For the first few years, I had been ashamed to tell her what happened with Tom, or in Reno. Then I hadn't called because I was embarrassed that so much time had passed. Then I told myself I had changed into someone she didn't know and might not like. I had become a real estate mogul and a Consciousness Circuit aficionado. I may have thought I'd gotten better than she was, which made me feel even more ashamed. It was also possible I'd convinced myself on some level that my life before San Francisco hadn't even existed.

I wanted to feel close to her again and to see the last place where I remembered being completely happy. The old neighborhood had deteriorated. The bar across the alley was all boarded up and looked like it had been that way for some time. Several of the businesses owned by Mollie's pals—the dry cleaner's, the mom-and-pop grocery, the shoe repair place—had gone derelict. Even the bakery looked shabby. Mollie would hate this. I felt a wave of guilt and sadness as I parked and walked slowly down the familiar stretch of sidewalk to our store.

Grime clung to my fingers as I pushed through the door. There were a few doughnuts and sweet rolls in the case, but nothing very special or appealing. It was so dark that I looked up to see which lights weren't turned on and realized it was just that they hadn't been cleaned. Decades of soot and dead insects dulled the light. Julie sat behind the counter, staring into space. There was a dark smudge on her yellow blouse, and she was wearing the same kind of makeup she had twenty years ago. It looked caked and pasty. The cheap blonde dye didn't completely cover her gray hair.

My whole body felt the shock of seeing her like that. It was like the dream in which it was final exam day, and I realized I hadn't gone to class all semester. I suddenly saw that I should have taken better care of her, and of the bakery, but it had never occurred to me until that minute. Julie had always been the tough, optimistic girl who knew the score, buoyed everybody up, and took care of *me*. I wanted to put my arms around her and take her shopping—then flood the bakery with Lysol, paint everything, and start making pastries.

She looked up as I walked in, but didn't recognize me until I stood smiling at her for a moment. There was a quick flash of her old self, and then a strange caricature of herself emerged, someone playing the person she used to be.

"Hi, hon," she practically yelled, getting to her feet unsteadily. I smelled gin. She wove around the counter and grabbed me into a bear hug. "Hey! Whereya been? Whereya been for...oh, I don't know...twenty years? Huh?" Her energy felt angry, but she kept smiling and clapping me on the back.

"I'm so sorry, Jules. I live in San Francisco."

"Where's your hubby? Tom, right? Good-looking guy."

"We split up a long time ago."

"Good! He was an asshole. Asshole! Hey! Come on upstairs and let's have a drink. You have to meet Steve." She held her left hand in my face so I could see the ring. Small diamond, flashy setting. "He's *my* hubby!"

She flipped the sign on the door to "Closed," not that it mattered, and we went upstairs to the kitchen. I ran my hand over the table where Mollie and I had sat the night I arrived. Grease and grime had cut deep into the wood. Everything was the same, only dirty and old.

Steve sat at the table in his undershirt and jeans. He was in his mid-sixties, hairy, overweight, and unshaven. The paper, a cup of coffee, an ashtray, and a beer were spread out on the table before him. Both he and Julie lit cigarettes as she introduced us, and the kitchen filled with smoke. Steve gathered up his things and lumbered out, throwing over his shoulder, "Let you girls talk."

"Thanks, hon," Julie called after him a little anxiously. She took down a glass for me and reached for a fifth of Scotch on the kitchen counter. "This good for you?"

"Ah...You won't believe this, Jules, but I don't drink anymore." She stared at me blankly, then poured a double and pushed it across the table to me. I moved it to the side. "I'm so sorry I didn't call you." She leaned back in her chair and looked at me sideways.

"You got your own life. No reason to bother with us here." I saw us all—Mollie, Julie, Loreen—sitting around this table for our family dinners, talking and laughing for hours, and my eyes filled up with tears. I walked around the table and hugged Julie from behind. She reached back and patted my shoulder, but looked straight ahead.

"Hey, wanna see your old room?"

"Sure." She led me down the hall, as Mollie had that first night. They had turned it into a storage area. Cardboard boxes, old books, and stray furniture were stacked everywhere. My bed was somewhere underneath it all. Sticking out of a cardboard box brimming with odd items was the little statue of Shiva dancing, kicking aside the Veil of Illusion. I touched it and had to wipe my hand on my jeans.

"Do you ever hear about Jeff?" I asked. To my surprise, this brought her to life.

"Oh yeah, he's a big deal now. All over the place. I keep telling Steve, we have to go sometime and throw cherry bombs at him, but Steve won't go." She peeked anxiously into the hall and looked at her watch. "I got a flier from the El station, if you wannit."

"Yeah." Back in the kitchen, she shuffled through a stack of dog-eared papers by the refrigerator and extracted the flier.

Jeff beamed a toothy, enlightened smile to the universe and beyond, even more gorgeous now than he had been a quarter century ago. His teeth had been capped and he wore an expensive-looking open-collar shirt and sport coat. A few lines around his eyes made him look like a person of substance, and a dusting of gray at the temples made him look wise. The effect was somewhere between George Hamilton and the Dalai Lama, but closer to George Hamilton. The photo took up about two-thirds of the flier. Below, in a typeface that looked sort of Gothic, sort of Sanskrit-y:

Meet Enlightened Master
Jeff Hackney
September 15, 7:00 – 9:00 PM
Hyatt Regency Chicago
151 E. Wacker Drive
$25 Suggested Love Offering

No more Suk—and the love offering had gone up.

"Hey, this is tomorrow! You and Steve want to go?"

She hesitated, then said, "Steve won't go."

"What about you?"

"Nah. Better not." She looked at her watch again.

"Okay." I took the hint, decided to call it quits for the time being, and made an excuse to go. She seemed relieved. I hugged her and said, "I'll call you." She nodded and looked away, but I knew I could win her back. Driving through the old neighborhood back to the expressway, I felt like crying. Instead, I planned outings with Julie. I would take her to lunch, to a spa for facials—and shopping, of course. I would make it all up to her. I would fix it.

☙

At six the next morning, I sat bolt upright. Holy shit, I was in Chicago, and possibly in no better shape to deal with Mother than I had been at the Custer Battlefield. I slugged back coffee and put on the beautiful dark green dress that I had bought in San Francisco especially for this next meeting.

By eight o'clock, I was heading into the Loop on the El—which, amazingly, went all the way out to the airport now. Dad still worked in the same building on LaSalle Street, even though he was almost seventy. I had kept tabs, calling the office every year or so and hanging up when they said they'd take a message. By nine thirty, well-dressed people were scurrying along LaSalle Street, their heads down, looking like they were preoccupied with weighty matters. The massive revolving door of Dad's building went *flop, flop, flop* as they pressed through it. I was whooshed into the somber, copper-toned lobby with its black marble floor. John J. Callahan, Esq. was in Suite 2800.

The elevator doors were copper as well. *Ding*. A door flew open and I was swept in. People reached around one another to press their floors until the there was no more room to reach. As they called out numbers, a young man standing near the panel pressed one button after another. His scrubbed pink neck was inches from my face. I peered over his shoulder and saw that twenty-eight was not lit.

"Twenty-eight." My voice sounded like a child's, high and squeaky. He looked back disdainfully and pressed the button. It lit up dark orange. I saw spots before my eyes. The elevator shot up, and my stomach dropped.

Suite 2800 was right by the elevator lobby, and Dad's name was etched into the sign on the door. My hand left a foggy little sweat mark as I pushed it open. A "ping" sounded as I crossed the threshold. The reception area was elegant—wall-to-wall plush carpet in deep taupe, richly upholstered maroon chairs, beautiful mahogany end tables and reception desk.

A stylish woman in her mid-thirties presided over it. She could have been a model, with her upswept dark hair, pale yellow suit, silk ecru shell, and conservative gold earrings. She was young enough to be eye-catching, but old enough to know all, see all. She seemed like she would be equally comfortable talking to cops on the beat or clients at a cocktail party.

"How may I help you?" Her smile was pleasant, but formal.

"Is Mr. Callahan available?" She raised her eyebrows and gave me a gracious but questioning look. "I'm his daughter." I wouldn't have thought anything could rattle this woman. She pulled it together quickly, though, and smiled as she stood.

"Have a seat, please. I'll check his schedule."

Surely she didn't need to leave her desk to do this, but she abandoned the reception area and disappeared around the corner. I sat in one of the maroon chairs, not knowing what to do with my hands or eyes. I could hardly pretend to be engrossed in an article on whales in the *National Geographic.* I flicked a spot of dust off my dress. Now my hands were sweating. The pale yellow suit appeared again from the back recesses.

"Will you come with me, please?" she said pleasantly, as if this sort of thing happened every day. When I stood up, dots formed before my eyes again. I felt like I might faint, but followed her down the hall. She held a door open for me, smiled, and motioned for me to go in. I walked through, and she closed the door as she left.

The air felt viscous, but I fought through it for a better look at the figure behind the expansive polished desk. He was about two-thirds the size I remembered him, slightly stooped, and almost completely bald. His skin looked pale and thin. I strained to see the person I remembered, vital and charming, his smile flying out in all directions—and saw a glimmer of it. In my mind, I made him stronger and bigger because he was my marker in the world. My anchor, my blood. I came from him. My heart felt like it would fly out of my chest and wrap itself around him.

He stood and started around the desk, moving almost like his old self. His eyes were hooded and surrounded by masses of wrinkles, but they were still piercing, glinting blue—and they still loved me. They softened and filled with tears as he came closer. By the time he got to where I stood, a tear had streaked down his right cheek. He was exactly my height now. When he put his hands on my shoulders, it seemed partly a caress, partly to steady himself, and partly to hold me still. His expression seemed somewhere between a grimace and a smile.

"Oh! Oh!" He put his arms around me and pulled me to him, hugging me tight. It felt just like it had when I was little, almost as if nothing had happened since then. My mind told me that this man had not protected me from my mother, had not looked for me very hard when I ran away. Yet I poured myself into him, and his love for me was palpable beneath my fingers, so precious that it erased everything else. I never wanted to let go, except that I wanted to see his face again. It was almost like looking into a mirror, despite the obvious differences. He touched my cheek.

"I love you. I'm so sorry," he said.

"*I'm* sorry. I love you." It seemed like that's all there was to say. Now that it had been said, we were both at a loss. Finally, he fell back on social skills.

"Here. Here, sit here." He put me in one of the expensive maroon chairs on the client side of the desk, and he sat in the other. We just stared at one another. Everything I started to say sounded stupid, and it looked to me like he was having the same experience.

"You're still working!" Stupid.

"Couldn't stop!" I had never seen him that nervous. Were we going to make small talk now? I figured as long as it was this awkward, I might as well throw the hardest thing into the mix.

"How's Mother?" He heaved back in his chair and sighed. Now we had something to talk about.

"Not very well." He didn't seem to want to say any more, so I used one of Joy's therapy tricks. If you wanted the other person to keep talking, you had to shut up. You didn't make appropriate conversational responses, just kept your mouth shut and looked expectant.

"As a matter of fact, we moved her into a wonderful care facility six years ago." I raised my eyebrows. "Up in Wilmette." I didn't even let myself nod. He must have known this same trick from depositions, but he kept talking. "About, oh, seven or eight years ago, she began acting not quite herself. Erratic. Forgetful. Unpredictable." He nodded to himself, looking at the floor, then glanced up to see if this satisfied me. It didn't. "We took her to specialists, but they thought it best for everyone if we let HeartStone give her the care she needed."

"Who is 'we'?" He shifted his weight forward, then to the other haunch, then pushed as far back in the chair as he could get.

"Elaine and I." This was a surprise. I smiled and cocked my head. "Uh, your mother and I were divorced just before her difficulties began." He looked up to gauge my reaction, seemed relieved, and continued. "Elaine and I were married six years ago." I smiled. He went from sheepish to almost giddy. "I want you to meet her. How long are you in town? Maybe we could have dinner. We could go to the Pump Room!" My old favorite. I smiled and nodded vaguely.

I had a stepmother? That felt very odd, but not unpleasant. I wanted to meet her, but not this trip. I had other plans, didn't want the distraction. The whole time, through all the words and information, it felt as if Dad and I were calibrating to one another on some unseen, unheard frequency. Letting those warm, lush lines of energy wash back and forth between us. I would have been happy just sitting there with him forever, and sensed he felt the same way. I kept the conversation where he obviously liked it.

"Tell me about her." He went over to the bookcase and took down a picture. Then, with a smile, he also took down the much smaller picture next to it. He returned to his chair with one in each fist, like a little boy.

He laid the smaller one face down on his desk and held the larger one in front of his chest for me to see, grinning proudly. Dad stood beside a grand piano in a tux, looking handsome and debonair, smiling as if he might burst, his arm around a beautiful redheaded woman about ten years younger in a stunning dark blue evening gown. She looked as pleased with the two of them as he did, leaning her head against his shoulder and smiling dreamily into the camera. She looked familiar, but I couldn't quite place her.

"This was at the country club Christmas party, the year we were married." He was smitten.

"How long have you known one another?"

"A long time. We've loved each other a long time." He hesitated, then gazed at the picture. "Actually, about thirty years."

It was a confession, one made out of love for this woman and, somehow, love for me. I stared into her face, and suddenly it hit me who she was. She could be the one I saw him with the day I left Chicago, when I snuck up here and saw him guide a woman into the elevator with his hand on the small of her back. I smiled at him, patted his arm, looked back at the picture, and began doing math in my head. They must have started seeing one another about the time I ran away. Maybe that was why he had been distracted. They had kept it secret all that time. I wondered if Mother had known.

"The divorce was very hard on your mother." He was talking fast, seemed relieved to be telling me this. "It started with the peculiar behavior, and I'm afraid advanced fairly quickly. She was arrested for shoplifting twice, and once for assault. Then involved in a car accident, so we knew she couldn't be left on her own. I still had her power of attorney, so we were able to care for her."

He had had her *committed*. I was only slightly bothered by how gratifying I found this, and kept nodding sympathetically, as if *of course, of course*. If he saw my ripple of schadenfreude, he ignored it and reached over to pick up the smaller picture. He held it to him, facing his chest, and smiled.

"Guess what this is." I had seen it the minute I walked into the room.

"What? Show me!" He grinned and held it tighter.

"Guess!"

I shook my head. He turned the picture slowly around for me to see. It was the same one I had in my pack back at the hotel, the one I had carried with me all these years. The two of us were sitting side by side on the concrete stoop of the Elmhurst house, gazing into one another's eyes. I took it from his hands, and tears filled my eyes to think that he'd had it all this time as well. He put his hand on my arm.

"Can I ask about you? Can you tell me what happened? Why you left? How you...I can't believe you're alive. We thought you...and now you're here."

I gave him an extremely abbreviated, Girl Scouty version of events that made my life sound like a series of mountain hikes and campfires, then nearly perfect romances, all capped off by a meteoric career in real estate and glowing with a rich patina of sophisticated spirituality. I could fill in the details later. I deliberately avoided talking about why I left. Today was about seeing if there was a possibility for us. There was, and I was laying our foundation with rocks—not glass or anything else that might break. Nothing difficult or fragile.

I couldn't help dropping that I had met Kevin Donnelly, the archdiocese lawyer. I wanted Dad to know that I knew something about what had happened, including that he hadn't looked for me very hard. "He told me about the search and settlement," I said. Dad shook his head and looked at the floor. I couldn't tell whether he was angry with Donnelly or felt guilty, or both.

"We should have tried harder to find you." That's all I wanted to hear. I would take him off the hook.

"I didn't want to be found, Dad. You never would have found me." He looked like I had just handed him the Hope Diamond.

I loved this man desperately, but I was on overload and couldn't take any more right then. I told him I wanted to meet Elaine, to see him again and spend time together—but not this trip. I told him I would come back to Chicago soon, and I planned to do just that. I did not tell him that I was going to see Mother. In fact, my instinct was to hide this information from him. I told him a deliberate lie, that I was meeting an old acquaintance that night and was flying home early in the morning. I didn't want him messing with my mission, and I had a feeling he might.

I gave him my San Francisco number and address, agreed to come back for Thanksgiving, and made sure the message was firmly in place: *I love you. I don't blame you. We will be in one another's lives.*

⍟

Emerging into the sunlight on LaSalle Street, I felt almost transparent and had trouble breathing—not because there was too little air, but because there was too much of it. When I put on my red jacket, stole all the money in Mother's purse, jumped on my bike, and rode away, I became an outlaw. I moved outside the white picket fence. I was someone who might find temporary sanctuary, as I did with Mollie, but who would never really belong with anyone or have a right to be anywhere. Now I was walking up LaSalle Street like a normal person. Somebody's daughter, a legit woman in a nice green dress.

Something inside me that had been clenched into a fist since the day I ran away had relaxed and uncurled. It felt spacious, but unsettling. Even dangerous. An open hand was more vulnerable than a fist. Sure, it could do more and had more options than a fist, but it wasn't ready for a fight.

I walked around the Loop, trying to get used to my new self and integrate what had happened with Dad. Up and down LaSalle Street, over to State and Madison, down to Grant Park and the lake, and back up via the Art Institute. I had lunch in the Walnut Room at Marshall Field's, where our bakery family had gone every year around Christmas. The huge crystal chandeliers and dark Russian wood paneling took me back to those safer, happier times. I ordered a Special Sandwich—turkey breast, aged Swiss cheese, Thousand Island dressing, bacon, egg, and tomato on rye—and topped it off with a piece of Frango Mint chocolate ice cream pie.

I bought some tennis shoes and socks at Field's and spent the rest of the afternoon meandering along the lakefront, stopping now and then to sit on a bench and stare into the waves. I thought about trying to find our old North Side apartment with the closet, but didn't know the address and didn't think I really wanted to see it anyway. I wandered over to the Michigan Avenue bridge and stood staring into the Chicago River, remembering when Dad took me to see it dyed green on St. Patrick's Day. I thought about Dad, about Julie, about Mollie, about the little baby, about Mother, and about Jeff, whom I was going to see that night.

Mostly, I was just curious about him. Did he still have the spiritual goods? What about Sally? Had she become a bronzy Chicago society matron—or was she long gone like I was, hanging out with some cowboy in rural Idaho while a younger, richer version of herself poured water at Master Jeff's events? And what of Saraswendy, the one *I* replaced?

I pondered all this over a petit filet at the Chicago Chop House, then walked up to the Hyatt on East Wacker Drive—a swank hotel near the Magnificent Mile with bright external lighting that danced on the Chicago River below it. Enlightened Master Jeff Hackney was in Crystal Ballroom C.

⅋

It was only six thirty, but a crowd of upscale, well-dressed Chicagoans milled around the Crystal Foyer, pressing up against a long sign-in table where five attractive women sat checking off names and collecting "love offerings." I edged along the periphery toward the table, watching Suk-y insiders glad-hand one another, hug, then hold one another at arm's length and talk through hard, bright grins. I'd seen this before. *We're in this together—and it's a good thing! Right? We didn't get suckered by this guy. We're better now, wiser. Maybe even enlightened. See how well we're doing?* The others, the newbies, stared at them warily and hurried into the ballroom to find a seat.

This was the Consciousness Circuit, gone Midwestern and trailing ten years behind the times. At least I was on familiar ground.

I coughed up the love offering and was asked by an elegant, silver-haired woman in a purple suit that cost at least a thousand bucks to fill out a card. Name, address, phone, where I had heard about Jeff (hah!), and where I could be contacted for future events. I said I'll fill it out later. She hesitated. I knew she was supposed to capture this information, no matter what, but I just looked at her like *Don't mess with me, lady! I hang out on the real Consciousness Circuit, and I'm not filling out the card.*

"Well..." She smiled uncertainly. "Just give it to an assistant, anyone with a purple name tag." I looked around. The "assistants" were standing at attention in strategic spots around the Crystal Foyer, wearing oversize purple name tags, objectless smiles plastered on their faces, holding stacks of cards in one hand, pencils in the other.

I nodded and smiled at her. She pressed a purple flier for the Foundational Course into my hand. Again, a huge picture of Jeff. The "FC" was two weekends long, starting the next weekend, right there at the Hyatt, and cost $2,495.

"Space is limited to 250," the flier said, so I heard several purple-tagged assistants urging people to "reserve their place" quickly. Preferably *right now*, with *them*, so they could get credit for the enrollment. I was in a time warp. This was ten or twenty years ago in San Francisco, with each new seminar trying to out-enroll the last, using the high-pressure tactics they had learned from Werner Erhard's est. The more enrollments you produced, the higher your standing in the organization—and with the guru personally!

So maybe Jeff was making it on his own, without Sally's father's help, if he were actually filling these courses. Surreptitiously, I did the math in the margin of the flier. 250 x $2,495 = $623,750. According to the schedule, he did these "FC's" every month. That was a lot of carrots and tahini.

I pinned on my name tag, as the silver-haired lady had instructed me to do, and saw out of the corner of my eye a phalanx of tall male assistants moving quickly, purposefully, along the edge of the Crystal Foyer. They had inside their moving shield, protected at the center, a presence I knew well and felt even from where I was standing. I cut across the foyer at top speed and intercepted them just as they were about to dart down a side corridor that no doubt led to "backstage." I planted my feet firmly between the lead guy and where he was going and looked into the center of their little nest.

He was even more gorgeous than in the recent pictures. Tanned and tricked out in an elegant navy sport coat and pale ecru shirt that set off his bright blue eyes, he was as magnetic as ever. It felt like a wave had hit me in the chest and sucked me under, tumbled me against the bottom of the ocean, and then tossed me up to the surface again.

"Jeff!" I said with as much command as I could muster.

One of the purple name taggers took me gently but firmly by the elbow and moved me to the side. The Enlightened Master looked down at the notes in his hand, as if he hadn't recognized me. I aikidoed away from the purple tagger and moved again into their path, staring directly at Jeff. He couldn't avoid it now. He overcame a nanosecond of fluster and pretended that he had just now recognized me.

"Mara? Mara, is that you?" He beamed and moved out of the phalanx, took me by the upper arms, and gave me a quick enlightenment hug. Full but very brief, then back to arm's length. "It's so wonderful to see you. I'm so glad you've come!" As if I were there only to hear his message again—having resisted for so long because of my ego limitations, but finally having surrendered to the Truth. I was perhaps a preferred customer, but a customer nevertheless.

"Do you have a moment after the program?" I asked genially, as if nothing much had ever passed between us beyond a few whiffs of incense. He looked mildly shocked, as if he were not used to people approaching him directly for appointments or making demands on his valuable time. As if I had dared something far above my station in his world, but also as if his humility and spirit of service were so vast that he could be gracious even under these inappropriate circumstances.

"Sure! Sure! A moment would be great! Al, will you make sure I see Mara after the program?"

Al was the guy who had tried to pull me out of the way, a big fellow with a $200 haircut, dressed almost identically to Jeff in expensive slacks, open-collar shirt, and sport coat. He smiled a bright enlightenment smile and took my arm, leading me very firmly back through the corridor and saying, "Hi, Mara. I'll meet you right here afterwards. *Here.*" He pointed to the carpet, then to the "Exit" sign above us. "Okay?" I nodded. "Blessings!" he said with a little wave, and made sure I was well into the Crystal Foyer before rejoining the phalanx.

I made my way into Crystal Ballroom C, which was almost full, and found a seat near the back. New Age music wafted from speakers along the walls, a harp and synthesizer plucking out random harmonious chords. The stage was flanked by very large potted palms with a soft gold backdrop. It struck me that he was using a grander, more expensive version of the same stage dressing I had put together for the Unitarian Church—the gold sheet and the much smaller palms that I had borrowed from the funeral parlor. An OM symbol glittered subtly in the fabric. One barstool sat center stage behind a microphone stand.

Even inside the auditorium, people wandered around greeting one another, introducing their "guests" to fellow "graduates." At precisely seven o'clock, the New Age music faded into a deep, basso OM—possibly a tape of Tibetan monks—and everybody scrambled for their seats. One by one, group by group, the audience joined in until Crystal Ballroom C thundered with one continuous OOOMMMMM. A few guys from the phalanx appeared onstage, OM-ing into hand mikes and encouraging the crowd, raising and lowering their arms like linebackers asking the stadium for more noise, pulling forth more and more energy from the audience.

After a few minutes, a flurry of Indian drumming from the wall speakers drowned out the OM-ing and people caught their breath. Enlightened Master Jeff Hackney bounded onto the stage and grabbed the mike from its stand. The crowd went wild, screaming and clapping. The assistants moved offstage in formation, like a high school marching band. E.M. Jeff waved and waved, threw kisses, and finally said in a deep, throaty voice amplified over the applause, "Thank you. Thank you. Hari OM! Krishna! Thank you." He waved some more, then stood perfectly still at the front center of the stage. The crowd hushed, and I could almost hear him breathing.

He began to speak, softly and slowly, his voice mesmerizing, and damned if he wasn't saying *exactly* what he had said twenty-five years earlier. It sounded a little different in Crystal Ballroom C, from a person fully clothed and expertly coifed, holding a hand mike and walking back and forth on the stage in Italian loafers—but it was the same. There was only one of us here, the I AM. Anything else was illusion and a source of suffering. The One I AM was aware of everything, judged nothing, abided in bliss and love. It was there always, unchanging, whether or not we noticed or believed in it, the stuff of which everything was made—of which *we* were made! We had only to put our attention on it to know that *this* was our true nature and identity, and to enjoy the bliss.

I let my eyes fall to the deep blue carpet and within seconds was enveloped in a deep, vast *samadhi*—just as I always had been in his presence. I wasn't the only one. The room was high in a way I'm sure very few of them understood. He still had the goods. I was utterly mystified by how someone as craven as I knew Jeff Hackney to be could produce this result in a room. It was completely beyond me how something so true, so right, could let itself be channeled through a person as squirrelly and venal as he was.

At the break, there were refreshments in the Crystal Foyer. The carrot-fest of years ago had morphed into fancy hors d'oeuvres and bottled water. Assistants cruised among the guests, enrolling them into the Foundational Course or, if they had already done that, the Mastery Course. The Mastery Course was "the next step"—four days from 9:00 AM to 9:00 PM, and guaranteed to "make bliss the place you come from, rather than the place you go to." At $3,500, it was only slightly more expensive than the FC!

I made a beeline for the ladies room, only to discover a female assistant working the line of captive women waiting for a stall. I returned to my seat, but there was no escape. The purple name taggers crawled among people who had returned early, asking radiantly, "Are you a graduate, or would you like to be in the FC next weekend?" I returned to the foyer and stayed on the move. One woman leaned against the hors d'oeuvres table, popping one shrimp-stuffed mushroom cap after another into her mouth. She was crying, which was probably why no assistants hovered around her, and wailed to her friend, "I just wish I could feel this way at home with my husband and kids!" The friend patted her on the shoulder. Finally the foyer lights flashed, calling us back to E.M. Jeff.

The second half was more of the same and ended with pitches for the FC and the Mastery Course. I slunk out as the audience surged to its feet, screaming and clapping.

Sure enough, Al was waiting for me right under the "Exit" sign. He looked a bit wary, as if he had been filled in on who I was. He did not take my arm as he led me to a smaller meeting room a few floors up, where there was another, smaller spread of hors d'oeuvres and bottled water. The Suk and Company green room. He put me on a small sofa, brought me a bottled water, and disappeared with a terse, "Jeff will be with you in a bit. He needs to speak to some of our guests."

Assistants rushed in and out on important business, urgent errands. Some gave me bright, cursory smiles. Others did double-takes at the intruder. I was not one of them. "May I help you?" a few asked through bright smiles.

"I'm fine," I said. "Al's taking care of me." They nodded, obviously relieved that I was under Al's supervision, not theirs, and rushed off again. One woman remained, collecting the enrollment cards and organizing them at a table in the far corner of the room. "Annalea," her purple name tag said. She did not smile; she counted.

Jeff sauntered in a half hour later, only half-covered by the phalanx. He smiled at me, got himself a water, and said to the room, "Thanks, everybody. We'll meet in fifteen." They seemed surprised at the dismissal, but gathered up their things and slunk out, looking over their shoulders at me. Jeff sat on the sofa next to me, falling back and sighing as if he'd just spent three hours on the cross and was ready for the Resurrection, or at least some compliments.

"Great program," I said.

"Thanks." He beamed at me. "Mara, I'm so glad you've come back. So much has happened!" He gestured around the room, as if still mildly surprised by his fabulous success. "I seriously want to acknowledge your courage. It can't be easy to come back and face your past."

My jaw went slack. Wait. Wasn't he the bad guy, the one who had told me to get lost after I'd put him on the map and killed a baby for him?

"We're doing such wonderful work now, truly serving people." My eyes narrowed. "Listen, I want to offer you something." He looked up at the ceiling, or maybe to heaven, as if checking out if it would be okay to give me whatever he was considering, then nodded to himself. "As a way of honoring your contribution early on, I want to give you a half-scholarship to the Foundational Course." He waited for a response, but I was speechless. Could he possibly think I was crawling back and wanted to be part of his shtick? "Once you've done that, I'd love for you to come back and be a part of the work. No hard feelings." I forced my mouth into a small smile, but realized it didn't matter because he didn't even see me. "We have a PR division now. Maybe you could help out there. Actually, Enrollment might be the best place for you. I think we might be able to find something for you there."

His voice trailed off and he seemed distracted. I couldn't tell whether he was imagining the numbers I could produce for him, or if he had suddenly become bored, or if he had figured out that we were not exactly on the same page—but it seemed urgent now that his entourage come back into the room.

"Listen, I'm sorry. I have to let these guys back in. Help yourself to some food. The mushroom caps are the *best*! Don't leave without saying good-bye..." He was on his feet, at the door, beckoning people back into the room. They swarmed in, congratulating him, and Annalea returned to her corner counting table to tally the latest results.

I looked around the room and was suddenly overwhelmed with gratitude. I was so lucky to be me and not Jeff Hackney. The horrible pain of being severed from this world now seemed like the best thing that had ever happened to me. With a small smile on my face, I edged toward the door.

In the elevator, I was flabbergasted and almost giddy. Enlightened Master Jeff Hackney was not a force of nature who had ruined my life, but a narcissistic, self-deluded guy desperate to be someone. He had the goods—who knew how?—but he himself was a true asshole. I had thought of him all these years as either a spiritual bully who deserved my hatred, or a spiritual hero and wise teacher who saw the evil inside me and was so repulsed that he couldn't bear to have me around. Both of those people were figments of my imagination. Fig Newtons, as Pastor Diamond had said. Like the red brick house in Elmhurst, he was smaller than I'd remembered. A shadow of the monster who had lived inside me.

I had been a naïve and desperate kid who put all her eggs in one basket and got burned. It had hurt so much that I murdered a baby trying to fix it—and that had only made it worse. Yet here I was, walking out into the crisp night air, the wind off the lake nipping at my cheeks.

I thought about Jeff and his purple name taggers, his scurrying minions and expensive haircut, his mushroom caps—and actually laughed out loud.

The El was comforting as I clattered back to the airport with the familiar old rumbling under my feet. It was like being inside my city's arteries. I rested my temple on the window, watching Chicago speed by on the other side of the glass with its nighttime sequins shining out of the darkness.

Chapter 20

I woke up nervous, filled with energy. Today was Wilmette, the ritzy North Shore suburb where Dad and Elaine had a house on the lake and Mother had a room at the HeartStone Care Center. I guessed I would see the house at Thanksgiving. As far as Dad knew, I was getting on a plane to San Francisco in an hour. I drove up to Wilmette slowly, trying to formulate a plan, but all the gears in my brain jammed. Cruising around the mansions and tree-lined streets, I didn't know any more than I had back at the Hilton. Or at the Custer Battlefield.

HeartStone was a two-story red brick colonial with white trim, spread out over the whole block like a sprawling, institutionalized version of our house in Elmhurst. I parked across the street under an arch of maple trees. Red, yellow, brown, and orange leaves drifted lazily into elegantly landscaped yards along the quiet block. Puffy white clouds scudded across a bright blue fall sky. A few middle-aged people plodded in and out of HeartStone—no doubt, the children of residents—sometimes accompanied by sullen teens and the occasional infant.

A breakfast of Denny's eggs and pancakes sat heavily on my stomach, and I could actually feel myself being pale—a fuzzy numbness and sinking feeling. My hands felt clammy against the steering wheel. Scenes with Mother rose up. Going up into the ceiling when she had sex with me. Looking back at her over my shoulder as Dad and I left the house to fly my kite, the fury in her eyes leaping out and grabbing me. Feeling her hatred as she watched me during dinner, waiting for me to do something wrong.

I was bigger and stronger than she was now, probably a lot smarter, and had faced down and survived more difficult things than I had encountered with her—but thinking about being in the same room with her sent a tsunami through my stomach.

What did I want here? The message I'd gotten out on my deck in San Francisco, the night I decided to make this trip, seemed far away. *Turn around! Go back and face her.* What did that mean? What was I thinking? I couldn't even sit in a car outside the place where she was institutionalized without fear or anger or shame. Pastor Diamond or some Himalayan monk who had spent sixty years in deep meditation might be able to do it—but not me.

Still, I had come this far. I had to grab whatever god or silver energy or holy person I could get my hands on and hold on for dear life. *The dark* started snaking around in me the minute I opened the car door. I could feel the sticky hatred rising in my heart, and stuffed it down. I conjured up a picture of me standing in her presence filled with *the bright,* I AM Oneness, whatever else I could wrestle out of the ethers and wrap around me. I pretended to know, as Pastor Diamond did, that there was a God and that He loved me. I had had all those good feelings, experienced all those gods at one point or another. I would stand in front of her and pull them out from wherever they were hiding, *make* them come to me.

If I could face her grounded and serene, I would know that I had not wasted my life. If I *couldn't* do that, I was no better than someone who had gone to Harvard Law School and become a partner at a fancy law firm, only to lose a case in traffic court.

I stood on the sidewalk, pulled my imaginary cloak of *the bright* around me, and reminded myself that I was an adult, five-foot-eight inches tall, rich, and very strong. I had ridden horses, shot people, dragged myself out of a Reno alley. If worse came to worse and she attacked me with her black energy and hatred, I could probably zap her back with enough juice to kill her. That's not what I wanted, though.

I pushed *the dark* down again, harder this time, and made one foot go in front of the other until I reached HeartStone's white paneled door and stepped through into the tasteful lobby. It was all cream-colored walls, colonial furniture, upholstered easy chairs, and plush dark-rust carpet that muffled sound and made the place seem quiet and genteel. Like a hotel lobby. In fact, the whole place was set up to look like a small, intimate hotel. The reception desk in the corner was a rich maple.

The woman behind it could have been the hostess at the Fairmont's high tea service or the history teacher at a posh North Shore girls' high school. She had thick, conservatively styled salt-and-pepper hair and wore a Pendleton skirt and sweater, rimless glasses, and pearls. Her name tag read "Mary Charleton, R.N." and you could bet she knew every move that anyone made in this place.

Her sharp gray eyes darted from a little family group in the corner—white-haired Grandma resident, earnest middle-aged son with what looked like his blonde trophy wife here for the introduction—to the entry, where an old gentleman with a walker was returning from Sunday brunch with his children and grandchildren, to me. I was the only unknown, so that was where she stopped. Keys rattled on a rubberized Day-Glo puce chain around her wrist as she put away her papers and shot me a welcoming, questioning look.

"May I help you?"

I gave her my best real estate smile. "Mrs. John Callahan? I'm her daughter."

She fell back slightly, suddenly losing her graciousness and then struggling to retrieve it.

"One moment." She smiled thinly and retreated to a file cabinet at the back of the reception area. She pulled a file and read it, then smiled at me and disappeared into the hallway behind the reception desk. Not good. She returned three minutes later carrying a cordless phone at arm's length.

"I'm sorry. We didn't list a daughter for Mrs. Callahan, so I had to call your father. He'd like to speak with you." She pushed the phone into my hand like a hot potato. Oh, brother.

"Hi, Dad."

"Honey, what are you doing up there? I thought you were going back to San Francisco this morning."

"Busted. Sorry. I was afraid you'd tell them not to let me in. You won't do that, will you?"

"Why do you want to upset your mother?"

"I won't upset her. I'm on a peace mission." A long pause.

"She may not see it that way."

"I know, but I want to try. Please let me." It was a good thing this man adored me, or HeartStone would be on lockdown to me already. "Please?" I was not above anything.

"Listen, you don't..."

"Please?" Another pause.

"Well." A pause. "Okay, but go easy. Don't upset her. If she gets agitated, leave. Okay?"

"Will do. Thanks, Dad."

"Yeah, yeah. Call me when it's over. Go easy."

"Okay."

I handed the phone back to Mary Charleton, R.N., who had been observing my side of the conversation with her arms crossed over her chest. She held the phone to her ear for a moment.

"All right, sir. Thank you." She pressed the off button and looked up at me. She seemed impressed, as well she might be.

"Come with me," she said, and led me down a long corridor that smelled like a dentist's office. In room after room, unspeakably old people lay with slightly arched backs, their eyes closed and their mouths gaping open toward the ceiling. Other residents lined the corridor, sitting in wheelchairs, staring into space. Tethered to one wheelchair was a red helium balloon that read "Happy Birthday Mom." The woman was almost bald, wore a dark purple robe, and yelled in terror as we passed. Young people in white swarmed her and wheeled her away. My hands felt clammy again. Mary walked beside me and must have sensed my fear. She put a hand on my arm in a professional way.

"Are you all right?"

"A little nervous, I guess." She gave me a sideways, sympathetic look.

"Well, we find that her bark is worse than her bite. Don't worry. I'll be right outside the room in case you need anything."

"That's not necessary."

"It's no problem." She looked at me as if I might have won the first round, but I had no idea what I was getting into and she was not going to budge on this. I nodded. Maybe it was a good idea.

Mary stopped us in front of Room 29. The door was half closed. I couldn't see inside. I looked at Mary. Maybe she would like to have lunch. Or a chat. Or a walk around the block. Maybe I should just sit with her for a while before seeing Mother and find out what to expect. Why hadn't I thought of that before? Definitely, I should do that. Just as I was about to suggest it, Mary opened the door all the way. I felt her hand on my back, gently shoving me in. My feet moved beneath me over the threshold.

The room had pale blue walls with pastel nature prints, a navy comforter on the bed, and a TV on the small table against the wall. In the far corner was a rocking chair, tipping slightly back and forth. Its rhythm was uneven, erratic. Sitting in the chair, the fulcrum of the jagged rocking, was an old woman—at first just a blur of red and white that took shape slowly into a bright red jogging suit and yellowish gray hair falling to the shoulders in long, winding chunks. Mottled, veiny hands clutched at the arm rests. The nails were manicured and polished an orangey red that made me think of mercurochrome. A shrunken, deeply lined face slumped to the side above the red collar.

I took a few more steps into the room, pulling the cloak woven of *the bright* and Pastor Diamond's energy more tightly around my shoulders. I pushed all that goodness out to encompass the bed, the walls, the pastel art—and then let it inch toward her, slowly softening the edges of the red and white, working its way in to touch her.

Her eyes moved up to meet mine as I got closer, tilting in their sockets without the head moving. They pulsed dully, a pale hazel. I pulled the cloak up around my neck and moved a little closer. A spark of recognition. She seemed to know that I was someone she ought to know and was casting about for who I might be. I doubted she could have said my name or how I was related to her, but she recognized something.

Her eyes opened wide and her mouth contorted into a grimace. Her head recoiled to the side against the back of the chair, either from revulsion or from fear. Her long, gnarled fingers snaked up off the armrests and wrapped themselves around one another over her chest into a tangled, writhing web of bones, liver-spotted skin, and mercurochrome polish. Her mouth opened into a silent scream that went on and on, until she was forced to rasp air back into her lungs. What was she seeing? What was I doing wrong? I sat down slowly on the bed, just a few feet away from her. Tried to wrap my mind around the fact that my body had come from inside the body in the rocker, that I had her blood and genes inside me.

I was shocked by how old she looked, how small and frail. This was not at all the person I remembered. This person in the rocker was in agony. She cringed in terror of something I couldn't see, something I was not sure even she could see. A mindless fury flailed out from her in all directions.

Then I saw it. Or rather, felt it. Snaking around inside her, feeding on her. *The dark.* She was in its grasp, half eaten and held down, powerless to stop it from doing whatever it wanted with her. It had her completely—had had her for a long time. It had taken her over and kept her. She hadn't run. She hadn't given up the "Mighty Fortress" God, even when it had stopped working. She hadn't taken a risk and gone looking for something better, and she certainly hadn't been willing to jump off the diving board into an empty pool to escape *the dark.* She had never turned to face it.

Compassion played around my edges. I wanted to comfort her. Without thinking, I felt out into her pain and was immediately swept into the self-loathing, the bottomless despair, the sense of not being human but only *food.* For a moment, I was myself as a little girl, trapped inside this woman's suffering, *the dark* coming at me full force, surging into me. I wrenched back from it and reached for *the bright,* the Pastor Diamond cloak. Pulled away from her and left her to *the dark.* She would never escape it, never know that she was anything other than it. I couldn't help her.

She kept wringing her fingers together, but her breathing eased and her eyes fixed on me. For a second, I felt a connection—some small flicker of caring, or maybe just sadness.

"Mother?" I sounded like someone else, a kinder and more self-assured person than I was. "It's Cathy." I forced a smile, pushed out *the bright* to envelop her, amazed that I could maintain it so long. As soon as I thought that, of course, it fell away and I was back to being just me, now only two feet from her. My reflex was fear, and suddenly *the dark* rose up in me again. I wanted to lash out at her, to punish her, but instead pressed myself back into the Pastor Diamond energy.

The dark and *the bright* both swirled around me. I was inside the storm, whipped around, out of control, with no idea which wind would pick me up next or what direction it would throw me. I dug deep for the compassion I had felt a minute earlier. Slowly, gently I reached over to touch her shoulder. I had never touched her voluntarily. My hand was only inches away. She watched it move toward her warily, with tears in her eyes. Her lower lip trembled uncontrollably. She stole a glance at me and our eyes met. It was frightening, but I held the look and so did she. It was like staring into some horrible, distorted mirror.

As my hand got closer, her eyes filled with panic. Her mouth opened again. The moan worked itself slowly, painfully up from her chest into her throat, then welled into a low animal noise. It wasn't loud, but it was inhuman and bone-chilling. The moan trailed off, and I let my hand rest gingerly on the red velour of her running jacket. She stared at it for a second.

Then, more quickly than my eyes could follow, her hand grasped my wrist. She pulled my hand to her face and dragged it desperately back and forth over her cheek. I thought she was going to kiss it, but instead— again, so quickly I couldn't follow—she shoved my two middle fingers into her mouth and bit down hard. Sharp pain shot up my arm. I pulled away and was stunned to see that the fingers were still attached. The skin was broken, and two jagged tooth marks began oozing blood.

I yelped in pain. She grabbed my wrist in both of her hands and tried to shove my fingers back into her mouth, bellowing low animal sounds again. I sprang to my feet and pulled away, but she was stronger than I could have imagined. She held on as I pulled my hand back. In the struggle, she started to fall forward out of the rocker. I straight-armed her back into the chair. She screamed again. I tried to soothe her, or to shut her up—I wasn't sure which—and reached to stroke her shoulder. That only made her yell more frantically. The long orange nails tore at my arms and hands.

The dark was in the room, in her and in me. I hated her. She was making it look like I was attacking an old lady! I wanted to smack her, then hold her close, and tried to fend off the flailing orange nails without hurting her.

Mary Charleton, R.N., rushed into the room and spoke calmly, but urgently, into a walkie-talkie. An orderly and attendant ran in and hauled Mother away. Mary pulled me out of the room and down the hall, one arm around my waist, the other holding my fingers away from my body and hers. We both looked over our shoulders at the staff dragging Mother in the opposite direction. She was howling again.

ॐ

Mary steered me into a treatment room and had me sit on the exam table. The pain in my fingers throbbed all the way up into my shoulder. I couldn't look at the bite. The lights were incredibly bright, bouncing off the pale gray walls, making it hard to tell if they were four feet away or twenty. I began to lose my sense of up and down.

"Put your head between your knees," Mary said. I stared at her. "Do it now!"

I put my head between my knees. Her saliva was in me. I had just made things worse! Mary was on the phone with a Dr. Sturgeon, who was apparently somewhere on the premises. The conversation was terse, short.

"Feeling better?" she asked, her hand on my shoulder, guiding me back into a sitting position.

"What will happen to her?" I asked, tears suddenly welling in my eyes.

"They'll evaluate her and decide."

"I didn't mean to upset her."

Mary shook her head. "We never know what will upset her." A pause. "I don't think it'd be a good idea to try this again." Me, neither. I nodded. The doctor shuffled in, so old he could have been one of the patients except that he was vertical. Mary introduced us, filled him in, and started to leave. I must have looked panicked, because she said, "I'll be right back."

He gave me a local anesthetic, poked around, cleaned my fingers, and applied bandages. Then he came at me with a bigger needle, and I freaked.

"It's just a tetanus," he said blithely, the smile never leaving his lips. His hand had a slight tremor, but I felt like I had caused enough trouble already. It hurt, but I didn't even care. I had made a mess here—for Mother, for them, for me. Mary bustled back in with a waiver, basically saying I had been treated for the bite and nothing that ever happened to me from that moment forward would be HeartStone's fault. I signed, and the doctor left with a sleepy smile. I thought he might be on drugs.

"Will you be okay now?" Mary asked, helping me off the table.

"Yes. I'm sorry for all the trouble."

She patted my shoulder as if all were forgiven, especially since I'd signed the waiver.

"Well, take it easy the rest of the day. Do you have somewhere to go?"

"I'm at the airport Hilton."

"Good. Just go back and rest." I nodded. Her beeper went off, and she frowned as she read the message. She hesitated a moment, then said, "I have to go. You can find your way out?"

"Sure, thanks," I said, trying to seem like a much more assured, less shocky person that I actually was. The message must have been urgent, because she took off at a fast clip down the corridor.

I was glad for the beeper call. The main thing she wanted right now was *me, out the door*—but I wasn't leaving. I didn't want to see Mother again, but I didn't feel finished here. The last thing I wanted was to drive back to the airport and lie down in a hotel room for the rest of the day. I had to sit here a bit, at least, and figure out what happened.

❧

I darted down the first corridor I saw. At the end of the hall was a little sitting room flooded with sunlight, with three easy chairs, a small sofa, a game table, and a TV. It was deserted. I sat on the sofa facing the courtyard and watched the autumn leaves scurry around the lawn. I had failed. I had stood there with both *the dark* and whatever god I could grab in the moment, but there had been no healing—and no raw silver energy. *The dark* still had her, and it was still in me no matter how well I had wielded the Pastor Diamond cloak. I had lost in traffic court. I felt empty and enormously sad. The anesthetic began to wear off. I just let my fingers throb.

Out of the corner of my eye, I saw someone coming down the hall toward my sanctuary. Damn. It was a patient—at least, I hoped it was a patient—moving unsteadily toward me on a wheelie walker with tennis balls attached to two of the legs. As she crossed the threshold of the sitting room, she flashed me a radiant smile filled with love and joy. She stooped a little, but I could see that she had once been tall and was still slim. She wore polyester jeans and a dark green turtleneck with jade green earrings. She had the crepe-like skin of old Irish women. Her hair, which looked like it was once auburn but was now gray, was piled on top of her head. There was something familiar about her, but I knew I had never met her.

Suddenly, I couldn't move a muscle. I just stared. This woman looked exactly as I imagined myself looking in forty years. She took her hands off the walker and raised them high above her head in elation and triumph, still beaming the huge smile.

"Evelyn!" she shouted in delight.

I half smiled and lifted my hand a few inches in greeting—not wanting to be rude, but not wanting to commit to being Evelyn, either. I snuck another look around the lounge to see if I had missed somebody.

No, she was looking directly at me. I stood so she could see that I wasn't Evelyn, but she only smiled more broadly and held out her arms. I moved closer, so she could see better—but when I got near enough, she grabbed my arm, pulled me to her, and hugged me. She looked right into my eyes, a foot away, and *still* thought I was Evelyn.

I played along and helped her sit down on the sofa, not sure how to proceed. I was clearly not good with these people and didn't want a replay of the shrieking and finger-biting. Plus, this woman was a lot bigger and stronger than Mother. I sat down gingerly beside her, and she held my good hand in both of hers.

"I'm happy you're here," she said, stroking my hand. How to stop this?

"Uh, my name is Cathy. Is Evelyn your daughter?" She bumped her shoulder against mine. She thought I was making a joke.

"You're such a kidder. *You're* my daughter." She stared out the window at the shuffling leaves. A squirrel darted up a tree, followed by another one, chasing it. She laughed, still stroking my hand. "I used to feed that squirrel," she mused. "Remember?"

I nodded, at a loss for what to do or say. Her hospital bracelet said Jeannie Armstrong. Maybe I should just slip out, before I did any damage. I was sure that's what Mary Charleton would suggest.

"On our honeymoon. I fed the squirrels." She seemed lost in space. Did she think I was her husband now? "Remember? In Brown County, the birch trees?" She looked at me anxiously, seeming desperate that I remember this as well. I nodded with another small smile and edged away, getting ready to stand up and leave.

"I have to go, Jeannie. It's been nice sitting with you..."

"No!" she wailed, clutching at my hand again. "No! You can't go. No!" I sat. Not only did I want to nip her hysteria in the bud, but I was strangely drawn to her. My impulse was to put my arm around her and try to make her smile. Still, it felt a little funny to be with her under false pretenses.

"Okay, I'll stay." She seemed relieved, a little embarrassed as she wiped away the tears with a trembling hand. I pulled a tissue from a box on the coffee table and handed it to her.

"Thank you. Thank you. I want to tell you something." Okay. I would be her daughter for ten minutes. Then I would get up and walk over to the lake, figure all this out. I let myself sink into the luxurious little nest where Jeannie wanted me to stay, and let her be my mother, someone with whom I was connected in mysterious and loving ways. She seemed to have lost her train of thought again, and was staring at my hair.

"Your hair is gray."

"Well, not *all* of it. It's just *starting* to get gray."

"Gray. Here, and here." She touched two places where there was more salt than pepper. She seemed like such a gentle soul. Her hand trembled—but she seemed completely relaxed, as if I really were her daughter and we really had spent forty years together on this earth. I started to relax, too. She might not have had much grasp of reality as Mary Charleton knew it, but that didn't mean she didn't love me, right in that moment. Or that I couldn't enjoy it and love her back. I leaned into it. What could it hurt? I'd had a tough morning, and this felt good. Besides, anything else seemed to upset her.

Where was the real Evelyn? Might she walk in on us? Did she visit Jeannie? Was she even alive? For the moment, it didn't matter. We just sat there, holding hands, watching the leaves and squirrels. It seemed okay not to talk. God knew where she was drifting.

I drifted back to what had happened with Mother. Tears stung in my eyes. For who she might have been before *the dark* got her and because I never knew that person. Because I knew now that *the dark* would never go away. Mostly, because I had to give up. Fighting *the dark* and finding the divine had driven my whole life. Now it was over. I had bet everything on the wrong number, and there was no more hope.

Jeannie turned to look at me. When she saw the tears, she put her arm around my shoulder and pulled me to her, held me like a child even though I was a lot bigger than she was. I let my head rest on her shoulder, and she stroked my hair. After all that had happened, I had wound up crying on the shoulder of a geriatric mental patient.

"Aw, poor baby," Jeannie murmured. I sniffled, feeling a little better after the tears, and just sat there watching the squirrels. Somehow, none of it felt quite so awful. In fact, it felt good just to lean back and let Jeannie hold and comfort me. Something inside me began to uncurl—not because I made it relax, but simply because it did. It was unnerving, like the "fist" that had opened up yesterday after seeing Dad. Only this wasn't just a fist; it was all of me. A soft warmth began to flow out from a place so deep inside me that I hadn't even known it was there, bathing my mind and spirit in rich, soothing nectar. It was like Pastor Diamond's trust and peace, like *the bright*, like the raw silver energy that had pulled me out of the Reno alley—but different. I felt as if I might dissolve.

I melted into that rich, winding river. In its warm flow, I sensed *the bright* and also streams of *the dark*. It held the energy behind Dad's eyes, Mother's scowl, Mollie's smile, and Tom's shoulder exploding into tiny pieces of flesh and blood. It held the stag in the Black Hills and the little tadpole baby, thousands of dark red votive candles and the sticky, gritty bricks of the Reno alley. The vast Montana sky, Jeff and Sally writhing on the floor, the roar of Avalanche Creek, the snake slithering across my windshield in the derelict Idaho barn, and churning streams tumbling down from snowcapped mountains through millions of trees to the ocean. We all merged together in that thick, silky river. Time and space collapsed, and we all breathed together, suspended in the shimmering flow.

The word "grace" filled my mind. Whatever that was, it was the thing I had been chasing all my life. If it disappeared forever in five minutes, I wouldn't care. I had felt it, seen it, taken it inside me and *been* it. This was the reality behind the curtain, the thing I'd been looking for in all the gods and all the people, in nature and the baby and booze and the mountains. It was what made life *be* and *go*. If I never felt it again, I would always know in my cells that it was there—and that I was a part of it.

I watched the leaves and squirrels for what might have been a minute or an hour. My back started to hurt from bending down to put my head on Jeannie's shoulder, so I sat up. Everything was at odd angles. The window, the walls, me. It was new and discomforting, but somehow I belonged in the picture. Some internal "reset" button had been pushed, and I had changed. *Change or die.*

Jeannie flashed me a bright smile and said, as if it had just occurred to her, "I'm glad I had you." I smiled back. I have no idea how long we sat there in silence. Jeannie began to nod out. I put my arm around her, and she fell asleep on my shoulder. Beyond the leaves and squirrels, visitors came and went along the sidewalk. Kids ran into the courtyard, chasing squirrels or just running around for the sheer fun of it. I had nowhere to go and was content just to sit there with Jeannie snoring away on my shoulder.

I heard someone coming down the hall toward us and turned to see a young black woman with a big smile and a staff name tag. Joanna.

"Jeannie? Is that my Jeannie?" She spoke loudly, to wake Jeannie up. Jeannie stirred and seemed to recognize her. She sat up and looked at me in a friendly way.

"Hello. Who are you?" she asked.

"Now Jeannie, that's one of your visitors. It's time for your lunch, honey. You come on with me."

Joanna helped Jeannie up and smiled at me. Jeannie planted her hands on the walker, then held one hand up, opened and closed it. "Bye bye." She smiled vaguely and clumped away with Joanna.

I watched them move slowly down the hall—but grace did not leave with them, as all the other gods had left with the people who brought them. It stayed, flooding the little sitting room. I felt a vast, echoing silence within me, a stillness I had never heard before. The sound of grace. Of home.

∞

Wind gusted off Lake Michigan, whipping up whitecaps on the dark blue water and stinging my cheeks. Way down the beach, a little kid flew a red kite.

I smiled and walked to the water's edge, set my faded pack on the sand, and took out the gun. Held it in my hand and looked at it. Then hauled back and threw it as far as I could out into the water. It splashed into a cresting wave and disappeared.

The sun was bright, but there were dark gray clouds all along the horizon toward Michigan. A storm was brewing out on the lake. The sharp, windy kind of fall thunderstorm that rattled everything and washed it clean, leaving it bare and ready for what was next.

Seagulls swooped above me, riding the updrafts, making minuscule wing and tail adjustments to keep themselves turned into the coming storm. Their heads darted from side to side, scanning. They let their fat, sleek bodies rest on the currents of air—an elegant instinct that saved their lives in a stiff wind. Their dance was all about course correction.

They rode for joy, in the now. Each of them my friend.

Join the discussion of Chasing Grace at
www.chasinggrace.net.

www.ingramcontent.com/pod-product-compliance
Lightning Source LLC
Chambersburg PA
CBHW022029240626
47154CB00007B/2331